THE COTTAGE ON NANTUCKET, A WOMEN'S FICTION MYSTERY

Nantucket Point, Book 1

JESSIE NEWTON

JEN Publishing

Copyright

Chapter One

Tessa Simmons walked inside the ferry station, her sensible weekender bag rolling along behind her. Her sister should be here already, as her flight to Boston had been hours earlier. Janey, however, rarely arrived anywhere on time, so surprise darted through Tessa when she spotted her sister standing at the counter at the cupcake shop, reaching for a cup of coffee.

She turned, the remnants of her smile still on her face, and Tessa lifted her hand as she changed direction.

"There you are," she said as she released her bag to hug her sister. Only fifteen months older than her, Janey stood an inch taller and at least thirty pounds lighter. She hugged her sister tightly, getting notes of clove and strawberry—her sister's preferred flavor of vape—coffee, of course, and mint. She chewed the gum to try to hide her vaping habit, but Tessa wasn't sure why. She wasn't on a business trip this weekend.

"I haven't seen you in forever, it feels like," Janey said, stepping back.

"Since the funeral," Tessa said, retreating to get her bag. She faced Janey again with a wide grin. She and her sister were cut from wildly different cloths, but they both had the Clarke barrel-like torso, a square, almost masculine face, and long, slender fingers that could bend and twist in weird ways.

Tessa had delighted and amused her friends as a teenager with her double-joints, but as a forty-five-year-old on her way to the summer cottage they'd frequented, that kind of thing didn't much matter anymore.

"I like your hair," Tessa said, smiling at her sister. "When did you put in the blue?"

"Last month, maybe?" Janey lifted her cup to her lips and sipped. She left dark maroon lipstick on the lid and started toward the ticket desk. "Did you get online tickets or do you need to buy one?"

"I got the app."

"I'll only be a minute then."

Tessa stopped by a bench and let her sister join the glut of people in line to buy a ferry ticket to Nantucket. Annoyance sang through her, but she tamped it down. She and Janey had already texted to death about getting tickets in advance, so they wouldn't have to arrive on Nantucket Point in the dark.

Tessa wanted to *see* the cottage. The whole point of this trip was to *see* the cottage. She told herself she had plenty of time, and the sun would rise tomorrow too. She wished she had something to sip while she waited. Instead, she watched Janey tap away on her phone, her long nails getting in the way several times.

Tessa had no idea how she did anything with the slender, pointed claws on her fingers. Janey's hair had been dyed what they used to call "vampire black" as teens, then highlighted with a deep, rich blue. Tessa did like it. In fact, she wished she were brave enough to do something like that with her hair.

Her dark brown hair—not the luxurious dark brown to be called a brunette, but just one shade past mousy—had started to get gray growing in it a few years ago. She'd decided she didn't mind. She was closer to fifty now, and she didn't need to hide it.

Janey wasn't hiding anything. She simply lived a more exciting life than Tessa ever had. She flew all over the country for her job, and she moved from hobby to hobby as if she had this intense drive to try everything before she died.

Currently, Janey rode with a group of women out of Jersey City, where she lived. On weekends and holidays, the group wore leather and bandanas as they took long road trips on their motorcycles. When Tessa had found out, she'd called her sister in shock.

"Motorcycles?" she'd asked. "Since when do you like riding a motorcycle?"

"I wanted to try it," Janey said. "It's so amazing, Tess. I feel so free."

Janey was always trying to feel free. Tessa had no idea

how she could afford a motorcycle, but she didn't ask. Her sister had had her fair share of financial trouble over the years, but she'd always managed to come out on top.

The line moved forward, and Janey did too, almost without looking at all. She wore a nose ring on the left side, bangles in gold, silver, and bronze, and a large pair of silver hoops in her ears. On the left side, studs dotted the lobe five or six deep, some with gems and some without.

Tessa had forgotten to put earrings on at all this morning. She wore mom jeans and a light blue blouse with tiny white butterflies on it. Janey wore loose, flowing pants like the beachcombers Tessa had packed. Her tank top flowed down over her barrel torso, with a shawl over that. She had long legs and long arms, and it was no wonder she was currently dating two men. At the same time.

Something gathered in the back of Tessa's throat, and she couldn't quite name what. She wasn't jealous of Janey. That ship had sailed decades ago. As her sister stepped up to the counter, Tessa realized she simply wanted more color in her life. Everything about her eastern Pennsylvania existence was so *dull*.

"Ready," Janey said, breaking Tessa out of her thoughts. They walked toward the line to get on the ferry, Janey asking about Ron and Ryan. Tessa gave a dutiful report on her husband and son, and asked Janey about her kids.

Their father had died years ago, and Mom just a couple of months now. Tessa had taken care of most of the funeral arrangements, though really, she'd just carried out

Mom's wishes. Their mother had been detailed almost to a fault, and both Janey and Tessa had owned a binder with what to do upon her death.

The last thing on the list before the pour-over will could actually be poured over was to go to the cottage on Nantucket and clean it out. Mom had been very specific in her instructions that the sisters go together, and that nothing would be released from the trust until the binder in the cottage was retrieved. They also had to meet with the lawyer on Nantucket that had prepared everything in Mom's estate.

They'd been given ninety days from her death to go through everything, and Tessa couldn't remember the last time she'd worked a full week at the library where she curated their adult mystery collection. Janey, however, had business trips and meetings, and she hadn't been able to just get away.

Tessa had gone through the New York City apartment alone, as well as visited the bank in the city and the one in Newark where they'd grown up to get the contents of the safety deposit boxes and check on the financial status of the accounts there.

Everything after that was fairly straightforward. Janey and Tessa had been named co-trustees, which meant neither could make a decision without the other. Janey had defaulted to Tessa's suggestions over the past six or seven weeks, and while they didn't see eye-to-eye on everything— or hardly anything—Tessa didn't anticipate a problem with the cottage.

"I can't wait to get there," Tessa said, standing at the railing on the ferry as it pulled away from the dock. "I love this ferry ride."

"Me too," Janey said with a smile. "Remember when Daddy brought doughnuts for everyone on board?"

Tessa grinned into the sky, the sun behind her in the west as the ferry headed east. "I wish I had a doughnut right now."

"We'll go to Distillery in the morning."

"Deal." Tessa glanced at her sister, finally feeling comfortable with her. Things always took a few minutes to settle inside her after she met up with Janey, and she wasn't sure why.

The ferry ride reminded her of simpler times, and Tessa decided to tuck away all the problems at home, the complete mundaneness in her life, and enjoy her time on Nantucket. After all, there were beautiful beaches to visit, the best restaurants in the world to eat in, and the cottage at the Point where she could relax.

Thirty minutes later, the sisters emerged from the taxi-van and stood in front of the bright blue beach cottage. The sun hung on the horizon, lighting the cottage from behind and giving it a halo.

It seemed bigger than Tessa remembered, but smaller at the same time. There were probably hundreds of flaws she'd never noticed before, and a shiver ran up her arms as she thought about going through more of Mom's stuff. Another binder. More clothes. Personal pictures and knick-knacks that meant so much to her.

She'd never come here without Mom, and a wave of grief threatened to drag her under an invisible surface where breathing was difficult. Her chest pinched, and when she pulled in a breath, it stuttered painfully down her throat.

Tears pressed behind her eyes, but Janey took a step down the sidewalk, and Tessa hitched everything tight, tight, and followed her older sister.

Chapter Two

"Thank you." Tessa smiled at her sister when she set the plate with the fast food on it.

"Nothing like fish and chips in Nantucket." Janey grinned too, turning to get the teapot she'd set on the stove. With that sitting in the middle of the table, she finally sat down. "The cottage is in better shape than I expected."

"Really?" Tessa asked.

"Yeah." Janey pulled her first fish fillet out of the paper bag. "No one came this summer."

Mom had died in the middle of May, only a few weeks before she'd planned on coming to the cottage.

"It's still summer," Tessa said. "We're only six weeks late."

"Mom always cleaned for days before we showed up," Janey said with a smile that could only be described as sad.

"I didn't see a binder," she said. "For some reason, I expected it to be sitting right in the middle of the kitchen

JESSIE NEWTON

table." Tessa gave a light laugh, glad when Janey's smile perked up.

"If only we could all plan when and where and how we're going to die." Janey glanced down at her phone as it vibrated. A frustrated sigh escaped her lips, and Tessa watched as she typed out a response to the message with the pad of her pointer finger. She looked up and said, "Sorry. My boss is trying to find something in my office."

"It's fine," Tessa said. "I get you're busy." She offered her sister a smile. "You never did say what Cole's doing in Atlantic City." They'd been interrupted by the need to buy tickets, and Tessa did enjoying hearing about her niece and nephew. She only had one son, and Ryan had two semesters left before he'd graduate from Columbia with a degree in civil engineering.

"He's working construction there," Janey said with a fast smile. "He also works on the docks in the summer, so he's really busy right now."

"What does he do with the boats?"

"Detailing," she said. "Inside and out. It's pretty intense, from what he's said."

"Good for him," Tessa said, hoping she didn't sound condescending. Neither of Janey's children had gone to college, and she knew her sister felt inferior to her about it. Tessa wasn't sure why. It didn't matter to her what Janey's children did.

"He likes it," Janey said. "Keeps him busy and out of trouble, and I like that."

Tessa laughed with her sister. "He's still living with McKenna?"

"Mm hm." Janey nodded as she chewed the last of her fish. After swallowing, she added, "Yep, they're still together."

"Do you think they'll ever get married?" Tessa asked, immediately wishing she could recall the question. She knew a lot of young people delayed marriage or chose never to enter into holy matrimony. She wasn't passing a judgment, but Janey sometimes thought she was, when Tessa was just asking an innocent question.

She sighed, and she actually didn't look too happy. "I don't know. I used to ask him all the time, but I stopped. He's twenty-one years old. He can do what he wants."

"Yes, he can," Tessa said with plenty of knowing in her voice.

"Is Ryan seeing anyone?"

Tessa shook her head. "He insists he has no time for dating, but I'm pretty convinced he doesn't even try." She didn't mention that she hadn't actually spoken to her son in almost three months now. When he'd first moved New York to attend college, he'd called every Monday, rain, shine, snow, busy, tired, bored, or whatever.

The further he got into his program, the less he called. The more he separated his life from his parents, the less he came home. She and Ron had funded his first year for him, to help him get off to a good start, and since he'd been working to pay his tuition and rent, the busier he became.

As it was, Tessa hadn't seen her son since Christmas.

Well, besides for a very brief few minutes during her mother's funeral.

She hadn't truly seen him or spent any meaningful time with him for six months. She hadn't heard his voice in almost three.

New York City sat less than two hours from her home in Easton, and Tessa's husband made the commute to the city every week. She'd asked him if he saw Ryan as they both lived there during the week, and he'd said no.

Tessa had often thought she should pack a bag and hit the road for the weekend. Let him know she was coming, and ask if he had time to go to lunch. Her treat.

She hadn't done it, because spring had hit, and Tessa spent a lot of time in the yard in the spring and early summer. She loved pruning back the overgrowth and cleaning up anything that hadn't gotten done in the fall. Walking outside and finding new, bright green shoots coming back after the winter made her smile. Every day held a new adventure in her garden, and she could lose hours with gardening gloves on her hands.

Which was fine. She didn't have to give an accounting of her time to anyone. Her husband, Ron, had been working in the city for two decades, and back when he'd first started, they'd lived much closer. Close enough that he could commute across the river every day and be home in the evening.

When they'd moved to Pennsylvania twelve years ago, he started staying in the city Monday through Friday and only coming home on weekends. Ryan had been ten years old, and he and Tessa had adjusted to the single parent life the best they could.

Rarely, Ron would come home mid-week for a concert or performance, but as time wore on, Ryan didn't even tell his father about them.

Tessa mindlessly finished her fish as she thought about her family, the familiar loneliness and sense of boredom filling her. Everything in her life was so quiet, and Tessa really needed someone to scream and wake her up. Wake up Ron to what their family and their relationship had become.

Dead.

Her lawn and garden might be a showstopper and town winner, but everything else in her life had died.

Despite Tessa's heroic efforts, her family and marriage were both hanging on by a thread, and she didn't know how much longer she could keep her grip.

She dusted the salt and crumbs from her hands, still chewing her last bite of chips, when someone rapped sharply on the front door.

Janey looked up from where she'd fully engrossed herself in her phone. "Who on Earth could that be?"

Chapter Three

Tessa stood up and left her empty cardboard container on the plate on the table. "I'm sure it's probably Bobbie." She crossed through the living room, a smile already lightening her step. Bobbie Friedman lived next door to the cottage, and she and her husband watched out for the house when no one was here.

When storms caused any damage, Bobbie called Mom and reported. As far as Tessa knew, Mom and Bobbie had been best of friends, and they'd spent a lot of time with Bobbie and her husband, Riggs, growing up.

Tessa opened the door, and sure enough, petite, blonde, blue-eyed Bobbie stood there. "Bobbie," Tessa said with a big smile on her face. Maybe too big. Maybe a little fake.

She stepped into the older woman's arms and hugged her. Her eyes drifted closed, because hugging Bobbie was almost like getting a hug from her own mother, even if the other woman wasn't Tessa's favorite person on Nantucket.

Bobbie tended to gossip too much and pry too hard, but she had a similar body shape to Mom, and she smelled just like her—like powder and sugar and fresh coffee. Another powerful rush of missing and grief flowed through her, and Tessa found she couldn't let go of the older woman. Everything spun at the speed the Earth rotated, and Tessa felt wildly untethered.

"There, there," Bobbie said, repeating the single word she'd said many times before. When Tessa had been stung by a jellyfish, Bobbie and scooped her up into her arms and said, "There, there, I know just what to do."

And she had. Bobbie knew a home remedy for every ailment, and Tessa wondered if she had something to cure a broken heart.

Without Mom, Tessa honestly felt like she had no one. Her husband had barely been present for the funeral, and Ryan had shown up late and left immediately afterward, his finals the same day she'd buried her mother. He'd texted to say he'd wanted to stay longer. That he'd make sure he got over to the cemetery to visit Mom's grave. That he missed them.

Tessa wasn't sure what she believed. She didn't want to think that her son didn't like being around her. She thought she'd done the best she could for him. She hadn't worked when he was a child, and she'd been there for every science fair, every concert, every parent-teacher conference.

He'd played rugby, and she'd gone to many of the games. Enough to be supportive, but not so many as to smother him. Ron made good money, and Ryan had never truly wanted for anything. She had no idea why her son had pulled away and refused to be reeled back in. Tessa simply didn't know what to do about it.

"Bobbie," Janey said from behind Tessa, and that got her to step away. Tessa moved to the side so Janey could greet Bobbie, taking the opportunity to wipe her eyes quickly. She desperately wanted a nightcap and the time to sit on the porch while she sipped it—alone.

But Janey invited Bobbie into the cottage, and the blonde woman went. Tessa was left behind to close the door, which felt about right to her. She'd often existed in Janey's shadow or two steps behind her sister as a teen. She'd taken that feeling into adulthood, having one less child than Janey, and getting married two years later.

She trailed behind the other two women, and waved Janey away when she offered tea. Bobbie took a cup while Tessa started cleaning up the remnants of their dinner. With that done, she joined Janey and Bobbie at the table. The furniture coverings needed to be removed and shaken from the sofas in the living room, and neither Tessa nor Janey wanted to do it tonight.

They'd agreed to open all the windows in the morning and let the sea breeze blow through the cottage then. They'd uncover everything and start wiping everything out and down. They had groceries to get—along with those doughnuts—and plenty of items to discuss to finish up dealing with Mom's trust.

"…such an amazing woman," Bobbie said, shaking her head. "We're really going to miss her around here."

"Yes, she did love being part of this community," Janey said diplomatically. She hadn't lied; Mom did love Nantucket, and she'd come for months at a time, especially once Dad had passed.

"She met Dennis here, you know," Bobbie said with a self-important wobble of her neck.

"She did?" Tessa asked, casting a look at Janey. "She said she met him at the theater."

"Yes, yes," Bobbie said. "The movie theater on the day cruise."

The sisters exchanged a glance, and this time, Janey asked, "Day cruise?"

"You know," Bobbie said, clearly exasperated. "The six-hour cruise that goes around the island? There's a movie theater on-board the ship. They met there."

Tessa wasn't sure what to say, though her mind moved a mile a minute. She wasn't the funny, witty sister, nor the life of the party. She liked to have a good time too, and she'd always participated in family parties and events. Happily.

"Are you sure?" Janey asked.

"Quite," Bobbie said, her blue eyes blazing. She leaned forward and set her teacup on the table. Looking between the two girls, she asked, "She didn't tell you that?"

"She said they met at the theater," Tessa said. "It obviously doesn't matter." She shot a look at Janey, who still wore a frown between her eyes. "They got along so well, and we were just glad she didn't have to be alone for very long."

Bobbie's countenance fell again. "Yes, Dennis's passing was hard for many here."

"Did he live here, then?" Janey asked, her face back to her normal placid expression.

"The Martins owned several homes here at one point," Bobbie said.

Shock spread through Tessa. Several homes? That meant money. A lot of money.

Janey crossed her legs and leaned back in her chair, though Tessa had seen this tactic before. She was interested but wanted to look like she wasn't.

"They didn't stay, though," Bobbie continued. "They rented their homes for years and years. I saw couple up for sale after Dennis died, but I don't think the sales went through."

"Hm," Janey said. "Mom did like living in the city."

Darkness and disgust ran across Bobbie's face. "You couldn't pay me to go back to the city."

Tessa laughed, glad when Janey did too. "We know," Tessa said. "You left forty years ago, and you're not going back." She smiled at Bobbie, who wore her islander spirit right on her sleeve. She never held back her opinion either, and Tessa had forgotten about her bluntness. That, combined with the "free advice" Bobbie tended to hand out, kept Tessa from wanting to spend much time with her at all. She certainly didn't want to tell Bobbie Friedman anything of any significance. She didn't need the mundane details of her life being spread around the island to strangers.

Sometimes she wished she could tell people exactly what she thought about them, but she rarely did.

"Well, I'll leave you girls to get settled," Bobbie said, standing. She placed her teacup in the sink and another round of hugs took place before their neighbor left. Janey closed the door this time, a sigh coming loudly from her mouth.

"She exhausts me," Janey said as she turned around. "I need a drink."

Tessa said nothing, though she'd like one too. She let Janey rifle through the cabinets until she found a bottle of rosé. She only knew she'd done that when Janey called, "There's wine," from the kitchen. "Rosé."

"Okay," Tessa yelled back, continuing to take her clothes from her weekend bag. Her sister wouldn't expect her to come drink with her, so Tessa finished unpacking and changed into her pajamas. She'd just plugged in her tablet and her phone when her sister leaned in the doorway.

"I'm going to bed," Janey said, holding her wine glass by the stem like a refined socialite. "We'll go downtown for groceries tomorrow. I desperately need coffee with caffeine in it."

Tessa smiled, because Mom had switched to decaf at least a decade ago. "Agreed."

"I'm not setting an alarm," Janey said, throwing back

the last swallow of her wine. Tessa's mouth watered, but she just smiled. "Good-night."

"Night," Tessa said.

Janey went to the next bedroom and closed the door behind her. To be safe, Tessa waited another ten minutes. She used the time to send a quick text to her husband that she'd made it to the cottage, and she'd hope to know more later.

He hadn't texted or called, though she should've checked in hours ago. He'd barely paid attention to anything in the will and trust, and Tessa didn't have final numbers for an inheritance yet anyway.

That was why she and Janey needed to be here. They had another bank to visit, that blasted binder to find, and a lawyer to meet with. Perhaps then, they'd get some final answers and be able to start dividing the estate.

Certain her sister wouldn't make a reappearance, Tessa went into the kitchen, noting that all the lights in the cottage still blazed as if electricity were free. She turned off lights as she went, finally leaving only a single bulb burning above the kitchen sink.

She poured herself a healthy serving of wine, picked up the bottle, and crept through the house to the front door. The porch wrapped around the front and side of the house, and around the corner sat two weathered Adirondack chairs.

Tessa sank into one of them and lifted her wine in a toast to the ocean she could only hear. Darkness stretched before her, but she imagined the water washing ashore just to say hello to her.

She gulped the wine before forcing herself to slow down, her unhappiness and discontent finally allowed to stream out of her. If she kept it bottled up inside, Tessa wouldn't make it through tomorrow, let alone the next few weeks, with her sister.

She let her mind linger on any topic while she drank glass after glass of rosé, allowed her tears to overflow, and then fell asleep right where she sat on the covered porch, her wineglass in her fingers.

Chapter Four

Tessa woke with a start, her head pounding and the remnants of a distinct sound still ringing in her ear. Her tongue felt like a thick sock in her mouth, and she groaned as she sat up. Darkness covered everything, the deep, thick kind that spoke of a time when no one should be awake, let alone out on a porch by themselves.

She stood, a chill covering her skin and making her shiver. She stepped on a piece of broken glass, and she cried out as she jerked her foot back.

The glass. That was what she'd heard. The wine glass she'd drunk from last night had fallen and broken, the shattering sound waking her.

Her stomach sloshed as she squinted at the deck, trying to navigate around any other broken shards. In the end, she made a big leap and got past the wreckage. She limped around the corner, awake enough now to realize she was leaving bloody footprints behind her.

She simply couldn't take care of it right now. In fact, she'd really like someone else to take care of something, for once. Just one time, she wanted someone else to do the dishes. Put in the laundry. Vacuum the straight lines into the carpet and pay all the bills.

Tessa was simply tired of taking care of everything.

She should go clean up her foot, but her head hurt so badly, and she was so tired, that she simply went into the bedroom she'd used for years and collapsed onto the mattress. Hopefully, she wouldn't bleed too much before morning.

———

THE NEXT TIME SHE WOKE, THE FIRST RAYS OF DAWN FELL across her face. A low pain echoed from Tessa's foot, and the events of the previous evening ran through her head. She took her time opening her eyes, as they suffered the most when she drank too much.

Finally, she got them open enough to adjust to the light, which was thankfully still fairly weak. With a groan and a sigh, she sat up and let her legs hang over the edge of the bed.

The mattress on this bed still caused a pinch in her back, and Tessa reached up and pushed her hair out of her face as she arched to get the pain stretched out. She didn't think for a moment Janey would be awake already, as her sister was notorious for sleeping very late, especially when she went on vacation.

Sure, she'd brought work to the cottage and they had plenty to do here, but Tessa knew she still viewed it as vacation.

Tessa went into the bathroom and drank two glasses of clear, cool water. She knew the best way to get rid of all signs of drinking was to hydrate, clean up, and get some food in her. Then the alcohol would dilute enough for her to function.

She got in the shower, dressed in clothes she could go to town in and go through closets in, and made herself a couple of fried eggs and a single piece of toast. After eating, she cleaned up the dishes, as well as the porch where the bottle had broken. If Janey asked about the wine —and she likely would—Tessa could simply say she'd brought it out here to have a glass and accidentally dropped it.

In fact, she'd mention the wine for sure before they went to town. Then they could get more.

Janey still hadn't made an appearance, and Tessa stood in the front part of the house, in the intersection that led to all other parts. To her right lay the living room and front door. To the left, the dining room and kitchen. Behind her, the hall that led to the bedrooms on this level, and the stairs that led up to the second floor.

The cottage had an attic too, and Tessa couldn't remember the last time she'd been up there. As children, she and Janey had loved the attic, because Mom and Dad had filled it with tiny, child-sized furniture just for them. A little couch and a little chair. A desk, and a table and chairs. When it rained on Nantucket, they'd happily have tea parties with all their stuffed animals or plan big birthday celebrations with plenty of cake and chocolate milk.

Tessa smiled at the memories, because she had so enjoyed coming to the cottage as a child. She hadn't even minded it as a teenager, though Janey had thrown a fit or two about leaving her friends for "months on end" in the summertime. Once she got old enough, she'd gotten a job, and she hadn't come to the cottage for longer than a week in the summertime.

The whole house needed to be aired out, wiped down, and opened up. The job would take one person a few weeks; Tessa knew. She'd done the apartment in the city by herself, and she wondered if Ron had even missed her. She'd stayed there, and while he worked in the city, he hadn't come to her mother's apartment after work. He'd gone back to his. She hadn't contacted Ryan, because she hadn't wanted to bother him.

"No," she muttered to herself. "You didn't want to hear whatever excuse he'd come up with for why he couldn't see you." Somehow, not asking her son to get together for a quick lunch was easier to digest than getting rejected if she did ask.

Pushing her husband and son from her mind, Tessa faced the living room. She could open blinds and doors, tear sheets off furniture and wave them out in the breeze to get the dust out, and sweep up anything that remained.

As she worked, she wished rooting out the dirty, hidden things in her life was as easy as taking a storage cover from a sofa. She wished she could beat her relationships against the porch railing and have them come out clean and ready to be used in the future. As the pile of sand, leaves, and a bit of other debris got swept into a pile, Tessa could identify each piece of her life she'd like to group together, pick up, and toss out.

With sunlight streaming through the front windows of the cottage and the living room clean, Tessa finally found a smile. It wobbled on her face, and she didn't know what to do with the swirling feelings inside her.

She fumbled with her phone but got it out of her pocket. She never called Ron during the week. Truth be told, she hardly texted. They lived two different lives, especially now that Ryan was grown and gone, and she honestly didn't have anything to tell him.

She tried, as evidenced by the string of pictures she'd sent in the past couple of months. The garden before and after. The new rose bushes she'd put in. The first bloom of the azaleas she'd planted especially for him. Other than that, she might tell him about a neighbor they'd known for a while who'd fallen ill, or something particularly unique that had happened at the library.

Whenever she asked him what was happening at work, he said, "The same old thing," with a sigh. She'd asked him if he ever explored the city, and he'd dryly said it was just a city, and no, he had no interest in exploring it.

He didn't use social media, and by all accounts and purposes, he went to work every day at a prestigious and very competitive law firm, put in eighty hours in five days, and came home on the weekends. Sometimes, when he had a high-profile case, he didn't return to Pennsylvania for Saturday and Sunday.

He'd made partner two years ago, and Tessa had thrown a huge party for him—in the city. All of his friends lived there, and she was the only one who had to commute to celebrate all of his hard work. She was proud of him, and if she thought about him for very long at all, she realized she did love him.

She simply wondered if what she and Ron called their life together was truly any way to live. Today, she went out onto the front porch and took a picture of the sun hanging over the water. The sky didn't hold a single cloud, and after snapping the photo to send to her husband, Tessa took a moment to close her eyes and breathe in the sunshine, the air, the life this new day promised to bring her.

She sent the picture to Ron with the message, *Wish you were here. This place is beautiful, and we need a vacation.*

He responded instantly. *We sure do. I do love Nantucket. Let me look at my schedule and see what I can do.*

Hope filled Tessa's heart, though she pushed against it. Ron had made such promises before, and sometimes his schedule simply didn't have any openings in it. Still, she leaned against the porch and whispered into the morning breeze, "Please keep him well, and bless us that we'll find a time to reconnect soon."

She could say the same prayer for Janey, so she did. Then she turned to go wake her sister. After all, Tessa wanted doughnuts, and Janey had promised they could get some that morning.

Chapter Five

"I just don't understand," Janey said a week later. "She said we had to come here, right? That there was something we had to go through?" She looked at the various items scattered around her, a frown pulling her eyebrows down.

"That's what she said." Tessa understood the frustration, because it had been running hotly through her for a few days now. Even the most delicious apple fritters and tiger tails hadn't alleviated her irritation that they had not found another binder. She'd shown Janey the instruction sheet from the first binder, and it was very clear there were instructions here too.

She sighed and picked up a vase that looked like it had been made in the seventeen hundreds. "So...do we take this stuff down to the antique shop? See what Mildred says about it?"

"If it's worth something, yes," Janey said.

"We don't know if it's worth something without going down there." Tessa put the vase in a box along with a black wire birdcage and a couple of crystal figures of sailboats. They looked like paperweights to her, but Janey insisted they were the work of a local artist and could be worth something.

Janey's only interest was in the things that she deemed worth something. Tessa understood the mentality, but her sister had been coming across as fairly cold as they'd gone through Mom's things. The clothes, shoes, and household items were easy. Tessa had kept a few of her mother's sweaters, especially the Christmas ones, as her mother had possessed a real affinity for the ugliest holiday sweater possible, and they made Tessa smile.

They'd come to the cottage for Christmas several times, and she could remember her mother laughing as they went to this holiday party or that Christmas Eve dinner. She'd won a couple of the ugliest sweater contests around town and in the neighborhood out here on the Point, and Tessa had wanted the sweaters for sentimental value.

Everything else got donated to Good Will, and after the third day of dropping off, the worker there had given her and Janey their own tags. Then they could drop off before or after hours without a problem.

"Maybe Sean will have it," Janey said, picking up a stack of books and putting them in the same box. The vase clacked and scratched against the birdcage, but Tessa opted to say nothing.

"I already called him," Tessa said, not for the first time.

She'd had to call Sean Masterson, their mother's lawyer, to set up a time to meet with him. He'd said he did have a few items to go over, and only he could release the safety deposit box keys to Tessa and Janey, and yes, they did have to come together to get them. "He said he had a few instructions, and no, they weren't in a binder."

"Then it has to be in that stupid desk." Janey glared at Tessa as if she'd locked the desk and lost the key on purpose.

"I'll go try that key we found last night." Tessa turned and left the study, where her mother had been collecting things for at least six decades. About half the size of the other three bedrooms, the study had held about ten times as much stuff as the rest of the house combined. Mom had two bookcases in there stuffed to the gills, as well as a china cabinet, a desk, and a chest of drawers that hadn't housed clothing.

She and Janey had been going through it for days, and with one or two more trips, Tessa hoped they could be done. They had found plenty of odds and ends—a jar full of buttons, none of which looked like any other. A Tupperware container of only quarters. Janey had theorized that Mom had used them for the laundromat downtown, and that made sense to Tessa, so she hadn't offered another idea.

Mom loved books, and they'd unearthed plenty of those with old stickers on them from the used bookstore downtown. They'd been taking all of them there, and the owner was delighted to see what they had that he wanted to add back to his collection.

In fact, John Lawrence had called that morning to ask if the sisters would be stopping by that day with more books. He had a couple in town who'd taken several of the others he'd bought back from them, and they were very interested in seeing what else the Clarke cottage on the Point would yield.

Tessa had told him they'd be by with a couple of boxes, because she and Janey had been eating downtown every evening. Bobbie had invited them for dinner a couple of times, but Janey didn't want to go. It had fallen to Tessa to get them out of the situation delicately, which she'd done. She didn't particularly want to spend a whole evening reminiscing with Bobbie and Riggs either, but she didn't want to be rude to someone Mom had loved dearly.

She plucked the small brass key from the dish on the kitchen table and faced the stairs leading up to the second floor. Thankfully, Mom hadn't put much up there, as she'd stopped using stairs for the past few years of her life. They'd found old clothing, a heap of towels that had been left behind at some point, and plenty of old National Geographic magazines—Dad's favorite.

There was only one bedroom on the second floor, and it seemed like that was where Mom had put all of Dad's belongings she hadn't been able to part with after he'd died. Janey and Tessa hadn't had a problem filling the trashcan or a box for Good Will, and the second floor had taken less than two hours to clean out.

She climbed the steps and glanced at the single recliner that sat in front of the huge windows overlooking the beach. Mom and Dad must've hauled it upstairs in a box and then assembled it up here, because it was at least twice as wide as the narrow staircase, and they couldn't have gotten it up here any other way.

Tessa and Janey had considered breaking it into pieces to get it downstairs, but in the end, Tessa had suggested they just leave it for now. They owned the cottage, and in her mind, she had no plans to sell it. The recliner was a hideous shade of orange, but otherwise clean, and one night, after Janey had gone to bed, Tessa had nursed her Coke and whiskey from the serenity of that recliner.

It could stay, as far as she was concerned.

Now, though, she turned away from it and faced the even steeper and more narrow set of steps that led into the attic. Despite her generous hips, she managed to get upstairs and through the door, where all the child-sized furniture had been cleared out long ago. This room had a bare wood floor, with a single window that overlooked the beach as well. The only item in the room was a student desk. Nothing fancy, though definitely assembled in the space as well. It was made of a dark wood and had three drawers total. One long, skinny one along the top front that slid open easily without a single squeal.

Two more ran down the side of the desk, the bottom one larger than the top. Both of those drawers could lock, and they were both currently locked.

Tessa and Janey had tried everything to get the drawers

open, to no avail. They'd lifted the desk to determine if there was even anything in the drawers, and the weight suggested there wasn't. Tessa had heard something sliding around in one of them, though, and they'd discussed calling a locksmith at some point, if they determined the drawer's contents to be worth discovering.

"We have to go," Janey called from the first floor, and Tessa glanced at her watch. One-fifteen. They were meeting with Sean that afternoon, an appointment they'd waited a week to get, so they couldn't miss or reschedule.

"I forgot," she called down. "I'll be two minutes." She quickly fitted the small key into the lock, already knowing it wasn't the right one.

The key was brass and the lock silver, and sure enough, the key didn't open either drawer.

Tessa went back downstairs and held up the key. "Doesn't work."

"I'm not surprised," Janey said dryly. She already had her oversized sunglasses on, and with her perfectly styled and dyed hair, her flowing fabrics and professional fashion sense, she looked like a model for the single, middle-aged woman. "You've got the original binder, right?"

"Yes," Tessa said, dropping the key back into the dish and reaching for the bright red binder she'd brought with her. "Let's go."

Janey drove, as Janey always did when they were together, and Tessa watched the waves greet the beach during the fifteen-minute drive to the downtown area of Nantucket.

Plenty of shops and restaurants had been crammed into the heart of the island, and in the summer, tourists clogged every street and sidewalk, every cruise out on the ocean, every hotel and bed & breakfast.

Tessa had often been one of those tourists, so they didn't bother her. In fact, she saw herself in the family of four riding the neon green bikes down the beach path or the mom and dad pushing a stroller away from the pop-up seafood stand in the corner of the parking lot.

Janey grumbled about not being on time—as if she had any room to talk about such a thing—and how many people had arrived on Nantucket over the weekend.

Tessa ignored her and let the breeze pull through her hair as Janey got them onto a side-street that led to a quieter part of downtown where Sean's office was.

Inside, the air conditioning kept everyone cool and comfortable, and his secretary stood to greet them. "You must be the Clarke sisters," he said, his smile far too wide for a lawyer's office, even a small island one.

Tessa and Janey hadn't bothered to correct anyone about their name. They'd been Clarkes once, yes, and though neither of them had used the name in a while, Tessa still felt like it belonged to her.

Surprisingly, Ron had said he had a week at the beginning of August where he could get out of the office, and he was planning to come to the cottage on the Point. Tessa had spoken to him several times over the weekend, and he'd commented on how good the yard looked at their home in Pennsylvania, and Tessa had swelled with pride and accomplishment.

Standing in Sean Masterson's office, though, she wished she could've bottled some of that feeling like she'd done something great to use right now.

"We weren't that late," Janey hissed, glaring down the hallway as if she had another pressing appointment she couldn't miss. "There's not a single car in the lot besides ours. What's taking so long?"

"Relax," Tessa murmured, because the walls in some of these older beach buildings were paper-thin. "Maybe he's on the phone or something."

"I hate it when people prioritize people on the phone over people in person."

"Janey, you literally do ninety percent of your business on the phone." Tessa shook her head. "It's fine. We've been here for two minutes."

Janey sighed and reached up to adjust her sunglasses on her head. "You're right. I'm so on-edge about this meeting."

Tessa was too, and she stepped over to her sister. She put her arm around Janey, and said, "Me too."

"I don't even know why." Janey stood rigidly for another few seconds before finally relaxing into Tessa's side. "I am expecting a call this afternoon from the CEO at AeroBlue. Remember?"

"Of course," Tessa said, though she had forgotten. "You'll be fine if you take it. We just needed to be here together initially."

"It shouldn't take long," Janey said. "Ten or fifteen minutes. I just have to walk him through set-up and give him a generated code."

Tessa pressed her lips together, wondering if she should've put on another layer of lip gloss before coming inside.

"Janey," a man said as he came out of the hallway. "Tessa. So good to see you two." Sean Masterson wore the same wide smile as his assistant, but he boasted a dark suit, complete with the jacket, shiny shoes, and a head full of dark hair that swooped just-so, as if the wind itself had sculpted it on the way to work that morning.

He laughed, a big, booming sound that actually made Tessa smile, and hugged them both as if they were old island friends.

It was the first time Tessa had met the man. She giggled and went with it, though, noting that Janey did too. In fact, Janey's smile had taken on a whole new hue, and Tessa could see the interest sparking in her sister's hazel eyes.

Oh dear, she thought as she followed Sean and Janey down the hall to the lawyer's inner office. Was her sister seriously entertaining the thought of a fling with their mother's Nantucket lawyer?

He held the door for them, and asked Cory, his assistant, to bring coffee, soda, and water. Once everyone was settled, Sean pulled a folder from his side of the desk and set it on top.

"First," he said, looking at both women, his smile slipping away. "Let me say how sorry I am about your mother. Lydia was such a good friend to everyone, and she is missed here on Nantucket."

"Thank you," Tessa said automatically, Janey a half a beat behind her.

Sean nodded and opened the folder. "I understand you read the will with her agent in New York City. I know there was a provision to come here to meet with me, go through the cottage, and complete the conditions of the will before it can be fully executed." He glanced up, and Tessa nodded as it seemed he needed the confirmation.

"I have an auxiliary to the will for both of you, sealed in my presence by your mother." He took out a large, legal-sized envelope that looked like it held a bit of paper. Maybe ten or twelve sheets, at least.

He slid it onto the table in front of Janey. "You can and probably should open them in private. Your mother wanted me to pass them out and read a statement." He took out an identical envelope and put it on the table in front of Tessa.

Her fingers itched to reach out and rip it open, privacy or not. Hers didn't appear to be any thicker than Janey's, but she hadn't gotten anything personal from the lawyer in New York, nor the binder she'd been through half a dozen times.

What were her mother's final words to her?

Chapter Six

S ean droned on about the legalities of the contents of the envelopes. "They're part of the official will, as auxiliary clauses added after the fact, while Lydia Clarke lived and resided here on Nantucket, in the cottage on the Point." He didn't look up from the paper in front of him, and he'd put on a pair of reading glasses to be able to see it.

Tessa's attention had wandered, but Janey seemed razor-focused on Sean.

"Each co-trustee shall have the opportunity to open their envelope in private, and neither has to disclose to the other what the contents contain."

Tessa perked up then.

"Each co-trustee can discuss the contents with the other co-trustee, but the will and grantor leaves that up to the discretion of the parties involved. All other conditions and requirements of the original estate and trust, filed on

August thirteenth, two-thousand-sixteen with Hammer-
stein and Associates, are binding and in force."

He glanced up. "Questions?"

Tessa could only shake her head, and Janey said, "No."

"Once the letters have been opened, the legal represen-
tative of Lydia Clarke, who is now deceased, Sean Harland
Masterson, will present the final documents to the co-
trustees, provided that they are both present to receive
them."

He cleared his throat and reached for his bottle of
water. "That's it."

"So there's more after we open these?" Janey tapped
her envelope.

"Yes." Sean looked back and forth between the two
sisters. "I have one more folder for the two of you. I don't
have to give it to you today. You can—"

"We want it today," Janey said firmly, picking up her
envelope. "We can open these now? Or…?"

Sean gestured for them to go right ahead, but Tessa
hesitated. "Janey," she said as the first sound of ripping
paper met her ears. "It said we can open them in private."

Janey looked at Tessa, plenty of electricity zipping
through her expression. "You want to open yours alone?"

"We don't even know what's in there." Tessa couldn't
even bring herself to pick up her envelope.

Janey's phone rang at that moment, and she startled as
she started to fish it from her purse. "I have to take this."
She stood and swiped on the call. "Bronson, I need just ten
seconds, please." Her whole demeanor changed, and she

tapped a button on her phone. She looked at Tessa and then Sean. "Is there a conference room or somewhere I can complete my phone call and open my letter in private?" She blinked at him as if he should've offered this accommodation from the beginning.

"Of course," he said, jumping to his feet. "Come with me." At the door, he looked back at Tessa. "You're free to stay right here. I'll close the door." With that, he left with Janey, bringing the door closed behind him.

Tessa took a deep breath and reached for her envelope. She'd barely slipped her fingers under the flap when the door opened again.

Sean re-entered, and this time, when he closed the door, he locked it.

"Mister Masterson?" Tessa asked.

"You haven't opened yours, have you?" He looked at her with wide eyes. "Good. Just a moment."

"Just a moment?" Tessa let her hand drop from the flap.

Sean pulled the cords on the blinds, sealing his office from anyone walking by. Combined with the now locked door, the closed blinds made Tessa feel claustrophobic and like they were about to do something illicit or illegal.

Sean rounded his desk again and reached into the bottom drawer of his desk. "I was instructed to give this to you—and only you—before you opened your letter, but after it was delivered." He gave a shaky laugh. "I have to admit, I've been stewing about it since I heard of your mother's passing. She gave no directions for how I should accomplish such a move, and having Janey's phone ring when it did was an answer to many nights of prayer."

He sank into his chair, his relief palpable.

"I don't understand," Tessa said.

Sean nodded to the second, much smaller envelope. "That is for your eyes only. I do not know what it is. Lydia gave it to me, and requested that I present it to you alone, after you received your initial envelope, but before you opened it."

"Okay." Tessa reached for the smaller, more normal envelope. It was white, like the type a regular letter would come in. The type she'd been opening to pay her electric bill for decades. It weighed nothing, and she wasn't sure which to open first. "Is there an order I should open these?"

"She didn't specify." He got to his feet. "I do need to leave you alone now. You can stay here, or I can show you to another room."

"I don't want to take your office," Tessa said. She got to her feet and collected her envelopes, tucking the smaller white one behind the larger beige one so no one would see it. "Show me where I can go through these things alone."

Chapter Seven

"This is it?" Janey reached into the safety deposit box and picked up a slim manilla folder the color of the ocean. She looked at the gentleman who'd escorted them into the vault, her eyebrows raised.

"Whatever is in your box, ma'am." He looked from her to Tessa. "Would you like to keep the box open? Or would you like to close it?"

Tessa looked at Janey, and her choice was obvious. "We'll close it," Tessa said, reaching into her pocket to extract her key. This box had required two keys—she and Janey had each gotten one in their envelopes from the lawyer.

Tessa's stomach writhed, and she knew it wasn't because she hadn't eaten enough that day. She hadn't had enough time to thoroughly go through everything in her envelopes—both of them—before Janey had texted to say she was ready to go.

Since Tessa didn't want to call any attention to herself, she'd packed everything up and joined her sister in the lobby. They'd come straight to the bank, as that was obviously what needed to happen next.

"I can show you to a room to go through things," the banker said.

Janey had already flipped open the folder. "No need," she said, plucking out the single sheet of paper. "It's the deed to the cottage." She tucked the official document back into the folder, closed it, and handed the man her key as well. "We'd like to close this, as my sister said. What do we need to do?"

Everything at the bank took forever, and Tessa found she couldn't sit still. Thankfully, Janey couldn't either, and they took turns pacing away from the Vice-President's desk while he closed the safety deposit box and their mother's bank account.

He finally returned while Janey had stepped outside for a moment. Tessa suspected she needed to calm herself with chemicals, and she'd likely smell like sticky, sweet strawberries from her vaping vapor.

He sat behind the desk and glanced from Tessa to the empty chair. "Is your sister still here?"

"Yes," Tessa said, half-rising from her seat. "Should I get her?"

"No, it's fine." He swallowed and pushed a piece of paper toward her. "This is the balance of your mother's account." He straightened and picked up another paper. "This is the balance of your account."

Tessa looked up from the first check, which bore an amount that started with twelve thousand dollars. That was at least six for her and Janey each, and while that amount of money wasn't anything to sneeze at, Tessa's heart wasn't ricocheting around her chest because of that.

"Excuse me?" she asked. "*My* account?"

"Yes," he said. "Your mother had opened an account for you many years ago. That's the balance, and it's been closed now. It had her name on it too, but I'm assuming the will details what to do."

It most certainly did not, but Tessa quickly swiped up the extra check, barely glancing at it, and tucked it in her purse. She rose to her feet, wishing she'd brought in the manilla envelope so she could hide the extra check more easily. "Thank you." She shook the man's hand and marched out of the bank.

Janey stood down at the end of the sidewalk, one hand pressing her phone to her ear and one holding a vape to her mouth. She was partially turned away from Tessa, so Tessa heard, "I understand that, Sunny. I should have some money soon." She turned her head toward Tessa, who held up the check. "I have to go."

Janey hung up and extinguished her vaporizer. "What's that?" she asked, her eyes hopeful yet cautious.

"The balance of Mom's account." Tessa smiled, though her mind spun. Janey clearly needed money for something. She'd never heard the name Sunny before, and she wondered if she could press. "According to the will, since we're co-trustees, we should split this right down the middle."

Janey took the check, a huge smile forming on her face. "Let's go eat first. We'll pay for it from this, then split it."

"Sounds perfect." Tessa managed to smile, because she needed to be alone to truly examine everything she'd received that day.

After they'd cashed the check and gotten a table at Seaside Manor, after Tessa had spread her bright white napkin on her lap and Janey had ordered her gin and tonic, Tessa looked at her sister. "What are you thinking about the cottage?"

"We should sell it, of course."

Tessa bristled at the semi-condescending tone, as well as the last two words. *Of course.* As if any other course of action would be ludicrous. She didn't normally disagree with her sister verbally, though they did live two very different lives, and the way Tessa chose to live likely commented on exactly how she disagreed with her sister.

She would never date a married man, for example, and Janey had done that at least once.

"I'd like to keep it," Tessa said.

Janey's eyes widened. "Why? You always complain about how much work it is to maintain."

Tessa shrugged, because she had said such things in the past. "I don't know." She looked out over the water. Here in the curve of the island, it lapped at the shore instead of washing over the sand. "I don't want to let it go." She reached for her water as the waitress set down Janey's drink.

The conversation paused while they ordered their lobster rolls and frites, and Janey put in another order for a Bloody Mary this time.

"I'd buy you out," Tessa said, wishing she had a glass of alcohol to hide behind. At the same time, she thought that perhaps it was time to stop hiding altogether. Hiding from what she really wanted. Hiding from her sister, her son, and her husband.

At some point, she was going to have to face them all and do what was best for her. She honestly wasn't sure when she'd last done that.

"We don't even know how much the cottage is worth," Janey said with a frown.

"That's easy," Tessa said. "We call a realtor. You'd have to do that to sell anyway."

Janey folded her arms and leaned back in her chair. "I just think it would all be easiest if we just sold everything and split everything right down the middle."

"Why does it matter if I buy you out? You'd still get half of the profit."

"Does Mom own the house?"

"You have the deed in your purse. I'm assuming she does, yes."

"You're talking hundreds of thousands of dollars to buy me out then." She cocked one eyebrow. "You and Ron have that much money?"

Tessa kept her expression even, as she honestly wasn't

sure how much she and Ron held in their accounts. He managed all of that, and Tessa always had enough to pay the bills and buy groceries. "I'll have to talk to him, of course."

Janey sighed and looked out over the bay too. "I need the money, Tess." A hint of embarrassment rode on her words, and she wouldn't look at Tessa.

She thought of the extra check in her purse and swallowed. "I'm sorry, Janey." Her sister had often struggled to make ends meet. She'd had her car repossessed four or five years ago, and it was only in the past twelve or fourteen months that she'd gotten a new one.

She'd asked Tessa and Ron to sign on the new car loan if she needed them to, but she'd been able to get it on her own. Tessa's heart went out to her sister, but she knew she couldn't save her. She also knew she didn't want to bend to her sister's will and sell the cottage just because *she* needed the money. She'd get the same amount whether they sold it to someone else or Tessa bought out her half of it.

"I just want this done, so I can go back to my regular life," Janey said.

"I'm so sorry our mother died and inconvenienced you." Tessa regretted the words the moment they left her mouth. But, poisoned as they were, they were also the truth. Janey hadn't done anything to clean up the estate, go over the will, or move either of them toward a final solution.

Tessa had cleaned out the apartment in New York City.

Tessa had gone to the other banks by herself. Tessa had met with the city lawyers handling her mother's estate.

Janey snapped her attention back to Tessa, who shook her head. "Never mind. Forget I said anything. Let me talk to Ron and figure out how much the cottage is worth, and then I can decide."

"Fine," Janey said, and thankfully, the shrimp rolls arrived—along with Janey's second drink—and Tessa allowed herself to get distracted with the food.

At least for a few minutes. The desk, the keys, the check, and the envelope meant only for her never truly left her mind, despite the delicious lobster and crispy, buttery fries she consumed.

Chapter Eight

That night, an hour after Janey had downed her second glass of wine and gone to bed, Tessa snuck up the steps to the second floor, the plain white envelope clutched in her hand. Every board creaked, and she tiptoed over to the recliner in front of the windows.

She looked out over the dark water, the tips of the waves barely catching the moonlight and throwing it back into the sky. The sand, usually beige, was a frosty color, and everything seemed still and serene.

A figure jogged along the beach, a headlamp attached to the person's forehead, and Tessa marveled that someone would be out at this hour, exercising. Of course, she didn't do any sort of formal exercise if she didn't have to, and running was completely foreign to her.

When she was sure Janey wasn't going to come upstairs and investigate any footsteps she may have heard, Tessa stood and went carefully up the dark, narrow staircase to the attic. Her lungs labored with the effort to move silently and slowly, and her heart pounded in the back of her throat, choking her.

In her second envelope, the one Sean Masterson had given only to her, she'd found a second key. It had been taped to a piece of paper with writing in her mother's hand. *For the desk upstairs. Open it alone.*

There had been no other notes. No letters of love and forgiveness. No instructions for what to do with the contents of the drawers in this desk. The key and single sheet of paper had been folded into a piece of cardstock to make the contents feel flat, and Tessa now took out the other item she'd put there while Janey had showered that evening.

The second check, which was in the amount of twenty-eight thousand dollars and some change.

Just for her.

She frowned at it. How did Mom only have twelve thousand in her main account, but Tessa had more than double that? Where had this money come from?

And more importantly, why didn't Janey have a check or an account like this?

The key fell from the envelope, landing on the bare wood floor with a clatter. Tessa slapped her palm over it so it wouldn't skitter anywhere, and she sucked in breath after breath, listening.

For what, she honestly didn't know.

"Calm down," she whispered to herself. "There's not going to be a body in this desk drawer."

She knew that, and it wasn't bodies she was worried about. Something thick coated her throat, because she felt like Mom was cutting Janey out of specific things, and there had to be a reason why. Tessa had been hypothesizing all afternoon, but sometimes even her worst fears didn't come close to the truth.

On the top drawer, she inserted the silver key into the silver lock, and it turned easily. She pulled in a breath, held it, and pulled open the drawer.

A cash box sat there, a gray item no wider than her small laptop and no thicker than a loaf of bread. With shaking hands, she removed it from the drawer and set it on the floor. Her forty-five-year-old knees didn't like this position, but she didn't correct it.

She unclasped the latch on the cash box and lifted the lid, almost flinching away even as she peered inside, lest any locusts come soaring out.

The air took on the scent of dust…and money.

The cash box held bills in all denominations up to the hundred-dollar bill, each laid out neatly from smallest to largest, from left to right.

Ones, fives, tens, twenties, fifties, hundreds.

She lifted the bill holder to check beneath it, as she'd volunteered many times for the PTA fundraisers and knew checks and coins were usually stored beneath the plastic insert. Nothing in the bottom of the cash box had her breath releasing from her lungs.

There were no coins in any of the slots for them, and Tessa picked up the stack of hundred-dollar bills. It had a decent weight and heft, which only made her heartbeat start to sprint again.

"Where did Mom get all this money?"

Dad had died twenty years ago. Yes, Tessa and Janey had been adults by then, and Mom had gotten a good life insurance settlement. But was it this much? Enough for her to live on for two decades, and have forty thousand dollars in a bank here on Nantucket? She'd had that much in her bank accounts in the city too.

Plus that apartment overlooking Central Park.

Nothing made sense. Mom had never worked a paying job, and the dollars and cents weren't lining up in Tessa's head.

"You don't know how much the life insurance was," she told herself as she closed the cash box. How was she supposed to hide this? She thought about stuffing her pajama pockets with some bills now and coming back for more later.

At the same time, Janey had said at dinner that she needed to get back to Jersey for a day or two, and then she was flying to Dallas for a business meeting. She wouldn't be in the cottage for much longer, and Tessa could easily move the money then.

Guilt ripped through her, especially when she remembered Janey's conversation outside the bank with someone named Sunny, and her admission at dinner that she needed the money. Would this cash alleviate some problems for her?

When Tessa looked at it, all she saw was more obstacles. More deception and half-truths.

She removed the key from the top drawer and slid it into the lock on the bottom one. It twisted just as easily as the first, and Tessa felt stronger as she opened the second drawer.

She straightened up on her knees to see down inside the drawer, and a gasp flew out of her mouth.

A dark blue binder lay there.

She reached for it even as her brain screamed at her. This binder bore a layer of dust that Tessa's fingers left prints in as she gripped it and lifted it out of the drawer. It didn't weigh nearly as much as the one Tessa already had in her possession, and she set it on her knees and stared at it.

Something nagged at her, and she jerked her head up.

She'd heard something downstairs. Her pulse crashed in her ears, but she tilted her head to the side, listening.

A moment later, she heard the noise again. Janey was up and in the kitchen, most likely.

Panic streamed through Tessa. She couldn't be caught up here, examining the contents of the now-open drawers. She hurried to replace the binder in the drawer, and she put the cash box on top of it.

She slid the bottom drawer closed as quietly as she could, cursing when it scraped and squealed. She relocked it and got to her feet, her mind racing.

At her feet lay the white envelope with the check resting on it.

Swearing again, she bent and picked them up, reopened the bottom drawer and slid them through the smallest crack.

"The top drawer," she muttered, making sure it was locked too. She slipped the key in her pajama pants pocket, a new thought paralyzing her.

Had she closed her bedroom door? Or would Janey know she wasn't in her room should she happen to look inside?

Chapter Nine

B obbie Friedman had obviously spent many days on the beach, her skin weathered and tan and wrinkled. She'd invited the sisters to have a picnic on the sand with her and her husband, and Tessa had been so out of it from her midnight romp in the attic that she hadn't been able to come up with a reason why she and Janey couldn't attend.

"How long will you girls be here?" Bobbie asked, opening a picnic basket complete with the red and white checkered cloth.

Tessa met Janey's eye. Today she wore a black swimming suit cover up that made her look like a queen, plenty of dark eye makeup she'd hidden behind her oversized sunglasses, and a smile.

"Until things are settled," Janey said evasively, and that was news to Tessa.

"Have you decided to sell the cottage?" Riggs asked, his green eyes bright with hope. He exchanged a glance with his wife. "If you do, we'd like to be the ones to buy it. We'll give you the market value for it."

"It's just so close to our property," Bobbie explained further. "We'd love to have it for our kids and grandkids. If you're going to sell."

For some reason, Tessa didn't want to sell the cottage to Bobbie and Riggs, though she knew they'd take good care of it.

"We haven't decided what to do with the cottage," she said, her voice firm and final. Thankfully, Janey remained quiet as she took a sandwich from Bobbie. She gave her a smile and unzipped the bag.

The unmistakable scent of tuna fish came from the bag, and Tessa almost gagged. She'd grown up on tuna fish sandwiches, because it was cheap, and Mom hadn't been the greatest cook. She certainly didn't eat it as an adult, but Janey took a bite without complaint. She watched the waves out in the ocean, leaving Tessa to carry the conversation with Bobbie and Riggs.

She did, deftly avoiding eating any of her sandwich by consuming a lot of fruit and potato chips instead. She watched Bobbie watch Riggs, and she watched Riggs watch Janey.

No one seemed to be paying any attention to her at all, though the three of them continued to talk about the happenings on Nantucket that summer, and the farmer's market the sisters might want to attend the following day.

"Your mother used to sell her jewelry there," Riggs said, and that brought Janey's attention from the water.

"I'm sorry," she said, her first contribution to the conversation. "Mom sold jewelry at the farmer's market?" She looked at Tessa, who had the same question. "When?"

"All the time," Riggs said, not meeting his wife's eyes. "All summer long, every time she came."

Tessa wondered how much she'd gotten for it. "What kind of jewelry?" she asked. If she sold it at the farmer's market, she couldn't have gotten that much. People sold their homegrown vegetables, handmade soaps, and crocheted potholders at the farmer's market. Not fine jewelry.

"Her work was exquisite," Riggs said, a hint of pride in his voice. It matched the smile on his face. Tessa supposed he could've been handsome in his younger days, as he still had a head full of now-silver hair that had once been dark brown. "She polished her own rocks and found her own pearls for each piece. She made bracelets mostly, but some earrings."

He fell silent then, and Tessa noticed the sharp look from Bobbie. It softened as she looked at the sisters. "You didn't eat your sandwich," she said to Tessa, who'd tried to cover it with an apple core and two empty bags of chips.

"Oh, I filled up on fruit," she said with a laugh and a look in Janey's direction.

Her sister's phone rang, and she pulled it from her lap. "It's my boss," she said. "I need to take this. Excuse me." She stood and answered the call, quickly pulling the phone away from her mouth. "Thank you for lunch, Bobbie. Good to see you both." She smiled as if she really meant it and walked away, her voice wafting back to them on the wind, though Tessa couldn't make out the words.

"I should go too," Tessa said, standing. "Thank you so much for lunch." She didn't give a reason why she needed to leave, but she did bend down and help the two of them clean up. After stuffing chip bags into a designated garbage sack and helping Bobbie fold up the blanket, Tessa noticed Riggs had wandered away too.

"Is he okay?" Tessa asked, and Bobbie looked up at her and then toward her husband.

"Oh, he's fine." The smile she put on her face was false and plastic, and Tessa wondered what she was trying to cover up. "He just loves seeing you girls so much. Reminds him of our daughter, and we don't get to see her very often." Her chin shook and her eyes welled with tears.

Bobbie grabbed Tessa in a hug, which only caused Tessa to experience another round of guilt for trying to get away from them and not eating the tuna fish sandwich. "Thanks for coming to a picnic with a couple of old loonies." She laughed and released Tessa, who could only smile.

As Bobbie walked away, Tessa wondered why her stomach wouldn't settle. She couldn't see Janey, and she hurried up the beach to the cottage. Once inside, she headed straight into the attic and over to the window.

"There she is." Her sister strolled far down the beach, the wind coming off the water pulling at her swimming suit cover-up.

Tessa hurried to unlock the bottom drawer and pull out

the blue binder. Then she sat in the recliner and balanced it on her knees. She checked on Janey's position, and she was still headed away from the cottage. A couple of other people had come to the beach that day—locals who owned the other cottages on this beachside lane. None of them would bother her.

She looked down at the binder, took a deep breath, and opened it.

Chapter Ten

It's up to you if you tell Janey or not.

The words haunted Tessa for a full day before she started to have other thoughts. She'd claimed a flu bug and stayed in her bedroom for most of the day, but she couldn't confine herself to the fifteen-by-fifteen-foot space for another moment.

The cottage sat in morning stillness, the sunlight trying to get through the slats in the blinds Janey had drawn over the front windows.

As the clock had just ticked to eight a.m., Tessa didn't expect to see her sister for a couple more hours at least. She took her coffee and a piece of toast out to the front porch and settled onto the top step.

After she'd finished her breakfast, she called Ron.

"Hey, sweetheart," her husband said when he connected the call. "How's the cottage?"

All of the fears and doubts Tessa had experienced over

the state of her marriage dried up. They'd come creeping back in, though, and she needed to start rebuilding the bridge between her and Ron.

"It's incredible," she said. "I'm looking out over the ocean right now." A smile filled her soul, and she sighed. "The first week of August can't come fast enough."

He chuckled and asked, "How are you getting along with Janey?"

She glanced over her shoulder, but her sister wasn't there. She had so much to tell Ron, and she didn't even know where to start. "Good enough," she said. "She wants to sell the cottage."

"I'm sure she does."

"What do you mean?"

"She never has any money," Ron said gently. "The estate, with the cottage, will be worth a lot more."

"Yes," Tessa said slowly, thinking of the check, the cash, and the binder. "Ron, I want to keep the cottage. I proposed to Janey that we might be able to buy her out." She went on to tell him about everything she'd found, the story rushing out of her in quick sentences told in a breathy, excited voice.

Ron said, "Wow, I need a minute," when she finished.

She understood that. She'd taken a whole day, and she still didn't know what to do.

"What are you feeling?" he asked, something he'd done early in their marriage when she was upset with him. She'd learned over time to tell him how she felt and what she was thinking, and then they could operate from a place of fact. They'd learned to work together.

"I'm feeling like we don't really need the money," she said. "I'd rather have the cottage." She stood up and went down the steps, her bare feet touching the warm sand on the sidewalk in front of the cottage. "I'm feeling distant from you, and I hate it. I feel like Ryan's been cutting both of us out of his life for whatever reason, and we need to do something about it."

She turned and looked at the bright blue cottage, her husband strangely giving her another moment. Sometimes he tried to tell her stories, and sometimes he let her talk. Tessa had learned it all had to do with how his week in the city had gone. If he felt like he was getting enough air time, getting listened to, in his office, he let her talk.

If he felt like he was being overlooked or his legal advice ignored, he talked over her.

"I'm feeling like I should tell Janey what I've found and let her see all of it." Her stomach twisted at the thought, because she didn't think Janey would react well to any of the things Tessa had received or found in the past couple of days.

"You need to do what you feel is right," Ron said. "I'll support you, Tess."

"Thanks," she murmured.

"We are a little distant," he admitted. "It's my fault. I'll be there in a few weeks though, and let me call Ryan and see what I can find out. Sometimes he tells me things he doesn't want to tell you."

That was true, no matter how much Tessa wished it wasn't. She'd told her son he could always tell her anything, but she'd been the task-master and the disciplinarian for him growing up, and he simply didn't tell her everything.

"Thank you," she said. "I love you, Ron."

"I love you too, sweetheart." He wore a smile in his voice. "Let me know how it goes with Janey."

"I will." She ended the call and turned around to face the water again. She couldn't quite see the edge of it because the sand swelled just across the street, but the smudge of water sat on the horizon.

"Good morning," Riggs called, and Tessa turned toward him. A fishing pole rested against his shoulder and a tackle box dangled from his hand.

"Morning," she called back to him, then watched him go along the path that led over the swell and down to the water. She wasn't sure if he ever caught anything. One summer, she and her cousins had tried to bait crawfish with raw bacon along the shore, and they'd only caught three.

She faced the cottage again and climbed the steps. She could see over the swell here, and she noted that Riggs wasn't on the path anymore. Where he'd gone, she couldn't say, as she didn't see him at all. Puzzled, but pushing him from her mind, she went back inside the cottage.

She set a pot of coffee to brew, and then she went into her bedroom to collect the key and the binder she'd gotten in New York. A trip upstairs retrieved the rest of the items, and Tessa laid them all out on the kitchen table.

Her fingers shook as she balanced the check made out only to her against the salt and pepper shakers that never left the table. She blinked, and she could see the letters inside the blue binder.

It's up to you if you tell Janey or not.

That had been the first line of the letter that sat on the first page inside the new binder.

It had been the last line too.

Tessa hated bearing this burden, and she'd thought long and hard about what she'd want if the tables were turned.

She'd want the truth.

Janey was her sister, and Tessa owed her the truth.

"What's all this?"

Tessa flinched and looked up to find Janey examining the items on the table. She reached out and picked up the check Tessa had just taken precious moments to balance. "What *is* this?" she asked again, her eyes wide and filled with wonder and fear now.

"We should sit down," Tessa said, her voice sounding very frog-like. She did, glad when Janey pulled out a chair and did the same.

"Mom had an account in my name," she said. "That was the balance from it." She nodded to the check. "I got an extra envelope from Sean Masterson too, and it had a key in it." She tapped the silver key, which lay next to the white envelope. "It opened the desk drawer upstairs."

Janey put the check down on the table and folded her

arms. She didn't look mad or afraid or upset, and the lack of emotion unsettled Tessa.

"She said I could choose to tell you or not, and I'm choosing to tell you."

"Tell me what, exactly?" Janey asked, her voice a bit acidic.

"It's easier if you just read it yourself." Tessa nudged the blue binder toward her. "I just want you to remember that you're my sister, and I love you."

Janey hesitated in her reach toward the binder. Her eyes softened, and she hadn't put any makeup on that morning. Tessa could see the true version of her sister, and she was kind and loving and Tessa's best friend.

"I love you too." Janey gave her a small smile and reached for the binder. "Am I going to freak out at what I find in here?"

"I guess we'll see." Tessa swallowed, inhaled, and held the air in her lungs as Janey opened the front flap of the new, blue binder.

Chapter Eleven

J aney opened the binder, but she pressed her eyes closed. She carried a huge weight on her shoulders and in her mind, and sometimes she felt like she could only move her arms. *Flail* would actually be a better word for how much progress she'd made in the past couple of years.

In a moment of time, she could think about a dozen things. The emails she needed to respond to. Her boss who expected her to call with her date of return this morning. The texts from Sean Masterson. The ones from her boyfriend in Jersey—one of them anyway. The three buckets in the house that caught any water that leaked through the roof. The payment due dates for a dozen different accounts. The airplane ticket in her cart she hadn't finished buying yet.

She couldn't, because she didn't have the money in her account. She needed the dates too.

Janey opened her eyes, a sense of sheer fury licking at her insides. She didn't have time to spend on Nantucket. She didn't want to be here, and as she looked down at this second binder, all it held for her was an astronomical amount of time.

At least it held half as many sheets of paper as the first one Tessa had gone through. Janey had let her do everything with the estate and the accounts, because she seemed to want to, and she had much more time than Janey did.

The words on the page blurred, and Janey looked up as she took another breath. "Maybe you can just tell me what it says."

She'd had plenty of experience with hiding away how she felt. No one ever got to see her upset or angry. Clients thought she was a barrel of fun all the time. Her boss got pure professionalism. Her boyfriends got a flirty, laughing woman who'd kiss them on the first date and go home with them by the third. Janey knew exactly what to show to precisely who, at the perfect time.

Sometimes she stood in front of the mirror in her messy bathroom and wondered who she really was. The bad girl who wore leather and rode motorcycles with her club? The professional woman who knew fashion and makeup and always closed the deal? The carefree woman who wore shorts that were too short and tank tops that showed off her arms so she could get free drinks and dance the night away?

"Mom explains it," Tessa said. "Just read it." She stood up and paced into the kitchen, where she poured herself another cup of coffee. Her younger sister sounded frustrated with her, and Janey wasn't surprised by that. Tessa never said anything, but Janey knew her late start to the day irritated Tessa, as did a handful of other things.

Janey looked at the first page in the binder.

My dear Tessa,

It's up to you if you tell Janey or not.

I want to put that first, because it's the most important thing. I'll probably repeat it a couple of times.

By now, you've visited Sean Masterson and gotten the key to the desk drawer. You've most likely been to the bank and received an extra check, from a bank account I put in your name only. Now you've found the binder.

I'm sure you're confused and probably a little scared. I hope this letter will address the first concern, and I hope all the documents contained herein will ease your fears.

I've taken certain steps to protect my assets from those who would like to take them from you. I didn't put these items into the trust, because they can challenge that, which I'm sure they have already. If they haven't, they will.

Janey paused and looked up. "Who's 'they'?"

"I don't know," Tessa said, and that contradicted what Mom had said about the letter explaining all the confusing things.

"Has someone challenged the trust?"

"Not that I'm aware of," she said. "Though we do have the ninety days to go through it and come to an agreement. Perhaps they will after that?" Tessa shook her head and faced Janey. She wore a pair of shorts that went all the way to her knee and an untucked blouse in a mustardy yellow that no one had worn for at least seven years.

Janey actually wondered what it would take to get her sister to loosen up. She knew she had money. Why didn't she buy clothes from this year? There were so many simple things she could do to...*what, exactly?* Janey asked herself.

Tessa was happy, and that was all that mattered. She didn't need to wear the newest fashions to meet a new man. She didn't go to bars and clubs looking for Mr. Right. She already had him, and no one at the Easton Public Library cared if she wore an off-trend color.

"Can't people challenge an individual will too?" Janey asked.

Tessa's husband was a lawyer, and she just assumed Tessa would know.

"Yes," she said.

Then the whole letter only added to Janey's confusion. She glanced at the check, her heartbeat cartwheeling through her chest at the numbers on it. Twenty-eight thousand dollars. More than double what Mom had left for the two of them to split.

Janey's tongue stuck to the roof of her mouth. Everything was so dry, and she felt like she'd put a handful of chalk in her mouth and tried to gargle with it.

Her vision blurred again, but she squinted at the letter.

I've created an addendum for my will for these specific assets, as that way, the legal ability of others to contest it are lessened. There has not been a will for these items before, and if no one else is named, they generally can't contest legally.

It's up to you if you tell Janey or not. She will have some decisions to make regarding what she tells you as well.

My hope is that you two will work together on the will and trust. I know the two of you haven't always been close, nor have you always seen eye-to-eye. I remember distinctly the day you said that you sometimes don't even feel related to her.

She has weaknesses and strengths, just like every other human being does. Just like you and I, Tess.

But you can decide what you'd like to do. The money from your account is yours, or you can split it with her. The assets in this will are yours, and you will need to decide what to do with them. All of the documents needed to transfer ownership or power are here as well, should you decide to include your sister in the decisions you need to make.

I will tell her the same thing, and hopefully this can be a bonding experience for the two of you. Something that will bring you closer together and remind you that you two do belong to each other, despite your differences.

That's all. The listed assets in this will are on the next page.

I love you, Tessa Marie. You were my baby, and I'm proud of the woman you've become.

Remember, it's up to you if you tell Janey or not.
Love, Mom

JANEY'S EYES BURNED WITH TEARS. SHE WANTED A LETTER that contained her mother's spirit and voice, telling her she loved her and was proud of her. Her chest pinched that she didn't have something like this, though her eyes did dart up and catch a few other lines.

I will tell her the same thing and *She will have some decisions to make regarding what she tells you as well.*

Janey had plenty of secrets, sure, but none of them were related to her mother's estate or assets.

She turned the page and saw a very short list of assets, but the first one made her eyes bulge and a squeak come out of her mouth.

Chapter Twelve

"The Hotel Benjamin?" Janey practically yelled. She swung her head wildly toward Tessa, who leaned against the counter in front of the sink, her arms folded. She barely saw her before spinning back to the binder.

The words sat there, in black and white. They hadn't reordered themselves.

"Mom left you The Hotel Benjamin? Like, *The* Hotel Benjamin in downtown New York City?"

"It seems so," Tessa said quietly. She could've shouted it and it would've been quiet in Janey's head. So much clamored inside her mind now that she could hardly see the next item on the list.

"The home listed at 4752 Shoreline Way, Long Island," Janey read, her chest starting to throb with the effort it took to breathe. She gasped for breath. Her mother had left her younger sister a hotel in New York City and a home on Long Island.

These were huge items. *Huge.*

This wasn't Mom's string of black pearls she'd gotten on a trip to Cozumel, nor a picture frame that held sentimental value. This wasn't even her car, which she and Tessa had agreed to sell and split the money. It had been sitting in a garage in the city, and the late-model sedan came from a top brand and had less than ten thousand miles on it.

Mom had lived in the city for the last several years of her life, and Janey had no idea how she'd come to own a home on Long Island or a five-star hotel, complete with a James Beard award-winning restaurant on the main floor.

The next item on the list was a bank account, complete with the account number, the name on the account— Mom's and Tessa's only—and the address of the bank. A note below that read, *This is a completely separate bank from the others you've been to. Sorry. I know it means another trip to the city, but I suppose all of this will require that.*

"I guess so," Janey said with a scoff. She hadn't gone to the city with Tessa the first time. First, she honestly hadn't been sure she'd have been able to handle it mentally and emotionally. The ache to talk to her mother hadn't lessened with time and distance, and right now, it intensified in such a way that Janey's head pounded.

She closed her eyes, trying to block out the light and sound that plagued her perpetually. She'd brought all of her medications to the cottage on Nantucket, and she'd been religious in taking them. She got up and went to the drawer where she'd stored her pill box. With a shaking hand, she got a glass out of the cupboard, and Tessa edged over so Janey could fill her glass with water from the sink.

She drank it all, the cold liquid helping her to focus. Her pills would do the same, and she refilled her glass and swallowed all of them in a single gulp. "This is insane," she said, her voice made mostly of air.

"What do you think it means?"

"It means Mom was buying stuff in the past few years, and she didn't tell us."

Tessa's eyebrows drew down. "Why do we suddenly own someone else's intellectual property?"

"What?" Janey hadn't made it that far, obviously.

Tessa moved over to the table, and Janey followed. Her pulse settled, and she didn't care if the pills were placeboes. They worked, and she set her glass on the table and retook her seat in front of the binder.

The last item on the page listed the intellectual property. "This is three series of science fiction novels," she said. "Cole used to read these, years ago."

"Do you know who DM Conway is?" Tessa asked.

Janey picked up her phone and started tapping to get to the Internet browser. "He's an author. He wrote those books."

"I gathered that," Tessa said. "But how did Mom acquire the ability to control his publishing rights? I looked it up, and you can earn on someone's books for seventy years after they die. *Seventy*."

Janey looked up from her search for DM Conway. "Seventy years?"

"That's—yes." Tessa pressed her palms together, spreading her fingers. Janey had seen her do such a move several times in the past, usually when she was trying to get her brain to think of something it hadn't yet. "We're talking about passing this on to our children, Janey. I'm not going to live for seventy more years."

"Depending on when this DM died," Janey said, and Tessa nodded her acquiescence. She went back to her phone and typed in the name. An author website came up, but there was no picture. She left that and went to the next link, though she never really believed anything on the user-curated websites.

"Isn't there something in the binder that will tell us?" Janey asked as the site loaded. The Internet out here on the Point could be flaky, and that was just another reason Janey didn't like spending too much time here.

She could work from anywhere, but the Internet was essential for that to be possible. She could download the docs and graphics she needed easily, but uploading took forever, and the crucial item she needed to send to Sunny back in the Jersey office still hadn't finished.

"I admit I stopped looking," Tessa said. "I read the first two pages, and then I made the decision to tell you." She met Janey's eye, and Janey set her phone aside. She rarely let herself be fully present with her family. Even her children sometimes sniped at her to put her phone away so they could tell her something important to them.

With her mom and sister, Janey could answer work emails and text her significant others, and they wouldn't say a thing. She knew she missed out on important details and bonding conversations, and her stomach swooped as she thought about why her mother hadn't left her an extra key that opened a mysterious drawer. Or a check singly for her in the amount of twenty-eight thousand dollars.

Her throat tightened, and the world spun for a moment.

Janey knew this feeling well. It descended upon her every time her phone rang and an unknown number sat there. It could be a creditor, asking her where her payment was. In fact, that was almost always what an unknown number meant for Janey.

She usually kept her notifications on silent, so she didn't have to explain why she wasn't answering calls. She had a visual notification set, and her phone flashed when it rang, but she could shrug it off as a text if she had to.

She thought about her leaking roof and the home equity loan she needed to fix it. The subfloor in her bedroom and the living room needed to be torn out and replaced too, because her last dog had been old and used any patch of carpet for a bathroom.

Janey's house was far too big for her, despite the fact that her twenty-year-old daughter and her boyfriend lived with her, and she desperately wanted to move. In order to that, she had some major repairs to do on the house so she could sell it for at least what she owed on it. And in order to do that, she needed the loan.

With her despicable credit, she couldn't get the loan.

She'd asked Tessa and Ron to be co-signers for her in

the past, but she hadn't wanted to do so again. She was almost forty-seven years old, and she hated the feelings of inadequacy at not being able to handle her own life that came when faced with her past decisions that determined her future opportunities.

The world pressed down on her. Further and further and further, until she felt like she couldn't move, let alone breathe.

"Do you want to look?" Tessa asked, her voice echoing in Janey's ears. "Or should I?"

Janey burst to her feet. "You know what? I need a minute." She swiped her phone off the table and dashed for the front door. She didn't bother closing it behind her. In fact, it slammed against the wall as she hurried down the front steps and hit the sand across the street in a dead run.

Chapter Thirteen

J aney pulled in the salty air, wishing it didn't hold the scent of her childhood. A burning rage existed inside her that she needed to scream out. Sometimes she needed to hit something really hard to get the fury out of her system.

Nantucket had no Crossfit gym, and no punching bag, and while Janey had brought her workout clothes, she hadn't sought out a gym or a yoga class. Heck, she could've taken a walk along the beach just to get some exercise in.

Because she hadn't done much more than sift through junk and fight her irritation for the past week, she couldn't run for long.

Her lungs burned and she finally fell into a fast walk, her breath panting in and out.

"A hotel," she said, the words exploding from her. "How in the *wide* universe of possibilities did Mom buy a hotel?"

There was no explanation for that. None. After Dad had died—"Twenty years ago," Janey reminded herself—Mom hadn't gotten a job. She lived off the life insurance, and she'd used the money from the sale of her house to buy apartment in New York. She hadn't wanted to take care of a yard, and she'd loved her one-bedroom place on the sixteenth floor of a building that overlooked Central Park.

Janey's mind spun around that apartment. It had to cost millions, and now that she took a moment to think about it, Mom shouldn't have been able to afford it at all.

"She obviously could," Janey muttered. "Maybe she's owned The Benjamin for decades."

If that were true, why hadn't she said anything to Janey or Tessa? They'd never stayed there. They'd never vacationed in the city.

No, Mom had always brought their family to Nantucket Point, to the little cottage she'd loved with her whole soul.

Tessa wanted to keep it, and while Janey had been looking at the situation from a purely financial point of view, with other assets in play, she could admit she didn't want to sell the cottage.

Before she knew it, she'd crossed the beach and arrived at The Lighthouse Inn. The old building had once been an operational lighthouse for the Point, and the Nantucket Historical Society had a plaque mounted next to the front door.

Now, the lighthouse served as a five-room bed and

breakfast, with full-time, live-in caretakers. Janey could still remember the day Phil and Margo Michaels had been named the operators of The Lighthouse Inn.

The entire population of Nantucket had come to the inn, and Mom had brought her and Tessa. She'd been sixteen years old and surly about being on Nantucket at all.

Over the years, though, Janey had come to the inn for an afternoon soda or to the beach that ran up to the overhang of rocks where the lighthouse sat.

Margo hosted games for guests on that beach, and she'd never turned away Janey and Tessa.

She wondered if she could catch Margo in her midmorning chores. Perhaps they could talk, as Margo had known Mom well.

Instead of heading toward the entrance, she wrapped her arms around herself and faced the wind that blew up off the rocks as if it were angry they dared get in its way.

She breathed in deeply and tried to clear her mind. Breathing never worked. Alcohol did. Her anti-depressants did too. But deep breathing? Yoga? Meditation?

Janey only did them to give her therapist the illusion that she was trying alternate treatments.

She walked around the three-story lighthouse that bore a fresh coat of light gray paint. She'd gone all the way to the door before she saw the sign taped to it.

Caretakers needed.

Janey pulled in a breath. The Michaels' didn't work here anymore—or wouldn't come November first.

She read the requirements to be the caretaker of The

Lighthouse Inn, as if she needed a new job. She didn't. She loved her job, and she was very, very good at selling software to huge companies.

The problem was, Janey spent more money than she earned. She always had, which meant she was operating with three decades of bad money decisions and constant financial pressure.

Her eyes caught on the third or fourth requirement: *Interested applicants should apply as a couple or partnership.*

"Well, that eliminates me," Janey said bitterly. She couldn't operate a boat either, but that could be learned. Finding a man her age who wasn't a total loser was a lot harder than learning how to sail.

She turned away from the inn, seeming to find disappointment wherever she looked. She needed to text or call Milford, her single boyfriend, and she already had a scheduled video chat with Curtis, her married one.

Just the fact that she had two boyfriends made most women's eyes widen. Tessa had sat on the other end of the phone line, utterly silent.

Then she'd said, "I can't even handle one man. How are you dealing with two?"

They'd laughed together, because it was a valid question. Janey hadn't answered it. The only thing she'd told Tessa after that was that yes, the two men knew about each other.

Milford knew more than Curtis, because Curtis didn't ask questions and didn't want to know.

Janey didn't see anything wrong with her behavior. She was honest about it. She wasn't cheating.

Curtis lived in an apartment in Jersey City, legally separated from his wife. The divorce just hadn't gone through yet. Janey wasn't wrecking any homes, and everyone involved was an adult.

Her walk back to the cottage took much longer than her march away from it, and Janey soaked in the sunshine, finally starting to calm down a little bit.

"It's not Tessa's fault," she told herself as the blue cottage came into view. "It's not Tessa's fault."

It wasn't.

Janey had a near photographic memory, and the letter had sounded like Mom was worried about someone else coming in and taking the valuable assets she'd hidden in this addendum.

Janey would be thrilled to never see another red binder again. At the same time, she couldn't help hoping she had one with a letter in her mother's handwriting just for her.

I will tell her the same thing.

It sure seemed like she probably did.

"But where?" she whispered, the words floating away on the breeze.

"Morning, Janey," a man called, and Janey turned toward the sound of the voice.

Riggs Friedman stood there, his smile far too large for someone holding a fishing pole and no fish.

"Morning, Riggs," she said, not wanting to be rude. She

got along with Riggs and his wife, Bobbie, but she didn't enjoy spending time with them. The couple was obviously lonely and starved for attention from their children, as they droned on and on about their daughter who was a judge in some city in Georgia Janey had never heard of.

If they weren't talking about Karla, Bobbie had a story about their son in Barcelona, who did some great big important thing for a sports team there.

As if both of those weren't bad enough, Riggs couldn't make it through a conversation without mentioning Janey's summer fling with Billy, their youngest. Yes, Janey had enjoyed kissing him, because he was a year older than her and incredibly hot. He still was, as she'd looked him up last week after Bobbie had stopped by the cottage on the first night Janey and Tessa had been on Nantucket.

She may have messaged him, just like she'd texted Sean Masterson.

Tessa would lose her mind if she knew Janey was currently talking to four men. Even she couldn't believe it.

"So." Riggs fell into step beside her, and Janey couldn't believe she'd let her guard down. "What do you think about breakfast?"

She glanced at him out of the corner of her eye. He'd obviously been talking while she'd been inside her own head, and she was at a severe disadvantage by not knowing what he'd said.

"I can't," she said. "Tessa and I have *so* much to do today. Besides, she already had blueberry muffins in the oven when I left for my morning walk."

There was so much wrong with that sentence that Janey nearly scoffed at her own statement. She couldn't remember the last time anyone had cooked in the oven in the cottage. Birds probably nested in it.

But Janey would say anything to get away from Riggs, who'd bring along an over-eager Bobbie.

"Janey," Tessa called, and relief rushed through her.

"The muffins are probably done." She gave Riggs her brightest, biggest smile, and lifted her hand to Tessa. "I'll be right in for those blueberry muffins."

Thankfully, Tessa knew how to deal with Riggs too, and she added, "Okay, but we don't have much time. We have to get all those boxes over to Good Will."

Chapter Fourteen

There were no blueberry muffins and no boxes inside the cottage. Janey almost wished there was, so she'd have something to distract her from the carefully lined up items still on the kitchen table.

"Are you okay?" Tessa asked once the door had been closed and locked.

"Yes," Janey said, keeping her back to her sister. She went to the fridge and got out a bottle of water. After uncapping it and taking a long drink, she asked, "Did you know the Michaels' are leaving The Lighthouse Inn?"

Tessa frowned and shook her head. "I didn't know that."

As neither of them were island locals, Janey wasn't surprised Tessa didn't know.

"What did Riggs want?" she asked.

"Something about breakfast," Janey said. "Thus why I said that about the blueberry muffins."

"We're going to have to eat dinner with them one night," Tessa said. "Might as well get it over with."

"Fine," Janey said, because her sister was right. "But they have to host it. If we do it here, they'll never leave."

"Agreed." Tessa sat down at the table and reached for the twenty-eight-thousand-dollar check. "Half of this is yours."

"Thank you." Janey sat down across from her sister but not in front of the red binder. "I need a new roof, and I can't qualify for the loan to get it. That will pay for it."

Tessa looked up and met Janey's eye. Nerves vibrated through her, along with plenty of embarrassment. Janey did her best to hold Tessa's gaze though.

Her phone rang, and Janey's eyes flew to it. She couldn't get it before Tessa saw Sean's name on the screen, and Janey swiped the call to voicemail.

"Are you going out with him?" she asked.

"He invited me to dinner," Janey said coolly. "I was considering it, yes." The man was a few years older than her and a lawyer, for crying out loud. Tessa might not have to think about such things, but Janey did. All the time. He was handsome *and* employed, and Janey knew that combination didn't come along every day.

"Are you still seeing Milford?" Tessa asked.

"Yes," Janey said with a small smile. "He's just gone on an assignment in Toronto for a few weeks."

Tessa nodded, pressing her lips together in such a way that expressed her displeasure silently.

Janey drew in a breath, wishing she'd been able to take

Sean's call. Perhaps they could've gone to lunch or dinner today, and she could get out of this cottage and find some answers.

She seized onto that single word—*answers*—and flipped open the blue binder again. "Okay, so maybe we should call this hotel and the bank." She looked up at Tessa, who seemed to be staring straight ahead at nothing in particular. "You know what?" Janey closed the binder again. "I'll do it. You handled everything else with Mom, and I can take care of these for you."

"The will is in my name," she said. "They might not talk to you."

Janey nodded and picked up her phone as she stood. "I'll see what I can do." She didn't want to go down the hall to her bedroom, but the front steps didn't appeal to her either. Riggs could wander by again, and Tessa could overhear her conversation.

So she went back down the hall to the bedroom at the end on the left, and she closed and locked the door behind her. Janey took care of dozens of business tasks on her phone, and her fingers had great muscle memory for exactly where to swipe and tap and type.

She found the number for The Hotel Benjamin and dialed it, putting the phone to her ear. She had no idea what to ask, or which button to push when she got an automated answering machine.

"Duh," she said quickly, remembering something in the letter. Mom had said she'd included contact information for the assets, and Janey hung up before she could decide if she should press one or two or zero.

She set the binder on the bed and knelt in front of it, gingerly flipping the page as if she'd rip it right out and all would be lost. Mom had done a very good job organizing everything, and a single sheet sat behind a divider that said THE HOTEL BENJAMIN in all capital letters across the top.

"Charles Burns," she read aloud, reciting the phone number typed below his name. It did not have a New York City area code, and that only added to Janey's puzzled thoughts. The address contained on the page listed him in Maryland, and Janey wanted to get on the next ferry that would take her back to the mainland, and then the very next airplane that would get her to Baltimore.

She typed in the phone number and tapped on the green icon to connect the call. Her pulse pounded with every millisecond that passed, and she had no idea what she'd say to Charles Burns should he answer.

He didn't, but his voicemail message identified him. "Yes, hello," Janey said, slipping into her businesswoman persona. She'd talked to hundreds of people, many of them CEOs. Janey could handle whoever Charles Burns was.

"My name is Tessa Simmons," she said, the little white lie rolling easily off her tongue. "I've just found my mother's will, and she's listed you as the contact person for an item that I suppose belongs to me now: The Hotel

Benjamin? Can you please call me at your earliest convenience?"

She recited her phone number and flipped the page as she ended the call. The next page contained the contact information for the bank, and Janey dialed the number. This time, Elle Wheeler answered her phone, and Janey launched into the same speech as before.

"Yes, of course," Elle said almost the moment Janey stopped speaking. "You'll have to come in with the account number and passcode. Then I'm to release the contents of the safety deposit box associated with that account, and I'll have a check ready for you."

"Really?" Janey asked. If this was what Tessa had been doing over the past six weeks, Janey didn't feel so bad.

"This is all detailed in my instructions from your mother," Elle said. "When you come in, I'm to have a check ready for you, and the account will be closed immediately. You get the safety deposit box, and it too is then canceled."

"Okay," Janey said. "I have quite a number of other items to deal with. Would it be possible to send my sister to take care of this?"

Elle didn't say anything, and Janey saw her opportunity to see what was in that safety deposit box start to smoke. She studied the page in the binder, the account number and passcode there, along with Elle's name, phone number, and the address of the bank.

"Ma'am, your sister is expected to come," Elle said, her voice filled with confusion. "Was that not listed in the will?"

"Of course," Janey said smoothly, flipping pages now, her eyes moving fast to find the information. She flipped to the next section, but it was about the hotel. Another flip and this section contained information on the house on Long Island. One more flip, and she arrived at the section about the bank account.

The same cover sheet that had all the information on it sat there, and Janey turned the page. *Tessa, if you include Janey in this process, send her to the bank in New York City. There is something for her to do there, and if you tell Elle Janey will be coming, they will authorize everything to her care for you.*

"I see it now," she said. "Janey will be coming to New York to deal with the account there."

"Yes, ma'am. Please make sure she has a valid ID when she comes. I work Monday through Friday, nine a.m. to five p.m., and she simply needs to ask for me when she arrives."

"Yes, ma'am," Janey said again, looking up and away from the binder.

The call ended, and she set the phone on the binder. She stared straight ahead, her knees reminding her that she need to focus. "No drinking," she whispered to herself. "Stay present. There is something for you to do in New York City."

Janey had no idea what she had to do in the city. She didn't live there, and she didn't go there if she didn't have to. Jersey was as close to the Big Apple as she wanted to get.

She had more questions than answers right now, but

she knew one thing. She needed to take this binder with her and get to the bank in New York City as quickly as she could.

Standing, Janey said, "Game face, Janey. It's okay to lie to her for the time being. You can tell her the truth once you know more of it."

She stepped over to the door and unlocked it, trying to find a reason Tessa would believe for why she needed to leave for the mainland instantly.

Chapter Fifteen

"I'll get it done as quickly as I can," Janey said as she lugged her carryon toward the front door. Tessa followed her, her displeasure as loud as a wail though she didn't make a sound. "It's just work. Sunny can't do anything with Rogers and Yardley without me, I swear." Janey made her voice as frustrated as she dared without going over the top.

She opened the front door and found her cab waiting in front of the cottage. Relief rose through her as quickly as the sun reared its face over the ocean each morning. Setting her suitcase on the ground, she turned back to her sister. "Three days, tops." She drew Tessa into a hug, ignoring the frown on her sister's mouth and eyebrows. She looked so much like Mom when she wore that expression, and Janey held her extra-tight as her emotions surged.

Moments like these, where she realized she'd never see that look on her mother's face again, snuck up on her, attacking out of nowhere and leaving her drained and exhausted for hours. She couldn't afford this setback right now, as traveling had started to wear her down the same way.

"I love you," she said, her voice almost a chirp it came out so high. She stepped back, didn't look at Tessa, and spun to pick up her luggage. She hurried down the steps and strode the length of the short sidewalk, her chest heaving as her eyes burned.

She slid into the back seat and cinched her arms across her chest.

"Ferry station?" the man behind the wheel asked.

"Yes, please," Janey clipped out, looking across the car to the beach opposite of the cottage. She couldn't stomach seeing Tessa standing on the porch, because Mom had often done exactly that. She'd lift one hand and yell to the girls to stay together and be home before dark.

Janey remembered the carefree days of her tweens, when she didn't mind so much that Tessa shadowed her everywhere. They'd collect shells from way out on the Point, where the shallow water was always warm and she could lay down in the soft sand and listen to the whisperings of the ocean.

She and Tessa would take turns burying each other in sand, building castles and then stomping them back into nothing but sand, and running as fast as they could when they heard the whimsical, almost circus-like music of the ice cream truck.

Mom always gave them a five-dollar bill for the day,

and Janey would buy them a corndog and fries to share so they'd have enough for ice cream sandwiches or the brightly colored rainbow pops that left her mouth stained a crimson red she shuddered at now.

The ringing of her phone pulled her from decades past, and she pulled it out of the pocket of her carryon. Sean's name sat there, and Janey quickly answered. "Sean, hello," she said smoothly, boxing up the emotions that had nearly undone her composure. "I hate to tell you this, but I have to return to Jersey for a couple of days."

"Something for work?" he asked.

"Yes," she said, feeling slightly bad about the lie. "Perhaps we can go to Rusty Bucket when I get back?"

"You're headed out now?"

"I'm on the way to the ferry station right now," she said. "I'm sorry, Sean." She did mean that, and she looked out the window at the quaint streets with houses dotting the horizon every so often. The cab left Nantucket Point, and fifteen minutes later, they'd arrive in the downtown area.

"It's okay," he said, and he sounded like he meant it. "I understand work emergencies, trust me." He offered her a chuckle, and she smiled though he couldn't see her.

"I'll be in touch." As soon as the call ended, she sent a quick text to Milford about her return trip to Jersey as well. She might as well cover all of her bases with the same story. It made everything so much easier to remember.

She sent him a picture of the beach and The Lighthouse Inn, saying she regretted she had to return to the office for even a few days. She frowned as she sent the same photos to her kids, asking them if she should keep the cottage so they could have summer vacations there.

She'd brought the kids as they'd grown up, but her marriage to their dad had ended before Rachel had turned three. Janey had been a single mom for sixteen years, despite a brief second marriage that had ended when her husband had physically disciplined Cole after she'd told him not to.

That marriage had ended seven years ago, and Janey's loneliness seemed to double by the day. That was why she couldn't go to Nantucket Point for a week without finding a man to go to dinner with, talk to, or think about.

She ended up not telling Cole and Rachel that she was leaving Nantucket. If she did, she'd have to tell at least Rachel where she was going, for her daughter lived with her and would certainly know she hadn't returned to Jersey for work.

Neither of them asked anything that required her to lie, and she told them about the beaches, the cottage, and the excellent seafood all the way to the ferry.

As the ferry made its way back to Hyannis, Janey texted Curtis to say she'd have to reschedule their video chat as she'd be traveling through it. He responded with a frowny face and the words, *Okay. Tell me when.*

She didn't, because she'd started to wonder why she should. Nothing was ever going to come of the relationship —besides amazing sex. Janey knew that; she'd known men like Curtis before, and they never truly left their wives.

Even though he was already separated, he wasn't divorced, and there was a reason for that.

Before she knew it, she'd joined the millions in New York City, each and every one of them walking with purpose and an exact destination in mind. Janey had once thrived on the energy in the city. Now, the tall buildings and the noise pressed in around her, though she did love to sit and people-watching, making up stories for each person who crossed her path.

Today, though, she had no time for sitting in parks and creating stories.

A huge clock in a square across from the bank rang four times, and Janey took a nice, long, deep breath. The letters above the doorway announcing the bank stared down at her, intimidating and imposing at the same time.

She reminded herself that she'd met with a number of CEOs, CFOs, and Cybersecurity experts. She'd led dozens upon dozens of meetings. She might not be wearing her skirt, slacks, or heels, but she knew how to put on a mask and pretend.

"Thirty minutes," she whispered to herself. "You just have to be strong for the next thirty minutes."

With that, she reached for the door and stepped inside Pinnacle Trust. The interior felt like a cave, with dark brick and dark hardwood on the floor. Low lighting reminded Janey of a club or pub, and she glanced to her right, where the long counter ran for tellers.

She looked left, and the space opened up, with desks dotting it at random. She definitely needed to go that way, and she pushed her hair off her forehead, wiping the thin sheen of sweat that had gathered on her walk here.

Janey stepped up to the first desk, already knowing it wasn't her goal. "Hello," she said pleasantly. "I'm looking for Elle Wheeler."

The man there looked up at her, no smile in sight. He seemed annoyed, and he probably had to field everyone who came in looking for someone more important than him. He indicated something behind her. "Elle's in the corner to your right."

"Thank you," Janey said crisply, turning and surveying the room. A fireplace took up the far end, and she wondered if the beautiful centerpiece worked. She'd often fantasized about having a home with a grand fireplace and mantel. To her, Christmas simply wasn't the same if she couldn't feed the discarded wrapping paper into the flames and watch it curl up, turn black, and smoke.

She hadn't been able to provide the same memories for her kids as she'd had as a child, and she vowed that her next house would have a fireplace, even if it was an electric one.

Elle's name sat on a plaque outside her office, and the door stood open. Janey stepped right up to the doorway and knocked on the frame. "Hello?"

A woman turned in her enormous office chair, rising a moment later. She didn't possess curves, but she did own designer clothes that made her thin body look normal. "Hello," she said in the same fluidly professional voice Janey had heard that morning. "Can I help you?"

"Yes," she said, committing to entering the room. She moved to the front of the massive mahogany desk separating her from Elle and extended her hand. "I'm Janey Forsythe. You spoke to my sister on the phone this morning." She added a smile to the statement, and the gesture helped settle her nerves.

"Janey, of course." Elle shook her hand. "Let me gather your items." She rounded the desk. "Can I get you anything? Water? Coffee? Soda?"

"I came from Nantucket," Janey said with a sigh, as if traveling to New York was such a chore. "Sparkling water would be lovely." She sat in one of the wingback chairs in front of Elle's desk and smiled.

"Sparkling water it is." Elle left her office, and Janey quickly got back to her feet and hurried to the door. The woman walked away without looking back, and she rounded the fireplace and went into the other office in the opposite corner.

Within five minutes, she'd returned with a sealed envelope and a key. "Come with me, if you would." She smiled, but she'd forgotten the sparkling water.

Janey scurried after her anyway, entering the vault after Elle had swiped her very important keycard through three checkpoints. She stood at the door while Janey found the box and put the key inside.

Her heart pounded harder than it ever had before, even more so than when she'd lost Rachel at an Easter egg hunt and couldn't find her for over an hour.

She finally twisted the key and opened the box, which

was one of the smaller ones. An envelope with her name written on the outside sat there, and she stared at it. How had Mom known she'd be the one to come to this bank?

It was in the blue binder, Janey reminded herself. Tessa was a rule-follower. If Mom said to send Janey to the bank, even if Tessa had wanted to go, she'd have sent Janey. She might have waited nervously in the street, but Janey would've gotten this envelope alone.

She reached inside and removed the envelope. A flash of silver caught her eye, and Janey reached for the necklace in the bottom of the box. A diamond-studded starfish hung from the chain, and Janey's eyes grew hot in less time than it took to inhale.

Janey had bought this for her mother for her fiftieth birthday. She hadn't been able to afford it then, but she'd had a number of credit cards, and Daddy had just passed away a few months prior.

She needed to get out of this vault and this bank. Dropping the necklace in her pocket, she quickly slammed the box back into its slot and turned back to Elle. She barely met the woman's eyes as she approached.

"Is that all?" Janey asked.

"Yes," she said.

Janey nodded as she went by, and she wanted to stop and tell Elle to eat something, because it wouldn't be worth saving the calories now in ten years.

Everything blurred around her. Faces, colors, sound, light, and all of her thoughts. She burst out of the bank and turned in whatever direction her feet took her. She needed somewhere safe and private to look through two envelopes...and then sob as she secured the starfish pendant around her neck.

She threw up her hand and a taxi came to the curb. She got in the car and said the first thing that came to her mind. "The Hotel Benjamin, please." Then she prayed she could press against her panic attack for just a few more minutes.

Chapter Sixteen

"I'll have the food sent up," Charles Burns said. "Once our timed safe opens, I'll bring up the envelope, Miss Forsythe."

"Thank you," Janey said, hoping she could make it through the door of the suite the man was currently taking her to. Her heels seemed to catch on the thick carpet, and she could barely keep up with him.

After she'd gotten him to the front desk, she'd shown him the page with his name and number on it, and the next thing she knew, he had two coded keycards and had said her room was on the forty-second floor.

Not a fan of heights, Janey swore she could feel the building swaying in the wind.

Charles unlocked the door to the suite and held it for her. She'd never stayed in a hotel this nice, and a long foyer showed her expensive artwork on the walls and the best bamboo flooring money could buy.

"I should be back in about fifteen minutes," he said, his dark hair salted generously. Janey sure liked a silver fox, but she reined in her thoughts. She wasn't going to start something with Charles Burns, the Vice-President of the Benjamin Foundation.

Pure exhaustion filled her as she crossed the threshold of the suite and entered it. Only when the door clicked completely closed behind her did she start to relax.

She pressed her back into the door and closed her eyes. *Breathe*, she told herself. *Just breathe.*

She kicked off her heels, sending them scattering down the hallway with loud clunks. She followed after them, stepping past them and into the suite. It was more of an apartment, really, with a wall of windows in front of her that overlooked the Hudson River. She could see into New Jersey, though the sun going down painted the buildings in glinting chrome and golden light.

An expansive living room filled the space in front of the windows, with a full dining room table that seated eight behind it, and then a gourmet kitchen. A hall led out of the room right beside the table, and she went that way to find a bathroom at the end of the walkway, with a bedroom on either side.

They both held huge beds, but Janey went into the one with another attached bathroom. Lilacs and cotton scented the air, and she sank onto the bed, her mind suddenly recalling what Charles had said. *Let me escort you up to the owner's apartment.*

"The owner's apartment," she repeated now. Her

shock and adrenaline wore all the way down, and her purse had gained about twenty pounds in the form of a letter and a locket. After releasing it from her forearm, Janey carefully took the sealed envelope Elle had given her from the front pocket.

She tore it open, her eyes not sending information to her brain fast enough. Her pulse pounded again as she removed a single check, made out to Tessa alone, for just over one hundred thousand dollars.

Janey sucked in a breath and pinched the check hard enough to crinkle the thick paper. She hated that Tessa's name sat there and not hers. Why send her to close an account that didn't even have her name on it? What was she supposed to do with it?

With her anger building, Janey slid the check back into the envelope so she wouldn't rip it to shreds. Tessa had already said she'd split everything with Janey; it didn't matter whose name had been typed on the line.

Her fingers shook with the amount of money she now had in her inheritance. She'd had no idea Mom had so much money. "There's this hotel too," she said. She could easily live here, in this two-bedroom apartment in the city. "There's a house on Long Island."

She removed the blue binder from her oversized purse and opened it again. The address for the house was listed, and she typed it into her phone's map app. She could see a traffic view or a satellite view, and the house sat right on the edge of the island, the road in front of it across from the Wide Ocean Beach.

"For crying out loud," she said, peering at the map. "It's almost in Southampton." She looked up, now-familiar shock coursing through her. They owned a house in the Hamptons.

She shook the thoughts away, because they felt so foreign. The house on the screen definitely wasn't a decades-old beach cottage in need of a fresh coat of paint. It was a two-story home, with a three-car garage and plenty of flat parking space. It looked well-kept and maintained, with an emerald-green lawn and black shutters against a charming light green exterior.

It was the type of home Janey only dreamed of or saw in magazines. It was where celebrity chefs lived or the housewife of someone who owned a huge, worldwide Internet storefront.

And it now belonged to Tessa.

Janey flipped open the blue binder to the section for the home on Shoreline Way. While she was here, she might as well catch the train out to Long Island and take a look at this house. Everything else had contained the names of people, addresses, and phone numbers, and Janey assumed this section would as well.

But behind the divider for the house, only a single sheet of paper waited. It bore the words, *More information for this house will be provided once you've gone to the bank and the hotel.*

Janey had gone to both. She had the money and the pendant. Her fingers automatically reached up to touch where it lay against her collarbone, her thoughts running far into the past for a moment.

When Charles had introduced himself, he'd said he had an envelope for her, but it was in a time-controlled safe that could only be opened once an hour, and they'd been inside it in the last sixty minutes. He'd brought her up here and promised to bring her the envelope once he could retrieve it.

She took out the one she'd found in the safety deposit box and opened it, deciding she simply needed all of the information as quickly as she could get it.

Mom's handwriting shone up at her, and Janey's breath caught in her throat. Tears burned her eyes, and the black, sloping lettering blurred. She pressed the letter to her chest, and let her emotions stream from her. She held something her mother had touched, and Janey cherished that.

"Thank you for my letter," she whispered. She'd been close to her mother, and she'd walled off the emotions of not being able to talk to her. Part of that strategy was letting Tessa deal with all the details of the inheritance, so Janey didn't have to feel any sadness, any missing, anything at all.

Now, though, she realized she needed to allow herself to experience her true emotions. Tears ran down her face as she did, and before she knew it, Janey had left the letter on the bed and gone into the master bathroom to find something to wipe them away.

She stood in the pristine, marble-endowed bathroom and sobbed. With a white towel pressed to her face, she slid down the wall and curled into herself as her emotions overcame her. She'd broken down like this several times in her life. The first time had been when her kids' father had left for good. He'd been traveling to Alaska for work for months previous to his final departure, and she'd been fine.

She knew the marriage had teetered on the edge of a knife for over a year before he'd finally said he wasn't coming home, but it wasn't until the finality of it had been spoken aloud that she'd allowed herself to truly feel the loss of her husband.

She'd had to deal with the fear of being a single mother. She'd had to face the fact that she wasn't perfect and that she'd contributed to the marriage's failure. She'd had to find a way to be strong for her then-toddlers.

Drawing in a long breath, Janey paused the way her therapist had taught her. *Just stop*, he'd said many times. *Stop and think: What's the worst thing that could happen now?*

She released her breath slowly and ran through the things that helped her focus on what she needed to do. She pictured her son's face, Cole's strong opinions and spirit making her smile. She lived for him.

She pictured his girlfriend's face. They lived together in Atlantic City, and Janey loved McKenna as a daughter, though her son didn't really believe in marriage. McKenna had literally saved Cole during a very trying time of his life, and Janey lived for her.

She thought of her daughter, and Rachel's sunny disposition and positive outlook on life made Janey smile. She worked at the supermarket, because she was terrified of becoming an adult. She'd graduated a year ago, and

Janey was in no hurry to have Rachel step out into the scary world. She lived for her daughter.

She thought of her friends in the Lady Tigers, the motorcycle riding group that she really enjoyed spending time with. They were important to her, and she lived for them.

When she thought of her significant other, one face came forward, and Janey wept again. She hadn't been thinking about choosing between the men in her life, but a crisis always forced her back to her core. Back to who she was, and what she wanted in her life.

Milford was the man she wanted, and she knew she'd need to let the others go.

Mom's face floated behind her closed eyes, as did Tessa, her husband Ron, and her son, Ryan. Her family had always been important to Janey, and that hadn't changed because she'd barricaded herself behind her emotional barriers.

She got to her feet and went back into the bedroom. The letter waited on the bed, and Janey was ready to see what it said.

Chapter Seventeen

M*y dearest Janey,*
I'm sure you are confused, scared, and angry. You have every right to be, and I hope you'll allow yourself to run through all of the emotions you need to feel.

I want to say that I will miss you terribly once I am gone. That must sound strange to have someone who has died say they will miss the one left behind, but it's true. I have been worried about how you will handle my death the very most, and I hope it will be a comfort to you to know that I will miss you.

You have been the very best daughter a mother could ever want. I hope you will not judge me too harshly once you learn everything.

You will get to decide what you'd like to tell Tessa. I don't know what she's told you and not told you. My guess is she'll share everything with you, simply because I know Tessa as if she were myself, and she loves you dearly and wants you to be happy.

But don't tell her anything just because she told you. There is no money involved with this, so you'll not be cheating her of anything.

Just so you know. Make your own decisions, Janey, based on what you feel is right.

I apologize for putting these new assets in her name only, but there is a very good reason. It's simply to protect them from Dennis's children. He has three of them, and they were all estranged from him for the past decade. Not one of them came to the funeral.

If you haven't looked at the packet from The Hotel Benjamin yet, all of the details and evidence you'll potentially need in a court case will be there. I won't go into them here.

Suffice it to say, his children did not care for him in life, and he did not want them to profit after his death. He left everything to me, and I've been managing it since his death two years ago.

I have left it solely to Tessa, purely because it will be easier for her to win should Dennis's children challenge my will to her. And they will, Janey. They have been contesting his will to me for the past two years, and I don't believe for a moment that they'll stop just because I am gone.

I apologize for not telling you and Tessa everything. It is the one major regret of my life, though I have had many, most of them surrounding you.

The first thing you need to know is that Dennis and I were married. That's why I got everything upon his death, and I've been able to keep his assets out of the hands of his children.

Please forgive me. I love you, and I have learned so much from being your mother. I am proud of the woman you are and the woman you will become after you discover all of my indiscretions. You are a strong person, Janey, though I know you feel weak. Don't listen to those negative messages in your head.

· · ·

LOVE, MOM

JANEY SUCKED BACK A SOB AS SHE RE-READ THE LAST paragraph and felt her mother's love. She'd told her to stay out of her head so many times in life, and Janey really wished her mind didn't try to sabotage her.

She gave herself a few minutes to absorb the information. She re-read the letter once more and shook her head when she got to the line about Mom being married to who Janey had believed to only be a boyfriend.

So much made sense now that she knew that detail. Dennis had been very wealthy, and that was how Mom had kept up her lifestyle. They had lived together in her apartment overlooking Central Park, and Dennis had obviously been paying for it.

The bank account, the hotel, and the home on Long Island belonged to him.

Dennis Martin was DM Conway, the science fiction author.

Relief filled Janey as all the pieces came together. At the same time, her fear remained, as did her confusion and anger. Why hadn't Mom been able to tell Janey and Tessa about the marriage? Especially after Dennis had passed away? Why wait until now?

"To protect the assets," Janey said, answering her own question.

Her phone pinged, and that was the notification sound for the app she used with Curtis. She sighed, but his face had not come forward during her meditation exercise to calm herself down and focus on what and who was most important to her.

He wanted to know if she was available that night, and with the time he gave, she knew he simply wanted to have phone sex. She drew a deep breath in and let her thumbs fly across her screen.

Curtis, I have enjoyed our time together so very much. However, so many things have happened, all of them pointing me in a different direction, and I don't think we should see each other anymore.

She paused, wondering if she should apologize. In the end, she didn't, and the message went flying through cyberspace. Her next breath entered her lungs so much easier, and she felt a great weight lift from her shoulders.

"Okay," she said, standing up. "I've got more information, with more coming." She nodded, folded the letter, and tucked it back into the envelope. She'd just put that away when the doorbell rang through the suite.

Janey lifted her head, her pulse right back to racing. "It's Charles," she told herself as she hurried out of the bedroom and into the living room.

He had an envelope too, and Janey needed the information in it to keep these new assets. She pulled open the door, expecting to see the silver-haired man who'd escorted her up to the owner's suite.

Instead, a blonde woman stood there, her eyes sharp sapphires and her lips painted in a deep, blood red.

Chapter Eighteen

Janey immediately stepped forward, almost out of the suite, and brought the door with her. "Can I help you?" she asked.

"Just delivering something." She extended an envelope toward her, but Janey refused to take it. She could barely handle the idea of taking another envelope from anyone, least of all this woman, who'd obviously dressed to deliver something deadly. She wore a black tank top that clung to her bony frame, along with a pair of cutoff shorts, and she was at least a decade younger than Janey. She looked as if she'd come to the forty-second floor from the beach, but she'd turn heads wherever she went.

Footsteps came toward them, and Charles appeared, much to Janey's relief. He slowed as he realized the blonde stood in front of Janey's door too, and his grip tightened on the thick, white packet in his hands.

"What are you doing here?" He scanned the other woman from head to toe. "I'm calling security."

"Don't bother," she said, dropping the envelope on the floor. "I'm leaving." She walked away, and Janey stared after her for a moment before looking up at Charles in surprise.

"I apologize for that." He bent to retrieve the envelope and stuffed it away inside his inner jacket pocket. He extended the packet to her, and she took that. "Do you need anything? Dinner? Anything you've forgotten in your packing?"

"Can I order from the restaurant on the ground floor?"

"Absolutely." He reached into his inner pocket again and withdrew a card, which she also took. "That number goes to our restaurant concierge. She'll take your order for Blackwidth, and you can find the menu on the screen on your television."

"Thank you," Janey said, giving him a smile. She backed up, then paused. "Who was that woman?"

"She didn't tell you?"

"No."

Charles shifted his feet and looked over his shoulder, clearly uncomfortable. "That was Aleah Martin."

"Ah." Janey nodded as if she was well-versed with the name and just hadn't placed the face to it yet. If she hadn't just read her mother's letter and seen Dennis's last name, it still wouldn't have meant anything to her. But it did now, and she was so glad she hadn't taken the envelope.

She lifted the packet. "Thanks." She slipped back into the apartment and locked the door behind her.

———

A COUPLE OF DAYS LATER, JANEY STEPPED OFF THE FERRY and back onto the island of Nantucket. She smiled at Sean as he reached for her bag. "How was the flight?"

"We sat on the tarmac forever," Janey said, shaking her head. "Sorry I was so late."

"It's actually better for me." Sean smiled at her, and Janey returned it. A shiver of guilt made her stomach vibrate, but she ignored it. She'd made her decisions for now, and she was going to stick to them.

Even when faced with Tessa, she told herself. *You're going to stick to what you've decided to do.*

Sean put her suitcase in the back seat of his car while Janey got in the front seat. He drove her the mile to The Harbor Gull, an upscale boutique hotel where she was going to be spending at least two nights.

She'd been in daily contact with Tessa, and she said she had something to tell her when she got back to the cottage. She did; that was true. She'd taken a picture of the check and sent it to Tessa. Using her bank's online tools, she'd been able to deposit the check with that picture, as well as the others.

Janey's bank account held tens of thousands of dollars now, and she hated that the increased amount really helped her smile more easily. But the truth was, money helped.

Money helped her stress level decrease, especially because she wasn't worried so much about who might be calling to get their money.

She'd gone home to get a few financial things sorted out, check on Rachel, and make a plan for the upcoming week on Nantucket.

After she checked in, she got in the shower while Sean made coffee and took it out to the balcony. Once dressed, she joined him, saying, "Thanks for making this." She sipped her brew, noting that he was very good at making coffee. "And thanks for keeping this between us."

"Of course," he said. "Did you find what you needed in the city?"

She nodded and gazed out over the bay, thinking back on the past few days. She had done about a half-day of work while she did laundry in Jersey and paid off the most immediate creditors.

"Did you see anything in the pages I sent you?" she asked.

"Nothing," he said, glancing at her. "I'm not sure why your mother thought it would be easier for Tessa to fight the Martin siblings alone, but other than that, the evidence your mother used to defend her husband's wishes regarding his assets seems very sound to me."

Janey nodded, and while she should feel nothing but relief, something still gnawed at her nerves. Her stomach grumbled, and Sean must've heard it, because he asked, "Would you like to go to dinner?"

"Sure," Janey said, standing. She looked right at him as

he got to his feet too. "Sean, I really appreciate you helping me. I know I started all of this by flirting with you, but I do have a boyfriend."

Surprise entered his eyes, and Janey regretted the person she'd been six days ago. She couldn't believe how different she felt today than she had when she'd first walked into Sean Masterson's office.

"Perhaps we can just be friends, then," Sean said, his smile slightly downturned. He dropped his head and turned to go back into the hotel room. Janey followed him, her thoughts firing at her. She'd had two boyfriends before, and Milford knew they weren't exclusive…

She pushed the idea away, promising herself that she'd revisit it later, when she wasn't in a highly emotional state.

She enjoyed dinner with Sean, and after he'd dropped her back at the hotel, Janey collected her beach hat and went out to the sand. Something about the soul of the earth touching her feet had always soothed her, and that was a characteristic she could trace back to her mother.

Her thoughts lingered and wandered around her mother and the years she'd gotten with her. She smiled out at the sky and the sea, feeling more like the person she was meant to be than she had in a long, long time.

———

Two days later, Janey arrived back at the cottage on Nantucket Point. Tessa rose from the steps where she'd been waiting, and she came down the sidewalk to help with

Janey's bags. She paid the cab driver and followed her sister back into the safety of the cottage.

It somehow seemed brighter inside, with less dust hanging in the air and the scent of coffee and cream more inviting than before. Janey looked around, realizing the cottage hadn't changed.

She had.

"Well?" Tessa asked after she'd set Janey's suitcase by the mouth of the hall.

Instant irritation flooded Janey, and she immediately missed the carefree hours of the past two days on Nantucket. Alone.

"I got the money," she said. "That account is all closed. The safety deposit box is empty. The hotel really is ours." She sighed as she sank onto the sofa. "You've changed the curtains."

"Yes," Tessa said, joining Janey in the living room. "The others were so heavy. These are much better." She smiled up at the sheer, off-white curtains that fell all the way to the floor. Tessa did have a way with beautifying spaces, whether inside or out.

"They are," Janey said. They were the reason the cottage felt full of light too. "Anyway, we'll need to figure out what to do with The Hotel Benjamin. Right now, Charles Burns is running it, and I met with him briefly. I don't know if you want to take that on. Perhaps Ryan would. Or Cole…" She let the sentence hang there, because there was a lot to discuss regarding the hotel.

Right now, it was a five-star hotel, with an amazing

restaurant on the main level. Not just anyone could step into the role of running it, and she actually thought her son would make a fool of himself if he tried.

"Definitely a lot to talk about there," Tessa agreed. "But it's ours? Mom didn't lose it to…whoever she claims will come after it?"

"No," Janey said. "And Tess, it's yours. Not ours. Mom left the assets to you, because she believed they'd be easier to protect that way."

"Okay," Tessa said, still confused.

"Tessa," Janey said. "Mom was married to Dennis Martin. He was her husband. The bank account, the hotel, the house on Long Island, and the intellectual property are his. He left them to mom—his wife—when he died two years ago."

Tessa's eyes grew wider by the second, and she reached up and covered her mouth.

"He's DM Conway," Janey continued, deciding to get the whole story out so Tessa could digest it all. "He has three kids who aren't happy that Mom got all of his assets."

She reached over to her purse and pulled out the thick, white packet of evidence she'd been given at the hotel. "Everything we need to protect the assets are in this."

She handed it to Tessa, who took it but didn't start to look through any of the pages.

"I think," Janey said slowly, because she'd had a plethora of time to think these past couple of days. "Once we win in court, then we can split these four assets."

"We've already split the money," Tessa said. "Didn't you get the deposits I sent?'

"I did, thank you." Janey smiled at her sister, remembering her mother's words. *I know Tessa as if she were myself, and she loves you dearly and wants you to be happy.*

She loved her sister too.

"Mom's been managing the assets. We can split them to do that now," Janey said. "Or you can do it. Or I can. I'm willing." She was strong enough now to do something more.

"I need to talk to Ron," Tessa said.

Janey nodded. "That's a great idea. Perhaps he can advise us on how to protect these assets and what to do with them in the meantime."

Tessa gripped the white packet of papers as she stood up. "I'm going to go call him." She bent down to hug Janey, who reached up to pat her sister's back. "It's so good to see you back." Tessa straightened, flashed her a smile, and hurried out onto the front porch.

Janey realized then that Tessa had probably thought she wouldn't return to the cottage. Janey could admit she'd thought about staying away, but as she looked around now, the cottage actually felt like home.

It felt like Mom was there, and Janey smiled as she closed her eyes and let herself feel sad that her mother was gone. At the same time, hope for her future filtered through her for the first time in a while.

Chapter Nineteen

B obbie grinned like the Cheshire Cat when she opened the door. "Oh, my dears. Do come in." She stepped back, and Janey led the way into the bigger beach bungalow that sat next door to their cottage. "Come in."

"This is lovely," Janey said, gazing around at all the white. White walls, white shiplap, white ceilings. Even the furniture was white as white could be. Bobbie had put pops of color in the room—turquoise, pink, and yellow—by using throw pillows, curtains, and rugs.

"It's very beachy," she added with a smile. She'd been gathering her energy for a week to be able to attend this dinner. That, and she'd taken half of an anti-panic pill twenty minutes ago. Everything felt floaty and fine, and Janey needed it that way to get through dinner with the Friedmans.

"Thank you," Bobbie said. "Come in. We're eating on the back patio." She led the way through the house, and

Janey spied stainless steel appliances in the kitchen to break up the white counters, white cupboards, and black and white tiled floor.

More color in that room, but Bobbie had moved from yellow to a bright peach color, and from turquoise to straight-up blue.

They went back outside, much to Janey's dismay. The humidity today had to be in the eightieth percentile, and she existed with a fine sheen of sweat on her skin at all times.

"There they are," Riggs boomed, and Janey gave him a tight smile. "Have you two met the Longs? They live on the other side of us." He indicated a couple in their thirties, and Janey suddenly wished she'd taken an entire anti-panic pill.

Because, right now, she was indeed starting to panic.

"David and Leslie Long," Riggs said. "They've got a couple of kids, but they're home with a sitter." He beamed at them as if getting a babysitter took great skill and courage.

Janey almost rolled her eyes, catching herself in time. She shook hands with David and then Leslie, wondering why Bobbie hadn't mentioned they'd be having another couple to dinner too.

"So, Janey," David said. "What do you do?"

"I sell software,' she said.

"Huh. Fascinating." David's smile and blank look did not make it seem like he was fascinated.

"She's one of the top sellers in her company," Riggs

said, and Janey turned toward him. How did he know that? She exchanged a glance with Tessa, who shook her head slightly, telling Janey not to make a scene.

"He's right," she said. "I'm hoping for a promotion next month."

"You don't just *hope* for a promotion," Leslie Long said. "You go out there and *get* it."

Janey gaped at her, then looked around for a glass of wine. She'd need alcohol to make it through this meal.

"Here we go," Bobbie said, rushing out onto the patio with a platter of steaming, yellow corn. "We've got lobster, corn on the cob, and shrimp salad. Let's sit down. Sit down."

Janey watched her scurry around to put napkins on the table and then rush back into the cottage to get serving spoons. Riggs did nothing to help her, and the nervous energy pouring from Bobbie made Janey squirm in her seat.

Riggs had sat right across from her, and David right next to her, making her feel trapped and insignificant. She took a lobster claw and a piece of corn, deciding to really go for as much butter as she wanted tonight.

"Have you ever thought about owning a timeshare?" David asked, and Janey looked up in surprise.

"No," she said flatly. She found it best to simply deny salesmen like him. She wouldn't even describe him as a salesman. He was just trying to make a fast buck.

"Why not?" he asked.

"I can barely pay my mortgage, for one." She pointed

her fork at him. "The cottage is my mother's. We don't actually have any money for a timeshare. Not only that, but with a timeshare, I have to also have time to travel, which I don't."

"Janey does a lot of traveling for work," Riggs said, and once again, Janey swung her attention toward him. How did he know *that?*

David continued to press her for why she wouldn't want a timeshare, and Riggs kept staring at her with a goofy look on his face. She ate as much as she could stomach, and quickly pushed the rest of the food away.

She really didn't like being around David and Leslie. They made her feel obsolete and like a complete failure of a human being. After all, Leslie was only thirty-five, with three children and one more on the way. She never stopped smiling, and she probably didn't ever do anything unladylike—like use the bathroom or pass gas. Ever.

Janey engaged in small talk, because Tessa tended to go silent when she was annoyed or out of her comfort zone. She was probably both tonight, and that left Janey to carry the conversation.

She did, but the moment they'd been there for an hour, she stood up from the table, which now only held the remnants of shells, cold bowls of butter, and entirely too much leftover shrimp salad for Bobbie to believe it was good.

By Janey's recollection, Bobbie always brought shrimp salad to the island potlucks, or even just over to the cottage when they'd all sat down together for lunch.

The shrimp salad hadn't been good then either.

"...now I get my nails done one week. My eyelashes the next, a pedicure the third, and my hair cut the fourth." Leslie trilled out a laugh about her spa schedule, and Janey couldn't look away from her.

What a joke, she thought, looking away. Women like Leslie Long weren't real. They were Stepford cutouts, and Janey had no use for them.

Her mind started pinging negative things at her, about her job, about her lack of a husband, about the healthy sum of money in her account now.

"Let's take our coffee out on the porch," Bobbie said, and Janey got to her feet in a fluid motion.

"We must go," she said, stepping over to Bobbie and giving her a quick kiss on both cheeks. "I'm so sorry, but we have an early morning tomorrow. Good Will is sending a truck for some of the furniture, and we still don't have it ready."

Nothing she'd said was a lie, so she didn't feel bad about anything. Though, if the dinner party had been anything better than insufferable, she might have stayed.

"So soon?" Leslie asked.

"Yes, regrettably." Janey started for the door. She didn't owe that woman an apology or a reason for why they had to leave before eight o'clock.

Back through the house and outside, and Janey could finally get a full breath. "That was horrific," she said to Tessa. "We can't do that again. Did you hear that guy trying to sell me a timeshare?"

Tessa giggled and nodded, and she'd clearly had a little too much wine with dinner. Janey hadn't had enough, but she didn't want to exist in alcohol-stunted awareness all the time. She also didn't want to be reminded of all the ways she'd spectacularly failed, and spending time with a couple like Leslie and David did exactly that.

She pushed against her own mind as it tried to send out dark messages about herself and how she wasn't worthy to own a cottage here on the Point. She wished she were back in the safety of her bedroom in the cottage, with the door locked. She could pull out the letter her mother had written her and remind herself of how someone else saw her, not how she saw herself through self-loathing eyes.

"I heard him," Tessa said, sobering slightly. "Also, how creepy was it that Riggs knew so much about what you did for work?"

"Scale of one to ten? Twelve."

They laughed together, but Janey glanced down the lane where the Friedman's cottage sat. Neither Riggs nor Bobbie stood on the front porch, but somehow, Janey still felt as if someone was watching her, watching Tessa, watching the cottage.

She shivered and hurried inside, locking the door behind her.

Chapter Twenty

J aney tucked her letter back into the envelope and slid that into her purse. She hadn't told Tessa about it, though she'd relayed most of the information she'd learned in New York City. They'd talked about Dennis's children, and Janey had told her about the visit from his thin, blonde daughter.

She did wonder what was in the envelope Aleah Martin had dropped on the floor outside the owner's suite, but Janey pushed it from her mind.

She finished packing and took her suitcase out to the kitchen. Tessa's bag sat on the table, and she stood at the window in the kitchen that looked out toward the ocean.

"Ready?" Janey asked.

Her sister turned from the window, a tired smile on her face. "Yes."

Janey poured herself a cup of coffee and set the pot in the sink. She washed it out, knowing she hadn't done as many chores around the cottage as Tessa had done. They'd worked hard to get it cleaned out and cleaned up. Together, the work had gone well, and Janey would stay if she didn't just need a breather.

"So we're going to keep the cottage," Tessa said. "Right?"

"Yes," Janey said with a sigh. "I think we should keep it. That settles out Mom's trust, right?"

"Yes," Tessa said. "I can call the lawyer when I get home. We'll go over everything again, and if there's anything we need to sign or do, I'll let you know."

"I can come help too," Janey said, finally meeting Tessa's eye. "I'm in a much better place now." She offered her sister a smile, and Tessa took it.

"I can see that." She rinsed out her coffee mug while Janey took her first sips of her morning brew. She made a face, because Tessa made her coffee so bitter. "You have to put sugar in it." She shook her head and laughed.

"I'll get some at the airport," Janey said. "We should probably go if we want to be on the ten o'clock ferry." She dumped her coffee down the drain and did a quick wash of the mug. They'd leave everything to dry on the thin towel next to the sink, because they'd be back in just a few days.

Janey picked up her bag and led the way out of the cottage. Tessa followed, and she locked the door behind them. "We should get one of those locks with the electronic code," Janey said. "No key required. Then anyone can come, and all we have to do is give them the code and they can get in."

The wind whipped along the beach that morning, trying to steal away Janey's purse and half of her hair. She quickly gathered the dark locks in her fist and looked toward the water.

"It's a lock?" Tessa asked.

"It's a whole doorknob," Janey said, staying close to the house as their cab hadn't arrived yet. "You just take the old one out and put the new one in."

"Sounds easy enough." Tessa met her eye. "We should do that, since there's only one key."

And Tessa had it on her key ring. Janey nodded, pushing against her irritation. She told herself that Tessa had taken her suggestion to leave for the weekend. Gather their thoughts. Make sure everything at home was okay. And then come back next week to start the repairs the cottage needed.

Janey had called Sean, and he'd given her the name and number of a local handyman, and she and Tessa already had an appointment with Brady Sturgiss on Tuesday morning.

Four days, Janey thought. She had a ton of work to catch up on, and she'd likely pull sixteen or seventeen-hour days between now and when she returned to Nantucket Point. If she did, then she could focus on getting the roof patched and clearing out the small garage next to the cottage.

The yard also needed a lot of work, and her fingers ached already.

"Let's think about how much we want to reinvest into the cottage," Tessa said as the car pulled up. "Okay?"

"Okay," Janey said, following her sister down the front steps to the sidewalk. The cottage could honestly do with a gutting and a complete renovation. New flooring, new cabinets, new appliances, new everything.

But every penny that went into curtains or carpet for the cottage came out of her bank account. Well, hers and Tessa's. Janey wanted the cottage to be a nice place to come visit, but the truth was, neither of them lived there. It didn't need high-end flooring or granite countertops. It just needed to be nice and functional.

She didn't say so right now, though, because it was probably going to be something she and Tessa didn't agree on—again.

"I'm going to bring Rachel next week," Janey said. "She talked to her boss and she got the whole week off. She'll be a big help."

"That's fantastic," Tessa said brightly, lifting her suitcase into the trunk. Janey handed her bag to the driver, who took care of it for her, and she rounded the car to get to the passenger side.

"Leaving already?" someone called, and Janey turned toward the sand, shading her eyes to find Riggs there, fishing pole resting against his shoulder.

"Just for the weekend," Janey said, putting her sunniest smile on her face. "I promise we'll be back to take care of the jungle between our place and yours next week."

He laughed, and Janey joined him briefly. "Thanks for watching out for us," she said, lifting her hand in a wave as Riggs came closer. She wasn't sure what about him rubbed her the wrong way. Maybe the perpetual smile. Maybe that he always seemed to be there—right *there*—hanging around the cottage.

Janey closed her eyes against the bright sun, and on the golden background of her eyelids, she saw Riggs in the cottage. He was angry, and he had Mom pressed up against the wall in the kitchen, right next to where the rotary phone hung on the wall. Janey was little—or at least shorter. She had to look up at Mom and Riggs, and when she'd said something to her mother, Riggs had backed off.

His eyes flashed angrily, but Mom had stepped between him and Janey, and the memory went dark.

She pulled in a breath and opened her eyes again. The scent of salt and musk and male cologne lodged in her nose, and she focused on Riggs, who now stood only a few feet away, the open passenger door between them.

He didn't look angry now, but Janey was just as afraid of him as she'd been as a child. He smiled, and the man had aged about four decades from the vision in her mind, and his wrinkles and gray hair made him seem innocent and grandfathery.

"Have a good trip," he said, looking from her up to the cottage. "We'll keep an eye on the old girl."

"Thank you," Janey murmured, and she slid into the

back seat. She closed the door, and the car eased forward to make a U-turn. They went past Riggs, who stood on the side of the road, a tackle box in one hand, and the other holding that fishing pole.

"Have you ever noticed that he never catches anything?" Tessa asked.

"Maybe he throws the fish back," Janey said, her eyes trained out the window. She'd never remembered waking up in the middle of the night and going down the hall to the kitchen in the cottage. She thought about it on the way to the ferry, trying to hang onto the pieces of memory so she could examine them. They blurred and slipped away like smoke, but she thought that memory—and possibly others—were the reason Riggs Friedman just didn't sit right with her.

———

"I'M HOME," SHE CALLED HOURS LATER. HER BLADDER HAD been unhappy with her for the past half-hour, so she darted into the bathroom while Rachel yelled to her from outside.

Once relieved, Janey went through the house to the back deck, where Rachel sat with her boyfriend, Travis. "Hey, you two." She smiled at them, the relief she felt at being home almost more than she could articulate.

She sank into an available Adirondack chair, sighing all the while. She looked out over the back lawn, noting that it had been cut. "Thanks for doing the yard, Trav."

"Yep," he said, giving her a quick smile.

Rachel didn't look up from her phone, and Janey found her ready for work. Her long, sleek, sandy blonde hair fell straight down her back and over her shoulders, partially covering the name tag she'd already pinned to her blue and white polo.

"What time do you have to work?" Janey asked.

"Three," Rachel said, looking up.

"Oh, so you have to leave really soon."

"Yeah, five or ten minutes." Rachel smiled at her, and Janey could see so much of herself—and Mom—in her daughter. "I got all the mail. There's a huge stack on the desk in the kitchen."

Janey smiled and closed her eyes. "Thanks, hon." She just needed a few minutes. A quick catnap. Once Rachel went to work, Janey would call Milford and tell him she wanted to be exclusive. She wasn't sure what his reaction would be, but she felt good about it. All she could do was hope and pray he would too.

"Tell her about that weird courier letter," Travis said, and that got Janey to open her eyes. She looked at Travis, the young man good-looking and so good to Rachel. They'd dated in high school too, and their relationship had simply continued afterward. He had dark hair and eyes, and couldn't seem to eat enough to put on a single pound. He worked for his dad at their family-owned deli, and Janey had benefitted from more than one Italian sub he'd brought to the house after one of his shifts.

"Weird courier letter?" Janey asked.

"Oh, right." Rachel stood up, her long legs clad in a

pair of jeans that barely held any blue at all. "Let me get it. Some guy dropped it off a few days ago. I had to sign for it, but he was mad it wasn't you." Her voice went with her as she stepped inside, and Janey sat up in the Adirondack chair, which was quite the feat.

Rachel returned with a slim envelope that didn't look nefarious in any way. Janey's heart seemed to know better, and it started to knock against her ribs. "It's from The Hotel Benjamin." Rachel look at Janey, her eyebrows up. "Did you stay there or something? It kind of looks like a check."

"The Hotel Benjamin?" Janey stood up and took the envelope. It did have a see-through window where her address sat, and it indeed did look like a check. She wasn't sure if she should tell Rachel she had stayed there a few nights ago or act like she hadn't.

Thankfully, her phone rang, and Milford's name sat on the screen. She smiled, lifted the device, and said, "Thanks, honey. I have to take this."

She took the envelope with her as she hurried inside. She swiped on the call from Milford and said, "Hey, baby."

"Hey yourself," he said. "Did you make it home okay?"

"Yes." Janey stepped into her bedroom and closed the door, her eyes trained on the return address on the envelope. "I wish you were in town. How much longer will you be in Toronto?"

"Assignment finished early," he said. "I'm at the airport. I'll be back tonight. That's why I'm calling. Wanted to take you to dinner."

Warmth filled Janey, and she tore her eyes from the envelope to say, "Yes, that sounds amazing."

"Great." Milford chuckled. "I've missed you, Janey."

"I've missed you too, Ford."

"Hey, they're calling my flight. I'll swing by around six?"

"Sure." Before she knew it, the call ended, and her attention went right back to the envelope. "Just open it," she coached herself. She slipped her fingers under the flap.

"'Bye, Mom!" Rachel called. "We're leaving."

Janey's fingers ripped right through the envelope as she flinched. She hurried to open the door and call, "'Bye! See you later."

She closed the door again and turned back to the envelope. It was open now, the edges along the top jagged and craggly, like the rocks along the cliffs of the Point.

She took a deep breath and pulled out the single sheet of paper.

My dearest Janey, her mother wrote.

Janey's eyes couldn't scan fast enough. She read the very short letter in only a matter of seconds, her brain misfiring on the words.

They were English, but they didn't make sense.

She looked up as she let the letter drop.

A scream came from her mouth, followed quickly by a wrenching sob. Crying freely now, she slid down the door and curled her knees to her chest, the black letters on the page burning behind her closed eyes.

Chapter Twenty-One

Tessa turned the corner and headed toward her house, finding Ron's SUV in the driveway. Her heartbeat went up and then down, and she wasn't sure if she was happy her husband was home or not.

They'd had some good conversations while she'd been in Nantucket, but sometimes integrating Ron back into her life for just a couple of days took so much work. She told herself they had plenty to talk about right now, and Ron would likely be exhausted from another week in the city.

She pulled into the driveway beside his car and got out, making sure she grabbed her library ID and purse. She didn't like to leave anything in the car, because then she couldn't find it when she needed it. Just inside the front door sat a small table, and it had two drawers on the front of it. Her keys and library badge went in one of them, and her purse went on the hook beside the garage door.

Tessa had a system and a routine for everything, and they brought her comfort in times when not much else made sense. "Ron?" she called, but he didn't answer. She found his briefcase on the desk in the office, and she went down the hall to the kitchen.

A vase of red roses sat there, as did a box of cronuts from her favorite bakery in New York City. Tessa smiled and reached for the velvety petals on the roses. She leaned over and inhaled their sweet fragrance, plenty of guilt stinging her stomach for not being thrilled to see Ron's car in the driveway.

She left the kitchen and went down the hall to the master suite, the sound of the shower meeting her ears as soon as she entered the room. "Ron," she said again.

"In the shower," he called. "I got a coffee on the way home, and then spilled it all down the front of me."

"Oh, no." Tessa went into the bathroom and inhaled the scent of his masculine body wash. "Should I order some dinner?"

"I already did," he said from behind the frosted glass in their shower. "I was craving The Boar's Head pulled pork. Or maybe their mermaid salad."

Tessa leaned against the countertop and smiled. "Definitely the salad."

"How was the library?"

"The library," she said, because it was boring. She'd shelved books and logged a few dozen new titles they'd gotten in while she'd been gone. Sometimes she had to work the check-out counter if they got busy, but today had been an easy Friday evening, and she'd stayed in the back to get caught up on the most important things she'd missed.

"I'll go put together a cocktail," she said, pushing away from the counter and then leaving the bathroom. She couldn't help the way her thoughts moved to Janey and the cottage on Nantucket.

The checks had cleared her bank without issue. Janey had learned a lot in the city, but she'd returned to the island several days later than Tessa had thought she would. She'd honestly thought her sister wouldn't return to Nantucket at all.

She hadn't wanted to keep the cottage when she'd left, but her tune had changed in the days she'd been gone. She also had another check, had been to the bank and the hotel in New York City, and she'd done all of that without talking to or asking Tessa about it at all.

Classic Janey, Tessa thought now as she had a couple of days ago.

Then, to top it off, Janey had suggested they take a few days back in their real lives before they came back to Nantucket to continue work on the cottage. They'd managed to go through almost everything inside, but the outside of the house and the yard needed a lot of work.

She got out ice cubes and gin, pulled some tonic water from the fridge, and quartered a lime. She put it all together in the tumbler and shook it up before pouring two drinks. She downed hers and poured herself another, the alcohol already moving through her, igniting her mind.

Janey had definitely been up to something more than catching up on her work when she'd left, and while she'd told Tessa a lot of information, she still had secrets.

Foolishness rushed through Tessa, because she'd told Janey everything. She'd been revealing her whole hand her whole life, and she hated that she hadn't learned better by now.

"Thanks, sweetheart," Ron said, stepping to her side and interrupting her thoughts. She pressed into his kiss against her cheek and enjoyed the heft and warmth of his hand on her waist.

"Thanks for the roses," she said. "They're beautiful." Her husband had brought her flowers every weekend for the first six months of his new job. She could admit that it had made his transition to working in the city and only being home on the weekends easier. Thinking about it now, she felt silly for thinking tulips and carnations could make up for living alone five days each week.

"And the cronuts," she said. "I'm not even going to need anything else tonight." Just sweets and gin. With those two things, she could easily stop thinking about everything she needed to do come Monday morning, and the fact that she'd be leaving again on Tuesday.

"Tell me how things went on Nantucket," Ron said, and Tessa started into the story.

Ron interrupted constantly, and that only set Tessa's teeth on edge. After the third or fourth time, with plenty of story left to tell, she just said, "And yeah. We needed a break from the island."

He was difficult to converse with when he interrupted like that, and Tessa tried to be patient with him. He'd likely felt obsolete at work this week, and this was how it manifested itself on the weekend.

"You mean from each other," Ron said.

Tessa shrugged, because he wasn't wrong. She loved Janey, and sometimes when she was with her, Janey felt like the only safe place in Tessa's life. Other times, she wondered how they could possibly be related.

She hadn't gotten to the second will or the four additional assets, and she poured herself a glass of wine while Ron went to get the door when the bell rang. She gulped it while he thanked the delivery driver for coming, and she poured another measure before he returned.

He said nothing about the drink, and if he'd known it was her fourth, he might have.

"My mom left me more assets," she said as he started unbagging the food. "Just me, Ron. She left Janey out of the addendum, but she said I could tell her what I wanted."

Ron looked up at her, surprise in his dark eyes. "Really? What did you do?"

"I told her."

Ron shook his head, which meant Tessa had done the wrong thing. Annoyance sang through her, and she swirled her wine and took a sip.

"And?" he prompted.

"We did some investigating, and we found out Mom was married to Dennis. He left her everything—these four new assets which are pretty major—and his kids aren't very happy about it. That's why she left them to only me. To protect the assets."

Ron scooped meat and mashed potatoes onto a plate for himself and rounded the counter to sit at the bar. Tessa thought about saying something about how he could've dished her some food too, but she bit back the words.

She didn't want to eat anyway. She just wanted to have another glass of wine and go to bed. If she didn't do that, she'd drink the whole bottle and wake up with a massive headache in the morning.

"What assets?" Ron asked.

Tessa told him, and he actually stopped eating, his eyes widened. "Tess," he said. "You should've called me before you told Janey. A hotel in downtown New York City? Why share that with her?"

"Because she's my sister," Tessa said with a hint of snap in her voice. "Mom left everything else to us fifty-fifty."

"Not this, though." He shook his head, and he didn't have to vocalize his opinion on Janey for Tessa to know it.

"She only did it so Dennis's kids wouldn't be able to get the assets." She stepped over to the desk and picked up the packet of papers Janey had given her. "She kept a bunch of records as 'evidence' so when his children challenge us, they won't win." She set it in front of Ron and picked up the spoon to put some mashed potatoes on a plate for herself.

"Can you help me go through it?" she asked.

He pulled the pages out of the envelope, a heavy look in his eyes. "You should've said you had this."

"I just did." Tessa glared at him, but Ron didn't look up. If he said "you should've" one more time, though, Tessa might do something she'd seriously regret later.

Chapter Twenty-Two

"So there's nothing else we need to do?" Tessa asked, standing at the window that showed her the entirety of her front yard. Ron had left for the city over an hour ago, after a weekend of reviewing the documents in the ratty envelope Janey had produced. He'd declared them "nearly useless," in a court of law, and Tessa had gritted her teeth and tucked the whole packet in the filing cabinet in the office.

Mom had obviously thought the documents would help, and Tessa wasn't going to dismiss them just because Ron said she should.

She felt a weight on her shoulders that hadn't been there before, because Dennis Martin's children would come after *her* for the assets, and she realized Janey had gotten off the hook again.

"Nothing," Marcus Hall, their mother's lawyer, said. "If you and Janey are in agreement about the cottage, then we can transfer the title into both of your names. After that, how you two split things—care of the cottage, who pays the electric bill, all of that—is up to the two of you."

Tessa thought of the key on her ring, and she added another task to her to-do list for the day. She'd promised Janey she'd make her a copy of the key, and she needed to at least do that.

"Great," Tessa said. "Thanks, Marcus." She hung up and looked out at her neighborhood. The sky shone with a brilliant blue. The grass on all the lawns up and down the street sparkled like emeralds. Flowerbeds bloomed in crimson, violet, and marigold. Tree branches and brilliant green leaves waved in the gentle breeze.

Everything felt serene and calm. Unrest bubbled inside her, though, and Tessa turned away from the tranquil scene. When her mood didn't match what she was looking at, she didn't know how to make everything line up.

She put a load of laundry in the washing machine and rinsed out her coffee cup before putting it in the dishwasher. She made the bed and opened her suitcase. She went through the clean items, refolding them methodically. When she did mundane tasks, she freed her mind to think about things that had eluded her previously.

"Why did Janey go to the city?" she asked herself as she tucked all the clean socks she had into her suitcase. She turned to get her swimming suit, an item she'd forgotten last time. She didn't have the gumption to play in the ocean the way she had when she was eight years old, but she did like to walk along the beach, and she could stand to get a little color in her skin.

"How did Janey get the money out of an account that had *my* name on it?"

Tessa picked up her all-black suit and the cover-up that went all the way to her ankles. She folded it nicely and put it in the suitcase, her eyebrows drawn down.

"How did she know who to talk to at The Hotel Benjamin?"

Janey knew so much, and Tessa sighed and put one hand on her hip. While she'd been buying new curtains for the cottage and putting off Bobbie Friedman, Janey had been doing who-knows-what in New York City.

"When she was supposed to be in Jersey and then Dallas," Tessa said. "Working." She turned and sat down on the bed, pulling her phone from her pocket. She tapped to call Janey, and her sister's phone went straight to voicemail.

She was either on another call, her phone had died, or she had lightning-fast fingers with swiping away Tessa's call. Tessa's bet was on another call. Not only that, but Janey wouldn't return her call, because she was so busy and she'd forget.

Tessa tried not to be bitter. She hated that her feelings resurfaced so easily, as she and Janey had left Nantucket on good terms.

"That was before you suspected she'd been lying to you." She started tapping out a few texts to Janey, asking the same questions she'd been thinking aloud to herself.

155

I told you I'd take care of it, Janey answered. *It was all laid out in the blue binder.*

Tessa hadn't read much more of the papers in the blue binder than the letter at the beginning. It had been too much for her to absorb, especially alone, and especially when she'd found it in the bottom of the desk drawer.

Janey had kept the binder too, so Tessa couldn't even take a closer look at it. Part of her wanted to let her sister handle everything in the will addendum. The other part really wanted to know how she'd managed to have conversations about property that wasn't hers in any legal way.

Oh, and Rachel couldn't come, Janey texted. *Her boss talked to her about being an assistant manager, and she decided she couldn't take a week off.*

Bummer, Tessa said, because she did love her niece, and Rachel was a hard worker. Right now, she had bigger problems than her niece not being able to come help with the cottage.

Tessa tapped to make another call, this one to Sean Masterson. His secretary answered, of course, and Tessa said, "It's Janey Forsythe," she said, making her voice slightly lower. "Is Mister Masterson available?"

"Let me transfer you."

A moment later, Sean said, "Janey, I thought your ferry was coming in at twelve-fifteen."

Tessa blinked, pure shock flowing through her.

"Janey?"

She quickly pulled the phone from her ear and hung up. Calls got disconnected all the time, and all she could do was hope Sean didn't try to call Janey back. "Even if he does, so what?"

Tessa couldn't sit still, and she got up and started pacing in the bedroom. Janey was returning to Nantucket a day early. Sean knew it and was probably going to pick her up. Maybe they'd go to lunch.

"She'll probably stay with him tonight." For some reason, that really bothered Tessa. Sean Masterson was supposed to stay neutral. He was supposed to advise her and Janey on all things legal, not start a secret relationship with a woman who already had two boyfriends.

Tessa had half a mind to get a ticket on the next plane leaving Pennsylvania and show up on Nantucket tonight too.

If Janey was arriving on Nantucket aboard the twelve-fifteen ferry, she was already on her way to Hyannis. The ferry took an hour to cross the bay, and Janey's flight took that long too. With transferring, she was probably at the airport now, or taking off.

Tessa wasn't sure why she felt so betrayed. Janey was a grown adult, and she could do whatever she wanted. She didn't have to call Tessa to get permission to travel or go on a date with a lawyer.

It was just that they'd agreed to meet back at the cottage on *Tuesday*. Tessa hadn't even thought to return early. What was the point of that? So she could do more work by herself?

Of course, if she had a new love interest, she wouldn't be working on the yard or roof of the cottage. She'd be sipping Mai Tais and watching the sunset. Eating lobster and salt and vinegar potato chips and hoping to catch sight of a whale.

Tessa suddenly didn't want to return to Nantucket at all. Maybe then Janey would get a taste of her own medicine.

Chapter Twenty-Three

Tessa didn't have to answer to anyone on Tuesday morning. She made coffee and puttered around the house, putting away a few things that had gathered on the desk. She mowed the lawn before the day got too hot, and she showered, scrubbed the bathroom, and double-checked to make sure she'd rescheduled all of her tickets appropriately.

She had not told Janey any details of her travel plans, so her sister shouldn't be expecting her at any given time. Tessa watched the clock as the day wore on, wondering when Janey would realize Tessa wasn't there yet.

This game made her angry, especially once the time ticked to four p.m. She reasoned that wasn't too early for a casual glass of wine, and she poured an aged red into a glass, made a batch of caramel popcorn, and put another movie on.

She'd already taken more vacation at the library. The

yard work was finished. Tessa's laundry was washed, dried, and folded. Her bags packed. She literally had nothing to do, but she set her determination, ate the sugary treat, drank her wine, and refused to change the movie even though she didn't particularly like it.

Tessa felt like her entire life could be represented in that moment. Everything always so buttoned up and done right. After she took care of literally everything, she needed sweets and alcohol to make it through an evening. Coupled with her sheer determination, Tessa lived like that day after day.

Where was her joy? What reasons did she have to laugh? How many years had she wasted in this state of sheer will to stay caged in this life?

Tears gathered behind her eyes, but she refused to let them out. She pressed her eyes closed, the hot water there burning. She would not let it escape. She had a good life, with plenty to be grateful for.

Her phone rang, and her eyes flew open. Janey's name sat on the screen, and a rush of vindication flowed through Tessa. She didn't answer, because she could just as easily send a text in a few minutes, which would indicate how *terribly* busy she was. No time for a call, just like Janey had done yesterday.

She finished her wine and set the glass on the end table beside the couch. Only then did she pick up her phone and tap out a text to Janey. *So sorry. I'm not going to make it to the cottage for a couple more days. Something came up.*

Reasonably vague, which was exactly what Janey

would've done. Tessa couldn't count how many times Janey had used the words, *Oh, it's just work*, or *I have so much going on right now* over the years.

Well, Tessa did too. For example, right now, she needed another glass of wine and a better movie. As she walked into the kitchen, a series of texts came in, making her heartbeat thump in a strange way.

She deliberately took a few minutes to poke through the fridge, hoping to find something already made and ready for her to eat. Of course she didn't, but it ate up a few minutes, so by the time she returned to her phone, she might actually appear busy.

Janey had simply said, *I hope everything is okay. Let me know what I can do to help.*

Tessa's guilt caught in her stomach like a fish hook. Someone on the other end of the line yanked, and she felt like she might throw up.

She wasn't sure why she'd gone down the passive-aggressive road, only that sometimes her sister drove her in that direction.

Ron had texted several times, triggering the multiple notifications, and Tessa tapped over to those texts. Her breath caught in her throat at the pictures he'd sent. He and Ryan were together in the city, sharing dinner it looked like. Her son wore a smile that felt real and bright, and Tessa reached out to tap on the picture.

It filled the whole screen, and she couldn't look away from it. Another wave of emotion hit her, and Tessa did let a single tear splash her cheek before wiping them away. She drew a deep breath and went back to the text string.

Ron said, *Having dinner with Ryan. He's doing great, Tess. He says not to worry about him.*

"That's great and all," she said. "But why doesn't he come visit? Why do we never go to see him?"

She looked up at the closing credits scrolling up on the television. She thought of The Hotel Benjamin, as well as the house on Long Island. Janey claimed she hadn't gone to the house and knew nothing about it, but Tessa wasn't sure that was entirely true. The assets had been left to her. Perhaps her son should use them.

"Maybe I should transfer them to him right away," she mused. Would that further protect them from Dennis's children?

She quickly tapped out a reply to Ron. *That's great! You guys are so cute. What's he doing these days?*

He's so swamped with the internship with Hyclone, Ron said. *Works fifteen or sixteen hours a day. But he said he's met someone.*

Tessa's heart warmed and she devoured Ron's next message as it came in. *I'm trying to get more details now. I'll call you later.*

Okay, she said, and Tessa leaned into the couch and kept her phone close so she wouldn't miss any updates about her son.

———

Two nights later, Tessa finally stepped off the ferry and onto the island of Nantucket. Hours of daylight remained, though she'd taken an afternoon flight and bought dinner from the concessions stand on the ferry.

She hadn't told Janey when she'd arrive, though she easily could have. Janey would've driven over in the ancient car Mom kept in the garage at the cottage, and perhaps they could've gotten dinner together downtown before going back out to the Point.

Tessa stepped out of the flow of people and took a deep breath of the briny air. It was hot and humid this evening, and she caught a hint of something fishy. Didn't matter. She did love being on the island of Nantucket, and the sound of water meeting the shore soothed her soul.

So much about this island ironed things flat for her, and she seriously considered moving here permanently. Ron could fly directly from the small airport here to New York; it couldn't be more than an hour flight. If that.

Tessa also knew a ferry went between Nantucket and New York City, because she'd considered taking it to return this time. It took six hours, and that would put her on the island closer to ten p.m.

In the end, she hadn't wanted to ride a boat for six hours, and she'd flown to Hyannis as she usually did. The flights directly to Nantucket cost twice as much, especially in the summer as tourists flooded the island.

She looked out over the bay, the brightly colored sails on the boats making her smile. Mom had loved to sail, and she'd used some of Daddy's life insurance money to buy a boat with a bright yellow sail.

She'd taken a couple of classes to learn to work with the wind, and Tessa relived the breeze in her face as she held a baby Ryan to her chest during a weekend trip she'd taken to Nantucket just to sail with her mother.

A sigh passed through her, and she whispered, "I miss you, Mom," just as her phone chimed.

Her ride had arrived, and Tessa pulled herself out of the past and stepped over to the curb. It was time to face Janey—face the future.

Chapter Twenty-Four

"I just can't believe you did this," Tessa said, still scanning the living room and kitchen she'd walked into.

"Well, something needed to get started, and you weren't here." Janey stood in the kitchen, several paces away, one hand on her hip. She wore jeans—something Tessa rarely saw on her sister's body—and a tank top that covered the barrel they'd been blessed with.

"You could've called." Tessa noted the curtains she'd put up remained, but that was about it.

"The furniture was old and disgusting," Janey said. "The floors too. All of the appliances were probably leaking antifreeze or something."

"We haven't even talked about what we wanted to spend here." And Tessa couldn't believe Janey wanted to spend anything to renovate the cottage. Heck, a week ago, she hadn't even wanted to keep it. Tessa had called Ron to discuss buying her out of it completely.

She'd erased so much of their mother already, and Tessa's heart pinched at the same time her frustration expanded. "Mom loved that orange settee."

"I didn't get rid of it," Janey said. "It's simply upstairs in the attic."

Relief hit Tessa, and she brought her eyes back to her sister. Her blue-black hair had been clawed back into a ponytail, but plenty of sections had come loose. She still looked amazing, as always, and Tessa wondered how she did that.

Maybe the huge hoops in her ears, or the half-dozen bangles on her wrist. No matter what, she could make dusty hands and dirty jeans look like a million bucks.

Tessa felt thrashed from a flight and a ferry ride, and she bent to pick up her suitcase. She'd dropped it just inside the door when she'd frozen at the sight of bare plywood on the floor. No furniture to speak of, not even the dining table and chairs.

No appliances in the kitchen, and the gaping holes where the stove, fridge, and microwave should be glared darkly at Tessa as she moved further into the cottage. "How much is all of this going to cost?"

"I got a great deal on the appliances," she said. "Sean manages a couple of rentals here on the island, and the owners are remodeling. They're barely used and made within the last five years. They'll be here tomorrow." She seemed pleased with herself, and she hadn't hidden the fact that she'd been communicating with Sean.

"Sean, huh?" Tessa asked, plenty of questions within that single one.

"Yes," Janey said, lifting her chin and the pitch of her voice slightly. "I've been in touch with him. He also hooked me up with Benavidez, who's redoing the floors. He had a surplus of this amazing bamboo flooring he's giving us for half-price."

Spending money was Janey's superpower, though she did seem to find good deals from time to time. Perhaps this was one of those times.

As the shock continued to wear off, Tessa said, "I wish you'd have told me. I didn't eat much on the way here, assuming you'd have something here. Coffee, at least."

"I do have coffee here," she said, and Tessa hated all the singular talk, as if the food and drinks that were here belonged only to her.

Tessa put her bag down at the mouth of the hallway again, her pulse crashing against her ribs when she noticed the rotary phone had been removed from the wall. "What did you do with the phone?" she demanded. "I wanted that."

"*Relax*," Janey said, and that only made Tessa want to fly across the kitchen and grab her by the straps on that tank top. "It's in your bedroom." She turned her back on Tessa and started making coffee. "I've got crackers here too. A bottle of wine, though I'm not trusting you with that again." She threw a small smile over her shoulder, but Tessa didn't take it or return it.

Exhaustion pulled through her as Janey continued to

outline that she had bread and butter, a toaster, and a couple of other items that didn't need to be refrigerated or cooked.

"We eat out anyway," she said. "The floors will be done in a week, and then Sean will come load the appliances."

A week. Tessa reached up and ran her hand through her hair, feeling it stick up in some places and gain too much electricity in others. She felt exactly like that inside, and she continued to look around.

"We should talk about what else we're going to do," she said.

"This is all I want to do," Janey said, finally turning back to face her. "The bedrooms are secondary, in my opinion. But having a nice main area to live, visit, socialize. That's what's important."

"The yard and garage will need a lot of work," Tessa said. "The roof might need to be replaced."

Janey's jaw tightened, but she nodded. "I waited to start going through those things so we could do it together."

Tessa bit back the words, *I bet you did.*

She'd taken on the fun projects—the ones she deemed necessary. The items that "in her opinion," needed to be done.

But the hard work? Pulling old boxes, tools, and toys out of the garage? Mowing an overgrown yard? Oh, Janey had left that so Tessa could help her decide what to do.

More like so Tessa could do it all herself.

She tamed her bitterness, because she didn't want to fight with her sister. She regretted trying to show her what it felt like to have someone not show up when they said they would. She should've just returned to the island on Tuesday as planned.

She didn't need to be anyone but the responsible, reliable Tessa she'd always been. Why she thought she'd needed to prove anything to anyone, she now didn't understand.

Her frustration morphed and aimed inward, and Tessa sighed.

"We still have the chairs on the deck," Janey said, approaching with a cup of coffee. "Should we go sit out there? I can catch you up on things here, and you can tell me why you're two days late." She looked so hopeful, her eyes wide and filled with concern.

Tessa fell into that spot where she belonged to Janey, and Janey belonged to her, and she accepted the cup of coffee with, "Sure, let's go sit outside." She'd taken two steps before she turned back to Janey.

"And bring that blue binder. I want to look at it."

———

HALF AN HOUR LATER, THE HOOK IN TESSA'S STOMACH HAD been joined by at least two more. Mom had outlined everything in this binder, and Janey had simply followed the directions. If Tessa had bothered to read it instead of downing a bottle of wine, she wouldn't have had to suffer with her unwarranted bitterness, frustration, and suspicions.

She'd finished her coffee a while ago, and now she simply sat watching the sun paint the sky with rays of gold, orange, rose, pink, and violet.

"How's Milford?" she finally asked into the silence. Thankfully, she hadn't accused Janey of anything.

"Great," Janey said, reaching up to touch something at her collar. She'd done so a couple of times in the past thirty minutes, and Tessa finally looked over to her.

"New necklace?" The silver starfish boasted diamonds along each of its five arms, and while it looked familiar, she couldn't place where she'd seen it before. Perhaps Sean had given it to Janey.

"New to me," Janey said. "Mom left it for me in the safety deposit box in the city. I found it when I went to close the account."

Surprise moved through Tessa, but she'd had enough experience to keep her mouth shut even when her thoughts begged to come out.

"I gave it to her for her fiftieth birthday," Janey said. "I guess she wanted me to have it back." She sniffled—actually sniffled—and Tessa's shock only grew. She hadn't seen Janey cry in years. She stuffed everything away from prying eyes, even Tessa's, and always remained the picture of perfection on the outside.

She reached over and took Janey's hand in hers, squeezing as she said, "I'm glad she gave it back to you. It's beautiful."

Janey nodded, her eyes still trained out on the sand, surf, or sky. Several minutes passed, and just as Tessa released her hand, Janey said, "I'm not seeing Sean."

"I didn't say you were."

"But you're thinking it."

"I wasn't actually thinking about anything but how early is too early to go to bed." She flashed her sister a smile, but it wavered at the top of the curve, quickly falling flat.

"Then I just wanted you to know." Janey sighed and slouched further in her Adirondack chair. "I also broke up with Curtis. I'm only seeing Milford right now, and he was able to come to Jersey for a couple of nights over the weekend."

"That's great," Tessa said, pleased with this personal update. "Are things…serious with him? Or are you keeping him in the outer box?"

Janey had once explained to Tessa about outer boxes and inner boxes. She kept men where she wanted them, so she wouldn't get hurt, and neither would they. She'd let too many into her inner boxes, allowing them to get close enough to her heart to break it, and she proceeded with much more caution now.

Tessa had simply nodded along like she understood, but she hadn't. She wasn't sure if she did even now, but she wanted to communicate with Janey in her own language.

"He's getting really close to the inner box," Janey admitted. "Especially now that I've told him I'd like to be exclusive." A smile touched her mouth. "He said, for him, we've always been exclusive. That he didn't want anyone but me."

"I bet that was nice to hear." Tessa wasn't sure what she needed to hear from Ron. They'd had a fine weekend together. Nothing special. Sleeping late on Saturday, then her work at the library, and brunch on Sunday. He'd gone running both days, claiming he missed the clear air and hated running on a treadmill in the city. He'd made love to her early on Sunday night, said he couldn't wait for their vacation right here on Nantucket in a couple of weeks, and he'd been gone before dawn on Monday morning.

"It was," Janey admitted while Tessa continued to evaluate her weekend. Ron often complained about his life in the city, but he'd been living it for over two decades.

Maybe it was time for a change, and a brand-new life bloomed right before her eyes. Perhaps even right here, on this deck. She imagined sitting here with Ron at her side, not her sister, as they talked about their day, what they'd do tomorrow, and when Ryan would bring his girlfriend home to meet them.

He'd not reported any more about who Ryan had met, citing that their son hadn't wanted to say much about it.

Her mind felt stuffed full, and Tessa needed a mental break. That was why she'd started drinking in the evenings. Too much to think about, and it weighed her down. The buzz of the alcohol removed all of that, and she didn't have to think so dang hard.

Sleep would do the same thing, and tonight, she simply

wanted to do that. "Well, I'm tired," she said. "I'm going to head to bed."

"You never said why you couldn't come on Tuesday," Janey said, standing with Tessa. Her eyes probed, and Tessa had never been able to lie to her sister very well.

"Oh, just a meeting at the library, and then some stuff with Ron and Ryan." She watched Janey's eyes round. "Minor stuff," she said.

"Did you tell them about the new assets?"

"Just Ron," Tessa said. "He went over the packet of evidence, but he wasn't terribly impressed." She shrugged, though she had brought the documents with her. "I'm surprised we haven't heard from any of Dennis's children."

"Besides Aleah showing up at my hotel room," Janey reminded her.

"Right, besides that."

"We need to talk about those assets," Janey said as she started for the corner of the house. "Tomorrow? While we're knee-deep in whatever's in that garage?" She glanced at Tessa over her shoulder, a teasing, sarcastic tone to her voice and a glint of it in her eye.

"Sure," Tessa said, tired from tomorrow's events already. "I also want to go see the house on Long Island." She thought fast, because for some reason, she wanted to make the trip alone. "In fact, I have a ticket to fly out on Monday morning to do that."

"You do?" Janey paused and turned around completely, and Tessa made her face as impassive as possible.

"Yes," Tessa said, watching her sister carefully. "Unless

you've already gone? I didn't think you had, and I want to see what we're dealing with there."

"I haven't gone," Janey said, indicating the blue binder in Tessa's hands. "It said more information about the house would be provided once we went to the bank and the hotel. Have you gotten anything?"

"Gotten anything?" Tessa repeated, thinking telling little fibs to her sister had somehow gotten easier. "No, I haven't received anything. You went to the bank and the hotel. Did you get anything?"

"No, nothing." Janey whipped around so fast that Tessa knew instantly that she was lying.

"Strange," Tessa said moving around the corner of the cottage to find Janey had already reached the door. It was almost as if she was running away from Tessa and the conversation.

Definitely strange—and her sister had definitely received something. Tessa just needed to figure out what, or how to bring up the subject again in a way that would get her the answers she needed.

Chapter Twenty-Five

"All of this is junk." Tessa exhaled and wiped the back of her hand up her forehead, clearing away the hair that had stuck there. Cleaning out a garage in the middle of the summer wasn't a treat, and trying to get the job done with her sullen, mostly silent sister only added tension to the chore.

"I agree," Janey said, coming to stand beside Tessa in front of the large bank of lockers that took up the entire far side of the garage. Ragged surfboards, boogie boards, plastic buckets and shovels, and beach chairs lay or stood haphazardly in the compartments. "Lord, look at those life jackets."

The end locker held an assortment of life jackets, all of them with frayed straps and faded colors on the padding. Several dark spots had bloomed on a couple of them, and Tessa backed up a step. "They're moldy," she said, looking at Janey. "We should've gone to get those masks."

She'd suggested it that morning, but Janey hadn't wanted to waste the cooler morning hours with driving downtown for protective masks. They'd been working steadily for a while now, and the temperature in the garage kept climbing.

At least she'd found some gloves on the shelf just inside the garage. Sure, they'd crinkled and cracked when she'd first put them on, but the gear had protected her hands. She started pulling things from the locker and loading them into the wheelbarrow Janey had found in the garden.

"We should probably talk about the hotel," Tessa said without looking at Janey.

"Probably."

"I looked it up online last night," Tessa said, fitting in one more life jacket before moving around to the handles of the wheelbarrow. "It looks amazing. Plenty of rooms. High ratings. A good restaurant on ground level."

"It was beautiful," Janey agreed.

"What do you want to do with it?" Tessa asked. She didn't want to make any suggestions today. She wanted Janey to talk, so she'd know what she thought and where she stood.

"I don't think Mom did anything with it," Janey said. "I think she hired a general manager, and he does everything at the hotel."

"Charles Burns," Tessa said as she left the garage. They'd ordered a massive haul-away Dumpster, and it sat right in front of the garage. She began tossing in the life jackets.

"Right," Janey said from inside. "He's got house-keeping managers, a restaurant manager, hospitality managers, a security manager, and then people working in all of those divisions."

Tessa had seen that on the website. With the wheel-barrow empty, she returned to the lockers, passing Janey as she carried two surfboards toward the Dumpster.

"The money flows up," Janey said. "Mom drew a salary from the hotel, the same way Charles does."

"Really?" Tessa tackled the sand toys, loading the brittle and faded plastic into the wheelbarrow.

"Yes," Janey said. "I spoke to him on Wednesday. That's what he said. So we can do the same thing. Split the salary each month. The only thing we'll need to manage is hiring someone should Charles ever decide to leave."

"How much is the salary?"

"Ten thousand per month," she said. "He assured me we could set it at whatever we wanted. The hotel makes plenty of money, and he put me in touch with the financial officer—a man named Felix Conrad."

Wednesday. Why hadn't Janey told her any of this then? She bit against the resentment, because she was the one who'd invented some minor crisis and had stayed away from Nantucket. Janey probably hadn't wanted to bother her.

"So I put a call out to him, but he's on vacation this week. His secretary told me he'd call first thing Monday morning."

"Okay." Tessa went back and forth cleaning out the

lockers toy by toy and piece by piece. Janey called her over to a tall trunk in the corner by the lockers.

"Mom's gardening tools."

They both looked down into the mess of rusted shovels, handheld rakes, and even an unopened bag of decorative stone Mom hadn't used yet.

Tessa could see Mom working in the garden, those bright green gloves on her hands. She'd loved gardening, and Tessa had loved toddling around after her with a rake small enough to fit in her hand as she "worked" with her.

"Let's get rid of that bag of fertilizer," she said. "But we could keep everything else."

"It should go out in the shed with the other tools." Janey looked at Tessa, who nodded.

Her sister reached for the bag of fertilizer, and it came free of the jumble of other items easily. "We can also stay at The Hotel Benjamin whenever we want," Janey said. "The owner's apartment on the forty-second floor is never rented out. Charles and some of the other higher-level managers use it also, so there is a schedule for reserving it. He sent me a link. I forwarded it to you."

Tessa nodded, though she hadn't been on her email in days. "And everything at the bank is closed."

"Yep."

"What about the intellectual property?" Tessa followed Janey toward the gaping mouth of the garage and picked up the handheld brush and dustpan it was attached to. She separated the two pieces and began sweeping out the lockers.

"That's actually managed by someone else," Janey said when she returned to the garage. "This literary agent listed in the binder. I called her. She said she managed the IP, selling it in various forms over the years. When royalties are due—and they come from different sources around the globe, at different times of year—then she takes her cut, and sends Mom a check for the rest."

"Wow," Tessa said. "What's her cut?"

"Twenty percent on international deals, like she sold Conway's first trilogy in Germany, and I guess it does well there. They pay out twice a year, she said. His books have actually been sold in twenty-one countries, and they all pay at different times. Sherryl—that's her name—said she sent Mom money almost every month. Sometimes it's a lot—like when Warner Brothers renewed their rights to make the movies of that first trilogy—and sometimes it's not."

Janey paused and lifted her water bottle to her lips. Today, she wore a tight-fitting tank top that showed off her muscular arms. She'd paired that with a short pair of shorts that hugged her thighs and made her look strong and sexy at the same time.

Tessa had opted to stay more covered, as she usually did. The extra weight she carried contributed to that, as did the fact that she didn't think she was young enough to pull off a pair of cutoffs that barely covered anything.

"Domestic deals are fifteen percent," Janey said. "That's print, ebooks, and audiobooks here in the US. Movie deals here. Comic books, graphic novels, merchandise. Anything that uses anything from his books, Sherryl sells. She takes her cut; we get the rest." She set her water bottle down and looked up at the bicycles hanging from pegs on the back wall. "We just need to give her our updated payment information, and she said she'll take care of the rest."

"Okay," Tessa said, actually impressed by all Janey had done. Familiar guilt crept through her, and she went to help her sister get the bikes down. "Flat tires everywhere," she said.

"Why didn't Mom get rid of these? I think these are the original bikes we got from that safety fair once." Janey gazed up at the dilapidated bicycles and then met Tessa's eye. "Remember that?"

Tessa nodded, because she'd been thrilled to finally have a bicycle here on Nantucket. A lot of people rode them, and there were miles of trails along the beaches. Mom and Daddy had taken them to a safety fair put on by the Sheriff's Department, and both she and Janey had brought a bike back to the cottage.

"These haven't been ridden in years," Janey said. "Should we toss them and get new ones if we want them?"

"Yes," Tessa said. They had to work together to heave the bikes over the top of the Dumpster, and Tessa felt the bond between her and Janey restitching and regrowing. When that job was done, Tessa once again wiped her sticky hair off her forehead. Her stomach growled, and her shoulders and back ached.

"Janey," she said, and her sister turned toward her. "Thank you for dealing with all of that."

"Of course," she said with a smile. "I said I would, and you've already done so much with the original will and trust."

Tessa smiled, glad when her sister made the first move and drew her into a hug. "We should put all of these things into the trust," she said. "That way, we're both trustees of it, and we can both pass them onto our children."

Janey pulled back, her eyes bright. "Really? Mom left them to you for a reason, Tess."

"But I don't know what it is."

Janey turned away and bent to pick up the stiff broom that had fallen. "I think Dennis's children will come after them. Once that's all settled, then yes. We put them in the trust—if you still own them."

She walked to the back of the garage, turned, and started sweeping the mess they'd made toward the wide door at the front.

"I'm going to order from Fisherman's Plate," Tessa said, pulling her phone from her pocket. "I'm starving, and I'm sweaty, and I need a break."

"Get me the salmon tacos," Janey said, the comforting *swish-swish-swish* of the broom somehow settling Tessa even further.

THAT EVENING, TESSA WATCHED JANEY WALK AWAY FROM the house. They'd taken it easy that afternoon, sort of puttering around the yard and making assessments for what needed to be done more than actually doing anything.

The shed that sat next to the cottage in the back yard held a variety of tools, most of them rusted or broken. They'd agreed to go to town in the morning and get proper equipment for tackling the yard, and then Janey had showered while Tessa had taken a nap.

She'd emerged from her bedroom wearing a gorgeous teal blouse and a pair of skinny jeans. She said she was going to take a walk on the beach, and she'd tucked her phone in her back pocket and pinched her sandals in her fingers before leaving.

Tessa didn't believe for a single moment that she was going to simply walk the beach in perfume, makeup, and jewelry. She was going to meet someone for dinner, despite her declaration that she wasn't seeing Sean.

"Maybe she met someone else," Tessa said aloud. She hated that the only chairs currently at the cottage sat out on the deck, but while they'd made good progress in the garage, the painters had been working in the house. Two-thirds of it now gleamed with an off-white color Janey had called oyster egg.

She shook her sister out of her head. Janey had said she and Milford were exclusive. She was allowed to go to dinner with whomever she wanted, and Tessa picked up her phone from the wide armrest on the Adirondack chair and swiped to get to her son's name.

Surprisingly, he answered on the second ring. "Mom," he said. "How are you?"

"Good," she said with a sigh. Relief streamed through her, along with so much love. "Dad said you're doing well. Busy." She put the phone on speaker and set it back on the armrest.

"*So* busy," he said, his voice filling the air around her. "But I love working with Hyclone. They just have a *massive* highway project going on this summer, and I've been right in the thick of it." He continued to detail the ins and outs and challenges of designing and implementing a major roadway between New York and New Jersey, and Tessa just listened to the sound of his voice.

She asked him a question here and there, and he finally fell silent. "Thanks for calling, Mom," he said. "And hey, thanks for not interrupting and trying to tell my story as if you know what I might say next."

Tessa burst out laughing, and she hadn't even had a drink yet. "Dad can do that sometimes, can't he?"

"He can do that all the time," Ryan said dryly. "It was fun to see him earlier this week, though."

Tessa smiled as the sun set even further, throwing navies and violets into the sky. "I'm glad."

"What's happening at the cottage?"

She told him about the garage and the house needing a new roof. That they were going to keep Mom's car, because while it was old, it also only had fifty thousand miles on it and ran great. That the remodel should be done by the end of July, and if he could get away, Dad would be on the island the first weekend in August…

"I might be able to make that work," Ryan said. "I'll need to check a few things first."

"That would be wonderful," Tessa said, debating whether she should bring up this new significant other Ron had mentioned. In the end, she didn't. Instead, she said, "Listen, my mother owns a house on Long Island. We think it's empty right now, and I'm wondering if you might be interested in living there."

"Long Island?" Ryan asked. "Wow. I didn't know Grams had a house out there."

"I didn't either. I'll be there on Monday to see what's going on with it. We might sell it. Who knows? I thought I'd find out what you thought so I could have all the pieces when I sit down to talk with Janey about it."

"I suppose it depends on how much it is," Ryan said. "And how far from my job and school. I only have a year left, and I'm almost certain I can get a job here at Hyclone when I graduate. They're the fastest-growing civil systems company on the East Coast. In fact, they just signed with the city of Raleigh to expand their bridge systems. That project doesn't start for another ten months though."

"It sounds like the house might not work for you."

"Sounds like it."

"All right," she said. "Well, I'll let you go."

"Love you, Mom," he said quietly, and Tessa felt the power of it stream through him.

"Love you too, Ry." Tessa reached over to tap the red phone icon, ending the call. She got up and moved to the railing, leaning against it and looking all the way up into the sky. The stars had started to prick through the near blackness, and a sense of peace and calmness came over her.

Rustling in the dry beach grass sounded to her left, and Tessa's gaze shot that way. "Hello?" she called, wishing the back of the cottage had lights on it the way the front did. Daddy had once wanted to put flood lights back there so they could play volleyball and badminton after dark. Mom had never done it though, as he'd died the next month.

Tessa's skin prickled as she searched the darkness. The wind always seemed present on Nantucket, and surely it had just disturbed the tall grass. "Or it was a cat," she murmured to herself. Still, she turned, grabbed her phone, and headed inside. She didn't need to make herself an easy target, that was for sure.

Chapter Twenty-Six

M*ore information for this house will be provided once you've gone to the bank and the hotel.*

Tessa hadn't received any more information for the house on Shoreline Way. She pulled up to the house in her rental car, the minty green exterior charming and quaint at the same time. This driveway could easily hold half a dozen vehicles, and then there was the three-car garage too.

She kept her sunglasses firmly in place as she rose from the car. The sound of the beach echoed behind her, and she turned around. Right across the road lay the beach, its white sand stretched toward a gorgeous blue slash of water.

"Unbelievable," fell from her lips. This house seemed false, and she couldn't believe she owned this.

Turning back to the house, she surveyed the crisp, green grass and the blooming flowerbeds. Someone took care of this place, but she had no idea who. All the other assets had names and phone numbers attached to them. This house had nothing.

Black shutters hugged the windows, completing the captivating feel of the house. Tessa felt woefully under-dressed to even be here, and if she'd ever been invited to this address for a garden party or a bridal shower, she'd have to visit a high-end boutique in the city to find the right clothes.

She had no key for the house, so she marched toward the sweeping staircase that led to the pillared porch. Up she went, and she didn't hesitate as she reached to ring the bell. A song played behind the closed door, and it hadn't quite finished before the bright white door opened.

A woman stood there, probably a decade or so older than Tessa. She wore a modest blue dress that had been ironed into precise lines. Tiny white dots covered the whole thing, and she wore a very sensible pair of black pumps.

"Can I help you?" she asked, her voice so proper it almost carried a British accent.

"Yes," Tessa said. "I own this house, and I'm wondering what you can tell me about it."

The woman had dark hair she'd cut into a stylish bob, and her makeup had been applied flawlessly. Simple silver hoops hung from her ears, and she looked every bit the part of a celebrity housewife for this pristine house along the beach, only blocks from the million-dollar homes in Southampton.

"You're not one of Dennis's," she said. "So you must belong to Lydia."

The mention of her mother brought hope to Tessa's heart. "Yes," she said. "I'm Tessa Simmons, Lydia's daughter."

The woman gave her a sympathetic smile. "Yes, I can see her in your eyes now." She stepped back. "Do come in. I'll do my best to help you if I can."

"Thank you." Tessa glanced down and stepped over the lip of the doorway, inhaling the sweet, citrusy scent in the house. "Do you live here?"

"Actually, no," she said. "My goodness, I didn't even introduce myself. I'm Minnie Martin. I'm Dennis's cousin. Second cousin…once removed?" She gave a light laugh. "I'm not really sure how to describe it. Dennis's mother and my father are step-siblings. They don't share any blood, so neither do Dennis and I, but we both lived in the city for so long that we became close."

"And you don't live here?" Tessa glanced around the house, which did possess a bit of dead air.

"No," Minnie said. "I come out every once in a while to make sure the management company has what they need, and they called to say the last renters had just moved out, and they thought we needed to replace a couple of rugs. I came to see those and give the approval."

"I see." Tessa hated that she'd fallen into this formal personality, but Minnie seemed to require it. "So you managed the property for Dennis and my mom?"

"Sort of," she said, stepping past Tessa. "Would you like something to drink?"

"Sure," Tessa said, following the woman out of the foyer and through a doorway that led into an immaculate sitting room that connected to a dining room and then a kitchen at the back of the house. She didn't see any rugs even close to needing replaced, but she didn't say anything.

Minnie opened the fridge and took out a bottle of water. "I'm afraid this is all there is." Her dark eyes flitted around the house almost nervously, and Tessa's anxiety grew as well.

"That's fine." She reached for the water and seized onto the cold plastic to anchor her thoughts. "So this house is rented out?"

"Usually," Minnie said, turning to the kitchen sink and flipping on the water. "The previous renters just moved out a week or two ago, and I don't believe there's anyone moving in yet."

"There's no for-rent sign out front," Tessa remarked.

"Signs on the lawn are not allowed here." Minnie flashed her a smile that didn't feel very happy. Tessa didn't dare sit down, though she wasn't sure why.

"Who collects the rent here?" Tessa asked.

"I do," Minnie said, still not looking at her.

"And you then give it to…my mother? Or…?"

Minnie finally put down the washcloth she didn't need. "Dennis and Lydia allowed me to keep it."

"Really?" Tessa asked, disbelieving her for some reason. "Rent for a beautiful house in Southampton? That must be thousands of dollars each month." She couldn't believe her mother would allow that. The bank accounts hadn't been extravagant, and even a salary of ten thousand dollars from the hotel didn't seem excessive.

"The rent here is forty-four hundred dollars," Minnie said. She faced Tessa with tears in her eyes. "Without the rent I get from this place, I would not be able to maintain my lifestyle in the city."

"I see," Tessa said, though a frown pulled through her whole body. "Well, I hate to tell you this, my mother left me this house in her will. I own it now, and I'm not sure I can keep giving you almost five thousand dollars."

Ron would be so proud of her, and Tessa's smile felt somewhat genuine on her face. "Can I look around? There's hardly any details on the house. I don't know how big it is or anything."

"Sure." Minnie put a plastic smile on her face. "I'll get you the card for the management company I've been using and wait outside while you do what you'd like."

"Thank you." Tessa watched her walk through another doorway, and she heard a drawer opening. She sipped her water in the kitchen, looking out a huge window that over-looked a brilliantly beautiful backyard. Green grass. An in-ground pool, as if the beach right across the street wasn't good enough. A pergola, and chaises, and two patio tables and chairs sat on a rocked patio.

A waterfall cascaded down boulders in the back corner of the fenced yard, and a built-in dog run sat next to that. This place was pure heaven, and if Tessa didn't move to the cottage, she thought she'd very much like to live here. It was closer to the city for Ron, and she could find something to do on Long Island. They had libraries here, right?

Minnie's heels clicked by, and Tessa turned in time to see her leaving the kitchen area. A few moments later, the front door opened and closed, and Tessa breathed a sigh of relief.

She started exploring, starting with the door right behind her. It led into the garage, where a single car sat. A very expensive Mercedes Benz, in fact.

Tessa's compassionate side fired, and she turned away from the garage. Minnie had walked into an office, and Tessa gaped at the massive oak desk in the middle of the room.

That attached to the master suite and en suite bathroom, and Tessa found the expansive living room with the television and pool table on the left side of the front door.

The steps led upstairs directly in front of the entrance, and she found four more bedrooms up there, two on each side, each with a bathroom separating a pair of them.

Everything seemed to be clothed in the best bedsheets. High thread-count towels hung in the bathrooms, with exquisite art on the walls.

If someone had lived her in the recent past, Tessa could not tell. Everything about Minnie's story seemed... odd, as Tessa didn't see any rugs that needed to be replaced either.

She returned to the master suite and opened the closet. A suitcase sat there, and several dresses and blouses hung on the rod. Minnie wasn't just here to check on some rugs. She *was* living here.

In the office, Tessa began opening the drawers in the desk. The last time she'd done that, she'd found something that had changed everything. Her heart pounded the same way now, but there were no envelopes, no binders, and no pages stuffed away somewhere.

Frustrated, and starting to worry about the time she'd been in the house alone, she straightened and ran one hand through her hair, pushing it back off her face.

Someone knocked on the window behind her, and she yelped as she spun around. Another woman stood there, her hair completely void of color and her eyes the same color as the ocean across the street. She gestured for Tessa to come open the window, but Tessa found she couldn't move.

The woman grew more animated, and she said something that Tessa couldn't hear through the glass. She looked to her left and when she looked back at Tessa again, her eyes were wide and afraid, and she pointed to the right.

Then she was gone.

Tessa remembered the several steps she'd climbed to get to the porch and into the house, and she wondered how that older woman could even reach the window. She hurried toward it now and pulled it up before looking out.

To her right, she saw the older woman jogging away in a track suit. To the left, she saw Minnie standing on the patio with her arms crossed. Besides the frown on her face, there was something askew about her that Tessa couldn't quite place. When Minnie's gaze switched to the window, Tessa quickly stepped away from the window and pressed her back into the wall beside it.

"Her hair was sideways," Tessa whispered. Minnie had been wearing a wig.

Chapter Twenty-Seven

Tessa kneaded the steering wheel as she drove away from the house on Shoreline Way. She'd found Minnie in the driveway in her car, her dark wig perfectly pristine. She'd said she'd be returning to the city, and Tessa had gotten her phone number.

She'd driven away first, because Minnie had said she needed to run inside and get the spare key to turn into the management company. Minnie had gone left while Tessa right, and she pulled into the first coffee shop she saw. She waited in line to get the caffeine she didn't need, because she needed time to pass.

She got her caramel mocha, and she mapped the way to the nearest public park so she could sip it and hopefully get Minnie off the island. She drove around the island, burning time and gas, finally returning to Shoreline Way.

Her nerves skittered through her like sunshine scattering over the beach. She went past the immaculate lawns and skillfully sculpted trees and bushes to the house next door. Peering through the windshield, she pulled into the driveway of another beautiful beachside home.

She gripped her purse in one hand and her cellphone in the other as she got out of the car and approached the front door. The stark white door opened before Tessa reached the stoop, and the older woman with hair matching the color of the door stood there.

"You came back," she said, glancing left and right. "Come in quickly." She backed up, and Tessa darted into the house. The door closed and clicked locked behind her, and she felt like dialing the first two digits for emergency services so she'd only have to tap a couple of times to get help.

"Who are you?" Tessa asked, turning back to the woman in the track suit. "What's going on?"

"You're Lydia's daughter," the woman said, reaching up and patting her almost icy blue hair. "I recognized you immediately, because I've spent plenty of time with your mother." She offered Tessa a warm smile, and the anxiety bleeding through Tessa ebbed away.

"You have?"

"She spent her time here, every year from Labor Day to New Year's." The woman moved past her and padded further into the house. Tessa turned, tried to decide if she should follow or not, and decided she wanted answers.

"What's your name?" she asked again.

"Oh, silly me," the woman said. "I'm Esme

Carmichael." She looked over her shoulder, and those blue eyes tickled something in Tessa's memory.

"You look familiar," she said, and the woman grinned. She had straight, white teeth, and all the pieces clicked together. "You're Esme Carmichael, the supermodel."

"Guilty," the woman said. "I don't model anymore, obviously. Well, from time to time, when they want to show that all women are beautiful, no matter size or age, I get called back in."

Tessa settled at her peninsula and accepted the cup of tea Esme offered her. "You knew my mother?"

"Oh, yes," she said, growing serious. "And I know that Minnie is not who she says she is. She's Dennis's oldest daughter, Minerva, and she has been collecting the rent on that house since Lydia passed."

"It's only been a couple of months."

"That's almost ten thousand dollars," Esme said. "Maybe you don't need that money, but I know Minerva shouldn't have it." She shook her head as if trying to get her hair over her shoulders, but it had been cut short and barely moved. "I call the cops every time she comes, but I think they think I'm going senile." She gave a light laugh. "This time, I saw you pull up only a few minutes after her, but I still called. They haven't even come yet."

"Does Mom really rent that house?"

"Only through the end of August," she said. "The family that was there left at the beginning of June, because the husband had another job in Egypt." She spoke as if everyone traveled the world and lived in a rental house in the Hamptons in their down-time. "Minnie's trying to get the management company to rent the house again, obviously. What did she tell you for why she was there?"

"Something about a couple of rugs that needed to be replaced," Tessa said, trying to wrap her head around everything.

"Right." Esme scoffed. "The family that was here had two teen girls that were nothing but respectful. The father works in cybersecurity, and the mother baked the most delicious cherry pies." Esme laughed again, and Tessa found herself liking the older woman. No wonder Mom had trusted her.

"Oh, anyway, I'm supposed to give you something." She practically danced out of the kitchen and down the hall. Tessa gazed into her cup of tea, trying to find the next step she should take. She should probably call Janey, and Ron, and the management company.

"The management company." She owned the house, not Minnie, and she'd tell them not to rent the house for the rest of the year, the exact same way her mother never had. Before she could dig the card out of her purse, Esme returned.

"Here you go, sweetie." She carried a box wrapped in brown paper, and Tessa took it with some measure of trepidation tripping through her. She was tired of opening things and finding surprises, especially because the surprises she'd been getting hadn't been the type she'd normally associate with something good.

"Do I want to open this?"

"I have no idea," Esme said. "She gave it to me a few weeks before she passed away, and she said to give it to you when you came to the house."

Tessa nodded, feeling the heft of the box. It wasn't light, but it also didn't weigh a whole lot. Anything could've been inside, and the only way she'd know was to open it. "Should I wait until Janey and I can open it together?"

Esme cocked her head. "Who's Janey?"

Tessa opened her mouth to answer, but nothing came out. Her thoughts wouldn't align, and the doorbell rang before she could come up with an answer.

Esme kept her pinned with a look for another moment, and then walked toward the front door. Tessa heard her say, "It's about time you showed up. I called over an hour ago."

She got up from the bar, leaving her tea behind, and followed Esme into the foyer. She continued to chew out the two cops who'd come to the door, while Tessa stood there listening, trying to explain about a sister she'd known her whole life.

Why hadn't Mom mentioned her to Esme? They obviously knew each other quite well.

"You come faster next time," Esme said. "That woman does not own that home, and she's trespassing whether she has a key or not." She closed the door after they agreed, and she turned back to Tessa.

"Now, have you had lunch? There's a great little place right around the corner here. Your mother *loved* it. Bluebird? Did she tell you about it?"

Tessa shook her head, because Mom hadn't told her about her life here in Long Island at all. She lived here for four months out of the year, and Tessa didn't know. How was that possible?

She'd visited her mom in the city at Christmastime. They'd gone shopping in November for Ron's birthday together. She'd never come to Long Island and Mom had never breathed a word about a beachside cottage.

"I have not heard of the Bluebird," she said weakly, fighting back tears and wishing she could throw the package into the churning surf across the street.

———

"I DON'T KNOW," TESSA SAID FOR THE FIFTH TIME. SHE SAT on the ferry, away from everyone else, her eyes trained out over the dusky water. "It's a package, Janey. I didn't open it, because I wanted us to be together."

"Okay," Janey said, resigned. She'd asked a dozen questions about Minnie, the house, the management company, and Esme. Tessa had told her everything she knew, and she'd told her she didn't know several times too, the last one about what was in the package.

The one question Janey had not asked was why Esme didn't know about her. Tessa hadn't been able to find an answer to that, nor had she been able to stop thinking about why. The only thing her mind had been able to come up with was that Mom had only put Tessa on the will for the house, as she was clearly trying to keep Dennis's children from getting it.

The story had to be complete and elaborate, and no one could know Janey existed.

But they already do, she told herself. Dennis's children knew about Janey, because one of his daughters had been at The Hotel Benjamin.

Janey said, "I'll be there to pick you up. Eight-forty-nine?"

"Yes," Tessa said, and the call ended as she lowered the phone to her lap. The last of the sunlight cast everything in gold and gray, and Tessa loved this time of night. She loved that it didn't get dark until late, and she loved that she didn't need a jacket at all.

She shook her head to get the thoughts to settle. She just wanted to clean up the garage and yard, make the necessary repairs to the house, and be ready to entertain her husband and son on Nantucket Point Beach. They'd enjoyed several summers there together, and she needed to get all of these questions answered and mysteries cleared up before they arrived.

From the look on Minnie's face as she rose from the car to meet Tessa told her that the fight for the hotel, the IP, and the house wasn't over—or even really beginning. But Tessa had Ron on her side, despite some of the irritating things he said. He was incredibly smart, and he'd always been a light in the darkness for her. An anchor when she wavered. A voice of reason when she turned irrational.

She'd called him after lunch with Esme, and he'd calmed her down, pulled the title for the house, and coached her through her meeting with the management company.

When the ferry docked, she disembarked and found Janey waiting inside the station instead of the parking lot. Relief filled Tessa, and she rushed into her sister's arms. "I love you," she whispered. "I'm sorry I've been irritated the past few days."

"It's fine," Janey said. "We're allowed to be annoyed with each other, with the situation, with anything." She held her just as tightly as Tessa gripped her, and the moment reminded Tessa of what mattered most.

Family.

"Okay." She took a deep breath. "Here's the package."

Janey took it, a dubious look on her face.

"I met with Abigail Methesda at the management company, and we're rekeying the house. They're not going to rent it until the New Year, unless we change our minds. They're not going to talk to Minnie or any of Dennis's other children." She exhaled heavily, glad the meeting had gone so well. Her possession of the title with her name on it had really helped.

"Mom never rented the house from September to January. She *lived* there during those months, Janey. That's how she knew Esme so well."

"She lived there from September to January?"

"That's what Esme said. She knew me on sight, and she knew a lot about Mom."

"Did she live there with Dennis?"

Tessa frowned. "Dennis didn't come up, actually." She met Janey's eye. "Besides Esme saying Minerva was his daughter. Other than that, she didn't mention him. Not at her house, and not during lunch. That's weird, right?"

Janey gave a one-shouldered shrug. "This is all a little weird, honestly."

"I agree." Tessa faced the exit and squared her shoulders. "Let's go open this package."

Chapter Twenty-Eight

"You do it," Janey said once Sean had left, but Tessa didn't want to. In the past few days, a new floor had been laid, and a new kitchen table and chairs had been delivered that day while Tessa was in Long Island.

She and Janey both sat at the table, the brown-paper package in front of them. "Tell me why Sean was here. You said you two weren't dating."

"We're not," Janey said. "I asked him to come last night, because I was uncomfortable staying in the house alone."

"Was he here last week too, before I came?"

"I stayed with him, actually." Janey regarded her coolly. "We're not involved in anything physical. We're friends. He helped me, because I heard something last night that scared me."

"What?"

"A car kept coming down the lane, parking, and then leaving."

"The same one?"

"No, different ones." Janey shook her head. "It was nothing. Sean came, and he slept in the master suite. I felt safe."

Tessa nodded, remembering the rustling grasses from the other night. "All right." She exhaled and reached for the box. She peeled the paper back to reveal an old shoe box. Nothing remarkable or expensive, and she cut a glance at Janey. "This can't be a pair of shoes, right?"

"I wouldn't think so," she said.

Tessa removed the last of the paper and lifted the lid on the box. Inside, envelope after envelope of photographs ran from one end of the box to the other. "They're pictures," she said, tilting the box so Janey could see. "From a film camera."

"Mom always had a camera in her hand while we were here at the Point," Janey said, reaching for the box. She took the first packet of pictures from the end of the box closest to her. "Twenty-four pictures per roll. Remember Daddy complaining about the cost?" She smiled as she looked at Tessa, and the memories streaming through her mind were sweet and special.

Janey flipped open the top of the packet, and the negatives had been tucked into the back of it. She pulled the pictures out and started flipping through them. "They're still in good shape too." She looked up and back down again. "Look, here's us building a sandcastle." She put the picture on the table, and it was more yellow than pictures nowadays. Grainier too, but Janey and Tessa were unmistakable.

"How old do you think we are?" Janey asked. "I look to be about eight. Look at my teeth."

Tessa picked up the picture and looked at it, getting transported back about forty years to that sandy beach, all of that sunshine, the blue sky, and the carefree days of building sandcastles with her sister. "That's got to be close. Did Mom mark them?" She flipped over the picture, but no one had written on it.

Janey examined all the pictures, front and back, and found no notes. "The envelopes have nothing on them either."

Tessa had sat silently while Janey looked through the two dozen pictures. She didn't reach for another packet. There had to be at least twenty or thirty of them packed into the box, and she wasn't sure what she was supposed to do with them.

Relive the past? Reminisce with Janey? Why couldn't Mom just give them these pictures herself?

Her head pounded, and she stood up. "I'm tired. I'm going to go to bed."

"Okay," Janey said, clearly distracted as she tucked the first packet back into the box and took out another one. Tessa went down the hall, hoping Janey would be able to find something in the box that would answer some of the questions today had produced. She was eternally glad she didn't have to deal with this cottage and all of these secrets alone, and her gratitude for her sister doubled as she laid down and let her thoughts finally settle into silence.

————

DAYS ON THE BEACH, BIRTHDAY CAKES, THAT ONE TIME WE had a picnic on the roof. Janey went on and on detailing the pictures in the box.

"So basically our childhoods here at the cottage," Tessa said, pulling the last item out of the shed. They'd been working all morning, and thankfully, the shed was shaded by a couple of very large trees that separated the cottage from the house behind it.

The new tools waited against the back of the cottage, and they started loading those in next.

"Yes," Janey said. "Dinner parties with Bobbie, Riggs, and their kids. Remember Dale and Joan Harton? They were in there. There were several packages of a time when Mom and Daddy came without us. We must've been adults, off at college."

"Mm." Tessa hadn't seen, heard about, or thought of the Hartons for decades. They'd been good friends of Daddy's from his days at the hospital at Johns Hopkins. Once Daddy had died, Mom hadn't talked about Dale or Joan at all.

Janey finished talking about the pictures, and said, "What about the house? Was it nice?"

"Immaculate," Tessa said. "Someone takes really good care of it." She smiled at her sister and ignored her growling stomach. "Honestly, I think one of us should live in it. It's one-hundred percent paid for. It's only fifty-seven minutes to Ron's office instead of over two hours. It's a longer commute for you when you have to go to your office, since you're in Jersey."

Tessa picked up the weed eater. "Do you want to trim or mow?" Their conversation would have to cease, but Tessa was ready for some silence anyway. Janey had been talking for *hours*.

Janey frowned, her dark features clouding over. "Sounds like you want the house on Long Island."

"I've mentioned it to Ron," Tessa said, her defenses flying up. The house was in her name, and Mom had left it to her. Technically and legally, she didn't have to discuss this with Janey at all.

She pushed against those thoughts, because she didn't want to go down that path. It felt dangerous and sinister, and she didn't want to find herself there alone.

Janey turned away. "I'll mow. You trim."

"Then can we take a break? I'm starving." Tessa pulled out her phone. "I got an email from the Nantucket Tourism Bureau, and there's a food truck rally at The Lighthouse Inn today. Started an hour ago and goes until two-thirty."

"You get emails from the Tourism Bureau?"

"Yeah," Tessa said. "I'm here, and I don't want to cook my own lunch." She flashed a smile at Janey. "Let's get this done and go find some mimosas and shrimp scampi."

Janey made a face again, but she smiled immediately afterward. "You get the scampi. I'll search for crab cakes."

"Deal." Tessa plugged the weed eater into an outdoor outlet, praying she wouldn't get electrocuted, and pressed the button. It started just fine, and she adjusted her sunglasses and got to work. The area around the house went quickly, and she buzzed her way down the white wooden fence that separated the yard from the beach, the tall grasses waving merrily on the other side.

She looked up as she approached the shed, crying out at the sight of a person in the grass. Crouched down. She dropped the weed eater, and she looked down as she jumped back, hoping her shins wouldn't get eaten. The machine whined before turning off, and the handle landed on her foot soft enough that it barely hurt.

Looking back to the grass, she searched for the individual who'd been there. Her mind screamed at her that someone had been in these grasses a few nights ago too. Listening. Watching.

Had it been a man or a woman? Tessa couldn't tell.

The roar of the lawn mower stopped, and Janey called, "What's wrong?"

"There was someone here," Tessa said.

"What? Really?" Janey came over, clapping her hands together. "Who?"

"I don't know." Tessa pointed to the grass, where she had definitely seen a face. "They were right there."

"Let's go look."

"Janey." But her sister had already started toward the

shed, twenty feet away. She slipped through the gap between the building and the fence, but Tessa wasn't sure she could.

She did, though, and she and Janey walked back along the fence when Janey said, "Stay over here. We should be able to see if the sand has been disturbed or not." She paused in front of the weed eater. "Right there?"

Tessa positioned herself the same way she'd been standing when she moved the weed eater back and forth. "Yes," she said. "Right there." Slightly to her left, and right in those grasses. She leaned forward and examined the sand. "There's definitely been someone here," she said, her heartbeat turning into hummingbird wings now. "The sand is all mushed up."

Janey peered at it, and when her eyes met Tessa's, neither of them had to say anything.

"Hey, girls."

Both Janey and Tessa yelped—fine, Tessa's cry was more of a scream—and they grabbed onto one another as they turned toward the sound.

Riggs Friedman stood there, his blasted fishing pole in his hand. His smile faded as Tessa took in the ugly camouflage bucket hat and his bright orange T-shirt. He probably scared the fish to death with that color and then reeled them in easily. "What's going on?" He looked at the grasses and then the yard behind them. "Is everything okay?" He seemed genuinely concerned, but Tessa didn't want to involve him.

"Yes," she said quickly, in tandem with Janey. "Just lost my…pendant. Janey was helping me look for it."

"Oh, I have a metal detector," he said. "I like to go along the beach after the tourists leave."

Tessa bet he did, and she wasn't surprised by his statement.

"I found it," she said, patting her pocket. "The clasp broke, so I'm keeping it safe in my pocket."

"Oh, good." He smiled again and whistled as he started walking away. Tessa stood very close to Janey as they both watched him until he couldn't be seen anymore.

"Was it him?" Janey whispered.

"I don't know," Tessa said. "He was wearing a hat, and the person in the grass wasn't."

"And that shirt could've been seen from space."

"Exactly." She still didn't turn away from where Riggs had gone. "Strange how he's *always* around though."

"More than strange," Janey said. "I'm going to ask Sean about him."

"Good idea," Tessa said, and with some reluctance, they finished cleaning up the back yard.

THREE DAYS LATER, THE GARAGE, SHED, AND YARD WERE done. Tessa laid on the beach, her legs straight out in front of her, while Janey cracked open a diet cola and tapped away at emails on her phone.

"The roofers will be here next Tuesday," Janey said.

"I can stay," Tessa said. "You can go back to Jersey if you need to."

"It's almost the weekend," she said. "I'll see how my meeting in the morning goes."

Tessa just nodded, though her sister wasn't looking at her. Her phone rang, and it took her mind several seconds to catch up to the sound of it. Janey said, "That's you, Tess," and she still didn't get the device out in time.

The call went to voicemail, but another one came in right after it. She had the phone in her hand now, and the billowy clouds and crystal blue sky didn't feel so lazy anymore.

"It's Esme," she said, sitting straight up.

"Answer it."

Tessa swiped on the call. "Esme," she said. "What's going—?"

"There was a man here," the older woman said. "I called the police, and they came quickly, by a miracle of miracles." She was panting as she spoke, and Tessa quickly put the call on speaker so Janey could hear.

"A man?" Tessa asked.

"An older man," Esme said. "I've never seen him before, but he tried to break into the house. He broke a window in the back, and I just happened to be in my jacuzzi and heard the glass shattering. I called nine-one-one, and he ran off when he heard the sirens."

"Did they find him?" Tessa asked, wondering if she'd need to go back to Long Island.

"No," Esme said. "But I got a picture of him. They'll find him, and he'll be brought to justice."

Tessa met Janey's eyes, and she had to work hard to suppress her giggle. "Can you send me the picture?" she asked, looking away from her sister so she wouldn't laugh.

"It's on its way."

"Thank you, Esme," Tessa said sincerely. "You're so kind to keep an eye on the house for me."

"The last thing I need is hooligans in this neighborhood," she said, and Tessa nearly laughed again.

She thanked Esme one more time and got off the call.

"Hooligans?" Janey repeated, giggling. "Be brought to justice?"

"She's a little eccentric," Tessa admitted. Her phone chimed, and all traces of laughter and smiling vanished when she opened the picture Esme had sent.

In fact, tears came to her eyes, and she emitted a high-pitched whine.

"What?" Janey asked. "Who is it?"

Tessa just handed her phone to her sister, her vision blurring and her heartbeat rippling through her whole body.

Chapter Twenty-Nine

"Who is Riggs Friedman?" Janey asked again. She paced from the far windows to the new dining room table, where Tessa and Sean Masterson sat. Dinner had been delivered an hour ago, but Tessa had mostly picked through her chicken Caesar salad.

Her appetite had fled earlier that day when the picture from Esme had come in.

She looked at it again. It was clearly Riggs Friedman, from the oversized nose to the wrinkled forehead to the wispy, thin hair.

"Why did he go to Long Island?" Sean asked, looking between the two sisters.

"To *our* house?" Tessa asked.

They'd been through this routine before, all the same questions being posed.

How would he even know about it? Had he been

following Tessa? Was the cottage here bugged? Janey had been asking questions for an hour, ever since Sean had showed up with dinner and a kit containing several security cameras.

They now had one on the front door, the back door, and the garage, and he'd shown Tessa and Janey how to access the feeds on their phones.

"Maybe you two just go next door and ask him." Sean closed his Styrofoam container and pushed it away, though he hadn't eaten anything out of it in a while.

Janey glared at Sean as if he'd suggested she give up diet cola for a year. She folded her arms and cocked her hip. "Come on. What if he's dangerous?"

"The guy carries around a fishing pole and a fake box of tackle," Sean said, giving Janey's attitude right back to her.

"How do you know it's a fake box of tackle?" Tessa asked.

"I'm assuming," he said. "You two just see him walking to and from the ocean with the pole and box. You don't actually ever see him fishing."

"Or ever catching any fish." Janey sighed and sat down. "Okay, look, I have something to show you." She cut her eyes in Tessa's direction without truly looking at her.

Tessa's stomach tightened and tried to flip, but it didn't get anywhere. She wasn't sure if she felt good or not, but she said, "Okay," slowly. In the past, before Mom had died,

Tessa would've quipped about it being a picture of Janey with her lady motorcycle club, all nine of them decked out from head to toe in black leather. If not that, then a screenshot of how much weight Janey had just done a dead lift with.

Tessa could barely get herself off the couch most of the time.

"I'll be right back." Janey got back up and went down the hall.

Tessa watched her go and then watched Sean. "You know what it is, don't you?"

"I think so," he said.

Tessa barely knew Sean, and she wished he wasn't here for all of this. Janey had obviously been leaning on him, though, and Tessa should be glad about that. Her boyfriend was out of the country, and Tessa had been absent the past several days.

She needed to get outside of her head. Her phone rang, and she quickly swiped on the call from Marcus Hall, her mother's lawyer. "Marcus," she said, surprised. "It's quite late, isn't it?"

"This can't wait," he said. "I was just working on your mother's will to move it out of probate and get it settled, and I can't. It's still locked."

"Okay." Tessa got up from the table and walked toward the front door. She didn't dare go outside, though, because Riggs could be there.

"Janey didn't sign it," Marcus said.

"I thought—yes, she did."

"My system is telling me she didn't. So I need her to get on and do that before we can get this sewn up."

"Okay," Tessa said with a big sigh. "I'll talk to her."

"The link I sent her the first time should still work."

"Thanks, Marcus. I'll let her know."

"I don't want to put too much pressure on you, but we only have until the end of the month. July twenty-ninth, in fact."

"Yes." Tessa turned back to the kitchen when she heard footsteps. "I'll make sure it gets done." She ended the call and went back to the table. Janey sat across from Sean now, and she had a couple of pieces of paper in front of her.

"What's this?" Tessa asked.

"I got a letter from Mom."

Tessa blinked, absorbing the words. Janey didn't look at her, and everything felt so black and white in that moment.

Her vs. Janey.

Just when she'd started to think they'd work everything out and everything would be okay.

Then she'd learned that Janey hadn't signed the documents to settle the will, and she'd been hiding a letter.

"When did you get this?"

"It was in the safety deposit box in New York City."

"Really?" Janey had gone to the bank in the city over two weeks ago.

Janey nodded, smoothed her hands down the front page, and lifted them up to Tessa.

Tessa's eyes could not move fast enough, and she forced herself to slow down so she could read and understand.

My dearest Janey,

I'm sure you are confused, scared, and angry. You have every right to be, and I hope you'll allow yourself to run through all of the emotions you need to feel.

I want to say that I will miss you terribly once I am gone. That must sound strange to have someone who has died say they will miss the one left behind, but it's true. I have been worried about how you will handle my death the very most, and I hope it will be a comfort to you to know that I will miss you.

You have been the very best daughter a mother could ever want. I hope you will not judge me too harshly once you learn everything.

You will get to decide what you'd like to tell Tessa. I don't know what she's told you and not told you. My guess is she'll share every-thing with you, simply because I know Tessa as if she were myself, and she loves you dearly and wants you to be happy.

But don't tell her anything just because she told you. There is no money involved with this, so you'll not be cheating her of anything. Just so you know. Make your own decisions, Janey, based on what you feel is right.

I apologize for putting these new assets in her name only, but there is a very good reason. It's simply to protect them from Dennis's chil-dren. He has three of them, and they were all estranged from him for the past decade. Not one of them came to the funeral.

If you haven't looked at the packet from The Hotel Benjamin yet, all of the details and evidence you'll potentially need in a court case will be there. I won't go into them here.

Suffice it to say, his children did not care for him in life, and he did not want them to profit after his death. He left everything to me, and I've been managing it since his death two years ago.

I have left it solely to Tessa, purely because it will be easier for her to win should Dennis's children challenge my will to her. And they will, Janey. They have been contesting his will to me for the past two years, and I don't believe for a moment that they'll stop just because I am gone.

I apologize for not telling you and Tessa everything. It is the one major regret of my life, though I have had many, most of them surrounding you.

The first thing you need to know is that Dennis and I were married. That's why I got everything upon his death, and I've been able to keep his assets out of the hands of his children.

Please forgive me. I love you, and I have learned so much from being your mother. I am proud of the woman you are and the woman you will become after you discover all of my indiscretions. You are a strong person, Janey, though I know you feel weak. Don't listen to those negative messages in your head.

LOVE, MOM

TESSA READ THE LETTER AGAIN, TRYING TO DECIDE WHAT she was supposed to get from it. "You told me all of this," she finally said, handing the pages back to Janey. She did like seeing her mother's handwriting, as it made her feel closer to her mom.

"There's a few things in there that point to something,"

Janey said. She picked up the pages. "I apologize for not telling you and Tessa everything. It is the one major regret of my life, though I have had many, most of them surrounding you."

She looked up. "Surrounding me? Why would she say that?"

"I have no idea."

"Maybe that's why she left all of the items in the addendum will to Tessa," Sean said. "There's something going on with Janey she still doesn't know about."

"She said it was to make it easier to keep everything away from Dennis's children."

"And then there's this," Janey said. "I am proud of the woman you are and the woman you will become after you discover all of my indiscretions."

"Yeah, that she was married to Dennis and had all of these extra houses and a whole hotel in the city."

"A marriage she didn't tell us about isn't an indiscretion," Janey said. She refolded the letter and tucked it into an envelope. She looked across the table at Sean and inhaled deeply. "I've been over everything in the binder, and I think we've been behaving exactly how Mom predicted we would."

She reached over and touched Tessa's hand. "You told me everything. I went to the city to the bank and the hotel, but you went to the house in the Hamptons."

Tessa thought of Esme, and the question she'd asked that had been plaguing Tessa all week. *Who's Janey?*

"She was married to Dennis and didn't tell us. She had

all of these properties and didn't tell us." Janey got up and retrieved a new can of diet cola from the fridge. "She leaves us all these old pictures. For what? Then we find out Riggs is up on Long Island. There's so much going on here that we don't know yet."

"Do you think Mom had an affair with Riggs?"

"I don't know."

Tessa put her face in her hands and tried to think. "Remember how Bobbie said Mom met Dennis here? On Nantucket? On one of those cruises?"

"Yes."

"And she told us she met him at the theater." Tessa wasn't sure where she was going with this. She couldn't find the path she needed to be on. "Maybe…maybe Riggs is related to Dennis too. Maybe he's trying to figure out what we have or what we know, so he can fight us for it."

"His last name is Friedman," Janey said. "Dennis's was Martin. Wouldn't they be the same?"

"Not if they're half-brothers," Sean said.

"Bobbie said Dennis's family had a lot of homes here. Remember?" Tessa really needed Janey to fill in the blanks, but her sister only looked confused.

"I remember," she said. "Do you think he still does? Mom didn't mention any of those."

"Maybe they could be the indiscretions." Tessa would grasp anything at this point.

Sean stood up. "Let me do some digging on this. If Dennis Martin lived here and had a lot of properties, I'll be able to find them."

Janey jumped to her feet too. "Bobbie said the Martins were really wealthy and had a lot of property here on the Point."

"I'll see what I can find in the records."

"You're leaving?" Tessa asked, following Sean and Janey toward the front door.

"I'll be back in the morning," he promised. He opened the front door and turned back to Janey. "Bye, beautiful." He gave her a warm smile that said he wanted to be more than friends and actually leaned down and swept his lips along her cheek. Then he was gone.

Janey stepped to the closed door and locked it, leaning into it and holding onto the doorknob for several long moments before turning back to Tessa.

"You said you weren't seeing him."

"I don't know what's happening," Janey admitted. "He's handsome and sweet and employed." She shrugged and smiled, and that was the smile that had gotten Janey all the boys in high school, and obviously got her the men in her mid-forties.

"Can you sleep with me?" Tessa asked. "I'm a little afraid."

"I'm so glad you brought it up first," Janey said with a nervous laugh. "Are you still a furnace at night? Because the blanket on my bed is suffocating enough as it is."

"I still run a little hot," Tessa admitted, and she let Janey tuck her arm against her side and lead her down the hall to the bedrooms.

They changed into their pajamas, and then Tessa rolled

toward the wall and started texting Ron. She really needed to unpack everything and have someone look at it objectively, and he was usually really good at that kind of thing.

Tonight, he didn't even answer, and it wasn't even nine o'clock yet.

Chapter Thirty

The thunder clapped again, waking Tessa fully this time. The windows held gray light, which meant dawn had arrived and full daylight wasn't far behind. She sat up at the first sounds of rain overhead, because they hadn't fixed the roof yet.

"Three days," she grumbled. Three more days, and the roof would be fixed.

"Janey," she said, surprised her sister hadn't been awakened by the thunder. "Get up. It's raining, and we need to protect the new floor." Tessa pushed herself to the end of the bed and stood, the floor sending a chill through her bare feet.

She ignored it and hurried into the kitchen to find as many bowls as she could. The buckets sat on the shelves in the garage, and she wished she'd checked the weather or done something to be more prepared for a storm.

"At least we're here," she muttered, craning her head

back to look up at the roof. Water didn't immediately start pouring down, and Tessa's adrenaline wore off.

The wind battled the glass in the front windows, and Tessa cinched her arms around herself. The cottage had heat, but they hadn't turned it on. Tessa didn't want to now either, because for all she knew, the furnace would blow out a puff of smoke if fired up.

Janey came down the hall in slippers and a bathrobe, her hair wisping in many directions. "Thanks for the six a.m. wake-up call."

"That was Mother Nature," Tessa said. "The roof is going to start leaking. You don't want this floor to get ruined, trust me." She bit back her irritation at her sister. She could spend far too much on floors in a beach cottage without consulting Tessa, but she'd leave it up to Tessa to protect those floors.

Janey harrumphed, and Tessa actually hoped there would be a lot of leaks. She heard the tell-tale sound of a drip, and she spun around. Vindication streamed through her, and she took a couple of steps toward the far wall, searching for where the water had hit the floor.

It dropped right in front of her, and she set the salad bowl down. "Right here," she said. "Janey, bring a towel."

Her sister did, and they spent the next half-hour hunting down the leaks and putting cups and bowls under them. All told, they found eight separate leaks, and exhaustion pulled through Tessa.

"What's the weather like until Tuesday?" Janey asked with a sigh.

"No idea," Tessa said. "You have a phone. Look it up."

Janey glared at her, but Tessa was too tired to apologize for sniping at her. She'd laid awake for a while, waiting for Ron to respond. He never had, and she wondered why. Then Janey had asked if she was still awake, and they'd talked for a couple of hours. Tessa hadn't contributed much to the conversation, because Janey had been in a railroading mood.

When she got like that, her opinion was right, no matter what anyone else said. Tessa had been dealing with Janey for her whole life, and she just let her talk and talk, because sometimes Janey just needed to be heard.

Tessa knew exactly how that felt, as she felt so removed from everything and everyone she'd once been so close to. She couldn't pinpoint when she and Ron had started growing apart. When had the texts become so stale? When had they started to go unanswered? When had their weekends together been one day of her working at the library while he did the previous week's crossword puzzle, and then a lazy Sunday brunch?

When had their Sunday-night sex become making love?

She still wasn't sure if Ryan would come to Nantucket Point, as he'd never texted or called with his schedule.

She was hot and cold with Janey, feeling close to her one moment and then distant and irritated in the next.

"The papers," she said, turning toward Janey. She wasn't standing in the kitchen anymore, and Tessa strode toward the mouth of the hallway. "Janey."

The doorbell rang, and Tessa spun back that way. Her heartbeat roared through her ears, because it was far too early for a casual caller.

"Janey," she hissed this time.

Her sister came toward her, open alarm on her face. "Who's at the door?"

"I have no idea." The two of them huddled together, turning toward the door as someone knocked. Their voice came through the door, and Janey looked at Tessa.

"It's Sean," she said, relinquishing her hold on Tessa's hand and starting toward the door.

"Janey," Tessa said. "Are you sure?"

Janey unlocked the door and pulled it open. Sure enough, a soaking wet Sean Masterson walked inside. "What in the world are you doing here so early?" she asked. "And did you walk? Why are you so wet?"

Sean walked away from her without saying anything, and Tessa actually edged closer to the silverware drawer in case she needed some sort of weapon. Forks could be used for stabbing, right?

"Sean." Janey closed the door and marched after him. "What's going on?"

He indicated the table. "You two need to sit down."

Tessa gripped the back of a dining room chair, but she couldn't sit down. Janey folded her arms, her dark eyes sparking with fire.

"What did you find?" Tessa asked.

"Nothing much on the Martins," he said, his voice somewhat wooden. "They did own a lot of land here on the Point at one time. The only thing left is this undeveloped piece of land on the other side of The Lighthouse Inn. The historical society has been trying to purchase it for years, but Dennis's sister won't sell."

Janey sucked in a breath. "Do not tell me his sister is Bobbie Friedman."

Tessa looked wildly from Sean to Janey and back. "Sean," she insisted when he didn't say anything.

"If you guys aren't going to sit, I am," he said, sighing as he pulled out a chair and sank into it. The refrigerator hummed, and the wind rattled the glass, and Tessa's heart beat like hummingbird wings in her chest.

"It's not Bobbie Friedman," Sean said. "It's an elderly woman who lives in the oldest building here on Nantucket." He closed his eyes and shook his head. "It doesn't matter. This doesn't matter."

"What does matter?" Janey asked.

"This." Sean reached into his front jacket pocket and pulled out a folded sheet of paper. It wasn't white or a regular piece of copy paper. It looked thicker, and it had multiple colors, like the legal paper titles and certificates came on.

"What is that?" Tessa asked, but Janey snatched it up off the table before she could take a single step toward it.

Janey unfolded it, and just from the back of it, Tessa knew it was a title. The title to what, she didn't know.

"This is the title to Mom's car," Janey said, looking up. "It's been signed over to me." Her eyes rounded, and she extended it toward Tessa, the color draining from her face.

All of the anger in her stance and expression had been replaced with either shock or fear, Tessa wasn't sure.

"Where did you get this?" Tessa asked, scanning the title. It was for Mom's car, and she'd signed it, which meant she'd done it months ago. "Wait. Why is Dale Harton's name on this title?"

He'd signed it too, and that made the car Janey's. But it also meant that Mom and Dale had owned the car together…

Janey left the kitchen, and Sean just stared at the table-top. Neither of those inspired any confidence in Tessa, and she felt a scream building way down deep in her gut.

"Someone better start explaining something," she almost yelled, letting her anger move past her shock and fear. She was not going to spend her time in Nantucket Beach huddled in the same bed as her sister, scared of every sound and every shadow.

Janey's footsteps came quickly down the hall, and she also clutched a colorful piece of paper in her hand. "Sean," she said, practically barking the name. "Where did you get this title?"

"A silver-haired man brought it to me early this morning. At my home," he said. "He didn't give his name, but Janey, he…said." He cleared his throat. "He said he's…"

"My father," Janey said, her voice flat and full of resignation.

The breath got sucked right out of Tessa's chest. "What?" she managed to gasp. She wanted to look at Sean and demand he deny it, but she couldn't look away from Janey.

Janey was her sister.

Of course she was. They'd grown up together, and there had never been anyone but Daddy in their lives.

"After I went to the bank in the city," Janey said. "That triggered someone to mail this to me." She handed the paper to Tessa, who could barely read it.

"It's my birth certificate," Janey said. "Mom's name is there, but the space for my father is blank."

Tessa blinked and blinked and blinked. No matter how many times she blinked, no name appeared in the box reserved for the father.

"Gregory Clarke was not my father," Janey said, sinking into the chair beside Sean. He reached over and took her hand in his.

A wail started in Tessa's head, and she gripped one horrible paper in each of her hands, her fingers tightening around them. If she could just get her fingers to unclench, she could rip both of these official documents to shreds.

The scream that had been gathering in her gut rose, and rose, and rose, until Tessa either had to let it out or swallow it back.

She took a deep breath, swallowed, and sat down. "What are we going to do now?"

Chapter Thirty-One

J aney needed a stiff drink and a hot bath. She needed
to figure out what to do with her life. She couldn't
believe she'd raised two children and made it to the
age of forty-six and still had no idea what she wanted.

Her hand in Sean's sure felt nice, though the mood in
the cottage was definitely not nice. Tessa, her sister, just
kept looking at Janey.

Looking and studying and watching.

Janey was tired of all the staring. She'd felt like
everyone in the world had learned of her sudden identity
crisis in the past nine days, and they were all watching her,
waiting for her to crack and break.

She hadn't told anyone about the birth certificate that
had come to her house. Not Rachel. Not her official
boyfriend, Milford. Not her unofficial boyfriend, Sean. Not
Tessa.

No one.

Janey was very, very good at keeping secrets.

What are we going to do now?

The question Tessa had asked hung in the air.

Janey didn't know how to answer it. She'd been asking herself the same thing for nine straight days. An ache started behind her eyes. Rather, the ache that had been infecting her for over a week intensified, and her hand in Sean's tightened.

His eyes moved to her face too, and Janey ducked her head so she wouldn't look at him. All at once, like water rushing over a tall cliff, she understood why Mom hadn't said anything about the hotel. The bank accounts. The house on Long Island.

She understood with perfect clarity how her mother's secrets had haunted her, weighed her down, and kept her silent.

She couldn't even tell Sean or Tessa about the birth certificate, and it wasn't even anything she'd done wrong.

What about the papers you didn't sign?

That question had been keeping her awake at night too, and she wondered how long a person could go without only a few hours of fitful sleep, plenty of caffeine, and a noose laced with secrets around their neck.

Not much longer, in her opinion. She felt two breaths away from picking up the nearest objects and smashing it on the ground. She took those breaths, and nothing happened. Then two more, hating this situation and everyone inside it—including herself.

Her phone rang, shattering the silence and making her

jump. She pulled her fingers from Sean and reached for the device on the table in front of her. "It's my boss," she said, her pulse leaping from the back of her throat, where it had lodged with the shrill ring, and practically out of her mouth.

Her memory fired at her, and Janey gasped. "My meeting." She ran down the hall to the bedroom, swiping on the call from Sunny as she went. "Good morning, Sunny," she said, a little breathlessly, but still professional.

"There you are," she said, her voice as bright as her name. "Running a bit late this morning?" Sunny understood late, as she was a single mom of three teenage boys. She and Janey had been good friends since the interview that had landed Janey the sales job eight years ago.

Sunny's boys had been little then, and Janey had been raising teens of her own. She'd pulled all of Cole's old clothes out of his closet and given them to Sunny, who'd broken down into tears. The women met for brunch on Sundays, worked out at the same Crossfit gym, and stayed late in Sunny's office eating Chinese food when they had looming deadlines.

"Yes," Janey said. "I'm so sorry. I just need five more minutes." She could tame her hair and put on a blouse, lip gloss, and a smile in five minutes. Janey could stuff everything away at the drop of a hat, but she knew she'd have to unpack it all eventually.

She usually did so while on the back of a motorcycle, or in bed with a man, or through a little too much liquor. Exercising helped, and when she was her most mentally sound, Janey talked to a counselor through an app, gave up all drink except water and wine, and for a week or a month or even six, she'd feel like she could conquer the world.

Her doubts always came creeping back. Her insecurities loomed around every corner. Her loneliness followed her like a hunter, and she always its prey.

She wasn't entirely in a good place right now, especially since Mom's death. That had sent Janey back to her mimosas, her motorcycle, and her men.

"No problem," Sunny said. "I'll call Reggie and meet back with you in ten? How does that sound?"

"Perfect," Janey said. The call ended, and she tossed her phone on the bed she and Tessa had slept in last night. Well, Tessa had slept, at least if the snoring was anything to judge by. Janey had wandered down the hall to the living room and curled into the couch, her knees close to her chest and her thoughts far, far away.

She first flipped open her laptop, because it took a minute to connect to the Internet here. Then she pulled off her pajamas and quickly dressed in a pair of slacks and the black and white blouse she'd brought specifically for this call. After darting across the hall, she brushed her teeth, washed her face, and ran her wet fingers through her hair.

She quickly redid her mascara and lip gloss and pulled the hair dryer out of the drawer. With her hair properly dried and slicked and presentable, Janey hurried down the hall, where Tessa now stood at the stove, frying eggs, and Sean hadn't moved from his spot at the table.

He looked awful, and her heart flipped at the sight of

the exhaustion in his face. She wanted to apologize for bringing him into her crazy—into this family drama—but she didn't.

"I completely forgot about my meeting this morning," she said. "I'm going to be at least an hour."

"Okay," Tessa said without turning around.

"I can't reschedule it," Janey said, though she didn't elaborate on why. "Can we meet up for lunch and talk then?" She knew Tessa didn't have anything on her schedule, so she kept her gaze on Sean.

He finally looked at her as if he'd just barely realized she stood there and speaking. "Sure," he said. "I'll go catch a few hours of sleep and be back here about lunchtime." He stood and pushed his chair under the table.

"There's all the food trucks at The Lighthouse Inn today," Tessa said, sliding her eggs onto a plate. The salty, almost plastic smell of them turned Janey's stomach, causing her to look away.

"Okay," Janey said. "I'll walk you out." She went with Sean all the way to the porch. She closed the door behind her and held onto the handle for an extra moment. Sean continued away from her, and Janey didn't want him to leave like this. "Sean, I'm sorry," she said.

He turned back, thankfully, and his smile did make him all the more handsome, as well as erased some of the tiredness from his eyes.

She moved toward him and wrapped her arms around him. "I'm really sorry."

"Why didn't you tell me?"

"I didn't know how," she said. "I was still processing, I think."

His hands drifted up her arms, and Janey's skin sang under his touch. "I like this blouse," he whispered.

She lifted her eyes to his and found his gaze trained on her mouth. Janey knew this look, as she had plenty of experience with men. She leaned further into him and tipped her head back a little more, a clear invitation for him to kiss her.

He dipped his head, his mouth against hers soft and seeking permission. Janey gave it, and kissed him properly, enjoying the slow, sensual way he stroked his lips against hers. He was different than most of the men in her recent past, and Janey sank into his strength and warmth.

He pulled back far too soon for her liking and said, "See you in a little bit."

"Bye," she said, letting him walk away from her and go down the steps. He climbed into his luxury car and turned around to leave the cottage. Janey moved to the edge of the porch and watched him.

The moment his car rounded the corner, Riggs Friedman came down his front sidewalk and turned toward the cottage. Janey ducked back into the shadows of the porch, then dashed back into the cottage, locking the door behind her.

Riggs hadn't had a fishing pole this time. He was simply watching all of the comings and goings from the cottage.

She didn't say a word to Tessa at the table as she

passed, compartmentalizing everything so she could focus on her meeting.

She sat down in front of the computer the moment the online conference call rang, and she tapped to answer it. "Sunny," she said, smiling for all she was worth. "Thanks for giving me a few minutes."

"Of course. How are things on Nantucket?"

They chatted for a few minutes, and Janey kept everything full of laughter and beach days and food trucks.

Then Sunny said, "Janey, I'm thrilled to let you know you're one of the top two candidates for the Senior Sales Manager position that's open. I'm going to loop in Shane and Dalton, and we'll start the interview. Okay?"

"Yes, ma'am," Janey said. "Thank you so much."

This was so much more than a meeting. This was the job interview of Janey's life, and she couldn't afford to be thinking about Sean, her mother's will, this cottage, Riggs and what he might be doing, or who her father was.

Later, she told herself, sewing everything away that she didn't need to get this job. As Sunny got her senior partners on the call, Janey opened a few documents she'd prepared for this interview.

Facts and figures and her sales history. She took a deep breath and focused. She needed this job, and she was going to do everything she could to get it.

She could figure out who she was and where she belonged afterward.

Chapter Thirty-Two

"Yes, Shane," Janey said. "I can see that, but no, I don't really agree." She kept her voice as passive as possible, while still trying to get her point across. "OceanAir *is* a huge account, despite the small number you see in the chart, and I'll tell you why."

She clicked over to her one-sheet on the company, though she had it memorized. "They only bought enough software for one of their airlines, because they wanted to try it first. I check-in with them every two weeks to answer questions and keep my relationship with the booking manager there current. Steven and I get along great, and the reason this is a huge account is because OceanAir owns thirteen airlines."

She looked up at Shane Farnsworth, the auburn-haired man who sat second-in-command at Janey's company. He didn't look happy as he peered down at something in front of him.

"OceanAir put the software on one airline that flies from Hawaiian island to island, and then two flights to Japan each day and two to the US. But really, they own sixty-four percent of the flights that happen over the Pacific." She leaned back and smiled her best professional smile at the camera. "I'm confident I can get our booking and tracking and financial software in *all* their systems within a year."

Janey had said such outlandish things before when she'd had no idea if they'd come true or not. This time, though, she spoke with some level of confidence. She'd spoken with Steven Isle only three days ago, and he'd put in an order for four more of their airlines.

She simply hadn't recorded the sale yet, because Steven still had some invoicing he needed to complete.

Shane looked up, surprise in his eyes. "A year?"

"Yes, sir," she said, glancing at the other man on the call with her and Sunny. Dalton sat at the head of the finance sector of her company, and she hadn't dealt with him much. She wasn't sure why he needed to be on this call at all.

Shane signed a paper in front of him and handed it to someone off-screen.

"I agree with Janey," Sunny said. "Not only is she exceptional at her customer service, she delivers when she says she will."

Janey's heart skipped over itself, but she kept her smile hitched in its spot.

"I've seen that in her file," Shane said. He'd been asking her about her sales, her contacts, and her goals for the future for half an hour. Janey's stomach flipped again, something it had been doing for the entirety of the interview. "Here's what I'm thinking." He paused for a moment, and Janey wondered when he'd last made a cold call to a massive corporation and tried to sell them expensive software they didn't want.

Probably not for years, she thought.

And if she got this Senior Sales Manager position, she wouldn't have to do that anymore either. She'd over see a *team* of people. Yes, there would be more paperwork and the same odd hours as she spoke to people overseas in various time zones.

She'd have an office with real walls, and she'd get to set her own schedule. She'd see an increase in pay by thirty percent, and she'd get to keep doing the things she liked most about her job—talking to her clients.

"You're clearly more qualified than the other candi-date," Shane said, lifting his eyebrows. On her screen, Sunny nodded, and gratitude and relief filled Janey.

"Thank you, sir."

"I think the position should be yours, and if you can get OceanAir to sign on the dotted line with all of their airlines for all three software pieces we sell, I'll bonus you a year's salary."

Janey's eyes widened to the point of pain, and her heartbeat fought against itself it went so fast.

"Shane," Dalton said, and that was all.

"We regularly bonus our people, Dalt," Shane said. "Let's make a note of this in Janey's contract."

"What if I don't do it?" she blurted. "Do I lose my job?"

Shane smiled and chuckled. "Not at all. I just think sometimes it's good to have a goal to work toward, with something attached to it."

Janey wasn't sure she believed him, but she couldn't find any malice in his face. "Thank you, sir."

"Sunny, get the paperwork done and pushed through. I want this tied up before the fiscal year ends."

"You got it, Shane," Sunny said.

Janey couldn't stop smiling. Dalton and Shane dropped out of the call, and she squealed with Sunny. Waves of adrenaline shot through her, coursing through her veins over and over. "Wow," she said. "That's a huge bonus."

"It sure is," Sunny said, still laughing at Janey's shriek. "I'll be sure to give you until the end of July to get OceanAir on-board," she said. "And the fiscal year ends August thirty-first, Janey, so you'll assume the new position on September first."

Janey drew in a breath, trying to quiet everything that had started rioting. "Okay, sure. Yes, September first." Her mind flew through the bills that were due before then. The roof that needed fixing. The fact that she really wanted to sell her house and get into something cheaper and smaller.

It's six weeks, she told herself. She'd gone months with the pressure of her bills and financial obligations in the past. Heck, years.

"Okay," Sunny said. "Go enjoy that island and the beach. I wish I was there with you." She waved, and her screen went dark in the next moment.

Janey just stared at the remaining words—Sunny Jones has left—her thoughts zipping over each other before one had even finished. As the adrenaline wore off, Janey realized she wasn't going to be lounging on the beach, chatting with her sister about her new promotion.

Excitement danced through her, and she wanted to tell someone about this amazing call. In the past, that someone was Tessa.

Now, she didn't even know who Tessa was to her.

"A *half*-sister," she murmured, and somehow that seemed so much less than who Janey would rely on, spend time with, or share her most intimate thoughts and feelings with.

Knowing she wasn't Tessa's full sister hadn't answered any of the questions about why Mom had to leave the hotel and other assets in the will addendum just to Tessa. Janey was still her mother's daughter, just as much as Tessa was.

Dale Harton.

The name entered her mind, and Janey strained against her memories to find some with him in it. He and his wife, Joan, had lived here on the Point for a couple of years. Or maybe they'd just had a beach house, the way Mom and Daddy did. Janey wasn't sure, because she'd been a teenager at the time.

The box with all the photographs sat on the corner of

her desk, and she pulled it toward her. She'd looked through every one of these on Monday night when Tessa had returned from Long Island, not knowing what she'd find or what she was supposed to find.

Until she'd seen the title for the car currently parked in the garage, she hadn't known Dale Harton meant anything. He'd been a friend of Daddy's, a doctor just like him. They'd gone to school together, and they'd both landed jobs at Johns Hopkins.

Daddy performed heart surgeries, and Dale had too. For a few years, at least.

A memory tickled her, and she reached into the box, now knowing she wanted to see all the pictures with Dale and Joan in them. She wasn't sure why, but she kept the pictures separated into their groups of twenty-four, taking out any with Dale or Joan and setting them on the desk in front of the packet.

Over and over, she sorted through them, trying to find a pattern in when Dale and Joan came into their lives.

They were there in the oldest of the pictures, when Janey and Tessa were tiny children, building sandcastles and wearing saggy swimming suits until they couldn't keep their eyes open for another moment.

Janey flipped through the dozen or so pictures with Dale in them. He had dark hair, like hers, with big, bushy eyebrows. She'd always plucked hers or gotten them waxed to keep them feminine and shapely.

She pulled in a breath on one with Dale laughing. He

tipped his head back in the picture, and the only other person in the photo was her. Dale and Janey as a child—maybe seven or eight years old—laughing about something.

She didn't remember what. She didn't remember talking to him when this picture was taken. The next one in the group was of her and Tessa walking with Dale. The three of them approached the camera, and the trio all smiled.

Janey was holding his hand; Tessa wasn't.

Tears gathered in her eyes, and she wasn't sure why. She wasn't happy to be learning these things. She wasn't relieved her father might still be alive.

She was angry. Oh, so angry.

She didn't want to know any of this.

Shaking, she swiped her hand across the desk, scattering the pictures she'd so painstakingly sorted. As they flapped and fluttered to a stop, she stood in the room, her chest heaving.

"I don't want to know any of this," she said out loud. "Do you hear me, Mom?" She looked up at the ceiling. "I just wanted to come here and get this cottage cleaned up so we could sell it. Why couldn't it have just been that simple?"

"Janey?" Tessa's light knock on the door had Janey wiping at her eyes quickly.

"Just a minute," she said, looking at the photos. "I'm almost done with my call."

"Okay." Tessa's voice came through the closed door she

hadn't tried to open, but Janey didn't hear her footsteps retreat.

She bent to pick up one of the fallen pictures. It was her and Tessa and Dale again, this time nearly smothered in darkness. A red-orange glow across the top of the picture illuminated their faces as they lay on a blanket on the beach.

"I remember this," she whispered. The Fourth of July fireworks, which could be seen from anywhere on Nantucket. Mom always took blankets out to the beach, followed by at least three picnic baskets filled with sandwiches, licorice, potato salad, krab salad, and fruit.

They ate as the sun went down, and Tessa and Janey drew stars and Liberty bells in the sand with sticks until it was too dark to see. The water lapped at the shore as it always did, and they tuned their FM radio to the feed coming out of downtown Nantucket.

When Neil Diamond's *They're Coming to America!* started, a cheer rose over the beach out here at the Point, where locals and tourists alike had gathered for the fireworks display. An assortment of patriotic music, as well as a spoken program, followed, with fireworks filling the sky with booms and pops and crackles—and light.

Such glorious light. Janey had loved the Fourth of July holiday on Nantucket Point.

In the photo, she lay against Dale's side while Tessa sat cross-legged on his other side. Again, the familiarity of the two of them spoke of a father-daughter relationship, and Janey wondered why she'd never realized it.

"The innocence of childhood," she said aloud, supposing that to be true. She knew better now, and the worst part was, so did Mom.

Mom had known who Janey's father was. Instead of leading her all over two states and this island collecting pendants and envelopes and letters, she could've just put everything in her blasted will to begin with.

Or better yet, had the guts to tell Janey while she'd been alive.

She dropped the photo and watched it fall to the ground. She didn't want to ruin these photos, but she didn't want to look at them right now.

She didn't want to break down. Not again.

She couldn't face Tessa. Not right now.

Janey quickly stuffed her feet into a pair of sandals, grabbed her phone, and turned toward the window.

She'd snuck out of this very bedroom while Tessa had slept in a nearby bed, and just because three decades had passed didn't mean she'd forgotten how. The frame lifted noiselessly, and Janey popped the screen out in seconds flat.

Twenty seconds later, she landed on the newly-mowed grass outside the cottage, and she strode away from it without looking back.

Chapter Thirty-Three

Janey hadn't taken the keys to the car, so she set off down the street on foot. She had her credit card stored in her phone, and she could use that to pay for whatever she needed.

She wasn't sure what she needed.

Her footsteps slowed as she approached the cottage behind Mom's. Bobbie and Riggs lived here permanently, and they took great care of their house. It had been pink for a while, and then yellow, and now it stood two stories tall and bright white.

Clean, and classic, and someone had put plenty of charm into the bright green shutters. Flowers hung from the eaves, and stepping stones and statues of frogs filled the garden surrounding the front steps.

Janey found herself moving down the sidewalk and standing in front of the stepping stones. They had baby handprints and footprints pressed into the stones, with names of grandchildren etched in as well.

Colored gems and rocks decorated the terra cotta, and Janey smiled. What a great gift from a child to a parent. She looked up to the house, which she stood very close to now. Panic seized in her chest, and she stumbled backward.

She didn't want to be here. She didn't want to talk to Bobbie or Riggs. She could tolerate them, because they'd been such good friends with Mom. But Bobbie liked to give advice Janey didn't want or need, and Riggs…there was something off about Riggs.

She pictured the older gentleman as she knew him in real life, and then from the picture Esme had sent from Long Island. Why in the world had he gone there?

Safely back on the road, she kept going away from the beach. Usually she ran toward the sand and surf. She loved the sound they made together when they met, as it had always soothed her.

She remembered walking the sand with her mother one afternoon. Just her and Mom. She couldn't remember where Tessa or Daddy had been, but Janey remembered her small hand inside of her mother's. They'd stopped near the lighthouse on the Point, and Mom had looked out into the vastness of sky and ocean.

"We're but small players on a large stage," she'd said. Janey didn't know what it had meant. She still didn't.

The words looped through her mind, and she searched the memories for any sign of sadness from her mother that day. She'd sighed, lifted her arms up high, and stretched them toward the water as she bent over.

"Stretch with me, little one," she'd said, her smile returning to her face. Janey had, and she remembered her purple-painted toenails. Mom had done them the night before while they sat on the porch and listened to Daddy tell stories about his patients in the hospital.

It had been years before Janey realized he cut into real hearts and not paper ones. She'd been very young in this memory, and she wondered if it was one of the first times they'd come to Nantucket Point as a family. Daddy had worked *so much* in Janey's childhood.

She wrapped her arms around herself as she let the memory go. The wind picked up as she turned the corner, and she headed down another finger-like lane that led to the beach. Out here on the Point, one could drive into a neighborhood and find a cul-de-sac of sorts, with streets leading off the circular center island, all of them lined with cottages, sturdy trees that could withstand the ocean breezes, and sand.

They dead-ended into the beach, and Janey did step onto the sand a few minutes later. It slid into her sandals and across her skin, bringing comfort in the oddest way. She didn't want the cottage here, but she did love the beach. The two thoughts warred with one another, and she didn't know how to make them line up.

She didn't deviate right or left but went straight out to the water. The sun had risen and already started to warm the sand while she'd been in her interview, but the water held a chill as she let it kiss her feet.

She drew in a deep breath, taking in the power of the ocean as she did, held it, and then exhaled it all back out. Mom had taught her this too, telling her to imagine how powerful all that water was, how it could tumble ships as if they were toothpicks, and how it could form massive landmarks like the Grand Canyon.

Take that power, Janey, and use it. Breathe it in, make it yours.

Janey had believed her mother when she was ten years old, and she'd breathed in all the power and held it.

You're stronger than you know.

The line from Mom's letter to her popped into her head. Maybe she was, and maybe she wasn't. "What do I do?" she asked. "How do I find the answers I need?"

She had one more question she didn't give voice to but which circled through her mind. *Why do I feel like I need to do this myself?*

She'd always felt like that, actually. She wanted to do everything herself, from learning to bake a birthday cake to changing her own oil. She'd learned over the years that she had strengths and weaknesses, and she now paid for the things she simply couldn't—or didn't want to—do herself.

She breathed in again, counting all the way to ten as her eyes drifted and then pressed closed. When she released her breath, she knew what to do.

———

"Mm hm," she said, her feet squishing in the wet sand. "That's fine, ma'am. I can do that."

"And don't be bringing any of that fake crab," the old woman said. "And don't ring my doorbell. I'm deaf anyway and I won't hear it."

Janey smiled into the sky, but it faded quickly. "Yes, ma'am," she said, wondering how she'd taken a call if she couldn't hear. "Tomorrow at noon."

"Don't be late," she barked, and the call ended.

Janey tucked her phone under her bra strap and against her shoulder bone and turned away from the water. She'd wanted to visit Viola Martin today, but the woman said her house wasn't fit for visitors. She'd also been very keen to know how Janey had gotten her number.

It was amazing what a professional voice and a quick call to the Nantucket Historical Society could yield her.

The Lighthouse Inn stood proudly to her right, and Janey gazed up at it. Built up on a cement platform, the lighthouse seemed to right straight up out of the ocean. The beach sloped around the sides of it, but the front definitely had a rock wall fifteen or twenty feet up before the ground leveled.

She'd never stayed in the inn, but she'd toured the place lots of times. She couldn't believe they'd closed, and she hoped the Historical Society would be able to find new caretakers and get the four-room inn reopened.

She even had the wild thought that she could do it.

That idea got dismissed quickly as she approached the

dock attached to the inn. Whoever ran the inn had to have nautical knowledge, and Phil Michaels had been a sailor in the Coast Guard before coming to the inn with his wife, Margo.

She'd often played in the foamy water under the dock here, though Mom didn't like it. She said sharp shells got deposited here, and Tessa had cut her foot on one once, long ago.

Today, a few fishing lines lay lazily in the water from the poles up on the dock. Janey heard people talking in voices muted by the water rushing ashore beneath the dock, where she walked, and she let her mind ebb in and out like the water.

She watched her footsteps appear in the wet sand, and then blur and disappear, especially when a wave came ashore.

Someone coughed, and this person wasn't up above her. Janey looked up sharply and froze at the sight of Riggs several paces away from her, standing next to a pillar holding up the dock, water up around his ankles.

His fishing pole had not been threaded with a line and hook. In fact, it stood against the pillar without even a reel of line in it. Janey couldn't see a tackle box at all, and she wondered if he hid it in the grass somewhere between here and his house.

Just the fact that she thought such things increased her heart rate, and she felt sure Riggs would hear the booming pulses as they moved through her ears.

He muttered something to the water and walked away from her, around the pillar. She wasn't sure what to do. She didn't really want to talk to him, but walking in the water would create some noise, which could attract his attention.

Her phone rang, and Janey's panic reared again. He'd hear that, and she struggled to get it out from beneath her bra strap. He rounded the pillar as she did, and she turned away from him quickly as if she hadn't seen him there at all.

"Hey, Tess," Janey said breathlessly, straining to hear Riggs's footsteps behind her.

"Where the devil are you?" Tessa asked. "I just got brave enough to go in your bedroom after you refused to answer me, thinking you might be dead or something!" She yelled the end of the sentence, her frustration and panic plain through the line.

"Sorry," Janey said, regret filling her. "I just needed a breath of fresh air."

Sloshing steps sounded behind her, and she forced out a laugh. "Just walking along the beach."

"You should've said something to me," Tessa said. "We're not fourteen years old anymore." That was a semi-nice way to tell Janey to grow up and stop being petty.

Her defenses flew into place, and her stomach tightened, especially when she caught movement in her peripheral vision. She turned toward Riggs and did her best to act surprised. "I know," she said. "Yes, I'll still meet you for lunch."

Hopefully, that would prevent him from grabbing her and dragging her under the water right here at the dock. Just the fact that Janey thought he might do something sinister made her flesh crawl.

"Now we're meeting for lunch?" Tessa demanded. "When is Sean going to be back?"

"Yes, Sean's coming," she said, smiling at Riggs now as he did as well. "He should be here any minute."

"Any minute?" Tessa repeated. "What is going on?"

"Listen, I just ran into Riggs. Can I call you back?"

"Riggs?" Tessa barked out. "Janey, where are you?"

"Yes, down by the dock." She kept her smile in place and trilled out a little giggle. "Okay, Tess, see you in a minute." She hung up while Tessa said she'd be there as fast as she could, and she gripped her phone as she faced Riggs. "Is this where the good fishing is? I see all the other poles up top."

"They don't know what they're missing down here," he said, lifting one hand to his lips in the universal sign to keep quiet. As he lowered his hand, he grinned and laughed.

Janey did her best to join in. "Catch anything?"

"Not today," he said, keeping his easy smile on his face. He must think her so stupid to not even know that pole didn't even have a line. For some reason, that made her really angry.

"Yeah, I bet it's hard to catch fish without a reel," she said. "Or any fishing line." She looked around as if the tackle box or a bucket of worms would manifest itself.

"Or even a hook."

Their eyes met, and Janey held very still, kept her shoulders boxy and strong, thankful for her Clarke barrel torso for maybe the first time in her life.

The smile vanished from Riggs's face, and his normally bright green eyes took on a shadow that sent a shiver through Janey's chest. She thought of the training she did in the Crossfit gym, and she'd run at a dummy before, ramming her shoulder into it and pushing it back.

Riggs was at least seventy-five years old, and Janey prayed she could tackle him if necessary.

Then, just as quickly as his smile had fallen off his face, it reappeared. "Yes," he said with an obviously false chuckle. "You're more observant than my wife, but I suppose I better do a better job of fooling her."

Janey stared at him, refusing to just laugh this off. "You come out here to get away from Bobbie?" Was that really what he expected her to believe?

"A man needs freedom to be himself," Riggs said, shrugging one shoulder, lifting his blue T-shirt. "I'd appreciate it if you didn't say anything to her."

Janey would say what she dang well pleased, but she gave Riggs a single nod. His smile brightened for some odd reason, and he started to walk away. "Have fun at lunch."

She watched him go until she saw Tessa hurrying down the beach toward them. She had a brief interaction with the man, and then she jogged toward Janey, who still stood in the water under the dock.

This next conversation wasn't going to go well either,

and Janey sighed as she turned away from her sister, needing a few more seconds before she had to start explaining.

Chapter Thirty-Four

"Thank you," Janey said, looking up at the waiter set her glass of Pinot noir in front of her. She glanced at Sean, who'd ordered a Diet Coke, and then Tessa, who'd opted for lemon water. Both of them were waiting for her, and Janey felt the tension inside her stretching and stretching.

"You tell him," she said to Tessa, who rolled her eyes.

"She ran into Riggs on the beach. He had his fishing pole, but no reel or hook, and she called him out on it."

Sean looked back to Janey, surprise in his eyes. He'd arrived for lunch several minutes ago, and Janey had suggested The Glass Dolphin, because she didn't want to carry her food in a cardboard container and eat it from her hand.

The Glass Dolphin was far too expensive, but neither Sean nor Tessa had argued with her.

"She shouldn't have done that," Tessa said. "Not when we don't know what he's capable of."

"What did he say?" Sean asked, lifting his cola to his mouth. Janey watched him, thinking of the kiss they'd shared earlier that morning.

She didn't regret it, but she didn't know what the next step for them was either.

"He made some excuse about needing to get away from his wife," Janey said, waving her hand, though she had been scared. "It was fine."

Tessa bristled across the table, but she kept quiet.

"Did you get some rest?" she asked Sean as if they had nothing better to talk about.

"A little." He picked up his napkin and put it on his lap. "How was the meeting?"

A smile sprang to Janey's face. "Great. It went...great." Why couldn't she share her promotion with them?

She cut a look to Tessa, who'd taken the glaring down a notch, and then Sean.

She knew why.

She didn't know who she was anymore. Did she belong to Tessa? Why should she share intimate things with someone who wasn't really her sister?

And Janey enjoyed Sean's company, but their relationship was still new. Perhaps she'd leave Nantucket Point next week and never come back. He didn't need all the intimate details of her life if she was never going to see him again.

"I saw the photos scattered all over your bedroom," Tessa said, actually lowering her voice.

Janey's eyes flew to hers, a pinch tight in her throat. She cleared it away, and said, "Uh, yeah, I looked through some of those after my meeting."

"Why?" Tessa pressed

Janey lifted her glass of wine to her lips to buy herself a few moments. She felt like someone had stuffed her with bees, her whole chest beginning to buzz. "I need to figure out who my father was. I thought he might be in the photos."

"It's got to be Dale," Tessa said.

"We don't actually know that," Sean said, and Janey waved to him as if to say, *There you go.*

"So you're thinking you simply don't know who it is." Tessa leaned back and folded her arms.

"The line was blank," Janey said. "So no, I don't know who it is. Just because Dale Harton shows up with a car title and *says* he's my father doesn't make it true."

Tessa glanced at Sean. "Why would he lie?"

"Mom died, and she has properties all over the Eastern Seaboard, for one." Janey folded her arms. "Maybe he thinks he should have all of that."

"But those came from Dennis," Tessa said, her dark hair swaying as she shook her head. "It doesn't matter. That doesn't matter." She leaned forward again. "Janey, you're my sister." She reached across the table and took Janey's hand in both of hers.

Janey appreciated the sentiment, but she didn't want Tessa to touch her. She wanted to fold her arms and enjoy an expensive lunch. Then she needed to get back to the rudimentary home office she'd set up in the cottage and get some work done.

Tomorrow, she'd tackle the bulk of figuring out her true origins.

She didn't pull her hand away, and she even gave Tessa a smile. "Thanks, Tessa."

"I'll help you figure all of this out," she said, swallowing and darting a glance in Sean's direction. "But Janey, you didn't sign the papers for the lawyer."

She did pull her hand back then, leaning even further from the table. She wondered how long it would take for Tessa to notice.

"Why?" she asked. "I thought we'd agreed to keep the cottage. You bought new flooring and appliances." She flapped one hand in the general direction of the cottage. "Why spend that money if you just wanted to sell?"

"I'm back and forth," Janey admitted. "When I did the renovations, I wanted to keep the cottage."

"But you hadn't signed." Tessa studied her, confusion and intensity in her dark eyes that Janey fully understood.

She was so confused herself. The honest truth was she was a huge mess. She made decisions based on single moments of time. When Tessa hadn't returned to Nantucket last week, Janey had been in a window of time where she wanted the cottage. So she'd called a handyman, and a flooring company, and Sean, and they'd ripped out the old and replaced it with new.

Janey loved nothing more than pulling out dirty and dingy and putting in bright, new, and clean.

It was a representation of what she wished she could do with her life. Rip out her dark mind and simply get a new one that operated the right way. A mind that didn't run to men to make herself feel good—or feel nothing at all. A mind that didn't spend money as if that could buy happiness.

A mind that functioned and thought through things, made smart decisions, and enjoyed downtime.

She shook her head. "I know. I don't know."

Thankfully, the waiter appeared, wanting to know if they were ready to order. Janey had barely glanced at the menu, but she ordered the seaside salad. "But no gorgonzola, please," she said, imagining herself to be one of the rich and famous who simply couldn't abide hard, crumbly cheeses.

Sean ordered surf and turf, and Tessa chose a pan-seared chicken with local vegetables.

"That sounds good," Janey said. "I want to try those."

"You're not getting out of this conversation," Tessa said. "If we don't execute that will by the end of the month, Janey, we lose the cottage. If you don't want it, just say so, and I'll buy you out."

Janey couldn't say it though. She hadn't been able to sign on the dotted line either. "What happens to the cottage?" she asked, reaching for her wine glass and swirling the red liquid.

"I don't know," Tessa said. "It goes to Mom's next relative or something."

"Who would that be?" Sean asked.

"I don't know," Tessa said, shooting him a glare. "You knew Lydia Clarke. Where would the cottage go?"

"I'd imagine perhaps one of her sisters, brothers, cousins..." He let the sentence hang there, but Tessa shook her head.

"Mom was an only child of an only child."

"Maybe someone on your father's side," Sean said, and Janey watched Tessa perk up.

"Daddy did have a brother," she said thoughtfully. "We didn't talk to him much."

"He lived in California," Janey said. "No way he'd want a cottage all the way across the world from him." She shook her head and sipped her wine. "He was older than Daddy besides. He could be dead."

"He could have children," Sean said.

"We need to find out, I suppose," Janey said. "Maybe she left it to the Historical Society."

"I don't want them to have it," Tessa said with a scoff. "What would they do with a beach cottage?" She shook her head and looked at Janey as if she were being difficult on purpose. Maybe she was. "Please, Janey. Either sign it or let me buy you out. I can get Marcus on the paperwork today if that's what you want."

"I don't know what I want," she said.

"Or Sean," Tessa said as if Janey hadn't spoken. "He's a lawyer too, and he can get the paperwork done for the buy-out to satisfy the will."

"I'd start it," Sean said. "Tessa, I'd get that paperwork

going. Then all Janey has to do is sign one or the other by the deadline."

"Okay," she said, standing up. "I'm going to call Marcus right now." She walked away from the table, her back straight and strong.

Janey couldn't quite look at Sean, and he let her have her silence for a minute or two. Then he said, "I don't think I should really be involved past this point, Janey. I—"

"Why not?"

"Why not?" His normally smooth tone took on a bite, which caused her to look at him. His dark eyes sparked with something akin to lightning. Dangerous but also exciting. "Janey, I'm you mother's lawyer. I was to execute her final instructions and that's it. The dinners, the staying over on my couch, and me on your couch, that's what friends do. Boyfriends." He cleared his throat. "I know you said you had one of those, but then you kissed me this morning, and I'll admit I'm confused."

His normal boisterous personality had been subdued lately. Janey had needed him. She hadn't wanted to sleep alone in the cottage when Tessa didn't return, and he had a comfortable couch.

"I don't need to be involved in any of this," he said. "Tessa's talking to the New York City lawyer, and I have no skin in this game."

She knew what he was saying. If she wasn't going to keep the cottage or ever come back to Nantucket, he could exit stage left, a single kiss between them.

If she did keep the cottage, perhaps he'd stay. See if he

could win her over and be her boyfriend instead of Milford.

"What if I want you to have skin in the game?" she asked.

"Then you have to make a decision," he said firmly. "And I don't just mean about the cottage, though I would certainly start there." His gaze never wavered from her, and Janey looked away, uncomfortable.

How did he do that? How did anyone do that? Look someone right in the eye and refuse to look away?

She shouldn't saddle a man like him with a woman like her. He was steady and strong, put-together with a good business here on the island. She was a walking basket case, holding things together with invisible strings until everything burst and she found herself sobbing on the bathroom floor.

"Whatever you've learned in the past couple of weeks about your mother doesn't change you and Tessa. You're letting it come between you. You're letting the fact that she might not be your full sister prevent you from sharing things with her."

"I share things with her."

"You don't," he insisted. "Anyone with two eyes can see you're hiding things. Even about something as simple as your meeting. I can hear it in your voice."

"I knew I shouldn't have started anything with a lawyer," she said.

Sean sighed, finally looking away.

"Sorry," Janey murmured.

"It's not me being a lawyer or not," he said. "Tessa's not a baby. She's not stupid, either. She knows too. So you need to figure out what you're doing here. From my perspective, you're pushing both of us away, refusing to make decisions that have huge consequences for Tessa, and acting like you're the victim in all of this."

Janey's gaze flew to him. "I *am* the victim."

Sean just shook his head, his eyes moving down to his plate now. "There are no victims, Janey. Your mother died. I knew her and loved her. Discovering she had secrets, honestly, is just part of what happens after someone dies." He looked up, his dark eyes bright again.

"I really like you," he said. "I'd love to get to know you better and have a real relationship, but I'm not going to share you. I'm also not interested in being an island fling whenever you decide to come to Nantucket, if you ever come back at all."

She nodded, because she expected as much from a man like Sean Masterson.

"Okay," Tessa said, sliding back into her seat. "Marcus is working on the buy-out paperwork. He's got a call out to a realtor so we can get the market value of the cottage. I called Ron, but he's in a meeting." She looked back and forth between Sean and Janey, her eyes soaking up the tension and silence between them. "I missed something."

"No," Janey said slowly. "You didn't miss anything. I kept it from you."

Tessa's eyes widened as Janey's whole body rioted against the words surging up her throat. "First, my meeting this morning was actually a job interview, and I got it. On September first, I'll be the new Senior Sales Manager at AccuSchedule."

Tessa's mouth dropped open, and her instant grin reminded Janey of just how much her sister loved her. That same bond—that sisterly bond—moved through her too, and she smiled as well.

"That's so great, Janey," Tessa said. "Congratulations."

"Yes," Sean said with a small smile. "That's wonderful, Janey."

She reached over and took his hand in hers. "Second, I kissed Sean this morning. I guess we are seeing each other."

Tessa looked back and forth between them, a bit more shock and a little less smile than before.

"Third," Janey said, because she didn't want to explain any more about Sean or Milford right now. She'd have to deal with that soon though. "I called Viola Martin, and I'm taking her lunch tomorrow at her mansion on the south side of the island."

"Viola Martin?" Tessa asked.

"Dennis's sister," Sean said.

Janey nodded. "I'm going to find out everything she knows."

Chapter Thirty-Five

The following day, Janey drover her mother's car—
her car now, if she'd simply sign the title and send it
into the DMV—around the Point and down to the south
side of Nantucket. The downtown area sat nearly directly
across Viola Martin's house, which defined the older estate
homes in the Wainscott neighborhood of the island.

"This is a mansion," Janey murmured as she pulled
into the elegant driveway and past the tall trees. This place
had been here for decades, but the white exterior looked as
if it had been power washed only yesterday.

She parked next to a pale yellow car from yesteryear,
her car brand-new compared to the classic beside her. Her
stomach clenched as she got out of the car and opened the
back door to get the food she'd picked up fifteen minutes
ago.

No fake crab, that was for sure. Her credit card knew
that.

Glancing around, she took in the detached garage with a covered yacht next to it. She wondered if the elderly woman ever went out onto the sea, and what kind of vehicles she'd find in that garage.

Everything sat pristinely, as someone definitely took care of everything, where Viola used it or not. Janey supposed that was what money looked like, and she couldn't wait to see inside the mansion.

She climbed the curved steps and rang the doorbell. It clanged through the house, meeting her ears easily. She wondered if that did have to do with Viola's supposed deafness. After several seconds of anxious silence, the huge, intricately carved door opened.

A man stood there in a white shirt and tie, and he couldn't be as old as Janey. In fact, she probably had a decade on him. "You must be Miss Forsythe," he said with a crisp accent that sounded slightly British and slightly Irish.

"Yes," she said.

"Miss Martin is expecting you." He reached for the food she carried, and she handed it to him. He backed up and she stepped into the house. The foyer stretched up toward the heavens, with a ceiling that had been carved and painted into delicate roses and other flowers.

The walls that ran toward them stared back at her with perfectly white faces, and the only art showed gardens and waterfalls. The hardwood floor absorbed all the color, and Janey would never pick a wood this black, but with the flowers, the walls, and the art, it all worked together.

"This is lovely," she said.

"Thank you," the man said. "My name is Miles, and I'll get the food onto plates and bring it into the library." He nodded to a wide, arched doorway to her left. "Right through there. Miss Martin is near the windows."

Janey faced the library, the scent of parchment and books already in her nose. She drew in a breath and told herself she needed answers. She knew Dennis Martin wasn't her father, but Viola was the only person connected to her mother she could talk to right now. She didn't trust Riggs or Bobbie, and Esme hadn't even known about her.

The library contained thousands of books, deep book-shelves, a grand piano, several rugs on the floor in a variety of colors, and a pair of windows and high wingback chairs on the far side that created a reading nook.

Janey approached that, and as she did, an elderly woman rose from the chair on the right and turned toward her. Janey put her professional smile on her face, the one she used to charm CEOs and CFOs and the toughest of financial supervisors who did not want to write checks with six figures on them.

"Miss Martin," she said, going with the name Miles had used. "I'm Janey Forsythe."

The older woman had bright blue eyes, and all the color in her body had settled in those eyes. With white hair, pale skin, and nearly zero body fat, she looked absolutely wraith-like. "You look lovely today."

Viola wore what Janey would describe as a kimono with loud, bright flowers covering it. The woman clearly adored flowers and gardens, and Janey wished she'd paid more attention to Mom as she'd talked and talked about the flowers she put in her garden at the cottage.

Janey shivered to think about telling Viola she and Tessa had pulled everything out of the garden, leaving the beds like raw, dark smudges against the house and around the trees.

"Where's lunch?" Viola asked, and Janey's smile faltered.

"Miles is bringing it in." She reached Viola and extended her hand.

Viola looked at it for half a beat and then shook it. "Do sit down," she said, her propriety taking over. "I under-stand you have some questions about my brother."

"Yes," Janey said, perching in the flowery chair and facing Viola as she practically fell back to her chair. "Dennis and my mother were together for several years before his death a couple of years ago."

"Yes, Lydia," Viola said, her head nodding. "Lovely woman. She—a" Viola cut off and looked at Janey. "My goodness, child. You look just like her."

Janey reached up and touched her dark hair, which had been very much like Mom's. "Do I?"

"Her eyes were a bit lighter," Viola said, and she seemed to come more alive for some reason.

"My father—" Janey cut off, her throat suddenly too tight to speak. She'd often told people her darker eyes came from her father, but now she wasn't sure she could say such a thing. She cleared her throat, getting enough of the emotion out of the way to make room for the words. "Did you know my father?"

Confusion furrowed her brow. "I don't think so."

"But you knew my mother. They came to the island for years. Decades, really, as my mother inherited the cottage from her mother, who bought it in 1950."

"I met Lydia in 2014," she said. "Dennis brought her to lunch here once. They lived in the city."

"Did you know they were married?" Janey asked, determined to keep her talking while she could.

The disgusted look on her face said she did. "Of course I knew. Now I've got all of his offspring calling me at all hours of the day and night." She reached up and touched her perfectly set hair. Footsteps approached, and Miles appeared with a tray with two plates on it.

"Lunch, Miss," he said, sliding the tray onto the coffee table between the two chairs. He continued to get the TV tray and position it in front of Viola, then he placed her plate on it. He did the same for Janey, who watched him with interest. How did someone like him get a job here?

"Thank you," she said once he'd put her halibut in front of her. He smiled and walked away, leaving Janey to watch Viola take her first bite of the crab cakes from Lester's she'd requested.

"Mm," she said, her eyes rolling back in her head. "The sauce for these is delicious." She swiped another bite of food through the thick, light green sauce.

"Dennis's children are calling you?" Janey asked, hoping to get back to the topic. She swiped up a piece of fish and rice pilaf, her mouth watering at the salty, warm scent of her food.

"All the time," she said. "Their in-laws, even all the bastards in the family."

Janey nearly choked, though her white fish was the most delicate morsel she'd ever put in her mouth.

"I'm sorry?"

"Oh, our family has quite the sordid past," Viola said, and Janey would eat her plate if there wasn't a bit of excitement in Viola's expression now. "Didn't you know?"

"I did not," she said with a smile she hoped would encourage Viola to spill all the secrets.

"My father had three wives," Viola said. "Some people got left out of his will. There have been vipers after the Martin fortune for decades."

Janey simply took another bite of fish, this time with a green bean stabbed on her fork with it.

"Lydia was Dennis's third wife too. Because the calls didn't start until now, I can only assume he left her everything."

"Seems like perhaps he did," Janey said.

"Mm." They ate in silence for a few minutes, and when Viola finished her crab cakes, she gazed out the window instead of moving onto her filet mignon. "I remember Lydia saying her first husband's father had been married several times as well."

"Oh?" Janey said, her synapses firing now. "But you didn't know my father."

"No," Viola said. "She just said that when they came

for lunch." Viola waved her hand and picked up her fork. "Of course, there's that infuriating man who won't leave me alone. He thinks he has a claim to my fortune through both Dennis *and* Lydia."

Janey's eyebrows drew down as she studied Viola. She cut her steak and wiped it through the sauce on her plate. "He claims to be entitled to a piece through Dennis, because he was my father's second wife's son. But he came along after their divorce." She shook her head and ate her steak.

Several pieces, in fact, each one accelerating Janey's pulse.

"And through my mother?" she asked.

"Really through your father," Viola said, delicately cutting her steak again. "One of his father's previous wives."

"So he and my dad were siblings?"

"No." Viola scoffed. "Step-siblings. If that. It's just like with my family. He came with one of the wives, then departed when the marriage ended. There's no blood relation at all. That's what I keep telling him. No blood. No money." She popped the meat into her mouth.

"Who is it?" Janey asked, almost not wanting to know.

"Richard Friedman." Viola practically bit the name out.

Janey fell back into her chair, her mind unable to truly make sense of what she'd said. Finally, she asked, "Riggs?"

"Loathsome man," Viola said. "I've got someone looking into him, and we strongly suspect the man spent some time in prison." She nodded as if rumors were fact, and that she alone would reveal the truth.

Janey had no idea what to say, and though she hadn't eaten even half of her food yet, she couldn't take another bite.

Chapter Thirty-Six

J aney clicked again and then again, trying to find the wives of Earl Clarke, her grandfather. She'd tracked down her grandmother easily. They'd been married for thirty-seven years before Mary Clarke had died.

Then Earl had married another woman named Donetta. No children between them, though she'd had four kids of her own from a previous marriage. All of the searching Janey had done at the library in downtown Nantucket had not revealed any Richards or Riggs.

So Earl had to have been married again. That would make Riggs and her father step-siblings.

And if he wanted to get technical, Riggs could say he was entitled to Lydia's assets through her first husband, Greg.

She sighed and sat back, frustrated with the tediousness of this search. "Maybe you should look into Dennis's father," she said. "If Riggs is saying he's entitled to the assets through both parties, wouldn't his mother have been married to both Earl and Dennis's father?"

She started typing and clicking again, and because the Martins were such a prominent family on Nantucket, their records were easy to find.

She jotted down the first name and clicked to reveal the others.

Betty Friedman stared back at her, setting her heartbeat clanging like a gong.

She wasn't sure how long she sat there staring at the computer screen, but once she came back to her senses, she clicked on the woman's name, and sure enough, she had two children. Both sons: Paul and Richard.

Her other marriages included one to Brian Friedman, who was the father to her two boys. Then Jonathan Martin. No children, and Janey noted that they were only married for three months before the divorce had been recorded.

Then Earl Clarke.

"So it's true," she whispered, and she suddenly felt like her lungs had way too much air in them. She tried to push it out and pull in new oxygen, but it didn't happen very easily.

She paused and pressed her eyes closed.

"Okay," she said, drawing in a deep breath through her nose. "Riggs and my dad were step-brothers, but only through marriage. No blood." She started drawing a chart on her note paper, putting Earl at the top and adding his wife and their children. That was the line Janey came through.

Supposedly, if Gregory Clarke was her father.

But Earl had married Donetta Downs. She had four children from someone else. They had no children.

Early had then married Betty Friedman. Again, she had two boys from someone else, including Riggs. They had no kids together.

On the other side of the paper, she listed Victor Martin and Julia Papilion. That was who Mercy, Viola, Dennis came from. Then he'd married Betty Friedman for three months—again where Riggs factored into the Martin side of the equation. Then another woman Janey hadn't investigated yet.

She didn't need to.

Riggs thought he should have access to Dennis Martin's assets, as well as Mom's assets through both sides of that marriage.

"What a nightmare," Janey said. She needed to talk to someone about this. She needed to know what would happen if he sued. Would he win?

She printed everything with Betty Friedman on it, paid the fee for using the computer and the printing, and called Sean as she left the library.

"I have to show you something," she said. "I need your legal advice." She wanted to say she needed him to comfort her, but the words wouldn't quite come out.

"I'm at my office," he said. "Come on over."

Chapter Thirty-Seven

He *absolutely could win.*

Sean's words rang through Janey's head when she woke the following morning. She'd met with Sean with her printouts, and she'd paced in his office while talking a mile a minute.

He'd reviewed everything and he said that yes, Riggs had a real case to make before a judge for why he should have some claim on anything belonging to the Martins or the Clarkes.

"At least if things are left up in the air with the wills," he'd said.

Janey needed to sign the papers to get the will executed and done. The problem was, she still didn't know which set of papers she wanted to put her name on.

No matter what, Riggs Friedman was not going to get his greedy hands on anything her mother hadn't wanted him to have. Not the cottage. Not the money. Not the house on Long Island.

Nothing.

She rolled over and checked her phone to find Tessa had gone to town to get bagels, smoked salmon, and cream cheese. She showered and went out to the porch with a cup of coffee, wishing she knew what move to make.

She watched the ocean, so she didn't see Riggs approaching until his stomping footsteps came down the front sidewalk. Janey pushed away from the pillar where she stood, gripping her coffee mug like it would transform into a sword she could use to defend herself.

We strongly suspect the man spent some time in prison.

"You got that car?" he demanded.

"Excuse me?" Janey asked, staying down in the corner of the porch, though there was no escape here.

"That is a Mercedes Benz, and it has hardly any miles on it."

Janey simply blinked at him.

"That is *my* car."

"I wasn't aware you bought it," Janey said coolly. "What are you going to do with a twenty-year-old car?" She laughed, which probably wasn't her smartest move.

Riggs took a step toward her, and she faced him fully. "Do not come any closer to me, Mister Friedman. You should leave."

Anger flashed through his eyes and raged across his face. "You girls can't keep everything from me."

The Cottage on Nantucket, a Women's Fiction Mystery

"I think we can," she said. "As Mom left it all to us, and there's nothing you can do about it."

He laughed, the sound cruel and high-pitched for a man with such a low voice. "You're such a fool," he said.

"Why do you think that car is yours? My mother bought it with someone else."

"Right," Riggs said. "Dale Harton, right?"

Janey didn't confirm or deny. It made sense that Riggs would know about Dale and Joan. They'd all been friends years ago. Janey had seen all of them—her mother and father, Dale and Joan, and Riggs and Bobbie—in the photographs.

"He's not your father," Riggs said, taking another menacing step forward.

She held up her hand, and he stopped again. "My father was Gregory Clarke."

"No, he wasn't," Riggs said, and he actually looked like he was enjoying himself. "I'm your father."

"No." Janey shook her head instantly, horror moving through her. "That's not true."

"Your mother only used Dale to buy the car, because he had so much money, and I'd just lost my job."

"Stop talking."

"Your dad had just died, and she hadn't gotten into the life insurance yet. She needed a car, and Dale co-signed. That's it."

"I don't care," Janey said.

"The Hartons left the island after that," Riggs said, and she wanted to throw her coffee mug at him. "He and Joan

285

sold their cottage, and they haven't been back to Nantucket."

"So what?"

"Bobbie and I thought it was actually Joan keeping them here, because she was in love with your dad, and with him gone…" He let the words hang there, and Janey's mind raced.

Dale and Joan had disappeared after Daddy's death. Janey had seen that in real life, and the photographs catalogued it too. Could it be because Joan was in love with Daddy?

Or because Dale didn't want to break up his marriage to be with Mom?

Or some other reason entirely? She hadn't kept up with the Hartons. They were her parents' friends, not hers.

"Are you going to keep the cottage?" Riggs asked.

"Yes," Janey said.

Riggs's face transformed into something frightening, and he growled. "I'm owed something from this estate," he said. "The cottage, the car, the bank accounts. Something."

"You're delusional."

"You're my daughter!" he boomed, and Janey flinched. She backed up, but she met the porch railing behind her.

"You need to leave," she said, her voice strong but her insides shaking. "Right now." She reached into her pocket. "I'm calling the police."

Riggs came even closer, and Janey worked hard not to

whimper. Her fingers shook as she tried to get her keypad up to dial.

"I just want the car and at least one hundred thousand dollars."

Shock coursed through Janey, enough to make her look up. "What makes you think we have that much money?"

"Please," he said. "I know what Dennis was worth." He gave her a cruel smile. "Give me the car and the money, and I'll leave you and Tessa alone."

"Get off my porch," Janey said.

"You'll throw your own father out?"

"You're not my father." Janey took a step forward. "Get off my porch right now." She suddenly didn't need the police. She was going to use the muscles she'd gained from all of her Crossfit training to rip this man apart right where he stood.

Riggs actually smiled as he stared at her. Then he spun and went down the steps, leaving the porch just as she'd demanded.

Relief sagged through Janey, and she actually slumped against the nearby porch railing. Her pulse rippled through her veins, and she pulled in breath after breath of air, trying to calm down.

"Riggs can *not* be my father," she whispered. "Please, Lord, anyone but him."

If not him, then who?

Janey needed to find out.

Janey needed to talk to Dale Harton.

Chapter Thirty-Eight

"Thank you for moving the money over," Janey said, folding a tank top and laying it in her bag. This trip from Nantucket felt entirely different than her last one, where she'd packed haphazardly and lied to Tessa to get out of the house.

She'd rescheduled a business trip to Dallas and gone to New York instead. She'd found a locket and a letter and a house in the Hamptons.

Surely more than three weeks had passed since she'd stepped foot on this island for the first time in a couple of years.

"Of course," Tessa said. "It's money we're both entitled to, and once all the expenses for being here and dealing with all of this are tallied and done, we'll split whatever is left right down the middle."

"You'll be okay here alone?" Janey turned toward Tessa. "Riggs is unhinged. He's dangerous." She'd told

Tessa about the encounter on the porch from a mere hour ago. "I'd feel so much better if you stayed in a hotel. There are plenty to choose from."

"Sean said the same thing," Tessa said, her hands worrying around one another. "Let me pack a bag, and I'll ride to town with you." She bustled out of the room, and Janey finished her packing. She sat on the edge of the bed and called Sean.

"Tessa needs a room tonight," she said. "Maybe tomorrow night too." She proceeded to tell him about the conversation with Riggs, her plans to fly to Maryland to visit Dale Harton, and that she didn't want Tessa to stay in the cottage alone.

"I've got a room at The Harbor Gull," he said. "It's no problem. Do you guys need a ride?"

"Tessa will have the car."

Her sister appeared in the doorway, her bag ready. "We're leaving now," Janey said. "I'll call you when I have more information."

"Janey," Sean said. "Be safe, okay? Think, please."

"I will." The call ended, and annoyance ran through Janey. She'd met Sean a few weeks ago, and she didn't need the lecture about being safe and thinking. He wasn't her father. He wasn't even really her boyfriend.

Confused and irritated, she stuck her phone in her purse and stood. "Let's go. Sean got you a room at The Harbor Gull."

"Really? That place is so nice. I'm surprised they're not booked in the middle of the summer."

"His office has a suite on standby all the time for clients," she said, smiling. "Now let's see if we can get out of here without running into Riggs."

A FEW HOURS LATER, JANEY NAVIGATED HER RENTAL CAR down a sleepy Baltimore suburb with houses as big as the mansion where she'd eaten lunch the previous day. The sky shone down with brilliant waves of azure and cream, and it was the type of perfect summer afternoon painters put on canvas. The type great writers stuffed into their literary masterpieces.

Right now, it was that sky that kept Janey grounded.

Her fingers had not rested for a single moment since leaving the cottage. She'd texted, called, searched, and recalled to find out where Dale Harton had ended up. In the end, it had been Rachel, her daughter, who'd found the right number at the right hospital to get a forwarding address.

Dale had finally retired last year, after his wife had become extremely ill. Janey's stomach quaked with adrenaline and nerves as she pulled into the drive of a huge, red-brick mansion with four tall pillars on the front porch. Baskets of flowers hung from the ceiling of the porch, and everything from the blades of grass to the bushes lining the sidewalks had been clipped and trimmed to precise measurements.

She sat in the car for a moment, trying to figure out

what to say. She'd been thinking about it for hours, and her mind was no closer to a solution now than she had been when she'd poured her coffee that morning.

With nothing left to do but take the next step, Janey got out of the car. The walk to the front door seemed to take forever, and she clutched the envelope she'd brought with her in one hand and the strap of her purse in the other.

The door spanned the width of two and looked like it had been polished in the very recent past. A doormat said that the dogs were the doorbell, but when Janey rang the actual bell, she heard no barking inside. She heard nothing but the whisper of the wind through the leaves in the trees and the beating of her own heart.

She reached up and pushed her hair back, wishing she'd gone to her hotel to freshen up before coming straight here. Doubts streamed through her, infecting her from the top of her head to the bottom of her feet.

"His wife is sick," she muttered even as she reached for the doorbell again.

More silence, and then just when Janey was about to turn and start to make a Plan B, the door opened.

Dale Harton himself stood there, and Janey examined him with new eyes. Eyes that wanted to see things in him that she'd seen on her own face for forty-six years. Eyes that could somehow see past skin and bone to blood, and even further to DNA particles.

"Janey Clarke," he said, surprise filling his voice. He swallowed as if nervous and glanced past her. "Did you come alone? Where's Tessa?"

"She had some business elsewhere," Janey said, her voice hoarse. She held up the envelope. "Did you deliver the title to my mother's car to Sean Masterson a few days ago?"

Resignation filled his expression now, and while his hair had turned gray and was going white in some places, his dark eyes still had plenty of life left in them. They sparked with an energy Janey had seen in Riggs's eyes, but she wasn't afraid of Dale.

"Yes," he said.

"You said you were my father." Janey tucked the envelope into her purse. "Could I come in for a few minutes? I understand Joan is ill, but I really don't think this is a conversation we should have on your doorstep."

Dale fell back a couple of steps, his profile getting washed away in the dim light inside. "Come in," he said. "Joan's asleep, so I have a few minutes."

Janey stepped into the house, thinking Dale definitely had her chin. Or she had his. Could he really be her father?

He showed her into a sitting room that held furniture that probably cost as much as Janey's whole house in Jersey. She wished she had something to drink, and then Dale appeared, holding out a bottle of water for her. He settled into the couch in front of the bay window and uncapped his own water.

Janey perched on the edge of the couch and guzzled hers, trying to find the right question to lead with. There was only one.

"Are you my father?" she asked.

Dale took a long, deep breath and blew it out, the seconds ticking by. Each one accelerated Janey's pulse and forced her throat into a narrow tube.

He finally said, "I don't know, Janey. I simply don't know."

Chapter Thirty-Nine

"Your mother was having an affair with all of us that summer," Dale said. He'd finished his bottle of water ten minutes ago, but he hadn't slowed down in his story. "Myself, your father, who was my best friend, and Riggs Friedman. We all knew about the other, and in the end, I honestly don't know what we thought would happen."

He wore a smile, as if the days of yesteryear really were that amazing. As if sharing one woman with his best friend and one of his enemies had been a real treat.

"A summer fling, I suppose." He looked at Janey, the smile vanishing. "When she found out she was pregnant, she essentially chose who she wanted to be the father. She chose Greg, and they got married literally the next weekend. You came along eight months later, and while I suspected you might be mine, I didn't push the issue. I'd met Joan by then, and your dad was happy with Lydia.

They were happily married, Janey. I saw no reason to disrupt that."

"What about Riggs?" Janey asked, her voice a bit rusted from the long listening spell.

"He left Nantucket the day after the wedding," Dale said with a shrug. "When I heard he'd married Bobbie, I was actually pretty stunned. He'd seemed so broken up over the wedding, but six months later, there he was, buying the cottage right behind Lydia's and Greg's, and Bobbie was pregnant within the first month."

"Did you...?" She didn't know how to finish, because she didn't know the question to ask. She struggled for a few moments, and then asked, "Do you think he knew the baby. Might be his?"

"If he did, he never said anything to me about it," Dale said. "Of course, Riggs and I weren't friends. We didn't talk about much of anything. Your mother loved Bobbie, and that was why they came to our picnics and dinners and all of that."

Janey nodded, thinking of the pictures. "You never got a DNA test? Paternity test? Anything like that?"

He shook his head. "When Greg died, I co-signed on the car to help your mother. She needed it, and she didn't have the money. I've wondered if you were mine for almost fifty years, but I never gave your mom any money or anything. I suppose that co-sign was me letting her know that if you were mine, and she needed help, I'd be there to help her. She never asked me for anything else, ever again."

"Do you think you're my father?" she asked. "I mean, I know you said you don't know, but surely my mom wasn't sleeping with all of you in the same day."

Dale shifted uncomfortably in his seat and finally got up. "She…I know your dad and I were with her together. It's entirely possible you're his or mine, and yes, that happened at the same time."

Janey did not need to know this. She shook her head, trying to get rid of the images that had suddenly bloomed to life inside her mind.

"Okay," she said quickly. "So the only way to know is a blood test."

"If you want to know that badly, yes," he said.

"You don't think I should know?" she asked.

"Why do you need to?" he asked. "I'm not going to interfere in your life. You've been living and operating with the knowledge that Greg Clarke is your dad. Why does it matter?"

Janey wasn't sure why it mattered, only that it did. "Well, legally," she said. "It matters, because Riggs is claiming he has a right to some of Mom's inheritance."

"You're kidding."

"There are medical histories to consider," she said, though that was a weak reason to want to know who she should be calling Dad, and she knew it. Peace of mind would be nice too. She wasn't sure what she'd do if she learned Riggs Friedman was her father.

She already felt like she didn't know the woman she saw when she looked in the mirror.

"I can order a kit from the hospital," he said. "I'll have it sent to you."

"How long does that take?" she asked.

"Once they have my sample and yours, it should only take a day or two," he said.

"Tell me where to go," Janey said.

"If we use Johns Hopkins," he said. "They'll have your father's DNA on file too. Then you'll know if it's him or me, at least. And if it's neither of us, then you'll know if it's Riggs too."

Relief filled Janey, though her stomach still felt like someone had inflated it beyond capacity and then tied a knot in it. She needed someone to pierce it with a pin, making it burst. Then maybe she'd be able to take a full breath. Then maybe she'd be able to function properly again.

"Okay," she said. "Johns Hopkins it is."

"Let me make a few calls," he said. "It's an hour drive. You're okay to do that?"

"Yes." Janey nodded and got to her feet. Whether she could drive for an hour or not was irrelevant. She *needed* to do it, therefore, she *could* do it.

"You can wait here," he said. "Let me go get changed and get a friend on the phone. Then we can get this done in a discreet way."

"Discreet would be great," Janey said, relieved Dale had received her so easily. Of course, he'd known about Mom's affairs. Heck, he'd had a threesome with her at some point in the past.

Janey shook the thoughts out of her head again, and she couldn't sit back down. She paced in the sitting room until Dale returned, a lab number at the university hospital and a confirmed time for one hour in the future.

Now, she just needed to get her blood taken, and then she'd know who she needed to deal with.

She'd know who *she* really was.

Chapter Forty

"Janey." Tessa lifted her hand, and Janey changed directions to head toward her sister. She said nothing as she stepped into her arms. She'd told Tessa everything over the phone last night, and she honestly couldn't go round and round the whole situation again.

The paternity test was only sixteen hours old, but Janey couldn't help feeling like the results should be back by now. Impatience ripped through her like a stiff sail on a boat, and it hit her so strongly that she felt it in the back of her throat.

"Let's go to lunch." Tessa linked her arm through Janey's. "I know you don't want to talk about anything. Let's go shopping, and charter a boat, and get drunk." She beamed at Janey, but she only smiled and shook her head.

"Tessa, you don't get drunk," Janey said. "I don't want to either. Just a couple of drinks to help me relax."

Tessa looked away, and Janey felt something pinch

behind her lungs. Could Tessa be hiding something from her?

You've hidden plenty from her, Janey told herself. She'd shown Tessa and Sean the birth certificate, but she hadn't disclosed the second letter that had come with it. Tessa had asked her if she'd received anything after going to the bank and the hotel in the city, and Janey had lied and said no.

Not just hidden something—she'd flat out lied to her sister.

It hadn't mattered in the end. Tessa had gone to the house, and Janey hadn't been surprised when the next-door neighbor hadn't known who she was. Mom's second letter to her had said as much.

My dearest Janey,

Tessa needs to take care of the house on Long Island. No one there knows about you, and once she's been there, you'll be able to go. But she needs to handle the house alone. I have no doubt a friend of mine there will give her all the details about the house, and because you've obviously been to the bank and the hotel, Tessa will keep you informed.

She'll come back with a package, and Janey, I know I owe you a lot of answers. I was too weak in life to tell you the truth, and all I can do at this point is pray that you'll find a way to forgive me. Write these letters and pray.

I love you, and I hope you won't think too badly of me once you know everything.

Love, Mom

· · ·

Janey didn't know what to think. She knew she didn't want to think of her mom having a sexual relationship with three different men in one summer. She didn't want to think about how she'd been conceived.

At the same time, Janey felt a deeper connection to her mother, surprising as that may be. But Mom had entertained multiple relationships at the same time, and Janey didn't have a problem doing that too.

She knew who the father of her children was, though, and that was a marked difference.

"Lobster mac and cheese?" Tessa asked. "Or one of those crab cakes you can't stop eating?"

Janey blinked her way out of her mind, which took several long seconds. She looked at her sister, wondering how she could tease at a time like this. Of course, Tessa knew who she was, as her heritage wasn't up in the air. She had a stable family life, whereas Janey still felt like she was akin to a flag, flapping this way and that, according to whichever way the wind happened to be blowing.

She hated being alone, and she couldn't even come to Nantucket without finding a man to accompany her, to text with, and to kiss.

"Mac and cheese," Janey said. "And lobster. I need Nantucket comfort food."

"You've got it." Tessa led her to the car that belonged to Janey, at least in title. "I know the perfect place."

"If it's a food truck, I'm out," Janey said. "You have me eating out of cardboard way too much."

"It's not a food truck." Tessa drove them to the edge of

downtown, on the northern side of Nantucket, to a restaurant that looked out over the Sound. Boats dotted the water, and the wispy clouds in the sky slashed through the light blue sky high above the deeper azure of the water.

Janey took a long, deep breath, feeling some of the bits and pieces of herself that had gotten knocked loose get put back where they belonged. She did love Nantucket. She loved the beach. She'd been conceived here, born in Maryland, and brought back here every year of her life until the age of sixteen.

She'd missed a few years in her late teens and twenties, but she'd been coming regularly in the past fifteen years or so too.

"I'll sign the papers," she said to Tessa the moment they'd gotten a table. Both chairs faced the water, and the gentle sound of water lapping the shore infused her with even more peace. The scent of salt, sunshine, and soup filled the air, and Janey's stomach grumbled at her for not eating in so long.

Tessa looked up from her menu. "Really?"

"Sorry I didn't before," she said. "I feel like I've been up and down, back and forth, in and out." She sighed and smiled at her sister in a wobbly way. "I know it doesn't make sense. When I first came to Nantucket, I was ready to put the island in my rearview mirror. I didn't need to come here anymore, especially if Mom couldn't be here."

Tessa reached out and covered Janey's hand with hers. "I understand that feeling."

Janey gave herself a couple of moments to miss her

mother, and she thought of her first letter, which had said Mom would miss her too. That brought a small, unhappy smile to her face, but it was enough for now.

"Then I started fixing up the cottage, which I know you weren't happy about. I apologize for that. I should've asked you first."

"I don't care," Tessa practically mumbled. "The truth is, Janey, I had nothing keeping me from Nantucket. I stayed away out of spite, because you seem to come and go as you please, and I want to as well."

Janey turned and gazed at her sister, shock flowing through her. "I'm not sure if I should apologize or not."

"It's my problem," she said. "Younger sister syndrome, still, even at this age." She gave a light laugh and shook her head. "It's ridiculous to still feel this way. I'm working on it." She sobered and met Janey's eye again. "You have a long shadow, and I'm still constantly trying to fill it."

Janey didn't know how to apologize for that.

"Drinks, ladies?"

Janey looked up at the waitress. "Yes, I'll take a gin and tonic. Tons of lime, please."

"A double for me," Tessa said.

Janey blinked at her sister again. "Tessa."

"I drink, Janey," she said, sighing. "In fact...I didn't drop and break the bottle of wine the first night we were here. I drank it all, passed out, and dropped my glass on the deck."

Janey could only stare at her sister, and it seemed like this lunch would be about sharing some secrets they'd kept from one another. Janey could do that. In fact, she'd like to unburden herself from some of the things she'd kept from Tessa.

Starting with the letter she'd received with the birth certificate. Her personal problems could be dealt with later.

So she started giggling, glad when Tessa joined in. They laughed and laughed, and their drinks hadn't even come yet. Whoever had said that laughter was the best medicine had been absolutely right. Janey felt better than she had in weeks, and she decided sitting right there at the table, overlooking Nantucket Sound, about to have a couple of drinks and a creamy lobster mac and cheese, that she and Tessa still belonged to one another, no matter who her father turned out to be.

———

Two days later, Janey held a legal-size envelope in her hand, her gaze moving from Sean to Tessa. They sat on the rocks at The Lighthouse Inn, letting the wind pull through their hair, because Janey couldn't stand the thought of opening anything at the cottage.

She had signed on the dotted line to execute the will and get it out of probate. She and Tessa would be co-owners of the cottage on the Point. They should be able to split the assets right down the middle, though they still needed to talk about who would do what, and when.

Who would manage the rental of the house on Long Island, for example.

Who would deal with the hiring and firing of any management at The Hotel Benjamin, for another.

The intellectual property was easy enough, as was the cottage—at least if they could keep them.

"This is it," Tessa said. "You're killing me."

"What if it's Riggs?" Janey asked, the same question spilling from her mouth which had been plaguing her for too many days now.

"Then we'll know," Sean said. "We can make a plan from there."

Janey paced away from them, wanting to release the envelope to the will of the wild wind. The Earth could have the knowledge, and she could bury it up in the mountains, or sink it into the depths of the sea.

She suddenly wasn't sure if she wanted to know. Did she really need to know who her biological father was? Perhaps Dale had been right. What would it change?

"Are you going to open it?" Sean asked, looking at her over his shoulder.

"I don't know," Janey said, moaning as the weight of the world pressed down on her.

"Give it to me." Tessa stood up and dusted her hands on her shorts. She approached Janey with an open expression on her face. She took her by the shoulders. "We are sisters, Janey, no matter what. Do you hear me?"

Janey nodded, her throat too tight to respond verbally.

"Sisters," Tessa said. "It doesn't matter what it says in this envelope. That won't change."

"It could make defending the will harder," Janey said.

"Maybe," Tessa said, leaning closer. "That's why we brought Sean along." She whispered the sentence, her smile widening. "Once we know who we have to deal with, we'll be able to make a plan. We'll know better what to expect."

Janey nodded again, because of course Tessa was right. She handed the envelope to Tessa, fell back, and folded her arms as if cold. But the July weather on Nantucket was nothing but gorgeous, with blue skies and plenty of sunshine. Harmless clouds and the kiss of the ocean breeze against her skin.

If she really wanted to enjoy her time here, she needed to know what that envelope contained. "Open it," she said.

Tessa held her gaze for another moment. Then she tore open the envelope that held Janey's paternity results.

Chapter Forty-One

Tessa had never felt so close to cardiac arrest. Her eyes seemed to malfunction, first only showing her white, then fading to a deep rich navy that didn't allow her to read the black type on the paper.

Rainbows of color streamed through her vision then, everything from brilliant emerald green, to sweeping hot pink, to a soothing, golden orange. She took a deep breath, hearing a voice somewhere beyond her awareness.

She looked up, and Sean Masterson stood in front of her. He'd been kind to her while Janey had been gone, and Tessa could see why her sister liked him. She understood why Mom had hired him here on Nantucket.

The summer events kept arriving in Tessa's inbox, and she hated that she and Janey weren't out there, experiencing the beach, the sailboat races, the rowing tournaments, the shopping walks, or the food tours. Oh, the food tours.

Tessa's mouth watered just thinking about the wine walking tour here on Nantucket, and instant anger hit her in the chest that she'd been huddled in a hotel room or this blasted cottage for weeks.

It was summertime, for crying out loud.

She also couldn't believe this was what her mind had chosen to focus on. Janey needed to know who her father was.

Tessa hadn't realized that *she* needed to know who Janey's father was.

She handed the paper to Sean, who gave her a kind smile and glanced at Janey. She sat at the new dining room table, looking calm and serene. Tessa wondered how on Earth she could pull that off. Tessa's hand shook as she pulled out a chair and joined her sister at the table.

The crisp scent of yogurt hung in the air, because she and Janey had ordered in from Daybreak, and they had the most beautiful berries in their yogurt parfaits. Again, Tessa found it extremely difficult to focus, and only when she reached over and took Janey's hand in hers did the world come back into clarity.

She needed to hold onto that. No matter what the paper in Sean's hand said, she could hold onto the past forty-five years of being Janey's sister.

No matter what, she told herself.

Sean cleared his throat and looked up from the page. He sat at the spot across from Tessa and right next to Janey. He kept his eyes on Janey, who likewise stared steadily back at him.

"Sean," she said, and the name definitely held a pleading note.

"I'm so sorry, Janey," he said, and he refolded the paper.

"No." The word sounded like a cross between a whimper and a whisper, and tears sprang to Tessa's eyes at the level of desperation and distress in her sister's voice.

"It's inconclusive," Sean said gently. "For either Gregory Clarke or Dale Harton."

"Which means it's Riggs," Janey said robotically.

"We don't know that," Sean reached across the table too.

"That's what Dale said," Janey practically hissed, pulling her hand away from Tessa and out of Sean's reach too. She didn't look at Tessa, and it seemed like she was deliberately refusing to make eye-contact.

Her phone rang, but Janey didn't even blink. Tessa looked down at the device on the table next to her sister, and she saw Dale Harton's name there.

"Janey," she said, already arcing her hand toward the phone. "It's Dale Harton."

"I don't care," she said. "He probably got the results today too."

Tessa picked up the phone. "I'm going to answer it." She didn't wait for permission, and she swiped up the phone icon to connect the call. "This is Tessa Simmons," she said. "Janey's sister."

The person on the other end of the line sighed. "She's upset, isn't she?"

Tessa got to her feet. "Understandably so." She walked away from the table, noting that Sean had managed to take Janey's hand in his.

"It's inconclusive," he said.

"You're the doctor," Tessa said, reaching the door. "Tell me what that means." She opened the front door and stepped onto the porch. The cry of seagulls above her and the quick lash of the wind against her skin reminded her that she wasn't in Pennsylvania right now.

Oh, how she'd loved this cottage growing up. She hated that these new memories were being made here now, and she wanted to rip the paper declaring the paternity results to little shreds and let the breeze scatter them across the vastness of the ocean.

"It means that I'm not her father, and Gregory Clarke isn't her father."

"But it doesn't mean Riggs Friedman is." Tessa kept her voice low as she looked to her right, down the lane toward the Friedman's house. Everything seemed so… innocent. Trees and flowers and sand didn't much care who Janey's father was. The breeze and birds didn't know of the crisis happening inside the bright blue cottage.

"It doesn't mean that, no," Dale said slowly. "Though if your mother was seeing anyone else that summer, I didn't know about them."

Janey had returned to Nantucket two days ago and told Tessa about her meeting with Dale. Apparently Mom had had a relationship with three men that summer, and Janey actually had confessed to some relief that she too couldn't narrow her male suitors to just one.

Tessa had barely managed to get one in the first place, and she'd simply listened to Janey, who'd needed to talk.

"So it's probably Riggs."

"I'd say yes, it's probably him."

"What should we do?" Tessa asked.

"I don't see why he's entitled to anything you girls have," Dale said, his tone equal parts confusion and darkness. "Your mother can leave her belongings to anyone she wants, and she and Riggs were not legally married."

"He claims to have a case," Tessa said. "My husband is a lawyer, and I'm having him review it all. Mom's lawyer here is too." She looked toward The Lighthouse Inn, which sat across the sand swells, and she longing for the carefree days of summer.

So many people wanted a slice of the pie. Tessa felt this great need to hold it all close, cover it all up, and make sure no one got a single penny of anything.

At the same time, she wasn't sure why she cared. Before Mom's death, she hadn't known about the bank accounts. The house on Long Island. The downtown New York City hotel. She hadn't known about her mom's marriage, or Dennis's intellectual property, or that Janey wasn't her full sibling.

If she lost it all, who cared? Why did she want to grip it all so tightly and make sure she didn't lose what she didn't even know she'd had two months ago?

Because of Mom, she thought. Her mother had been so adamant in her letters about making sure Dennis's children didn't get anything of his, and it was Tessa's sworn duty to make sure that didn't happen.

But so what if it did? Dennis wasn't here anymore. Neither was Mom. They couldn't actually turn over in their graves, and Tessa wanted to open her fingers and let it all go.

She knew she couldn't. She'd never been good at letting things go. She could compartmentalize them, sure. Think about them when she chose or ignore them for decades. But she could not let them go, not when Mom had been so strong in her convictions for the estate.

"Tessa?" Dale asked, and she blinked her way back to the porch where she stood.

"Sorry," she murmured. "I was thinking about something else there for a minute."

"I don't want to add more to it," he said somewhat apologetically. "I wasn't going to say anything, and I didn't tell Janey this when she came to visit. But with this new knowledge—or at least a very good assumption—I think you should know."

Tessa nearly threw Janey's phone out onto the sand. She'd fly after it and stomp it to smithereens, because she didn't want to know what Dale was about to say.

"Are you still there?" he asked, and Tessa took a deep breath.

She could do this. She *had* to do this. Janey wasn't

strong enough to shoulder anything else on her own, and Tessa could. She'd always been strong when Janey was weak, and her sister had always picked up the slack when Tessa was struggling.

"Yes," she said. "I'm still here."

Chapter Forty-Two

"I can't do this," Tessa said, not for the first time. She had no idea how much time had passed since she'd gone down the steps at the cottage, and an unfamiliar notification met her ears again.

Then again.

She finally realized the beeps came from the phone she carried in her hand, and she lifted it to look at it. The sunshine glinted off the screen, nearly blinding her, and she winced away from Janey's phone.

Janey's phone.

Tessa spun, her mind stuck in some sort of hamster's wheel that couldn't produce coherent thoughts.

The device rang, and Tessa used her body to shield the sun so she could see who was calling. She was calling, and a moment of being inside some sort of vortex sent a vein of whiplash through her.

"Of course," she said, getting her bearings. She'd gone east from the cottage, and surprise darted through her when she saw how far she'd come. She'd left the house without shoes or a hat, and she'd probably be burnt and lame by the time she returned to the cottage.

The phone stopped ringing, but it immediately started again. This time, Tessa swiped on the call from herself and said, "Hello?"

"Where did you go?" Janey asked. "What did Dale say?"

What did Dale say?

Tessa didn't want to repeat what he'd said, but she couldn't keep such a massive secret. She started the walk back to the cottage, her breathing hitching in her lungs. "I apparently went for a walk," she said.

"You didn't know you went for a walk?" Janey asked. "With my phone?"

Tessa didn't appreciate the dry, accusatory tone, and her fury started to build beneath her ribcage. "Dale got the paternity results too," she said, quickly relaying what his suspicions were regarding the identity of Janey's father. "He said the only way to know for sure would be to get Riggs to submit to a test, but he's fairly sure if it's not him or Dad, that your father is Riggs."

"I already know that."

Tessa swallowed and reminded herself that Janey was going through a lot more than she was. At the same time, though, Tessa was dealing with all of the same information as her sister. She had to deal with her mother's past behavior too. She had to shoulder the responsibility of the estate, and it would be her name on the lawsuits.

The fact that Mom didn't have a squeaky clean past only complicated things, and Tessa wondered if Janey had even considered that. Maybe. Maybe not.

One thing Tessa needed to stop doing was making assumptions.

"Janey," Tessa said.

"Ron's called twice," she said. "Are you headed back?"

"Yes," Tessa said, her pulse playing leapfrog with itself. "I'll be back in ten or fifteen minutes." The fact that Janey had let her go for that long astounded Tessa. Her sister must have really fallen into a funk and lost track of time as well.

The thought of telling her sister what Dale had told her face-to-face made her stomach boil, and Tessa needed the openness of the sky to tell her. "Janey," she said, her throat so dry. "Dale said we need to be really careful with Riggs."

"I think we know that."

"No." Tessa shook her head, irritation and desperation coiling together and making her vision blurry again. "Just listen for a minute." She was so sick of everyone talking over her. Telling her stories when they didn't even know them.

"He said Riggs has never had a real job. He said he's a con man. He gets people to sign over their accounts and assets to him for management, and he swindles them out of everything."

Janey said nothing, and Tessa knew the feeling. Her stomach still felt like it was coming back into its proper position from when it had fallen to the soles of her feet.

"He apparently took Dale for quite a bit of money forty years ago, and he says Riggs can be quite violent when he doesn't get his way." Tessa couldn't believe she'd never seen such behavior in all the years she'd known Riggs and Bobbie.

She felt so naïve and sheltered, and she hated that almost as much as being interrupted and spoken over.

"He once got the cottage from Mom, but she managed to get it back. Dale thinks Riggs has been lying in wait to get whatever he can from her, and that he'll go to any length to do it."

"Perhaps we should stay somewhere else," Janey said. "He did threaten me on the porch a few days ago."

"I thought he was just angry. Did he issue a threat?"

"No, you're right." Janey sighed. "Just get back here so we can make a plan."

"I'm on my way." Tessa returned to the cottage and hugged her sister.

"Let's spend the day downtown," Janey said. "It'll appear normal, and we can figure out what to do without the constant threat of Riggs overhearing."

Tessa nodded, because she didn't want to make any big decisions right now. She exchanged phones with Janey and went into her bedroom to pack a few overnight items into her oversized purse. They didn't want Riggs to think they wouldn't be at the cottage that night, but leaving with their purses shouldn't cause any alarm.

Ron called again the moment she closed the door behind her, and Tessa sank onto the bed with a sigh. She hadn't spoken to him in a few days, as every time she'd called, he hadn't answered. She thought about that as she realized he'd called three or four times in the space of only a few minutes, and her heart blipped out fast beats as she swiped on the call.

"Hey," she said, some measure of relief in her voice. Ron could have some maddening moments, but he'd always been her anchor in life's storms. "Sorry. I was out on the beach."

Ron didn't say anything, and Tessa pulled the phone from her ear to check to make sure the call had gone through. It was still connected, the clock on the call ticking up second by second.

"Ron?"

"Tessa." He sounded like he'd been hurt, and panic struck her right behind the lungs.

"What's wrong?" She jumped to her feet, wondering if she had another compartment for whatever had happened to Ron. "Are you okay?"

"I have to tell you something."

"Okay." Tessa couldn't wait another moment, and she wanted to rage at him to *spit it out!*

She took out a pair of clean shorts and a sleeveless

blouse with blue and white stripes. Folding them, she said, "Ron, I'm in a bit of a hurry. Sorry to rush you, but—"

"I've slept with someone else," he blurted out, and Tessa's voice died right there in her throat.

Her vision blurred again, moving to the horrible whiteness, then that darkness, and all those rainbow colors. She didn't know how to breathe, and a horrible wheezing sound filled the bedroom she wanted to burn to the ground.

She wanted to rewind this whole day and go back three months to when Mom was still alive. Then she wouldn't have to know anything about Mom's past. Anything about Riggs Friedman. Anything about Janey not really being her full sibling.

She wouldn't have to face the collapse of her core family and the sisterhood she'd relied on for so many years.

She wouldn't have to listen to her husband sniffle and admit that he'd been seeing someone from his firm for the past five years, and he simply couldn't keep living two lives.

He finally finished talking, and Tessa hadn't interrupted him a single time.

"Say something," he finally said, and Tessa's fury knew no bounds.

Instead of screaming, throwing her phone, and bursting into heartbreaking sobs, she simply drew a breath and hung up on her husband.

Then she opened the door and went down the hall, where Janey stood in Sean's arms, receiving comfort from him.

"Ready?" Janey asked as she turned toward Tessa.

Tessa wasn't sure what would come out of her mouth, as she hadn't quite compartmentalized everything the way she needed to yet. So she simply nodded and followed the happy couple out the front door.

Chapter Forty-Three

"Five years." Tessa stood at the huge floor-to-ceiling window, the glass separating her from the world outside. She reached out and touched the pane, the warmth from the sun seeping into her palm. Funny how something she could see right through could hold the heat at bay, keep the wind from coming inside, and protect her from rain.

Of course, it wasn't raining today. Not in the middle of July, on a gorgeous island in the ocean.

Tessa breathed in Nantucket, the cobblestone streets, the duned beaches, the meticulously pruned privets that bordered the homes on the island. She held the charm of the ocean, the joy the breeze always seemed to have, and the brilliance of the blueness that existed everywhere around her right inside her lungs. When she exhaled, the place did not leave her soul.

Mom had loved this place, and Tessa completely understood why.

"Five years," she said again, pulling her hand from the glass and folding her arms again. She almost felt like she existed outside of her body, as if her mind and physical form had somehow separated, and she was looking down on herself from an awareness that existed above. "What am I supposed to do now?" she asked.

Tessa didn't worry about money. Ron had supported her and their family for almost twenty-five years, and she knew she'd get alimony. She also had more money now due to her inheritance. Heck, she had a paid-for house on Long Island. She could get a job somewhere nearby and live a simple, single life.

Is that what you want?

The thought ran through her mind, unbidden.

She suddenly connected to Janey, though her sister had chosen to stay in The Harbor Gull, in the room Sean kept for his firm's clients. Tessa hadn't been able to get a room in the same hotel, but she had found one only half a block away, with four charming restaurants between them.

The sisters had joked that they'd eat at all of them over the next few days as they stayed downtown and dined, shopped, and sleuthed behind closed doors. Tessa had separated from her sister with the brightest, best smile she'd been able to produce, and she'd escaped to this suite on the fourth floor of The Sandbar.

She needed a holiday, and she reminded herself as she

stood staring at the swirling sea and sky that she was on a holiday.

Not only that, but Ron was supposed to be on Nantucket in less than two weeks' time. She did not want him here, and as she stood and watched the unrelenting waves as the white tips of them kept rolling on, she actually felt part of her heart harden. Just seize right up, with a wall going around it to protect her.

Five years, her brain wailed at her. Ron hadn't closed himself off from Tessa. She'd detected no change in his behavior whatsoever. He didn't stay weekends in the city when he shouldn't. There were no charges on their credit cards that indicated he'd been buying gifts or staying in hotels.

"He didn't need a hotel," she said. "He lived in one during the week." She shook her head, the foolishness cascading through her now. She should've *known*. How could she *not* know?

Janey was right. Tessa was so naïve and so inexperienced. She'd dated here and there in high school and college, but Ron had been her first serious boyfriend. The only man she'd ever been intimate with.

She cinched her arms tighter, trying to keep the memories and emotions inside. Contained. Controlled. If she did that, she'd be fine. She could make a plan and execute it. She was very good at making plans and carrying them out.

Knocking sounded on the door behind her, and Tessa turned toward the noise. She sniffed, realizing a bit of water had started to leak out of her eyes. She reached up quickly and wiped her face, sighing out heavily as she ran her hands through her hair.

"Game face," she coached herself. "Get your wallet out, Tess. You need new clothes to get through the next few days. And you can eat whatever you want while you do it."

Determined with her two-step plan—major shopping therapy and eat every buttery, fried thing she could find—she headed for the door. She expected to see Janey standing there, wearing something fabulous that would establish her as one of the rich socialites that lived on Nantucket full-time, and holding a fruity drink.

Instead, a man who looked close to her age looked up from the ground. He studied her with a dark-eyed gaze, his hair the color of the rich earth she dug through to plant her flowers. He seemed to spend time in the sun, as his skin had a healthy, tan glow, and he wore clothes that hadn't come from just any department store. No, his dark slacks and short-sleeved shirt screamed professional, and the color of his shirt mirrored the summer sky. He wore a tie loosely knotted at his throat, but it didn't seem to go with the rest of the package.

It was too wide at the bottom, and while Tessa had once thought any color could go with blue, she now knew differently. This black and white checkered thing did not fit with the rest of this man's ensemble.

Thinking him to be a manager at the hotel, she asked, "Can I help you? Did I leave something somewhere?" She'd only had her purse, and it currently rested on the bed in the suite. Because of the bulging population on

Nantucket in the summer months, the only room Tessa had been able to find near Janey had been a two-bedroom suite. She didn't mind, and Ron could foot the bill for her. She'd never have stayed somewhere like this without asking him first, but that was before the conversation she'd had with him only forty minutes ago.

"Are you Tessa Simmons?" the man asked, his voice low and rolling through the vowels in such a way that indicated he wasn't from the Northeast. He didn't have the harsh accent or the crassness she heard in some Bostonians, New Yorkers, or Jersey folks.

Where Tessa would've just said yes before, the past few weeks had changed her. She'd changed so much that she hesitated and asked, "Who are you?" instead of confirming her identity.

"I'm Landon Allen," he said. "Attorney-at-law."

Tessa's eyes widened as they dropped to his shiny shoes. Had Ron filed for divorce already? What was the point of him calling her then? Did he not want to work through anything?

Did she? Would she forgive him? Could she?

"Okay," she said, not sure what else to do or say.

"If you're Ms. Simmons, I have a copy of a complaint that's been filed against you in the state of Massachusetts." His perfect eyebrows lifted, and Tessa supposed that indicated another question as to who she was.

"I'm Tessa Simmons," she said.

He reached into his back pocket and pulled out a tri-folded piece of paper. "Don't shoot the messenger." He extended the paper toward her, and Tessa took it. "You have a good day now."

Tessa felt the smooth paper beneath her fingers, but it felt so, so heavy. Landon had already walked away when she regained control over her thoughts. "Mister Allen?" she called, and he turned back to her. "How did you find me?"

The whole point was to lay low. She'd been at the hotel for all of fifteen or twenty minutes.

"You used a credit card, ma'am," he said. "I just landed on the island, and my secretary called me." He smiled at her, and he surely devastated women with a grin like that. Dimples and everything. "You saved me a trip out to the Point, though I hear it's beautiful out there."

"It is," Tessa said automatically. She shook herself. She wasn't single, and she wasn't going to be friends with this man.

She fell back a few steps and let the door close between her and Landon Allen. She twisted the deadbolt and returned to the huge window. Using the natural light, she read the complaint.

Minerva, Lyons, and Aleah Martin had sued her for the intellectual property belonging to Dennis Martin, aka DM Martin.

The house on Long Island was not listed, nor was The Hotel Benjamin. The bank accounts Janey had cleaned out in the city were likewise absent.

Tessa frowned, wondering if she'd get four separate lawsuits. Would three more men come knocking on the door of this hotel room, able to find her so easily because she'd used her credit card, with similar papers, charming smiles, and sophisticated clothes?

"So what if they do?" she asked herself. She'd been expecting this, and while her first call would normally go to Ron, this time, when she lifted her phone, it was to call Sean Masterson.

She could've contacted the lawyer Mom had used to file her original will and trust with in the city. But he didn't know about the addendum, and Sean did. Mom had been dealing with him on all of these extra things, and he was local, available, and familiar with the situation.

"Tessa," he asked breathlessly. "Are you okay?"

Tessa paused, her mouth open. A frown pulled at her eyebrows as she asked, "Why wouldn't I be okay?"

"We're coming to you," he said, definite anxiety in his voice. "Don't leave your hotel room. I'll explain when we get there."

Chapter Forty-Four

"Is this legal?" Tessa asked, kneeling in front of Janey again. She pressed the cold, wet cloth to her sister's skinned knees. "People can't just run over each other, even on a bicycle."

"She claimed it was an accident," Sean said, but he hadn't stopped pacing since he and Janey had arrived five minutes ago. Janey had been hobbling, weeping, and bleeding from both knees.

Tessa glared at the wounds on her sister's knee, though she'd cleaned up plenty of injuries just like this over the years Ryan had grown up. "So she just ran into you?"

"Yes," Janey said. "Another woman came to help me, but the moment I sat up, she gave me this." Janey fisted a paper in her hands, and Tessa knew what it was without looking at it.

She'd been sued too.

"So Aleah hit you with the bike," Tessa said, looking at Janey as she nodded. "And you think it was Minerva who gave you the complaint."

"I think so," she said. "Based on what you've said she looks like. I met Aleah in the city when I went to The Hotel Benjamin."

Tessa groaned as she got to her feet. She washed out the cloth in the kitchenette sink and handed Janey another tissue. She held it to her second knee, and Tessa picked up the box of bandages Sean had gotten from the front desk.

With Janey's knees cleaned up and taken care of, Tessa sank onto the couch beside her. "I guess I got off easy then."

"What do you mean?" Sean asked. He took a seat on the couch across from the sisters, his dark eyes wide and probing. "Why did you call?"

"I got served with a lawsuit too," she said. "But I had a lawyer simply knock on my door."

"A lawyer? Who?" Sean demanded. He gripped his phone and looked down at it.

"Landon Allen," Tessa said, frowning as Sean started to tap in the name. "You don't think he was a lawyer?"

"No," Sean said. "I think that was Lyons Martin." He glanced up briefly, nowhere near long enough to make eye contact, and went back to his phone. "Why would the Martin sisters stage this elaborate scene to knock Janey to the ground, but send their lawyer here?" He shook his head, his expression growing darker and darker. "Did he say which firm he was with?"

"No."

"There aren't any Landon Allen's within three hundred miles." Sean looked up, his frown smoothing out. "Lyons Martin, however, is an attorney."

"He said he was an attorney-at-law," Tessa said.

"I think it was him." Sean turned his phone toward Tessa, and the man sat on the screen, smiling out at everything and everyone, in a very professional headshot. "Was it him?"

"Yes," Tessa said.

"Lyons Martin." Sean sighed, his shoulders releasing as he relaxed. "Okay, so the three of them are here, and we know they're willing to inflict hurt on you two."

"Can I see that?" Tessa gently took the paper from Janey's fist. She opened the paper and smoothed it against her lap. She read quickly, and said, "They're suing you for the house on Long Island and The Hotel Benjamin."

"That makes no sense," Janey said. "I don't own those things. You do."

"They don't know that," Sean said quietly, bringing Tessa's attention to him. He looked from her to Janey and back. "They don't know that," he said louder. "And you'll be able to get that lawsuit dismissed easily. They sued the wrong person."

"Why would they split it?" Tessa asked.

"Maybe because I went to the hotel," Janey said.

"But I went to the house." Tessa refolded the paper and set it on the armrest next to her. She looked out the window, her thoughts drifting for a few moments. "Can you get it dismissed?" she asked Sean.

He sighed and nodded. "I'm sure I can. You two have to understand that I don't spend a lot of time in courtrooms."

"You can, though, right?" Janey asked.

"I can," he said. "I'm a licensed attorney in the state of Massachusetts and the state of New York." He heaved another sigh. "I just don't do a lot of cases like this. I help people with their estates and tiny legal disputes here on the island, usually over land or property."

Perhaps Tessa would be better off getting someone more familiar with defending someone in a probate case. Her thoughts pinged around, unable to settle onto any one thing. She wanted to call Ron, but she absolutely would not. He had not tried to call her either, nor had he texted, and she needed to be alone to figure out what to do about him.

"Okay," she said, standing up. "I'm going to stay right here in this room for the next few days, and I only brought a single change of clothes." She walked into the bedroom to collect her purse. When she returned to the sitting area, neither Sean nor Janey had moved. "I'm going shopping and to lunch. Who wants to come?"

"Shopping and lunch?" Janey asked, her eyebrows up. "Seriously, Tessa?"

Fire roared through Tessa's bloodstream, igniting her anger and resentment. She worked hard to tamp it back before she breathed it all over everyone in the room. "Yes," she said, nearly barking all she'd heard tumble from her husband's mouth. "We can either sit here and feel sorry for ourselves, or we can talk about what we're going to do while we find a cute blouse to wear to dinner tonight."

She gripped the straps on her purse. "I'm choosing the blouse."

Janey got to her feet gingerly, taking extra time to find her balance. "Okay," she said. "I'll come shopping."

"Great," Tessa said, glancing at Sean, who also stood.

"I'm going to go back to my office and see what I can learn about these complaints." He picked up the wrinkled paper from the armrest, and then the one Tessa had tossed on the coffee table.

"Okay," Tessa said. "Call one of us if you need anything."

Sean nodded, and he wore such a troubled look that he stepped past both of them without touching or kissing Janey goodbye.

"He seems worried," Tessa said.

"I suppose," Janey said.

"You didn't think so?"

"I barely know him," Janey said, shrugging. "Aren't all lawyers concerned when their clients get sued?"

Tessa wanted to ask her how she kissed a man she barely knew, and she swallowed against the urge to do just that. Words crowded in her mouth, and she didn't know how to get them out.

She left the suite with her sister, the stiffness working itself out of Janey's stride with every step she took. The hotel had no elevator, and Tessa reminded herself of that as they went down the gleaming white steps to the street.

Outside, she took in a long breath of the summer air, the scent of corndogs and spicy mustard meeting her nose. Her stomach growled, and she thought that would be the perfect, greasy food to start accomplishing her two-step plan.

"Tessa?" Janey asked, stepping right in front of her. She wore displeasure on her face, her frown angry. "Why are you ignoring me?"

"Sorry," Tessa said. "I didn't mean to." She looked around for the corndog cart. "Do you think we could find—?"

"What's going on?" Janey asked, not giving Tessa a single inch.

"I just want a corndog," she said, trying to move past her older sister.

"There's more to this than that," she said, finally giving Tessa enough room to edge between her and the hedge lining the sidewalk that led to the cobbled streets. "You've been acting weird since we left the cottage."

Tessa didn't want to admit anything, not right now. It wasn't in her plan to spill her guts, cry over her cheating husband, or get unsolicited advice from Janey. She wanted to eat and shop. That was all.

Her sister meant well, Tessa knew. She also thought she knew everything, especially when it came to what Tessa should and shouldn't do.

She had been through two divorces, though, and Tessa

cut a look at her sister out of the corner of her eye as they reached the street. Fifty feet to the right sat the corndog cart, and Tessa turned that way. "I want a corndog," she said. "And I'm going to tell you something, and you don't get to give me any advice."

"Okay," Janey said, easily keeping up with Tessa as she walked toward the cart. She wasn't in a hurry, and that helped.

"Maybe some advice," Tessa said, her mind whirring now. "Maybe a yes or no answer."

"Yes or no," Janey said. "Got it."

"Did Kurt cheat on you?"

"That I know of?" Janey sighed. "I'd have to say no. But the man has five children with four different women. My guess is, yes, he cheated on me."

"Would you have left him just for that?" Tessa cut another look at Janey and lowered her voice. "For cheating on you?" Now that she'd spoken, the dam broke. "If that was the only thing he'd done. But he still took care of you, and paid all the bills, and was *there*. But he also did this other thing. And it's a bad thing, sure."

"A bad thing," Janey repeated slowly, and she certainly possessed enough intelligence to know where this conversation was headed.

"But in every other way, he's been loving and kind, and you still love him." Tessa had started crying again, and she didn't even know it until she sniffled. Horrified, she turned away from Janey and wiped her face.

Crying was not in the plan. Crying didn't go with corn-dogs. Sniffling didn't go with shopping.

"I don't know," Janey said, and *her* voice was loving and kind and it tore at Tessa's heart.

She drew her shoulders up and back as she took a deep breath. Turning, she faced her sister. "Yes or no?"

"Tess—"

"Yes? Or no?"

Janey was much more black and white than Tessa had ever been. She knew grays existed in every situation, and certainly in this one. Why she was pressing for a definitive answer only an hour after Ron's confession, she wasn't sure.

She just wanted someone to tell her what to do. Anyone.

The desperation for such a thing clawed at her insides, leaving them bruised and bleeding. She stepped away from Janey with a scoff, her new goal to get two corndogs and enjoy them at the water's edge on the small wharf beside the whaling museum.

She wasn't sure why she'd thought Janey could help. "Forget it," she tossed over her shoulder. "I don't know why I asked you. You can't make decisions to save your life."

"You know what?" Janey called from behind her. "You can go shopping by yourself."

"Fine," Tessa yelled, not slowing or stopping. "I do everything by myself anyway," she muttered. "This is just one more thing. It's fine." She arrived at the corndog cart and met the man's eyes there. An instant fake smile popped onto her face. "Two, please."

"Fifteen dollars," he said.

Tessa started to reach into her purse with shaking fingers.

"I got it," a man said, and she looked up and into the dark eyes of Lyons Martin.

Chapter Forty-Five

Tessa's heart leapt around in her chest, sending out painful beats to her extremities. The world narrowed to just the man holding out a twenty-dollar bill. Loud noise roared through her ears, and Tessa knocked his hand away from the vendor.

"You don't need to do that," she said, stepping in front of him so her hip nudged him out of the way. She dug in her purse and found her debit card. "I'm perfectly capable of paying for my own lunch."

Or whatever time it was.

She handed her card to the corndog vendor, who looked from her to Lyons and back. He took her card and ran it while Tessa cast a glare to the man next to her. He'd at least moved left a little, and she had room to breathe air that wasn't scented like his cologne and the expensive silk suit jacket he now wore.

"Aren't you hot?" she asked, eyeing the jacket. "It's July."

Lyons just smiled, and Tessa took her card back. A moment later, the vendor handed her two corndogs in a wide cardboard container. Tessa stepped away from the cart to the small table set up right next to it.

She added a healthy squirt of spicy brown mustard to her tray and kept moving. A glance down the lane showed her that Janey had indeed left, and Tessa focused on the pier. She wasn't sure why, but she didn't think Lyons would hurt her, so she didn't look over her shoulder to see what he was doing.

She walked away with her treat and found a patch of grass along the sidewalk, wishing she didn't feel the weight of the world on her shoulders. The weight of someone's gaze wouldn't go away either, and Tessa did her best to eat her corndog as if nothing was wrong.

As if she hadn't just been sued.

As if her sister hadn't just been knocked down.

As if her husband hadn't been unfaithful for the past five years.

Her chest hitched, and all of the strength she'd accumulated over the years crumbled into dust. Her next breath shuddered as it entered her lungs, and Tessa was sure she'd break down in the next moment.

Yet she simply took another bite of the greasy corndog, dunked it in the spicy mustard, and repeated the motion.

When she finished the first dog, she dusted off her

hands and looked at the second. She could eat it, but she wouldn't.

Lyons sat beside her, his own cardboard tray filled with mustard and two corndogs.

Tessa didn't have patience for this. She wasn't going to be stalked on Nantucket, and while a former version of herself would've scurried back to her hotel room and hunkered down until the police came, Tessa wasn't that woman anymore.

"What do you want?" she asked.

"Nothing," he said.

"Why did you guys knock down my sister?"

Lyons looked at her, and Tessa reminded herself of the name he'd given her. Landon Allen. "Tell me, Mister Allen. Who were those women?"

"I've spoken with them," he said. "I apologize."

"Oh, you've *spoken* to them," Tessa said with a heavy dose of sarcasm. "Well, then, I'm sure everything will just be peachy now." She glared at him, using a maternal one she hadn't had the opportunity to bring out in a while. "I could call the police and press charges against them, you know."

"You won't," he said calmly, taking another bite of his lunch.

Tessa fumed, but she didn't contradict him.

"What do you want?" she asked again.

"I'm just eating lunch." He cut her a look out of the corner of his eye. "Is that allowed?" He looked around. "Others seem to be doing the same."

Tessa refused to look away from him, and he gave an almost imperceptible shake of his head. "*What?*" she demanded.

"Act normal," he said. "Casual, as if we don't know each other."

"We *don't* know each other." Tessa picked up her corndog and practically stabbed it into her pile of mustard.

"I know what Aleah and Minerva Martin want," he said, actually looking away from her. "I know what Richard Friedman wants too." He finished his corndog and set his cardboard container on his other side.

"What do they want?" Tessa asked, keeping her voice low and her face out toward the water. Her heartbeat wasn't sure about this conversation, but Lyons didn't seem threatening. She had at least fifty pounds on him, and it seemed unlikely that he'd drag her into the water and drown her with so many people around.

The laughter of children met her ears, and the warmth from the sun painted her bare arms with heat and the sense of safety. Nothing bad happened underneath bright sunshine, right?

"They want everything," he said. "I don't think they'll stop, despite my advice that they do so."

"Why would you advise them not to sue us?" she asked. "Isn't that how you make your money?"

"I prefer to represent clients with a good cause," he said, yawning. A real yawn too. He kicked his legs out in front of him and laid down on the grass as if he'd take a nap. His eyes closed and everything.

"Plus, I like taking on cases I know I'm going to win."

"You don't think you'll win this one?" Tessa reached up and tucked her hair behind her ear.

"Maybe," he said. "Maybe not." His mouth barely moved, and Tessa fought the urge to stare at his face so she could read his lips if she had to.

A sigh filtered out of her mouth. "Why are you telling me this?"

"Do you know who I am?"

"Yes," she said, but she didn't give his real name.

A smile touched his face, and Tessa did notice how handsome Lyons Martin was. "I figured. You and Janey are smart." Several seconds of silence passed, each one driving Tessa closer and closer to pure insanity.

Finally, Lyons said, "I'm glad you're not staying in the same hotel as her, Tessa. It'll make things easier for us to get together."

"Why would I get together with you?" she asked.

"Because I'm going to give you everything you need to get my sisters off your back." He yawned again and stretched his arms above his head. "Richard too."

The fact that he called him Richard and not Riggs stung at Tessa's mind. That had to mean something. He didn't know Riggs personally; he only knew the name from somewhere.

"Tonight," he said. "One a.m. Meet me right here. Bring a bag big enough to hold some files."

Tessa's pulse bounced through her veins again. "Tonight?"

"Go now," he said as something chimed in his pocket. "Right now, Tessa. Go."

She wanted to stay and ask more questions, but the slight pitch up in his voice told her to leave. She collected her cardboard tray and walked away from the seemingly snoozing man. She didn't go toward the hotel, or down to the small beachfront here. She didn't return to the cobbled street either.

Instead, she headed for a boutique only fifty feet away, each step filled with the fear that someone would dart out from a doorway or ram into her from behind on a bicycle.

When she arrived at the high-end boutique, she tossed her uneaten corndog in a trashcan and finally dared to turn back to the pier.

Lyons still lay on the ground, but both Aleah and Minerva had joined him. They sat cross-legged on either side of him, and Aleah ate the corndog as if she hadn't seen food in years.

Tessa pulled in a breath and ducked inside the shop before any of them could turn and look at her.

As she browsed through blouses and knee-length shorts appropriate for women of class and status, Tessa's mind raced in circles. She ended up buying a few things—or rather, Ron bought them for her—and when she left the boutique, the Martins were gone.

"One a.m.," she muttered to herself as she passed the meeting spot. The next thing she needed to do was decide if she'd tell Janey or Sean about the upcoming meeting.

She made it all the way back to her hotel room without

incident. Her phone rang, and she picked up Janey's call, her anger and frustration gone now.

"Janey," she said. "I'm sorry about—"

"I'm on the ferry," her sister interrupted. "I had to leave, because Sunny and the VP at AccuSchedule want to meet with me about the promotion."

Tessa's mouth hung open, and she wasn't sure what to fill it with.

"I'll call you later," Janey said, and with that, the call ended as quickly as it had begun.

Tessa let the phone drop to her lap. "I guess I'm not going to tell her." She got up and looked through the things she'd purchased. What did one wear to a middle-of-the-night meeting with a handsome, yet possibly sinister, stranger?

Tessa straightened. "Don't be ridiculous," she said. "You're not going to meet him anywhere at one o'clock in the morning."

Was she?

Chapter Forty-Six

"You need some dark clothes," Tessa said to herself later that night. The hours had passed impossibly slow that afternoon, as Tessa literally had no one to communicate with. She could've spent hours texting Ron in the past. Or Janey. Or Mom.

Her chest had gone tight then, and she'd put on her swimming suit, left her phone in her room to charge, and gone down to the tiny swimming pool at The Sandbar. It only stretched twenty feet long and maybe ten wide. It had been fully fenced and shaded, with the sound of the surf coming from the beach close by.

She'd been alone there for a while, and then an older gentleman had joined her. They hadn't spoken, but he looked happy with a quick smile and plenty of gray hair. He'd swam the length of the pool, back and forth, for at least a half an hour, while Tessa sipped her way through three cocktails.

Hours later, she still felt a bit tipsy, but that could've been nerves from still being awake an hour past the time she normally went to bed. She'd first decided not to go meet Lyons. The thought of what he might have to show her called to her, though, like a siren's call.

At the moment, she was going to go, because it felt like an opportunity she wouldn't get any other way.

"An opportunity for your death," she muttered, wishing she didn't like crime dramas quite so much. She loved watching them on television and movies, or reading treacherous tales in books. She loved a good cozy mystery, and she'd read plenty of murders and probably knew more motivations for killing someone than she should.

Money was a huge reason to knock someone off, and she stood between the Martins and their money.

She pulled on the sweatshirt she'd bought in the lobby of the hotel though it probably wouldn't be cold. The wind could make the temperature much worse than the thermostat said, something Tessa knew all too well.

After double-checking that she had her room key, she stepped out into the hall, her phone gripped in her left hand and her car keys splayed through her fingers of her right hand. She'd learned a few self-defense tips too, thank you very much.

Outside, darkness had definitely settled over the island of Nantucket. Pinpricks of starlight gleamed down from above, and plenty of light came from the street lamps too. The hotel was downtown, after all, and the tourism here would suffer if people didn't feel safe.

The pier stood only about a hundred yards away, but Tessa hesitated before walking in that direction. She strained to hear anything abnormal for this time of night, but all she got was the sound of the waves, the wind, and the night insects who slept during the day and cried all night.

She stuck close to the shadows as her phone started to buzz, telling her she had five minutes before the meeting began. She'd barely reached the end of the building when someone said, "Right here's fine, Tessa."

"Lyons?" she hissed, though she recognized his voice. It was smooth as velvet and rich as butter, and she supposed he made a very good lawyer with a voice like that.

"Yes," he said. "I'm right around the corner, but I'm not going to come out."

"Are you alone?'

"Yes. Are you?"

"Yes." She didn't tell him Janey had left Nantucket. Knowing him, he probably already knew.

"Take this." His hand came around the corner, and he held a cigarette in his palm. "You don't need to light it, but it's a good excuse if someone comes by."

Tessa took the cigarette, feeling dirty as she did. She didn't smoke, and she didn't understand why anyone would. But she'd seen movies, and she knew how to hold it should the need arise.

"I only have one thing for you," he said. "If you stop by the front desk tomorrow sometime after noon, a man named Casey will have it for you."

"You're kidding," Tessa said. "So I had to come out here in the middle of the night for that? Why didn't you just tell me so at the pier today?"

Not only that, but he'd told her to bring a bag to carry files, which now made no sense.

He didn't answer, and Tessa took a step forward, almost but not quite daring to turn the corner and come face-to-face with Lyons.

"I'm trying to cover my tracks," he whispered. "It is so much easier to tell the truth than a lie, and if I didn't tell you anything at the pier, I didn't have to lie to my sisters."

Tessa had no idea what he was talking about. "Why are you doing this?"

"Blood isn't always thicker than water," he said. "That might be something for you to learn too. Anyway." He extended his hand again, this time lower. "I'll leave that item for you at the front desk. I can't do all the work either, but you should look for a couple of documents."

"Doesn't all evidence have to be given to both sides in a trial?" she asked.

"Only a criminal trial," he said. "This is a civil matter. You don't even have to show up to the hearing, though you absolutely should."

"Do I need a lawyer?"

"Not necessarily. Your husband could do it. Or coach you how to represent yourself. Most people get a lawyer for peace of mind, and because we do know the law."

Tessa leaned against the building as a dog started barking. Somewhere—and it could've come from anywhere—a car door slammed. The water surrounding Nantucket had a way of capturing a sound and throwing it around in the sky, making it hard to pinpoint where it had come from.

At least she could see in every direction. The blackness out at the point draped much thicker over the world, which was why there were two lighthouses out there. If she could get past this building and the delicatessen next door, she'd be able to see their beams.

"What should I look for?" she asked.

"Birth certificates," he said. "Of everyone involved. Me, you, Janey, Richard. Everyone."

"Do you already have them?"

He didn't answer, which Tessa actually took to mean yes. Why couldn't he just give her copies of those too?

"What else?" she asked, thinking she'd get every legal document she could. Birth certificates. Death certificates. Marriage licenses and certificates. Dates of divorce, any knowledge of wills, anything she could.

Mom had left some items for Janey, but Tessa hadn't really looked through them. She'd given them to Ron, and then Sean, to look through. Her husband had said they were useless. Sean hadn't given his opinion.

Lyons didn't answer, and Tessa edged forward again. "Lyons?"

Footsteps came toward her, but they were decidedly not male. Tessa shrank back, pressing into the ridged building and hoping whoever it was would keep going right past her. She stepped into the bushes just as a woman cleared the corner of the building.

"Who's there?" she demanded, looking left and right. She didn't bother to keep her voice down, and Aleah Martin looked mad enough to commit those murders Tessa had read about.

She pulled in a slow breath and held it, not daring to move her foot another inch, though she could definitely be more concealed by the privets here.

"What did he give you?" Aleah demanded. She swore under her breath when only the crickets and katydids talked back to her. Aleah's phone rang, and she yanked it from her pants pocket. Janey had described a tall, rail-thin woman who hadn't been wearing anything in New York.

Tonight, Aleah wore a pair of black pants with a short-sleeved turtleneck sweater the color of pumpkin pie filling. "Yes," she barked into her phone. "I know he's not in his room. I swear, Lyons is the slipperiest little eel." She spun on the heel of her sneaker and went back the way she'd come, leaving Tessa to expel the air from her lungs in one horrible gasp.

She pulled in another breath, and then another, trying to even them out and catch up on the oxygen she'd deprived her body of.

Don't stand here, her mind screamed at her, and she crashed out of the bushes and vines and hurried toward the entrance to The Sandbar. Three minutes later, huffing and puffing, she arrived in her room.

She closed and locked the door behind her, pressing her back into it and letting her eyes drift closed as she continued to suck at the air.

When she finally felt settled enough to open her eyes and take the next step, her foot came down on a piece of paper.

Another gasp flew from her mouth, and she clapped her hand over it as if she needed to be quiet up here.

Her fingers trembled as she reached for the single sheet of paper that had been folded in half and clearly slipped under the door.

She opened the note and read the words, *Come see me at the Point tomorrow. We need to talk. ~Riggs*

Chapter Forty-Seven

Tessa did not return to the Point the next day. She didn't have to jump when Riggs said to. She didn't have to ask him how high.

She spent the morning at the library tucked around the corner from the supermarket, trying to find birth records for Riggs Friedman. Richard Friedman. Anyone.

She couldn't find them.

She found the woman named Betty Friedman who'd been married to Dennis Martin for a brief stint, as well as to Tessa's grandfather, Earl Clarke.

Tessa frowned as she went back to the beginning and tried again. The genealogy website she was using allowed her to click on individuals and see more information. Instead of glossing past Betty, she clicked on her.

A whole new world opened up. Someone had kept up with their family history, because Betty's profile had pictures, documents, and notes attached to it.

Tessa started with the documents, and she clicked on the woman's birth certificate. Betty Friedman had been born Betty Morris, and she'd married a man named Peter Friedman. The marriage certificate looked authentic, with the ripped edge in the top right corner, and the thick, loopy handwriting from years past.

Tessa had helped many people use the computers in the library in Easton to find their ancestors, and she clicked on the oldest child. Paul Friedman's birth certificate looked good too, with the mother and father all filled out. He had pictures attached to his profile too, and Tessa paused on them for a few minutes.

There was something off about them, but she wasn't quite sure what it was. Old black and white photographs could be grainy, and when scanned in, and they could become downright blurry.

She clicked on Richard next—who was Riggs. His birth certificate looked good, again all the lines filled in. He only had a few photographs, and the last one showed him with his siblings, Paul on his right, and Barbara on his left.

The caption said: *The Friedman kids before Richard passed.*

Tessa blinked, sure she'd read it wrong. She went over the words again and then again, her pulse pounding faster with each time she read the simple words.

"Richard's dead?" she whispered. The note had been added by the profile Joy Friedman, and Tessa hurried to copy it down on the paper she'd been taking notes on.

She clicked and clicked again and sure enough, his death certificate had been attached to his file. She opened that, and this particular Richard Friedman had died when he was only twenty-three years old.

A few clicks later, and she had the name and location of the cemetery. She could probably find it online, as she knew more and more cemeteries had online catalogs now. Real pictures of the graves and everything, so people didn't have to travel long distances to find their loved ones.

Her stomach pinched, making her uncomfortable, but Tessa couldn't stop searching now. She printed the legal documents for the whole family, including Paul's and Barbara's, and then printed the picture of the three of them where Richard was definitely in his early twenties.

She continued with her research, pulling and printing any birth or death certificate she could for anyone involved. Earl Clarke, his wife Heather.

Gregory Clarke, and his wife Lydia.

Tessa had her own birth certificate at home in Easton, and she'd taken a picture of Janey's.

She'd just started researching the Martins to pull anything she could from Dennis's line when she heard yelling from the direction of the front desk. She had no reason to believe it had anything to do with her. Probably someone who'd had too much to drink at lunch and wandered into the library. Tourists could consume copious amounts of alcohol at any time of day.

In fact, Tessa could use a drink right now.

Her chest tightened as if someone had encased her in rubber bands and kept pulling, pulling, pulling them. She struggled to breathe, and when her ears heard her name, she got to her feet. Stuffing everything into her purse as quickly as possible, she left a twenty-dollar bill on the desk for the computer fee and printouts and ducked out the side door.

She kept her head down as she strode away from the library. The ferry station was a good mile from the library, but she didn't want to return to the hotel for the car. They'd have to get it out of the valet parking, and she didn't want to wait. She didn't want to use her credit or debit cards either.

Would Riggs be able to find her everywhere she went?

"I didn't use my debit or credit card at the library," she said. "How did he know I was there?" She hadn't seen him, but as her body calmed and the adrenaline wore off, she was able to place the angry voice in the library as Riggs Friedman's.

Except he wasn't Riggs Friedman.

At least not the one that came through Betty, who'd been married to Earl. He couldn't be.

Tessa wasn't cut out for danger or intrigue. She much preferred it in her television, movies, or books. She'd seen enough to know she needed money, and she needed to collect facts before she approached anyone.

At the ferry station, she risked using her credit card to get as much money from it as she could, which was five hundred dollars. Enough to get a ferry ticket and rent a car.

She waited until the very last minute to board the ferry, watching to make sure Riggs didn't. She darted on as the workers started to untie the plank, and she was the last onto the boat.

Hurrying around to the opposite side so Riggs couldn't see her if he happened to show up in the next five minutes as they got far enough away from the dock to really get going, Tessa found an empty spot on a bench and sat down. She clutched her purse in her lap and stared straight ahead.

Her stomach ached with the want of food.

Her mind spun.

Her watch bleeped out an alarm, and she looked down at it.

Noon.

She was supposed to stop by the front desk at The Sandbar after noon to pick up some mysterious item from Lyons Martin.

Anxiety spiked inside her, because what would happen if she didn't? Would Riggs be able to get it? Would Lyons simply take it back?

She didn't have the man's phone number, and she wouldn't use it if she did. Her guts tightened as she pictured Aleah's angry face in the moonlight and heard her say that her brother was a slippery eel.

Were she and Minerva holding him somewhere against his will? Perhaps he hadn't even been able to get over to The Sandbar by noon.

She silenced the alarm and folded her hands again, ever the proper middle-aged woman simply riding the ferry back to the mainland.

Nothing to see here.

Absolutely nothing.

Her phone rang, and Tessa fished it out of her purse, nearly dropping it when she saw the name on the screen.

Bobbie Friedman.

Chapter Forty-Eight

"He's really dead," Tessa said, looking down at the headstone. "I'm looking right at the grave."

Janey exhaled heavily, and Tessa was just glad her sister had picked up her call. "And you're in Boston?"

"That's right." Tessa looked up and out toward the ocean. The cemetery where Richard Friedman was buried sat on a hill, and she felt like she could see the entirety of the world from this single vantage point. "If he's not Richard Friedman, who is he?"

"He could be anyone," Janey said, the desperation and helplessness in her voice painting through Tessa with thick, dark strokes. She had not told her sister why she'd decided to look into the birth certificates and other legal documentation of Riggs. She'd simply said she'd "done some digging," and discovered that Richard Friedman was in fact, dead.

"He knew Daddy and Dale," Tessa mused. "I wonder if he'd know more about him."

"Uh." Janey held onto the sound, as if she was trying to think really hard. "Dale said something about him being a friend of Daddy's from college. But Dad had gone on to med school, and I guess Riggs had dropped out."

"Daddy went to UMD," Tessa said. "So this guy must've as well."

"Yeah, along with thousands of other people," Janey said, plenty of snap in her voice.

Tessa didn't let it strike her nerves, the way she might have in the past. She almost felt numb, and she hadn't even had a drink that day. The sun glazed everything in a hot haze, and while Tessa normally worried about sunburn sweat, today, she just stood in front of Richard Friedman's grave and soaked in the sunshine.

She felt like it couldn't touch her, and she wasn't sure if she should be happy about that or not.

"I'll dig around some more," she said.

"Or we could just ask Riggs who he is," Janey said.

Tessa almost scoffed, but she managed to turn it into a sigh. "Are you in Jersey?"

"Yep," she said. "At lunch with Milford."

"Oh, I'm sorry." Tessa wasn't really that sorry. If her sister didn't want to be interrupted, she certainly knew how to send a call to voicemail. She'd done it plenty of other times before.

"It's okay," Janey said with a sigh.

"Are we not liking Milford anymore?" she asked, feeling

like this was the last thing she should be worried about. Her sister's personal life meant nothing until Tessa knew who Riggs Friedman really was. He'd been living a stone's throw from the cottage on Nantucket for decades. Why? What did he want?

Bobbie and Riggs had offered to buy the cottage. Full market value. No questions asked. No repairs needed. Could there be something inside it that Tessa didn't know about? Something valuable?

She'd let Bobbie's call go to voicemail, where she'd promptly listened to the message the older woman had left.

Just wondering what you girls are doing this weekend. The Hawden House is having their summer tea parties this next week, and I wondered if you wanted to attend. Lydia used to love going so much.

She'd let the words hang there, and she'd certainly sounded sad to be speaking about Mom. Bobbie had then cleared her throat and ended with, *Let me know. I'd be happy to get tickets and go with you two.*

She seemed just as kind as she'd always been, and Tessa had actually felt guilty for thinking the woman was calling just to figure out where Tessa was.

She'd silenced her phone since, and turned off the GPS, just in case. She had no idea how someone would trace a phone, but she'd seen it done in Hollywood, and she firmly believed there was truth in those spy movies.

"I like Milford, yes," Janey said.

"I'll keep you updated with things," Tessa said.

"Tess," Janey said. Seconds of silence poured through the line. "I'm sorry I left."

"Yes," Tessa said, clearing her throat too. "I'm sorry I snapped at you yesterday. I was…somewhere outside of my head."

"Boy, do I understand that." Janey gave a light laugh, but Tessa couldn't return it. She didn't like this new layer of plastic wrap she existed inside of. It was almost like she'd taken everything she'd ever felt, piled it together, and then secured it into one giant ball beneath layers and layers of the best restaurant-grade plastic wrap. She'd have to peel back her control one thin layer at a time to allow her feelings out, and she wasn't anywhere near that right now.

"I can come back," Janey said.

"Whenever you're ready," Tessa said. "I'm going to stay here tonight if I can find somewhere cheap." She didn't want to use her credit card, and she'd used one hundred and sixty dollars to get to Boston via ferry and rental car.

She still hadn't eaten, and she thought she could spare ten bucks for lunch and then find a cheap motel to hole up in.

At the same time, she simply wanted to return to the cottage on Nantucket. The bright blue house had always made her smile, and she shouldn't let a man as despicable and vile as Riggs drive her away.

She was so done with letting men influence her decisions.

The call ended, and Tessa made her way to a sandwich shop in downtown Boston. She ate, and things started to come into focus a little bit better.

Back in her rental, she said, "Fact. Riggs Friedman is a fraud. Two, he went to UMD with Daddy. Three, once Mom and Daddy got married, he ran away from Nantucket and returned with a new wife. Four, he claims to be Janey's father."

Tessa needed to figure out who he was, and she put the car back in drive and started south again.

She wasn't going to stay in Boston that night.

She had a box of photographs at the cottage she needed to examine. Janey had said she'd gone through all of them, and they were just everyday happenings of their summers in Nantucket.

"But there has to be more," Tessa said. Everything Mom had left for her and Janey had been more than what it had first seemed. The box of photos surely would be too.

Three hours later, Tessa arrived back at the cottage, parking the dark green Mercedes Benz in the detached garage and sitting in it for a moment. She'd passed the Friedman cottage without seeing Riggs or Bobbie out front, and she had security cameras on the house now. They'd triggered when she'd pulled in, so Janey would know she'd left Boston and returned to the cottage.

Tessa didn't care. She didn't have to provide a minute-by-minute accounting of her thought processes for her sister.

Drawing in a deep breath, she got out of the car, scanning the open area beyond the door. Nothing. Just the wind and whisper of relaxation this place had always held for Tessa.

She certainly wasn't relaxed as she hurried down the sidewalk and around to the front door. Up the steps she went without trouble. Inside, she found the house exactly as she and Janey had left it.

Her heart pounded like a big bass drum, and a trickle of foolishness pushed against her adrenaline and nervousness. She was being silly. "What did you expect?" she muttered. "Riggs to be sitting here, an axe in his hand?"

She shook her head and set her purse on the kitchen table as she passed.

Janey had kept the box of photos in her room, and Tessa collected them and took them back out to the living room. Her sister had scattered them at some point, and Tessa found she didn't care.

She simply wanted to examine every single one with Riggs in it. Riggs and her father. Riggs and Mom. Riggs and Bobbie. Riggs, Bobbie, and Dad. Whatever combination she could find, if he was in it, she separated the picture into a new pile.

She also started pulling out pictures with Daddy in them, not sure why. Only that she'd found one with Daddy and Bobbie—just the two of them—and it intrigued her.

After that, as the sun started to set, turning the light inside the cottage a dull gray and then a melancholy navy, Tessa began to sort the pictures into a pile for Mom. Any that weren't already in Riggs's or Daddy's pile that contained Mom went into a new stack.

She had to pause and get up and turn on the lights so

she could continue, and her stomach pinched at her again, reminding her that she'd last eaten clear back in Boston.

Honestly, that felt like a different day, not only several hours ago.

She didn't pause to eat though. She went through the entire box of photos, sorting out Mom. Then she went through them all one more time, just to make sure she'd created the three stacks she wanted.

She took them to the kitchen table one by one before opening the fridge to see what she and Janey had left there. After setting two pieces of bread in the toaster, she returned to the table. She removed the photos of Riggs and Mom to the counter and started spreading out the ones with Daddy in them.

He appeared the most with Bobbie and Joan, followed closely by Dale. There were hardly any of him and Riggs.

"If they were step-brothers, wouldn't there be more of them?" Tessa murmured as she looked at another photograph of Daddy sitting in a beach chair, a beer bottle in one hand, and a smile on his face as he laughed at something someone else had said.

Bobbie sat on his left, and Dale sat in the background, both of them with pure delight on their faces too.

Tessa frowned at the picture, trying to see more than what it showed. She closed her eyes and put herself in the scene. She felt the evening air, heard the crackling fire they'd built on the beach, tasted the salty sea air right before she swallowed a gulp of beer.

What were they laughing about?

Why did this intrigue her so?

"Riggs," she muttered, realizing she'd completely forgotten about her toast. She should be focusing on *Riggs*, not her father.

Yet she couldn't stop looking at the photos she'd laid out across the whole tabletop. She sighed, stretched her back, and stepped over to the toaster to throw away the now ice-cold toast. She needed something mindless to do for a while so she could let her synapses think, and she began to make coffee. Gardening often provided the mental downtime she needed to work out problems and find solutions.

And she sure could use a bunch of solutions right now. A solution to her marital problems. A solution to her legal issues. A solution to her familial tensions.

"Family," she said, lifting her head from the filter and the coffee grains she was measuring.

Everything came back to family.

She spun from the counter, her heartbeat doing a new kind of tap dance behind her ribcage. It threatened to burst, and Tessa pressed one hand to her chest as she returned to the table and peered down at the pictures again.

Janey had said none of the pictures had writing on them. *At least the ones I checked*, she'd said.

Tessa picked up the picture of Daddy with Bobbie and Dale. With shaking fingers, she flipped it over, tearing her eyes from their laughter and clear joy.

Nothing.

Her hopes nosedived, and she set the picture back in the spot it had vacated.

She picked up the one with Daddy and Bobbie, his arm slung around her shoulders and both of them beaming right out at the camera. They had to be in their mid-twenties, and Daddy wore that hideous tank top with the wide, thick ribbing in bright red—but it was his mustache that gave away the era.

Her memory fired at her and she dropped the picture and bent to pick up her purse. She took out the picture she'd printed at the library that morning. The one of Paul, Richard, and Barbara Friedman.

The three of them stood in a similar pose, but with only two of them instead of three.

Tessa sucked in a breath, and the whole world whooshed by her.

She cleared a spot next to the picture of Bobbie and Daddy and carefully laid the printout next to it. No, it wasn't crystal clear. Yes, it was a bit grainy and slightly blurry—and true black and white while the picture that had come from the box was yellow with age.

Tessa fell into the chair, because her eyes and brain needed all of her energy.

Bobbie Friedman was the same woman as *Barbara* Friedman.

Her brain screamed at her that Riggs had married his sister, only to correct her in the next moment that Riggs was *not* Richard Friedman.

Bobbie and Daddy had been step-siblings, not Riggs

and Daddy. If anyone had any claim to his inheritance, it would be her, not Riggs.

"No wonder Mom loved her so much," Tessa whispered. "They really were like sisters-in-law."

The numbness from the realization ebbed, and Tessa reached out and picked up the photo. This time, when she turned it over, she saw *Barbie and Greg* written in her mother's hand.

"Barbie," she said, touching the letters with her fingertip. How did she go from Barbie to Bobbie? She'd never heard either of her parents, or Bobbie or Riggs, or *anyone*, call Bobbie anything other than Bobbie.

The next question in her mind had her looking at the clock to find out if the hour had grown too late for her to call Bobbie.

Almost eight. Surely she'd still be awake. Tessa hadn't located her phone yet when someone knocked smartly on the door.

Tessa yelped and actually jumped away from the front door, though she stood back in the kitchen. Her eyes flew toward it, and she wondered if she'd locked it. Paralyzed by surprise and a bucketful of fear, she held very still.

When the person knocked for a second time, Tessa could only categorize it as a pound.

Chapter Forty-Nine

"I know you're here," Riggs called from the other side of the door. He hadn't come through it yet, but every cell in Tessa's body said he would soon if she didn't answer him.

Thinking fast, she swept the photos she'd painstakingly laid out on the table into a pile and tapped them together.

Another demanding pounding of his fist against the door. "Tessa!" he yelled. "I can see the car in the garage, and there are lights on."

"Just a minute," she called. "I just got out of the shower." She dashed over to the countertop where she'd been making coffee and yanked open the drawer. She put the pile of pictures inside, and added the two other stacks she'd carefully sorted.

"I'm not going anywhere," Riggs said, and it sounded like a threat.

Tessa hurried into the living room where she's started

the sorting project. All of the photos went back in the box, and she ran down the hallway with the whole thing tucked under her arm. She slid it under her bed and faced the doorway.

Her pulse sprinted as if she'd just run a marathon, and she tugged at the end of her blouse. "Shower," she groaned, and she quickly stepped out of her khaki shorts and into her casual pajama pants. Down the hall, she ran her hands under cool water and ran them through her hair until it gleamed with a decent amount of dampness.

Only then did she head down the hall to the front door. *Ask him who he really is.*

Do not even get close to asking him anything.

You need to know, and he's right here.

She wasn't going to find him at UMD. None of the photos had shown anything before Mom and Daddy's marriage, though Janey had said Riggs was here and had been with Mom the same summer as Dale and Daddy.

Tessa unlocked the door and opened it six inches, keeping one foot right behind it and leaning her body weight into it. "What do you want?" she asked the tall, gray-haired man on the porch.

"We could help each other," he said.

"I seriously doubt that."

"You have no idea what you're dealing with."

"Why don't you tell me then?" Because no, Tessa didn't know what she was dealing with. Or rather… "Or who I'm dealing with?" She cocked her eyebrows, glad the porch had motion-sensor lights that shone with the force of the sun.

Riggs's jaw jumped as he pressed his teeth together. For once, he said nothing.

"Who are you?" she asked, raising her voice.

He actually looked to his left and back to her, as if he didn't want anyone to overhear them. "Keep it down," he said, almost under his breath.

"Tell me who you are."

"I'm Richard Friedman," he said.

"Try again." Tessa inched the door closed another measure, her fingers starting to ache for how hard she gripped the doorframe. "I know you're not Richard Friedman. At least not Betty Friedman's son. He died when he was twenty-three years old. He was Bobbie's brother!" She yelled the last sentence, her chest heaving now.

All at once, a bone-chilling thought entered her mind. "Oh, my word. Did you kill him?"

"Don't be ridiculous," Riggs said, scoffing. He looked down the lane again, giving Tessa a moment's relaxation.

He lunged toward her, and though Tessa carried extra weight, she was no match for a grown man, old as Riggs was. She stumbled backward, flailing for something to grab onto.

There was nothing, and she fell backward, her tailbone meeting the new bamboo hardwood floors in the cottage and sending blinding pain in all directions.

"I told you to be quiet," he growled. The door closed behind him, and though Tessa's eyes streamed with instant tears from her fall, she definitely heard the distinct click of the lock. "She'll come down here if you don't be quiet." He started to reach for her, but Tessa scrambled backward, thrusting her feet toward him.

"Don't touch me," she yelled. "Get away from me!" She screamed, because she needed help now that Riggs was in the house.

He threw himself on top of her, flattening his hand against her mouth and cradling her head. As she flopped backward with his added weight, his hand hit the floor and not her head.

Not your head, was her only thought.

"Tessa," he said, his voice very angry but very quiet. "You have to be quiet. I will tell you everything, but you have to be quiet."

Tessa looked into his eyes, hers as wide as they could go.

"I'm going to let you go," he said, his dark eyes flashing with danger. "Quiet."

She nodded as much as she was able, the awful, somewhat fishy, somewhat oily scent of his skin right up in her nose.

He lessened his grip on her head, and the moment she could, she slipped away from him. They both got to their feet, and Tessa didn't dare take her eyes from him for more than a breath of time.

Tears still filled her eyes, but this round had come from fear, not pain. "What are you doing here?" she asked, her voice tinny and high-pitched now.

"I asked you to come see me today," he said, staying over by the door, on the opposite end of the couch.

"You don't own me." She reached up and wiped her eyes, her strength returning to the center of her being. "I don't have to come when you tell me to."

"Where did you go?" he asked.

"None of your business." Tessa lifted her chin and stared into his eyes. He really did wear danger there, and she couldn't stop the shiver as it ran up her spine and across her shoulders. "Tell me who you are."

Riggs swallowed, and he looked around the cottage. Tessa had no idea what he was looking for, but she was reminded of how he and Bobbie had offered to buy the cottage. "What's here that you want?" she asked.

She'd certainly feel better if she stood closer to something—anything—she could use to protect herself. She took a step back while he continued to take in the changes they'd made in the cottage.

"I met your mother here," he said, his voice much softer than it had been a few moments ago. "Right here, at this cottage."

"How?" Tessa said. As far as she'd seen on TV, the more a perpetrator talked, the better the survival odds of the victim.

"I'd come to Nantucket with Greg," he said. "We were in the same stats class at UMD." A ghost of a smile crossed his face, and Tessa wondered at all the memories she could tell him about her father. "We needed a weekend away, because our midterms were an absolute bear."

Tessa edged backward again, getting closer and closer to the kitchen, where they kept the knives. Riggs returned his attention to her, and she stilled.

"Your mother was here, on her own break of sorts. It was cold—only the beginning of March—but she said we should come that summer. She was beautiful, your mother. I fell in love with her instantly." More of that smiling, and Tessa didn't like it one little bit.

She felt like he'd opened a door that was too intimate for her to walk through. She didn't need to know these things about her mother.

"Unfortunately, Greg did too, and Lydia was a big flirt. We came for two summers, though I'd dropped out of college by then and your dad had moved on to med school. He brought Dale with him that third summer, and Lydia…" He cleared his throat. "Let's just say we all had a good time that summer."

Janey had already relayed as much. "Why do you go by Bobbie's last name? When did you assume her brother's identity?"

Confusion furrowed his brow. "I didn't assume his identity."

"You must think I'm so stupid. You just happen to have the same name as her brother? Her *dead* brother?" Her voice raised again, and he held up one palm.

"Everyone called me Riggs when I was younger, because I worked as a boat rigger the first few years of college," he said. "I ended up dropping out to open my own boat repair shop, which I lost a couple of years later in Hurricane Joan."

"Joan? As in Dale's wife?"

"As in Dale's wife," he said darkly. "The woman ruined me, and then *they* had the audacity to sue *me*."

Tessa didn't need all the history. She didn't even want it. "Stick to you," she said. "You and Bobbie. You and my mom. You and my father."

"Well, Lydia got pregnant, and she chose Greg to be the father. The moment Janey was born, I knew she was mine. I knew. Greg knew. Lydia knew, but she refused to do anything about it, despite my pleas. I said I'd marry her. I could take care of her and the baby."

A horribly dark storm filled his face, and he shook his head. "She said no, and she said if I came near her or Janey, she'd do everything in her power to make sure I never saw my daughter again." He chuckled, but the sound carried only malice. "Your mother could be a mean woman when she wanted to be."

Tessa bristled and used the opportunity to fall back another step. "So you left Nantucket and met Bobbie. Married her and came back to live next door to the woman you were really in love with? For almost fifty years?" Tessa shook her head. "You'll pardon me if I don't believe it. Why? *Why* would anyone do that?"

Her mind fired more questions at her. "Why are you two Bobbie and Riggs *Friedman*? Why didn't Daddy or Mom ever tell me Bobbie was my step-aunt? Why would

Bobbie want to live next-door to the woman you loved when *she* was your wife?"

"Bobbie and Lydia were very close," Riggs said. "Two peas in a pod, those women." He didn't sound happy about it. "Bobbie was only Greg's step-sister, but she got along great with him and Lydia, of course. Everything was her idea."

"What do you mean? What was her idea?" Tessa had finally reached the cusp of the kitchen, and she settled her weight evenly on both feet. If Riggs came at her again, she could lunge for something. Pull the chair out to slow him down. Open the fridge to hide behind it. Fumble through a drawer for a knife. Something.

"Your dad was a heart surgeon," Riggs said. "Bobbie knew he had money, and over the years, she grew bitter and calloused. He'd told her he'd always be there to take care of her, but he wasn't. He doted on Lydia, and about the time Greg died, Bobbie started planning a way to get the fortune he'd built one way or another." Riggs sighed and looked down at his hands. Tessa didn't know what to do with the vulnerability.

"She's been planning the same for several of her other step-siblings."

Dots began to connect in Tessa's head. "Dennis Martin."

Riggs nodded. "When he sold his first book, Bobbie added him to the list."

"She set him up with Mom."

He nodded. "You're quick. That way, she said, she'd

have a finger in each side of that inheritance once Lydia passed."

"There's not much inheritance," Tessa said.

Riggs looked up, his dark eyes shining like stars in the midnight sky. "Oh, but there is. There's millions in Lydia's estate."

Tessa frowned, her mind racing. Her exhaustion would catch her at any moment, and she really just wanted to go to sleep so she'd stop thinking. "No," she said slowly. "There really isn't."

"There is," Riggs said, but before Tessa could argue with him, someone knocked on the door again. He spun toward the door, and Tessa took that opportunity to grab her phone and dial Janey.

She dropped her phone in the pocket of her loose pants just as Riggs turned back to her. He wore quite the expression of fear as he said, "I'm sure it's Bobbie." He strode toward her, and Tessa backed up until she pressed into the counter.

"I didn't have a chance to explain everything," Riggs said, his voice low. "Just agree with her, Tessa? Okay?" His expression blazed with urgency, and he didn't back away when Tessa remained silent.

The light knocking happened again, and Riggs barked, "Tessa."

"Okay," she said. "I'll agree with everything she says."

Chapter Fifty

"Janey?" she whispered, her back to Riggs as he walked away from her. Every cell in her body screamed at her to turn around. "Can you hear me?"

"Yes," her sister said. "What's going on?"

"Too much to explain," Tessa said. "I'm going to leave the call going. Can you record it?"

"I'll figure it out."

The door behind her opened, and Tessa said, "Gotta go," and slipped the phone back in her pocket as she turned toward Bobbie Friedman as she entered the cottage.

Tessa wanted to put a smile on her face, but found she couldn't. Bobbie did though, and she came toward Tessa as if they were simply old friends who hadn't spoken for a while.

"I meant to call you back," Tessa said, taking a few steps to meet Bobbie at the cusp of the kitchen. "I've been so busy, and I have this massive headache." She stopped talking there. She had been busy, so that wasn't a lie. She found it so much easier to keep her voice in the normal range when she didn't lie.

"Have you eaten?" Bobbie asked as she hugged Tessa. She drew back but kept her hands on Tessa's shoulders, as if she needed to be touching her to assess how she really felt. "You look a little gray."

"I haven't eaten," Tessa said with a weak smile. "I got really engrossed in this article Ryan sent me, and I went to Boston for some shopping today, and I'm not even sure what we have in the house."

Bobbie's blue eyes missed nothing, and Tessa noticed the sharpness in them in a whole new way.

"What are you and Riggs up to tonight?"

"Oh, nothing," Bobbie said. "I made fish stew. You should come next door and eat, Tessa. You don't look good." She finally stepped back, and Tessa couldn't see this woman being anything but a bit eccentric in her hairstyles and the perfect grandmother.

She cooked, she cleaned, she let her husband go fishing whenever he wanted. Tessa darted a look toward Riggs, who'd come back into the house but not very far. He wore a mask as an expression, and she couldn't tell what was happening in his mind.

Agree with everything she says.

"I'm really tired," she said, swallowing. Another weak smile. "We stayed downtown last night, and the bed was *terrible*."

"The beds here can't be that great," Bobbie said, her soft expression hardening considerably.

"They're not bad, actually." Tessa turned back to the kitchen and opened the fridge, pretending to look for something inside it. "I'm sure I can find something here." Every fighting instinct inside her screamed at her. *Don't go with Bobbie. Do not go next door.*

She had no idea what she'd find there, though she'd eaten dinner with Bobbie and Riggs at their cottage several times in the past. She and Janey had been there only a week or so ago.

"No," Bobbie said, and the next thing Tessa knew, the fridge door came flying toward her. It hit her in the calf, and then her hip, and she yelped as pain exploded through her leg from where the corner of the door had hit her.

The fridge slammed shut with a terrible rubber *thwapping* sound, and Tessa looked at Bobbie even as she reached to rub her leg. "What are you doing?"

Bobbie wore a look on her face Tessa had never seen before. "You don't have anything to eat here," she said, her bright blue eyes sparking with dangerous, hot flames. "You need to come next door to our place, and we'll feed you right up."

Like Hansel and Gretel, Tessa thought, still searching Bobbie's face for any sign of the woman she'd known for decades.

She didn't seem to live inside the petite blonde woman, and Tessa stepped backward. Her heartbeat crashed like cymbals in her ears, and her adrenaline flowed through her body with the power of river rapids.

Could she get a knife? Could she even cut another person if she did?

"Don't make a scene," Bobbie said. "I'd hate for something to happen to your brand-new floors." She smiled in the creepiest way possible, her light red lips curving up and out far too much to be comfortable—or normal.

"Come on," Riggs said roughly, opening the door behind him. "We have a lot to talk about tonight."

Bobbie rolled her eyes and turned her head to the side. She didn't try to look at Riggs at all. "No, we don't," she said. "We have nothing to talk about tonight." She returned her attention to Tessa.

Her instincts told her to get away from this woman, and fast. It was incredible how different she seemed tonight compared to every other time Tessa had seen her. "If we have nothing to talk about, I really can find something to eat here," she said. "Or I'll order from that soup shack."

"Soup in the summer?" Bobbie trilled out a high-pitched laugh. "Don't be ridiculous."

"But you made fish stew," Tessa said, her voice sliding into a whisper by the end of the sentence. Bobbie's smile slid right off her face. In that moment, she knew Bobbie had, in fact, *not* made fish stew for dinner.

Maybe you're the fish, she thought, a new brand of terror moving through her and wrapping her heart in tight, icy fingers. It struggled to beat, each one coming closer and closer to the one in front of it as they all tried to sprint through her veins simultaneously.

"And it's delicious," Bobbie sang out. She reached out, but Tessa sidestepped her hand. Anger flashed in the blue depths of her eyes. "You need to come with us."

"Why?" Tessa asked, her eyes darting to Riggs. "Tell me what's going on."

Bobbie settled her weight on one foot and folded her arms. Tessa didn't dare look away from her again. "It's really very simple, Tessa. You have something we want. We want to make sure the Martins don't get it, so we'll need your help with that. And then, you'll be giving us what we want."

"There's nothing to give you," she said. "I already told Riggs that."

Bobbie swung around to face her husband. "What have you been telling her?"

"Nothing," he said, holding up one hand. "I haven't told her anything."

There's millions in Lydia's estate, he'd said, and Tessa wondered *where*.

Bobbie shook her head in what could only be a show of disgust. "You better not have." The blonde woman turned back to Tessa. "Come on."

"I'm not hungry," Tessa blurted out as Bobbie started to twist back to the front door of the cottage. "I'm just going to take some painkillers and go to bed."

Bobbie changed direction fluidly, and she came at Tessa with the speed and precision of a rattlesnake. Her arm lifted, and Tessa had enough peripheral vision to see the syringe in her hand.

Go! she thought. *Move!*

She could do neither as Bobbie's left hand latched onto her forearm and the right one plunged that syringe straight into Tessa's neck.

The pinch there was more like the pain of someone slamming a toothpick into her jugular, and she cried out. "Stop it," she said. "Stop!"

She batted at Bobbie's hand in the space between her shoulder and her face. "What was that?" Something cold spread through her body, which was very, very strange, as the point of origin of the needle pulsed with white-hot pain.

"Help," she said, her mind clinging to only one thing. "Janey." The name came out weakly.

"We'll find her too," Bobbie said, her voice oh-so-chip-per. "Don't worry, dear. You're going to feel better when you wake up. You just rest now, and I'll take care of everything."

Tessa took a step toward the countertop, reaching out to steady herself and missing it completely. She wasn't anywhere near close enough to it, which was so, so odd, because it looked so close.

"Janey," she wheezed again as her throat started to close. "I'm going to need help." She fought against the blackness crowding into her vision, and she flailed to find something she could hold onto. Anything.

Otherwise, a fall was in her very near future.

"Help," Tessa said one more time. "I don't want to go next door with them."

"I'm so sorry," Bobbie said with plenty of falseness in her tone. "But you simply have to." She turned away from Tessa and barked at Riggs. "Get her before she hits her head."

Riggs strode toward Tessa, catching her just as she started to topple. They both went to the ground, where he knelt and cradled her against his thighs. "Bobbie, what was that stuff?" He shook Tessa a little bit, but her eyes had drifted closed, and she floated now, on a cold and hot sea filled with foam, lily pads, and the cheerful cadence of amphibians.

"You can't just be injecting people with things all the time," he said, his voice warbling in and out of Tessa's ears.

"She'll be fine," Bobbie said. "We needed some time, and she wasn't going to come."

Help, Tessa thought, hoping her sisterly connection with Janey hadn't been severed because she'd snapped at her sister yesterday.

"Now," Bobbie said. "Let's get her next door, and I'll keep my eye on her while you come back here and start looking for that trunk. It has to be here; it wasn't anywhere else."

"I really don't think Lydia kept stacks of hundreds in a trunk here at the cottage," Riggs said, and Tessa groaned inwardly as he picked her up in his arms. The movement made everything swim, swim, swim in her head, all of her thoughts floating by like cotton blowing in the wind.

"You don't know anything," Bobbie said. "She won't be out forever—at least with that. We'll tear this place apart board by board if we have to. I know there's cash in this cottage. We just have to find it."

The world moved, and Tessa begged for a release of the kaleidoscope of colors streaming along the backs of her eyelids. Her stomach swooped, and she retched.

At least she thought she did. She honestly wasn't sure what was going on, and thankfully, there had to be a God in heaven, because He stole her consciousness from her, and Tessa didn't have to fight against the tide any longer.

She sank into blissful oblivion, her last thought the hope that Janey would have the good sense to end their phone call before Bobbie realized it had been connected.

Chapter Fifty-One

Janey hung up, her mind racing. "Call Sean," she barked at herself, abandoning the work on her desk. When Tessa, her sister, had called about fifteen minutes ago, Janey almost hadn't answered.

Now her sister had been injected with something, five hundred miles away, and there was nothing Janey could do about it.

Except call Sean.

She jabbed at the screen to get to his name, her fingers shaking. She needed an airplane ticket to Nantucket. She needed to pack. She needed to call her daughter and make sure the cats got fed.

Thoughts streamed from one side of her mind to the other as Sean's line rang. "Janey," he said. "What—"

"They have Tessa," she practically yelled. "Bobbie and Riggs Friedman. She called me, and I was listening to the whole call, and Bobbie injected her with something."

393

"Whoa, what?" Sean said. "Slow down. Start at the beginning."

"There's no time to start at the beginning," Janey said. "You need to call the cops and get to the cottage. Bobbie and Riggs took Tessa!"

"Took her where, Janey?"

She paced in her office, trying to find the memories. She had such a good memory. Why couldn't she think?

You can't just be injecting people with things.

"Riggs told Bobbie she couldn't inject people with things," Janey said. "Tessa's speech was slurred at the end. She gave her something to make her pass out." She walked toward the window, forcing herself to go slow. To think.

"She told Riggs to 'get her next door.' They must be taking her to their house."

"That doesn't seem smart," Sean said.

"They know I'm not there." Janey stared out the window, regret and guilt cutting through her that she'd left Tessa on Nantucket alone. Nothing bad was ever supposed to happen on Nantucket. It was a place of sunshine and tea parties. The best beaches in the world, and the Christmas Stroll, and pristine restaurants and high-end boutiques.

It was quaint and charming. Lovely and scented with flowers.

Janey had enjoyed her time there as a child, and then as an adult. No one enjoyed anything in their teen years, did they? She hadn't, and Janey tried very hard not to reflect on that time of her life.

"I'll call the police," Sean said. "How do you know all of this?"

"She called me, and I heard everything. I recorded the conversation."

"I'll get help out there."

"I'm getting a direct flight," Janey said, hurrying back to her desk and her laptop. "I'll text you the information."

"Okay."

They both paused, and Janey looked up from her screen. "Sean," she said. "Thank you."

"Of course," he said.

"Don't go there," she said suddenly. "I know I just said you needed to get there, but the Friedmans are obviously dangerous."

"What was Tessa doing?" he asked.

"Call the police first," Janey said. "I'll call you back."

"I have them on the other line," he said. "My secretary called. Give me a second." His end of the line went silent, and Janey started clicking on her laptop. Three minutes later, she'd found the earliest flight from New Jersey to Nantucket, and she had two hours to get to the airport and be at her gate.

She put the phone on speaker and picked up the carryon she hadn't fully unpacked yet.

"They're on their way," Sean said, and Janey gave an audible sigh of relief.

"Thank you," she said. "My flight is in two hours. I'll be on the island in three."

"I'm on my way out to the Point," he said. "I'll keep in touch."

"Text or call me with everything," she said. "Please, Sean."

"I will," he promised, and the call ended.

Janey sighed, because she hadn't left Nantucket on the best of terms. Not with Tessa. Not with Sean.

She didn't want her last words to her sister to be "I'll figure it out."

Tessa had said, "I don't want to go next door with them." She'd asked for help.

That couldn't be the end.

Janey was going to help her, and she took a moment to press her eyes closed and pray. *Please protect her until help arrives. Please.*

Bobbie had done something to make Tessa cry out in pain. She'd threatened her by saying she didn't want anything to happen to the brand-new floors in the cottage. Bobbie had said Tessa had something she wanted.

"What is it?" Janey asked, tossing in a pair of shorts without even looking at them. She added socks, a pair of sandals, and dashed into her bathroom to get a stick of deodorant.

She seized in front of the mirror. "A trunk. Bobbie had said she would sit with Tessa next door while Riggs returned to the cottage to look for the trunk."

She blinked rapidly, her own dark eyes looking back at her. "And he said…"

He'd said he didn't think Lydia would keep stacks of hundreds in the trunk at the cottage.

If not, then where?

"Did we come across a trunk?" she asked herself. There had been a cedar chest, but they'd donated that to Good Will. There hadn't been any money in it.

"No time," she whispered, and she hurried back into the bedroom. Tossing in the deodorant, she told herself she could buy anything else she needed on the island, and she zipped up the suitcase.

She tapped on her app to call a car, and then she texted Rachel that there was a major emergency on Nantucket, and she needed to return immediately.

Her daughter called as Janey went out onto the front porch. "Mom, what's going on?"

"Aunt Tessa is in trouble," Janey said, looking up and down the street for her cab. "I have to go back, and I know you're off this weekend, and I'm so sorry." She and Travis had gone to Atlantic City for the weekend to visit Cole and McKenna.

"It's fine," Rachel said. "I'll call Sydney. She'll come take care of the cats."

"Thank you," Janey said as a dark blue car rounded the corner. "I'm headed to the airport now, and I'll keep you updated."

"Is she okay?" Rachel asked, her voice wavering. "Like, is she in the hospital? Was there an accident?"

"I don't know all the details yet," Janey said. "I got a

weird phone call where she said she needed help. Don't worry, baby. I've got the police on their way, and I'm going right now."

"Okay," Rachel said. "I'll tell Cole. Should we call Uncle Ron?"

"I will," Janey said, towing her suitcase down the steps as the car came to a stop in front of the house. The driver got out, and Janey said, "I need to go. I love you so much. Tell Cole I love him."

"We love you too, Mom," Rachel said. "You're scaring me."

"I'm okay," Janey said, though she wasn't sure if she really was or not. She had no idea what the cottage on Nantucket held for her. What she'd find there scared her too. "I love you guys."

"Call me as soon as you know anything else," Rachel said, and Janey let the driver take her suitcase. Her daughter was so good and so kind, with a big heart. She was simply afraid of becoming an adult, and she had no idea what she wanted to do with her life. Janey could relate, and she loved living with her daughter despite Rachel's graduation from high school a couple of years ago.

She slid into the back seat of the car and said, "I need to make a flight in less than a couple of hours. Can you hurry, please?"

"Yes, ma'am," he said. "Newark? La Guardia?"

"La Guardia?"

"I'll do my best."

The airport sat thirty minutes from Jersey City, and then she had security to deal with. She looked out the window, her stomach one giant knot. She couldn't do anything more than she'd done.

Except pray.

Chapter Fifty-Two

J aney had to wait for another plane to leave the gate before hers could pull in. She had to wait for all those in front of her to disembark. She had to wait for a cab despite calling one the moment she landed.

Darkness had covered everything, and Janey couldn't *see*. She hated not being able to see.

After forty-six years of life, some of which had not been all that kind to her, Janey had learned an inkling of patience. It had abandoned her today, and by the time the elderly man driving her cab turned onto the lane where the cottage sat, Janey's scream sat in the back of her throat, a centimeter from her vocal cords.

"Oh, dear," he said in a voice that indicated he'd smoked heavily for a lot of years. "I don't think I can get down there."

No less than six police vehicles crowded the street, each with their spotlights on, blue and red lights flashing in the darkness. One had been parked in front of each house on the street, with probably three in front of the little blue cottage Janey had been visiting her whole life.

"It's okay," Janey said, reaching for her purse. "I can get out here." Even as she spoke, an officer approached the vehicle. He held up his hand as she opened the door.

"Ma'am," he said. "Get back in the car."

"I live here," she said, ignoring his instructions. "That's my—"

"You can't go into any of these houses. This area of the beach is closed."

"My sister has been taken," she said, and that got the officer to cock his head. "From the blue cottage on the end there. Sean Masterson called the police, because I was on the phone with my sister when Bobbie and Riggs Friedman abducted her."

"Come with me," the officer said, starting to turn away from the cab.

"I need my luggage."

He moved to the trunk, and the driver opened it for him.

The trunk.

Lightbulbs flashed in Janey's mind. Little snatches of conversation she'd heard on the phone while Tessa had been passed out or on the way there.

You come back here and start looking for that trunk.

I really don't think Lydia kept stacks of hundreds in a trunk here at the cottage.

Her heart pounding, Janey looked down the lane to the

cottage. Men and women in uniform moved up and down the sidewalk, casting shadows through the bright spotlights. They went up to the porch and inside. She didn't see anyone going toward the garage, which sat in darkness, where Tessa had assumedly parked their mother's dark green Mercedes.

Janey hadn't gone through the car. It had been in pristine condition, save for a bit of dust on the dashboard and a heavy layer on the exterior. They'd driven it through a carwash downtown and called it good.

To her knowledge, neither she nor Tessa had opened the trunk. They'd hardly bought any groceries while they'd been here, and when they'd left the cottage a few days ago to stay downtown for a bit, they'd tossed their bags in the oversized back seat.

"Ma'am?" the officer barked, causing Janey to jump. A gasp flew from her mouth, and she pressed one hand over her heartbeat as it accelerated. Tears flew into her eyes, and she looked at the taller man next to her. "What's your name?" he asked in a much gentler voice. "I'm Officer Flint West."

"Janey," she said, swallowing back her emotion and pressing against the hot liquid burning her eyes. "Forsythe. Tessa Simmons is my sister. We own that blue cottage at the end of the lane there." She didn't even stumble over the word *sister*.

Tessa *was* her sister. She had been for decades, and a paternity test and a single sheet of paper—no matter how fancy it was—couldn't change that.

He nodded, his dark eyes kinder now but still full of edges that allowed him to stay sharp amidst chaos. "Come with me. The Deputy Chief will have some questions for you."

Janey saw Nantucket Police painted on the sides of SUVs and cars, but also a couple with Nantucket Sheriff on them. She honestly didn't know the difference, but she did know the Sheriff was higher up on the scale.

She remembered attending a bicycle safety fair the Nantucket Sheriff's department had put on years ago, and she and Tessa had each gotten a new bike that summer. They'd thrown away those very bicycles when they'd cleaned out the garage. There had been so much junk in that garage. Everything from home improvement supplies to bins of beach toys, lockers full of moldy chairs and life jackets, and—

Another cry flew from Janey's mouth as she remembered the grimy trunk full of Mom's smaller gardening tools. Handheld shovels and rakes, nozzles for the hose, sprinklers, and even a half-used bag of fertilizer. They'd thrown that away, but Tessa had wanted to keep the other things despite the rust and cobwebs on them.

"They're Mom's," she'd said. "And they're not in terrible condition."

They weren't, because the trunk rested inside the garage, in a corner where the roof didn't leak. Not the shed, where all the other gardening and lawn tools were. Janey hadn't found the location of it odd last week. She did now.

Why didn't Mom put the trunk in the shed with everything else? There had been room. Could it have something valuable in it, buried beneath the mundane?

"Are you okay?" Officer West asked, and Janey moved her eyes to him. Everything seemed to be moving so fast and yet so slowly at the same time. She needed all of these people to leave so she could figure out what to do next. So she could go through the trunk of the car and the trunk of handheld tools she and Tessa had not moved into the shed yet.

Would Riggs think to look in the garage? How much time had he had before the police had arrived?

"Leo," Officer West called, and Janey realized he'd asked her a question she hadn't answered. She watched another tall man turn from a conversation with another officer, this one with a yellow lab at his side. The canine wore a police dog vest and seemed utterly unconcerned about the events unfolding around him.

"This is Janey Forsythe," Officer West said. "She says she owns the cottage there, and it's her sister who's gone missing." He looked at Janey and let go of her arm. She hadn't realized how much she was using it to anchor herself until his touch was gone. "Janey, this is Deputy Chief Leo Trivett. He's leading the investigation, alongside Sheriff Cochran."

"Get Anne over here, would you?" Leo asked, his eyes locked on his officer. He then extended his hand toward Janey. "Nice to meet you, ma'am. I understand you have a recording of the abduction?"

"How did you know that?" Janey asked, but she was already fishing through her purse to find her phone. And where had her suitcase gotten to? She caught sight of it near her feet, and she marveled at what her mind chose to think about in a crisis.

"Mister Masterson mentioned it."

"Of course." Some of Janey's numbness wore down, getting replaced by the professional air she'd perfected over the years.

"I need to hear it," Leo said.

"Have you found Tessa?" Janey asked, procuring her phone. Finally.

"No, ma'am," Leo said. "She wasn't in the cottage, nor next door, as Mister Masterson suggested she'd be. No one has seen her."

Janey noticed little groups of people clustered in front of houses, the red and blue flashing lights painting everything in strange tones through the darkness. The world had been narrowed to only what the police vehicles could illuminate, and everything else didn't seem to matter.

A woman a few inches taller than Janey joined her and Leo. "This is Anne Cochran," Leo said. "She's the Sheriff for Nantucket County."

Janey shook her hand, tired of the formalities and ready to give and get information. Tessa had been drugged over three hours ago. No one knew where she was. Every muscle in Janey's body strained, and she held up her phone. "Have you found Bobbie or Riggs Friedman?"

"No, ma'am," Anne said. "Their house was empty, same as yours."

"No signs of a struggle?"

She and Leo exchanged a glance. "Definite signs of a struggle," Anne finally said. "We found vomit in the cottage, but otherwise, everything seemed normal when police first arrived."

"We have it all on video as well," Leo said. "It's part of our new initiative for crime scenes. Then we don't miss anything. I have my photographers here too, and if there's any clue—no matter how small—we'll find it."

He nodded to Janey and then down the lane. "I noticed you have security cameras on your cottage. Can we access that feed?"

Janey noticed that he did not assure her they'd find Tessa. She handed him her phone. "There's an app that will show you the security tapes. It records any time there's movement." She took a deep breath, because she hadn't thought to check that, as the cameras were still so new.

"I also have the recording of Tessa's call. It took me a couple of seconds to figure out how to record, so I missed some of the beginning."

"Do you remember it?" Anne asked, reaching for the pen she'd tucked behind her ear. She'd pulled her dark hair into a tight ponytail, and she wore more gear around her waist than Janey had ever seen. She must have an incredibly strong back and core to be able to hold the guns, radios, and pouches who who-knew-what in them around her waist.

She plucked a notebook from one of those pouches, just like detectives did on TV.

"Uh, let's see where it started," Janey said. She really didn't want to listen to the conversation again, though she'd been tempted to do so on the flight here.

Her stomach shook, reminding her that she wasn't a police officer. She was a saleswoman, and saleswomen didn't deal with abductions and syringes and trunks full of cash.

She didn't know the dirtier side of Nantucket, with its public lewdness or public drunkenness. All towns had their problems, but Nantucket was generally safe. Everyone loved coming here to visit, and things worked like a well-oiled machine.

Beach permits and fishing licenses could be obtained online. The miles of walking paths were maintained. The beaches never had trash on them.

She tore her attention away from the pristine life that existed in fairytales and to her current situation. She tapped on the recording she'd made and closed her eyes.

Chapter Fifty-Three

"...Look a little gray," Bobbie said.

"I haven't eaten," Tessa said. "I got really engrossed in this article Ryan sent me, and I went to Boston for some shopping today, and I'm not even sure what we have in the house."

A pause, and Janey let Anne take the phone from her without opening her eyes. The whole world swayed in this sea of blackness, and Janey just wanted the tide to take her out, and push her back in once everything was settled. Once everything had gone back to normal.

"What are you and Riggs up to tonight?" Tessa asked.

"Oh, nothing," Bobbie said. "I made fish stew. You should come next door and eat, Tessa. You don't look good."

Another pause, and Janey could only imagine the thoughts running through her sister's mind in that few moments.

"I'm really tired," Tessa finally said. "We stayed down-town last night, and the bed was *terrible*."

"The beds here can't be that great," Bobbie said, and something switched in her voice. Janey cocked her head, listening harder.

"They're not bad, actually." The phone's speaker rustled, indicating Tessa had moved.

Janey opened her eyes, and the world stilled. "She put the phone in her pocket," she said. "That's why there's that scuffling. I think she moved at that point."

Both Anne and Leo nodded, and the Deputy Chief stepped in closer, leaning his head down as if to hear better.

A squelching sound came through the recording, and Leo looked at her again.

"I think that was the refrigerator opening," Janey whispered, because she knew what came next. Her hands shook no matter how hard she pressed her palms together.

Leo stopped the recording, but Janey had already heard the cry of pain that would come from her sister's mouth in only a few seconds. Her near-perfect memory was a blessing and a curse. In times like these, Janey just wanted to forget. She'd give anything to be able to forget.

"She doesn't need to hear this," Leo said quietly. "Janey, I'm going to give you to my best sergeant. He's going to ask you some questions while Anne and I listen to the rest of this, okay?"

"Do you remember what came before this recording begins?" Anne asked, shooting a look at Leo. He ignored her and lifted his hand in the air, as if indicating to a waiter he'd like his check now, please.

Janey closed her eyes again. "Yes," she said slowly. "I was at home, working. Tessa called, and I almost didn't answer it. See, we hadn't left things on the best terms, but I'd spoken to her earlier that day."

That day. It was still today. Her conversation with Tessa just after lunch felt like a lifetime ago.

"She'd gone to Boston, because she'd learned that Richard Friedman was dead. She went to his grave. She told me she was going to stay in Boston. I'm not sure why she came back here." Janey frowned, so many questions piling on top of one another now.

You'll ask Tessa when you see her, she told herself. She refused to believe she wouldn't see, hug, and talk to her sister again. Clinging to that hope, she continued. "I answered, and Tessa was already whispering. She asked if I could hear her. I said yes and asked what was going on. She didn't explain anything. She asked me if I could record the conversation and keep the line open. I said I'd figure it out, and she said 'gotta go.'"

Janey opened her eyes and met Anne's dark ones. They harbored fire, and Janey liked her spirit. "There was quite a bit of rustling, and I'm assuming she put the phone in her pocket. That's what it sounded like. Her voice wasn't as loud as before, but I could still hear her. She told someone she'd meant to call them back, but she'd been busy, and she had a headache."

She nodded to the phone in Anne's hand. "It was

Bobbie Friedman, because she asked Tessa if she'd eaten, and that she looked gray. That's where it starts."

"So Bobbie Friedman called your sister."

"I'm assuming so," Janey said. "I left Nantucket yesterday afternoon."

"You don't know what Tessa was doing in Boston?"

"Yes," Janey said, frustrated. "I do. She went there to see Richard Friedman's grave. See, we thought Riggs Friedman—Bobbie's husband—was Richard. But Tessa had found some documents at the library that said Richard had died in his twenties. She found the burial records, and she went to the cemetery."

Anne's eyebrows went up, but she didn't ask another question. Janey honestly couldn't explain this whole situation. It would take hours, and she currently stood out on the street in the middle of the night.

"Do you know where Sean Masterson is?" she asked, beyond exhausted. "I'm assuming I can't stay at my cottage."

"That's an active crime scene," Anne said. "So no, I'm afraid you can't stay there."

Janey nodded, pressing her lips together into a tight line.

Leo indicated an approaching man. "This is Sergeant Conway Rilleti. He's going to take you to Sean, and the three of you will talk. Okay?"

"Okay," Janey said, because what other choice did she have?

Leo nodded to James, and thankfully, there wasn't any

more hand-shaking Janey had to do. The sergeant led her down the street toward the cottage, but he veered down the side driveway of the last cottage on the right-hand side of the lane, which sat only two houses down into the cul-de-sac. Janey's house was three more down, on the other side of the road. But the beach embankment came right up against this driveway on this side of the road.

A man jumped to his feet, and out of the shadows, Sean said, "Janey. Thank God." He strode toward her, and Janey's tears overflowed at the simple sound of his voice. She let him gather her right into his arms, and she clung to him like he alone could save her from this nor'easter storm that would whip the waves into towers that would drown them both.

She cried into his shoulder for a few minutes, and then he stepped back without removing his hands from her waist. He reached up and stroked her hair back, and she finally got the assurance from someone.

"They're going to find her," he said kindly. "I just know it." He didn't smile, and Janey wasn't sure how she ever could again.

She nodded, and Sergeant Rilleti said, "I hate to do this, but it's best if we ask you all our questions as soon as possible after the incident. We usually get the best information that way."

Sean slipped his fingers through Janey's and tugged her gently down the driveway a bit further. "Come sit down. We'll tell him everything we know, and they'll find her, Janey."

She followed him to a bench that had been placed right against the house.

"The Lowers aren't here right now," Sean said. "My mother knew theirs, and I called to see if we could use their cottage for a few days. They said yes, and I'm just waiting for their management company to bring me the key."

"I can stay here tonight?" Her gaze slid to the right, where the Friedman's cottage glowed under the spotlights of at least two police vehicles. "I don't know about that."

"I'll stay with you," he said, squeezing her hand.

"We'll leave officers here with you too," Sergeant Rilleti said. "They'll be going through the two cottages for a while anyway."

Janey didn't want to think about what would be left behind once all the police left. Dirty bootprints and finger-print dust. The vomit in the cottage—would someone clean that up? Open drawers and cupboards, and the contents of closets spilled onto the floor.

She didn't say anything, because she didn't know what the future held. Sergeant Rilleti asked her to start at the beginning and tell him anything she thought was important —anything at all.

"No detail is too small," he said. "It could be something you think is insignificant that helps us figure out where they took her."

Janey cleared her mind of her questionable paternity. Her workload waiting for her in Jersey. The trips to the bank and the hotel and the house on Long Island.

She needed to focus on Riggs and Bobbie Friedman, and their role in her paternity, the business she'd conducted in the city, and why they wanted Tessa.

Janey exchanged a look with Sean. "I'm not sure where the beginning is," she admitted. "My mother died, and apparently, she had a lot more money and assets than anyone knew about."

Chapter Fifty-Four

Tessa Simmons moved back and forth, back and forth. The lulling, quiet, almost peaceful swaying nearly coached her back to sleep, but panic ran through her mind, telling her to struggle to stay awake.

Or get awake.

She blinked, trying to grasp onto the threads of thought wafting through her mind. She couldn't fall asleep again. The surface beneath her pitched to the right at a more violent clip, and Tessa's elbow hit a wall. She woke further, and her head cleared a little bit more.

Memories streamed through her mind, and the pinch of a needle in her neck sent a shiver through her body. Heat engulfed her, and sweat broke out along her forehead.

She sat up slowly, her pulse increasing as she remembered all that had happened in the cottage. A moan started low in her stomach, but she kept it contained.

Because someone was coming.

She quickly lay back down, the world around her spinning.

"…have to go back at some point," Riggs said.

"We can't," Bobbie said. "I'm telling you, we need to get to Miami."

"I've got the boat headed that way." Riggs's voice came so close that Tessa's muscles seized. "I've never driven this yacht, and she's not used to this speed, I can tell."

He touched her forehead, and it took every ounce of willpower Tessa had not to move. Not to reach out and grab his hand, bend it back, and demand they take her home. "She's still out," Riggs said. "I can't believe you knocked her out so completely. It's been hours, Bobbie."

"She'll be fine," Bobbie said. "She'll wake up soon, and then we'll have to decide what to do with her."

"What if she's not fine?" Riggs hissed. "We weren't going to hurt them, and now we've stolen a boat too."

"They've been nothing but difficult." The sound of Bobbie's voice moved away from Tessa. "We didn't even have time to search that blasted cottage."

Riggs said something after her that Tessa couldn't catch.

After the silence had settled, and the boat swayed back and forth for several long moments, Tessa sat up again. Every second that passed brought more awareness. She looked around the room where she lay, most of it shrouded in darkness. A night light shone orange from the direction of what looked like a galley bathroom, and Tessa put her feet on the floor and stood.

Giving herself a moment to see if she could stay steady, Tessa then padded across the room to that orange light and stepped into the bathroom. She found a cup there on the tiny sink, and she grabbed it. After filling it, she gulped cool water, then splashed some on her face too.

The fogginess in her head cleared more and more, and only a minute later, Tessa felt ready to tackle her most pressing issue: getting off this boat.

She had no idea where she was. She didn't know what time it was. She didn't even have shoes on her feet, and she couldn't remember if she'd had them on at the cottage or not.

"Doesn't matter," she muttered. "Get off the boat. Shoes can come later." She reached into her pocket, but her phone wasn't there. Bobbie or Riggs had probably found it in her pocket and gotten rid of it.

She hoped Janey wasn't worrying too much, though she probably was. She'd at least called the authorities, as Bobbie and Riggs hadn't had time to search the cottage. They hadn't found what they wanted.

The boat pitched again, and Tessa fell to her knees. A grunt came from her mouth, and the moment she was able, she looked toward the direction Bobbie's and Riggs's voices had gone. A door sat across the room, and as far as Tessa could see, it was the only way out of here.

She got up and made her way to it, pressing one hand against the wood. The vibrations from the water filtered through her fingers, and she took precious seconds to listen. She couldn't hear anything, and she finally dared to crack the door.

Again, she paused and listened.

Again, nothing.

She stepped to the side of the doorway and peered through the four-inch gap, hoping to see what lay beyond. A narrow hallway, that she could tell. Light spilled onto the floor, and Tessa nudged the door open a little farther.

She could span the hall in only three steps, and she did so quickly. Stairs went up, light touching just barley kissing the bottom one.

Tessa took a deep breath and went up, each step painstakingly slow, her ears straining to hear something. Anything.

She heard nothing.

At the top of the stairs, she paused, mostly because the sound of her heart pounding in her ears needed to be quieted before she could go on. The low murmur of voices came from her left, and that prompted Tessa to go right.

Another few steps got her topside, and Tessa scanned the landscape. Darkness stretched in every direction, and she hated the ocean at night. It sucked color from the world, drawing it deep below the surface and refusing to let it go.

The moon wasn't nearly as powerful as the sun, and while the silver light charmed her when she caught it dancing through the slats of her blinds in her bedroom, she did not like the way it undulated on the tips of the waves before getting sucked under.

Nothing to the right. She needed to see lights upon the shore. She'd jump over and swim if she had to. The water wouldn't be warm, but it shouldn't be too cold either.

But she wasn't leaving this vessel if she didn't have another destination in mind.

You can't go to Miami, she thought. If she did, she didn't think anyone would ever find her again.

For one terrible moment, she wondered if anyone would even care. Ron had someone else now. Ryan didn't seem to care if he spoke to her or not. She had a few friends at the library that may miss her.

She had Janey.

The thought of her sister grounded Tessa, though she wasn't anywhere near solid ground.

She turned to her left and went to the railing on the boat. Lights winked in the distance, and Tessa had no idea how far away they sat. That was another thing about night-time on the ocean—it obscured distances in a horrible way.

Voices sounded behind her, and Tessa had less than a second to decide. She climbed up on the railing and over it, hearing Bobbie say, "...find her."

Before they could catch sight of her, she jumped.

She barely had time to pull in a breath before she hit the water, and shock hit her like a lightning bolt. The boat had been taller than she'd thought. The water colder than she'd estimated.

She'd gone under much farther than she'd imagined, and it seemed to take a very long time and plenty of effort to get back to the surface. She finally broke free, gasping and coughing. Part of her brain told her to be quiet, while the other part told her to do whatever she must to keep breathing.

She wiped her hair out of her face, her feet kicking to keep herself aloft. Salt water went in her mouth again, and she heard a shout from somewhere outside her awareness. Bobbie and Riggs might know she'd jumped, and she quickly rolled to lie on her back.

Floating, she checked over her shoulder to see where the lights on the shore had gone. "Straight...ahead..." she gasped, still trying to catch her breath and settle the quaking in her lungs.

She began to flipper her feet, moving closer and closer to the shoreline.

Or so she thought.

A very long time later—hours if Tessa truly thought about it—she finally felt her feet touch sand. Relieved and exhausted she turned over and knelt as the waves broke around her.

Tears came to her eyes, and she repeated the same phrase she'd been saying since the moment she'd began kicking toward shore. "You can do this, Tessa."

She looked up, found the strength to stand up, and she walked up the beach. She needed to figure out where she was, what time it was, and where she could find a phone.

Chapter Fifty-Five

Janey didn't think enough coffee existed to revive her energy levels. She'd been up for a couple of hours, the TV flickering in the darkness as it started to turn gray. She sipped her lukewarm coffee, but her stomach had started to boil, and she'd have terrible heartburn that day.

Only one of a series of mistakes she'd made recently.

Sean had stayed in the cottage on the lane with her, but in a separate bedroom. She'd wanted to curl into his strength and take it as her own, but Janey needed to rely on herself. She couldn't go running to the closest man—no matter how handsome and how employed—when things went wrong.

Been there, done that.

She finished her coffee—her third cup—and got up to put the mug in the sink. Vowing she wouldn't have any more, she looked out the window. This cottage overlooked the beach too, but in a different way than the one Janey was familiar with. The swells of dunes sat in front of her, with a few twinkling lights to her right where The Lighthouse Inn, the dock, and a couple street lamps stood.

"Where are you, Tessa?" she whispered. Closing her eyes, Janey tried to reach out with her awareness. She'd once told Tessa that they were so connected that she could feel when her sister was in trouble. They'd been at the beach, and Tessa had gone out into the sound. Janey hadn't felt like getting wet and salty that day, and she'd stayed on the sand to sunbathe.

After only a few minutes, the hairs on Janey's arm pricked up, and she sat up, scanning for her sister. She couldn't see her. Even once she'd stood, Tessa wasn't anywhere to be found. The girls often came to the beach alone, so Janey had no one to help.

She marched straight out into the sound, finally catching sight of her younger sister floating away on her inflatable raft. She'd been caught in a current, and her ten-year-old arms hadn't been able to fight it.

Janey opened her eyes, because the story had a happy ending. She'd run down the beach and flagged down a fisherman just setting out in his boat. She'd pointed out her sister, and he'd rescued her.

Reunited, Janey had told her they were connected. That she'd felt something when Tessa had been in danger.

Why hadn't she felt anything last night? She almost hadn't answered Tessa's call.

"But you did," she told herself, leaving the kitchen. She walked toward the TV, not really focusing on it. All she could think about was that she and Tessa weren't full siblings, and therefore perhaps their connection wasn't as strong as she'd once believed.

She didn't want to think that. She wanted to have somewhere she belonged, and she'd always belonged with Tessa. They might not have always agreed, but they'd had each other. She didn't want to lose that.

Janey reached for the remote control to turn off the TV, studying it for a moment to find the power button. She pointed it at the television at the same time the anchorwoman said, "A woman was found washed up on Cape Cod this morning, bleeding and disoriented. Massachusetts police have been notified, and while they're not saying, it could be the same woman who went missing from Nantucket Point yesterday evening, she does fit the description put out by the Nantucket Sheriff's Department."

The blonde turned to her co-anchor. "What are they saying, Paul?"

"No official word from the police department yet," he said, turning his attention to the cameras again. Janey would've turned this off had it simply been speculation about where Tessa had disappeared to. That was all the late-night news had been. Horrible rumors that Sean had finally clicked off before taking Janey down the hall to the master suite.

But Tessa had been found.

Janey let her arm drop to her side, not quite daring to believe it. Why hadn't the police called? Didn't they have an officer right out front? One quick call on the radio, and he could come tell her the good news. Right?

Maybe Tessa's not alive, she thought, and that caused her to sink heavily onto the couch while Paul the anchorman outlined the situation on the Point last night. He actually got most of the story right, and then he threw the story to a woman named Teresa, who stood on the beach in a flowery shirt.

"The woman was found on a bench on this beach along Cape Cod's southwest end," she said, starting that slow walk reporters did. "She was wet, with cuts on her feet, and the couple who found her said she wasn't making any sense. They called the police, who don't believe she's a danger to the public or anyone else. Once they know her identity, they say they'll contact the family." She looked like this story would make or break her career, and as she said, "Back to you in the studio, Paul and Linda," Janey turned off the TV.

Every hair on her arms had stood up. "That woman was Tessa."

Just like she'd once marched out into Nantucket Sound to find her sister, Janey strode toward the front door of the cottage, fumbled with the lock until she released it, and continued out onto the porch. A police cruiser sat in the driveway, and as the sun continued to brighten in the sky and lend sight to the day, Janey could see the man's face behind the wheel.

He looked up as she crossed in front of the car, and he

got out as she rounded the corner. "Ma'am," he said. "What's going on? Have they contacted you?"

"I think she washed up on Cape Cod," she said. "There was a story on the news." She cinched her arms across her chest, feeling a bit foolish to be outside in her billowing robe and bare feet. She normally didn't present herself this way.

Officer Bayless frowned. "I'll call over to the Chief."

"Thank you."

"Come sit in the car," he said, indicating the other side.

Janey did, noticing the gravel beneath her feet for the first time. She walked with a much more hesitant step to the passenger side and slid into the seat. Officer Bayless was already on the radio, and he said, "I'll tell her."

He looked at Janey, his eyes wide and sparking with an emotion Janey couldn't identify. If she'd known him better, she might classify it as hope. Laughter. Positivity? Something.

"They think the woman found on Cape Cod is your sister," he said. "The Sheriff is on her way to the island now, and the Chief is coming here. They'll do a video call, and hopefully we can make a positive ID."

Relief rushed through Janey, and tears pricked her eyes. "I know it's her already."

"How?" Officer Bayless asked.

"I can just feel it," Janey said, sniffling as she wiped her face. She looked the officer straight in the eyes. "She's my sister."

Chapter Fifty-Six

Deputy Chief Leo Trivett looked like he'd been up all night. Janey knew the feeling, and she hoped this would all be over soon. Then he could go home to his family, and she could be reunited with Tessa. She needed to talk to her, and not just about this abduction. She needed to know what Tessa had been doing back at the cottage, and she needed to know if Bobbie and Riggs had found anything there.

She paced in the small cottage that felt so foreign, waiting with the Chief for Anne Cochran, the Sheriff, to call. Sean sat in a chair facing the street, a cup of coffee in his hand that he didn't drink from.

Janey could admit she was glad she didn't have to go through this alone. She'd called her children last night, as well as Ron, and they were all on their way to Nantucket this morning. She gripped her phone, because she hadn't called Milford.

She honestly didn't know what she wanted. With every-thing that had been going on over the course of the last month—really since Mom's death—Janey had shouldered it alone. Milford traveled for work a lot, and she only involved him in her personal life when it meshed well.

That said something to her, but she wasn't sure what.

She did know she was terrified to be alone. Alone in the world without a blood relative—without Tessa. Alone in the world without someone to call and kiss at night. Alone in the world with only her job for company, and a boss she knew superficially to get tea with.

She wanted *more*, but she feared she'd been going after all the wrong things trying to find it.

"When do you think she'll arrive?" she asked Chief Trivett. Anything to get her mind to stop and her nerves to settle.

"Should be soon, Janey," he said, glancing up from his device. "I'm just going over all the notes. Looking at public records. Did the Friedmans have a boat?"

"I suppose," Janey said, frowning. "How else would Tessa have ended up on Cape Cod?"

"A fishing boat? A yacht?"

"I have no idea. Not a yacht," she said. "I've never seen a boat that big at their place. Riggs pretended like he fished, but I only ever saw him from the dock."

Chief Trivett nodded, a concerning line appearing between his eyes. He studied his device again. "And we don't know Richard's real name?"

"I don't," Janey said. "I have to assume Bobbie's is hers."

"There's no boat in her name," the Chief said. "Or any Friedmans."

Janey turned away from him and walked toward Sean. She hesitated when she reached him, but when he looked up at her, such softness and concern in his expression, she put her hand on his shoulder. "Where could they have gotten a boat?"

"You said they didn't have much money," he said.

"They were older than Mom," Janey mused. "Retired for years. I haven't been here in a while, but no, I don't think they had enough for a yacht or a sailboat."

"And you wouldn't really sail to Cape Cod," Sean said. "It's thirty miles. You don't do that in a fishing boat either."

"What about Viola Martin?" Janey asked, pieces clicking together inside her head. "She had a big yacht at her place."

Sean got to his feet as he set his coffee cup in the windowsill. "She did?"

Janey spun toward Chief Trivett. "What about Viola Martin?" She strode the few steps to the officer. "She had a boat when I went to visit her a week or so ago. Or two weeks." She pressed one hand over her pulse, which raced through her chest. "She had a big yacht parked on the side of her garage."

"Viola...Martin," Chief Trivett said, typing the name

into whatever he was looking at. A few moments later, he looked up. "Yes, she has a boat."

"Riggs had threatened her," Janey said. "She told me he kept coming around and trying to get her money. She had people looking into him."

The Chief lifted the radio from his shoulder. "All units, who's closest to the Wainscott neighborhood?"

Crackling came through the speaker, and then only silence. "Unit two-seven, Officer Gillford and Officer Barnes," a man said. "We're a couple of minutes from Wainscott on the south side of the island. Come back?"

"I need you to check at 3745 Church Drive," the Chief said. "We're looking for the owner, Viola Martin, and a boat or a yacht on her property."

"It was a yacht," Janey said, seeing the hulking shape beneath the tarp. "Covered up, parked beside the garage. She had a man living there with her. A younger guy. A butler or assistant of sorts. His name is Miles."

The Chief relayed all of that information, his dark eyes bright with hope now. "If they took this boat, we can alert the Coast Guard from here to Europe," he said. "It's registered, with distinct markings."

Janey nodded, not quite daring to be as hopeful at the Chief. She clenched everything tight inside herself as she folded her arms and turned toward Sean as he stepped to her side. His hand slid along her back and rested on her hip, and she leaned into his tall strength.

She wanted to pace to get out some of the nervous energy accumulating inside, but she wanted to be right beside the Chief when his officers came back with news from Viola's house.

Her phone rang, and she glanced at it to see Dale's name on the screen. Her stomach tightened, and she looked at Sean.

"Answer it," he said. "He's probably heard something about Tessa and is worried."

She nodded and took a few steps away before swiping on the call. "Hello, Dale," she said.

"Joan just got a call from Margo Michaels," he said. "They still live on the island though they've retired from The Lighthouse Inn, and she said there's something going on with Tessa?"

"Yes," Janey said.

"Joan is so upset, she can't speak clearly enough to tell me," Dale said in a near-whisper. "Is she okay?"

"She's been abducted," Janey said, her voice surprisingly strong. She often shocked herself with how calm she could be, but she never knew if she'd teeter one way or the other. She lived on the edge of a knife, a breath away from a perfect presentation or a blink away from a complete breakdown. "Riggs and Bobbie knocked her out and took her somewhere. We're waiting to hear if the woman that was found on Cape Cod this morning is her or not."

"Dear Lord," Dale said. "No wonder Joan is beside herself."

Janey cocked her head. "Why would Joan be beside herself?" she asked. "She hasn't spoken to Tessa in years. I haven't seen her since Dad died and you two left Nantucket."

"Janey, there's something I didn't tell you," Dale said, his voice heavy with regret.

"Janey," Sean said, and she spun back to him. "They've arrived at the house."

"I have to go," she said to Dale.

"Wait," he said.

"Chief," came through the radio. "It's Anne Cochran. We're with the woman. Are you ready to transmit video?"

"Unit two-seven," came through immediately after that. "We're approaching the garage door, which is ajar. There's something wrong here. Requesting back-up of at least three units."

"There's blood here," another officer said.

"No sign of a yacht," the first officer said. "Though there's definitely evidence that there *was* a yacht here."

"There's a man down," the second officer said, her panic plain even over the radio. "We need medical."

"Chief Trivett?" Sheriff Cochran asked.

"Janey?" Dale said over the phone.

Chief Trivett looked at Janey, his eyes wide.

She said, "I'm putting you on speaker," to Dale, and then said, "Get back-up to Viola's house and let's get this video call going while your officers figure out what happened on the south side of Nantucket."

Chapter Fifty-Seven

"A n ambulance is on the way to 3745 Church Drive," the radio chirped.

"Unit one-four en route," a man said.

"Unit oh-seven is five minutes out," another said.

"Unit two-six is on-scene," one more said.

"Anne," Chief Trivett said. "We're ready for the video."

"Calling," she said, and his phone went into a medley that sounded like a merry Christmas tune. He swiped and held up the phone so they could all see the Sheriff.

"We've arrived at the station on Cape Cod," she said briskly. "The woman is in custody and being taken care of. The detectives say she's disoriented and in some state of shock, as she won't stop shivering. They've called medical, but she's refusing treatment. She keeps saying 'Miami, Miami,' and then she'll go silent."

Janey's heart clenched. She pulled in a breath and held

it. She had to close her eyes as the camera jostled and Anne went through a doorway. When she opened her eyes, the picture had settled, and she saw a barren room with a table in the middle of it.

A woman sat in a chair, and as Anne sat across from her, she came into focus.

"Tessa," Janey blurted out, and the dark-haired woman looked up from where she studied the tabletop. "Tessa, it's Janey. What happened?"

Something lit in Tessa's eyes, and she reached for the phone. The Sheriff let her take it, and Tessa peered right into the device. "Janey?"

"Tessa, you're okay," she said, tears flowing down her face. "You're okay now. You need to tell them everything so they can find Riggs and Bobbie."

"Miami," Tessa said. "They're going to Miami."

"What else can you tell us?" the Sheriff asked. "Were you on a boat?"

"Yes," Tessa said, still staring at Janey. "A boat."

"Did they hurt you?"

"My head hurts," she said, her face crumpling. "She injected me with something."

"She needs to be in a hospital," Janey said angrily. "Why is she at the station? Get her to a hospital and figure out what they injected her with." She spun to Chief Trivett. "Right now."

"Anne," he said.

"They're calling now." Scuffling came through the call,

and the phone jostled again. "It's best if we talk to her as soon after this as possible."

"Let me talk to her," Janey said, taking the phone from the Chief. "Give her the phone again."

The transition was made, and Janey said, "Tessa, listen to me, okay? We have to know everything that happened after they injected you. I got the whole conversation recorded after you called me, but that's it."

"I woke up…" Tessa got to her feet, not bothering to keep the camera on her face. Janey lowered her device too and looked out the window. The tree limbs swayed in the breeze as if everything were normal. Janey didn't understand how the sun had even dared to rise this morning.

"I woke up on a boat," Tessa said. "The water was fairly smooth, but I got tossed around a bit. Riggs and Bobbie came to check on me." Her voice lowered and turned more haunted. "Riggs seemed upset that Bobbie had injected me. He said the plan was never to hurt us."

"Good," Janey said. "What else can you remember?"

"She said they didn't have a chance to search the cottage."

"Good," Janey said.

"He said he had the boat pointed toward Miami, but it was an old boat—and they'd stolen it." She lifted the phone back to her face, and her eyes looked much clearer now. "He touched me, and it was so hard not to move. But I didn't. Bobbie said I'd wake up soon, and they'd have to decide what to do with me then. I knew I needed to get off the boat."

"And you did," Janey said, smiling at her sister through watery eyes. "How long were you in the water?"

"All night," Tessa said, pressing her eyes closed. "I just kept kicking and kicking. I stared up at the sky and I thought, don't stop. They're going to Miami. Don't stop. Miami." She shivered again.

Janey cried openly now as she said, "You did so great, Tess."

"My feet hurt," she said. "I was on a beach, but there were all these broken shells I didn't see. It was still a little dark, and I think I walked across a bed of coral too. Someone finally found me, and I'm so tired and so hungry." Tessa cried now too.

"We'll bring you some food," the Sheriff said off-camera. "Come sit down, dear. They're going to take you to the hospital right now."

"Janey," Tessa said. "You'll come, right? To the hospital?"

"I'm on my way," Janey said, desperate to keep Tessa on the line. But she knew the call would end any moment. Sure enough, the Sheriff took the phone back and centered it on herself.

"We'll take care of her," she promised. "She'll be in Mercy General on Cape Cod. I'll stay with her personally and make sure her feet are tended to and that all the right tests are run to find out what drugs are in her bloodstream."

"Thank you," Janey said.

"Cochran out." The call ended, and Janey handed the Chief his phone with numbness spreading through her.

She sank onto the couch in the living room and put her face in her hands. *You need to get to Cape Cod.*

The sofa beside her moved, and she sniffled as she looked at the Chief. "What's going on at Viola Martin's house?"

"They found a man in the doorway of the garage," he said quietly. "The paramedics are there, and he's alive."

Janey nodded, her mind not truly absorbing everything. "That has to be Miles."

"That's our assumption, but we'll confirm his identity before releasing anything."

"And Viola?" Sean asked, sitting on Janey's other side and handing her a cup of tea. She sipped it with shaking fingers, the warmth of it soothing some of the ragged edges inside her.

Chief Trivett didn't answer right away, and it took several second for the horror to sweep through Janey and make sense inside her mind. When it did, she gasped. "Did they kill her?"

"No," Chief Trivett said. "Well, actually, we don't know. She's nowhere to be found on the estate."

———

JANEY ENTERED THE CURTAINED OFF AREA TO FIND HER sister sitting up in the armchair against the wall. "There you are." She rushed at Tessa and bent to hug her. "How are your feet?"

"Good," she said, clinging to Janey. "Not as bad now that I have some painkillers and they got all the debris out."

"No stitches?"

"Nope."

Tessa didn't have an IV either, and she wasn't a patient. They'd done all the cleaning and dressing of her feet as an out-patient in the emergency room, and she was only waiting in this area for her blood results. If she had something serious come up, the doctors would need to decide if she'd need an antibiotic or something to counteract whatever Bobbie had put in her bloodstream.

"You seem more coherent."

"I am," Tessa said, tucking her hair. "It's amazing what food, water, and painkillers will do." She flashed Janey a smile. "Have they found Riggs and Bobbie?"

"No," Janey said. "At least not in the past couple of hours." It had taken her that long to get all the information from Chief Trivett that was available, and then get on a ferry to Cape Cod. "But they know—or at least suspect—that they're on Viola Martin's boat. They don't know where she is."

Janey looked at Tessa, watching for any sign of recognition. "Was she on the yacht with you, Tessa?"

"I didn't see anyone but Bobbie and Riggs," she said. "But I didn't explore everywhere. My goal was to get off the boat as fast as possible."

Janey nodded. "That's what I told the Chief. If you'd seen her, you'd have said so on the video."

"She's not home?"

"She's not. There are signs of forcible entry, and her assistant—remember that guy I told you about? Miles?—he was knocked out in the garage. He was on his way to the hospital on Nantucket when I left to come here. As far as I know, the police haven't been able to question him yet."

"So they could have Viola."

"Possibly," Janey said, though in her mind, it was the truth. They'd abducted Tessa after knocking her out. Gone to Viola's once they realized the cops were coming, and they'd stolen her boat, taken Viola with them, and knocked out Miles to get away.

Janey sighed just thinking about everything Bobbie and Riggs had done. And for what? Some money? They'd been waiting in that house next door for years and years. The cottage sat empty most of the time. Why hadn't they simply searched it while Mom was away at one of her other homes?

So much still didn't make sense.

"Sean hired a cleaning service for the cottage," Janey said. "They agreed to come today, so when you're ready to go, we can grab some lunch and make our way back to Nantucket."

"What about Riggs and Bobbie?" she asked, fear in her eyes.

"The cops are watching their place. They set up

cameras on the house across the street," Janey said. "They won't come back there anyway, Tessa."

"They really fooled us," Tessa said with a sigh as she leaned her head back in the armchair. "Mom loved Bobbie so much."

"Bobbie's behind everything," Janey said. "Right? Isn't that what you found out?"

"Yes," Tessa said.

"What were you doing at the cottage, Tess? You said you were going to stay in Boston last night."

"I went back," she said. "Because I needed to go through the photos." She started a tale that began with her at the library looking up the genealogy, then going to Boston to verify Richard Friedman's death, and then back to the cottage to sort through the pictures of Daddy, Bobbie, and Riggs.

"It was Bobbie—whose real name is Barbara—and Daddy that were step-siblings," Tessa said. "That's why they were so close. That's why Mom loved her so much. She was the sister Mom never had."

"And we don't know who Riggs is."

"I don't," Tessa said. "But Bobbie once went by Barbie, short for Barbara. I put all the photos in the drawer next to the fridge. I still need to go through the other stacks."

"We need to find whatever trunk they're talking about," Janey said. "I've had a couple of ideas about that."

"Yeah?" Tessa actually closed her eyes and yawned.

"Yeah." Janey regretted that her sister couldn't just lie down and sleep until tomorrow morning. *She can*, she told herself. *Get her back to the cottage, and you can go through the garage yourself.* "You rest. We can talk about it later."

"No, tell me." Tessa opened her eyes.

"Okay, remember that trunk we—" Janey cut off as the curtain got pushed aside again. This time, a man stood there. Janey rose to her feet, her eyes locked on him. "Ron." She cast a quick look at Tessa before she moved to stand in front of her. "What are you doing here?"

Chapter Fifty-Eight

"Really, Janey," Tessa said. "It's fine." She'd have to deal with Ron sooner or later. She'd rather it not be in a hospital emergency room, with only curtains separating her from other patients, doctors, and her sister. But she didn't get everything she wanted.

Her older sister glared at Tessa's husband. "I'm going to get a soda from the machine," she said. "That's how long you get to talk to her." She walked out of the curtained-off area, and Ron moved to pull the yellow, billowy drapes back into place.

He faced her, pure nerves on his face. "What did you tell her?"

"I haven't told her anything, actually," Tessa said. "I did ask her if her first husband had cheated on her and if she thought she could forgive that." She wasn't going to sugarcoat things. Not with him. Not when he'd been lying to her for five years.

And probably longer, she thought.

"What *are* you doing here?" she asked, a measure of exhaustion in her voice. She really had been awake all night long, and she wanted nothing more than to sleep.

"She called and said you'd been kidnapped. I got on the first plane out this morning."

Tessa could only look at him. Before his confession, she'd think him heroic and romantic. Right there, exactly when she needed him. "I'm fine," she said now, unable to look fully into his eyes. Hers kept flitting all around the room, and she finally fixed them on her hands in her lap. "Did you call Ryan?"

"Yes," he said. "He's the one who told me you'd been found here on Cape Cod. So I came here."

Tessa nodded, her mind firing all kinds of questions at her. *Who is she? Why is she better than me? Why couldn't you have just told me what you wanted?*

She asked, "Why, though? Why did you come here?"

"You're my wife," he said. "I love you."

Tessa simply shook her head. "I don't believe you."

"You don't think a man can love more than one woman?"

"No, Ron," she said, plenty of acid in her voice now. "I don't. And if that's what you wanted, you should've told me, so I could've made a decision that didn't leave me heartbroken and betrayed."

"Sometimes things—"

"Don't you dare tell me sometimes things just happen," Tessa said. "They don't. You *choose* to do certain things.

From that, you choose to feel a certain way." She looked at him then, hoping her eyes threw fire at him. By the way he dropped his chin to his chest, she thought they did.

"I don't want you here," she said in a much quieter voice. "I'm fine without you. I don't need you."

"Tessa," he said.

"Please, Ron."

"Is that it, then? We won't talk about it?"

"I don't need to talk about it," she said. "You told me everything I needed to know."

"Are you going to file for divorce then?"

"I haven't thought that far ahead," she said. "I've been a little busy, in case you didn't notice."

He nodded, his eyes hard marbles now too. "Okay. I'll go. You let me know what you want to do. I can clean out my stuff in the house in a few days at most."

"I'm sure you can," she said. "You hardly lived there."

"You can have the house, if you do decide you want a divorce."

Tessa bit back a sarcastic reply and simply nodded instead. Ron looked like he might say more, but in the end, he just nodded too, turned, parted the curtain, and walked away.

Fitting, she thought. He'd walked away from their marriage and life together a long time ago. She'd been the one clinging to everything for the past several years. But knowing that didn't make the betrayal sting any less, and it didn't make the tears dry up any faster.

———

Tessa stood back while Janey bent to lift the garage door. She'd endured dozens and dozens of questions, first from the Sheriff and then the Chief of Police. She'd answered everything she could for Janey and Sean once they'd returned to the cottage.

She'd slept a lot the second day, and today, on the third, she and Janey had blocked off their morning for one purpose: to find the trunk full of money Bobbie and Riggs had thought existed on this property.

Janey and Tessa had whispered in the dark about the things they'd been thinking about, and they had two possibilities. The trunk of the Mercedes, and the trunk of garden tools in the corner of the garage.

"Close the door behind you," Janey said, her voice almost getting whipped away by the wind. Sometimes the weather coming off the Sound wasn't as quaint as the idea of Nantucket, but Tessa loved the scent of the sea the breeze brought with it.

She followed her sister into the garage and reached for the rope connected to the door. Pulling hard, the door ground against the tracks and filled the space with a grumbling that Tessa hoped wasn't indicative of what they'd find this morning.

"Do you want to start with the car?" Janey asked.

"Sure," Tessa said. She just wanted to follow her sister's lead today. Her brain felt stuffed full of information, coffee, or painkillers, and she didn't want to lead the search today.

Janey opened the front door and pulled the lever to release the trunk. Tessa reached for it, her heart thumping like she'd find a dead body inside. She waited until Janey stepped to her side, and then she lifted the trunk lid and peered inside.

"It's empty," Janey said, bending down to look all the way to the back. There was nothing there. Not even a hint of lint or a speck of dust.

"Do you think there's a spare tire?" Tessa asked, her eyes tracing the outline of the felt-like rug that sat on the bottom of the trunk. She reached for the edge of it on her side of the car and pulled it back.

It didn't come easily, and Tessa frowned. "I think you're supposed to be able to lift this piece up." She tried again, and a ripping sound met her ears. She stopped pulling and looked at Janey. "It feels like it's been glued down."

They stared at one another, several statements being made without a single word coming from either one of them. Tessa slid her fingers further under the rug on her side while Janey reached for the edge of it on her side.

Pulling together, they ripped the rug off the bottom of the trunk.

Where the spare tire should be sat what one would expect to find—a spare tire. Disappointment cut through Tessa, cooling some of the adrenaline racing through her. "Shoot," she said. "I thought there'd be something here."

"Does this look like the right spare tire for this car?" Janey asked. She tried to remove it, but five bolts held it in place.

Tessa kept pulling on the rug, removing it all the way to the back of the trunk, which went quite far under the slanted back window. Suddenly, the rug came loose quite easily, and she stumbled backward a step or two before regaining her balance.

She'd heard something too. Something that had sounded like a plastic bag getting wrinkled.

She returned to the trunk and bent down, peering as far back as she could. "I can't quite see. Can you shine your flashlight back here?"

It took Janey a couple of moments to get her flashlight on, and when she shone it back into the trunk, she bent over too.

"Oh," Tessa said, holding onto the end of the word for a few long seconds.

"What is that?" Janey asked, her voice little more than a whisper.

Tessa didn't answer except to stretch toward the white plastic bag that had been revealed with the removal of the rug.

The plastic was thick and smooth, like the bags she used to mail packages to Ryan. This one certainly looked as if Mom had received something in it at the cottage, and she'd torn the perforated tab to get the contents out.

Dark gray duct tape kept the bag closed now, and Tessa straightened as she pulled the bag out. The contents of it shifted, and she knew instantly that she was holding stacks of money. "Janey," she said. "Feel this."

She gave the bag to her older sister, and the recognition lit Janey's eyes. "I'll get the garden shears." Tessa stepped over to the trunk in the corner with all the garden tools, and she pulled out a pair of rusted shears.

She handed them to Janey, who just stood there with the shears in her hand, looking down at the package she'd set in the trunk. The package was about three feet long and two feet wide, and only a single stack of bills high. Long and thin and easy to slide into a suitcase without anyone questioning anything.

"Open it," Tessa said.

Janey took a deep breath, and she pinched the corner of the package to make the first cut.

The scent of musty money filled the air, and five seconds later, Janey had the bag sliced open down the side, and stacks and stacks of bound bills spilled into the trunk of the car.

Janey panted as if she'd just run a race, and she didn't look at Tessa. They both stared at the cash, and Tessa's heartbeat sprinted through her body.

"How much do you think it is?" Tessa asked.

"I don't know." Janey started putting the money back in the bag. "I think we should leave it here for right now."

"Why?" Tessa asked, her fingers tingling and she hadn't even touched the money yet.

"I just don't know if we're secure yet," she said.

Tessa cast a glance to the closed garage door, wondering if they'd ever know what had happened to

Bobbie and Riggs. The boat had been found abandoned at a port in Maryland, and Viola Martin had been rescued. Alive, but a bit shaken up and definitely still a little bit under the influence of whatever drug Bobbie had given her.

She had not returned to Nantucket yet, but Janey had already said she'd go visit her as soon as she did to get more of the story.

Bobbie and Riggs were nowhere to be found, and police in Maryland were now coordinating with Chief Trivett as they continued to search for the couple.

Janey stepped back from the trunk and closed it. "Let's go through the gardening tools."

Tessa went back to the trunk, which she'd left open. She took out small hand rakes, hand shovels, a garden hose, and a bag of potting soil. Janey took something out for every item Tessa did, and soon enough, they'd filled the bench in front of the storage lockers on the side of the garage.

The scent of mold and damp earth and dust filled the air, and the items in the trunk seemed to go on and on. "This this is like Marry Poppins' bag," Tessa said, reaching for yet another pair of galoshes. "Why didn't we throw this stuff away?"

"You said you didn't want to," Janey said. "You being a gardener and all. You wanted to go through these things and keep what you wanted, since it belonged to Mom."

"Mm." Tessa pulled out another hose that shouldn't

have fit so easily in the trunk. "Oh, my goodness. This trunk goes right into the ground."

"What do you mean?"

"I mean, someone's dug a hole down through the cement and clear into the ground." She looked up and into her sister's eyes, her own wide as fear ran through her. "Come look."

Chapter Fifty-Nine

Janey stepped next to Tessa and looked into the trunk again. She was absolutely right. The bottom of the trunk had been removed, and the hose Tessa held in her hands had fresh dirt on it. Only a few items remained in the trunk, and Janey pulled a metal watering can from the side.

A cigar box fell down without the support of the watering can, and Tessa sucked in a breath. Janey did too, dropping the watering can on the cement at her feet. She flinched with the noise, but she'd already started reaching for the wooden cigar box that was about the size of a shoe box.

She lifted it out and stared at the top of it. CLARKE had been carved into the lid, and she lifted her eyes to Tessa's. "Daddy carved this."

"Looks like it," her sister said without moving her lips.

Janey lifted the lid, which wasn't locked, nailed shut, or

otherwise sealed closed. "There's money." Only a few stacks of hundreds this time, but still probably ten thousand dollars. She moved over to the bench in front of the lockers and sat down, balancing the box on her knees.

"This you can hide in your purse and take to a bank or something," she said. There was probably a quarter of a million dollars in the back of the trunk, but much less here. Certainly not the "millions" Riggs had indicated would be found here.

She lifted out the four bundles of money and handed them to Tessa. "There's something else here." She removed a legal-sized envelope from the box, her fingers shaking slightly.

"I don't know if I can take it," Tessa said.

"Hey, it's not a binder." Janey smiled at her sister as she took a seat next to her. She breathed and opened the envelope. Inside lay a single sheet of paper, and it appeared to be a map. "It's a map of the yard," she said. "Where Mom put her bushes and trees."

Janey frowned at the map, wondering why this was the most important item in the cigar box. Which had been inside the trunk, down inside the ground. Out in the garage.

"Why couldn't Mom just leave us a bank account with all the money in it?" she asked, shaking her head. "All of this could've been avoided."

"And Riggs and Bobbie would have it all by now," Tessa said. "She did what she thought she had to do to keep the estate safe."

Janey's phone rang, startling her, and she took it from her pocket to find Dale's name on the screen. "I've been avoiding him," she told Tessa.

"Answer it," Tessa said, taking the map from Janey.

Janey frowned, but she did what her sister said. "Hello, Dale."

"Janey," he said, and his voice was definitely somewhat more crisp than it had been in the past. "Where are you? At the cottage?"

Janey didn't want to say yes, but she had a feeling she better not lie. "Yes," she said. "Why?"

"Joan and I are here, and we need to speak to you and Tessa, if at all possible."

Janey got to her feet. "Here? Right now?"

"The cab just dropped us off," he said. "We knocked and rang the bell, but no one answered."

"We're out on the beach," she said. "We'll come in."

"Could we go in the house, by chance? Joan doesn't do well in the wind." He spoke in a much softer and quieter voice now, and Janey's heart wept for him.

"Of course. We put a new doorknob on the front door, and it has a code. It's 3-2-8-4."

"Thanks."

The call ended, and Janey turned to face Tessa. "Dale and Joan are here. Remember I said he had something to tell me?"

"Here?"

"I said we were on the beach." She glanced down the bench where all the tools sat. "Let's put that in the trunk

457

with the other money and go see what they want. We can try to make sense of it once they leave."

With that done, the trunk locked, and the garage closed tightly again, the two sisters went around the back of the garage to the beach side of the house and approached the cottage from the direction of the Sound. No one seemed to be watching for their approach, and Janey entered the house first to find Joan leaning back on the couch while Dale made coffee in the kitchen.

"Joan," Tessa said in a placating, professional voice, and Janey went to greet Dale.

"You should've said you were coming."

"I did, in one of my messages," he said. "Why didn't you answer?" He cast a glance toward Tessa and Joan in the living room.

"We've been dealing with a lot here," Janey said. She didn't have to explain anything to him, and she lifted her chin as if challenging him to ask her another question. He seemed to get the hint, because he simply got down two more mugs and offered them both coffee.

"No, thanks," Janey said, but Tessa accepted a cup. Janey perched on the edge of the love seat with Dale, and everyone looked at Joan.

"I just found out about Lydia," she said, her voice shaky. "I didn't know she'd died."

"A few months ago now," Tessa said gently. "I know you two were good friends."

"I've been so ill," Joan said. "I don't even know what day it is most of the time, especially with the treatments and medicines I'm taking. But I heard Dale on the phone a few days ago, and I realized she'd died."

She gave her husband a weak smile, and though she clearly had more to say, she didn't continue.

Dale returned his wife's smile. "Joan reminded me that the two of us were your legal guardians should your mother and father pass away while you were still minors." He looked between the two sisters. "And Joan remembered something Lydia had specifically asked her to do upon her death."

"Even now?" Janey asked. "We're not minors."

"No matter when she passed," Joan said, her voice half the volume it had been previously. "She told me who your father was, Janey, and she asked me to tell you once she'd gone."

The air in her lungs seized, and Janey had a hard time pushing it out to get more. "Who?" she practically gasped.

"It's not Riggs," Joan said. "Or Dale. Or Greg. It was a man she'd met on a weekend trip to Long Island."

"Long Island?" Tessa asked, looking from Joan to Janey.

Long Island, where Mom had a secret house on Shoreline Way.

"Yes," Joan wheezed. Her eyes drifted closed. "His name is Ryan Harper. He's still alive, I believe, and he still lives in Southhampton."

Janey opened her mouth to say something, but she had no idea what. Her brain misfired, and she ended up simply gaping at Joan.

"So Janey's father is not Riggs Friedman," Tessa stated, hope dancing in her dark eyes. Janey felt it moving through her too, along with a heavy dose of what she could only describe as relief.

"No," Joan said. "Lydia gave me a picture of your dad." She nodded to Dale, who reached into the inner pocket of his sports jacket. "She wanted you to have that too. She said he never knew about you, but that you should know."

Dale handed Janey a black and white photograph of a man with a strong jaw and a bright light in his dark eyes. She felt like she was looking into a mirror, recognizing the shape of her face in this man's, and the way her eyes crinkled the way his did.

"Thank you," she said quietly, not sure what to do with the information. Should she contact this Ryan Harper and reveal her identity to him? Why hadn't Mom told him about his own daughter? Had Daddy known?

Janey looked up at Dale. "Did you know about this man?"

"I did not." He shook his head. "Lydia went to Long Island a few times that summer. She said her step-sister lived there. She'd go for a day or two and come back. I never suspected anything."

Janey nodded and looked back at the photograph again. "Thank you," she said again, not sure what to do now.

"Would you like to stay for lunch?" Tessa asked, rising to her feet. "I can call The Glass Dolphin and order a delivery." She glanced at Joan, clear worry on her face.

Janey let her take over, because she couldn't think quite clearly enough at the moment to play the perfect hostess.

She now knew who her father was, and she had to figure out what to do about it.

———

"I'M REALLY SORRY, MILFORD," JANEY SAID, WATCHING THE waves come ashore only a few feet away. In a few hours, the tide would be up, and if she still stood in this position, the waves would cover her feet and rise to her ankles.

"I don't know who I am anymore," she said. "I need some time to myself to figure it all out."

"I understand," Milford said, but Janey wasn't sure how he could. She barely understood why she needed to break-up with him. She'd spoken true—she had no idea who she was.

Gregory Clarke's daughter.

Ryan Harper's.

Milford's girlfriend.

The perfect saleswoman.

Tessa's sister.

Sean Masterson's "special friend."

She didn't know who Janey Forsythe was, and she was tired of the other labels put on her.

The only one she was willing to keep at the moment was Tessa's sister. She knew that deep down inside her soul, and nothing that had happened over the past few weeks had or could change that.

Everything else was up in the air, and Janey needed time to let all the balls come down so she could examine them and make sense of them.

"I'm so sorry," she said, her voice breaking. "Maybe when I have things sorted, I'll be in a better place to be the girlfriend you deserve."

"Janey, you're a great girlfriend." Milford sounded frustrated, as he should be. He and Janey had been dating for about ten months now, and while it hadn't always been exclusive, they had gotten along really well.

"I'm sorry," she said again. "I just need some time."

"Take the time you need."

When the call ended, Janey let her hand fall to her side, and she allowed the wind to push and pull her caftan-style cover-up around her arms and legs. She took in a long, deep breath, closed her eyes, and held it. Blowing it out slowly, she tried to clear her mind as well.

With twenty minutes of meditation behind her, Janey turned back to the cottage. Dale and Joan had left yesterday afternoon after visiting for a few days, and Sean had stayed away and given the four of them time to talk, get answers, and make sure everything was clear between them.

She saw the lawyer walking toward her now, his head bent against the breeze as he came closer and closer. He wore a pair of black slacks despite the summer temperatures, and a pale blue shirt open at the throat. No tie right now, but he'd likely put one on before they arrived at Viola's house.

Janey started toward him, glad he'd agreed to accompany her to Viola's house. He sometimes heard things she didn't, and he thought of questions that didn't even cross her mind. Plus, she simply didn't want to go alone, and Tessa had gone to Long Island to talk to Esme and find out more about what Mom had done when she'd visited the pale green house on Shoreline Way.

Janey too had spent plenty of time on the Internet and in the genealogical archives of both Massachusetts and New York to learn more about Ryan Harper. His name was quite generic, but having a location so specific had helped her find out more about him.

The man was still married to the same woman he had been for the past fifty-two years, and he had three children—two daughters and a son.

His eldest daughter, Julia, was only six months older than Janey. He would've known his wife was pregnant with their first child when he slept with Mom, and she'd have known it too. Could that have been the reason why she hadn't told him? She didn't want to disrupt his life?

Mom had kept a lot of secrets, worried as she was about making sure everyone lived a peaceful, easy existence.

Janey actually disliked that about her, and she'd spent a couple of hours ranting at her mother as she walked up and down the sand out here at Nantucket Point Beach.

"Hey," she called as she got closer to Sean.

He lifted his head, a smile spreading across his handsome face. "Glad you're coming in," he said. "You said Viola hates it when people are late, and we're right on the cusp of about-to-be-late."

"I know," she said. "I'm coming." She smiled at him as she approached, and while she would've normally taken his hand, today, she didn't. She did like Sean, and she could see herself dating him easily. But she'd told Milford the truth, and she wasn't looking to hitch herself to another man right now.

They drove over to Viola's neighborhood in relative silence, and Janey wanted to ask Sean what he was thinking. He'd known her mother well, and she thought he might actually have some insight into Mom's life that Janey didn't.

She hadn't asked him yet, but it was definitely on her to-do list.

First, she needed to talk to Viola, and she glanced over to the garage where the boat had been before. A scar sat on the land where it had been parked, and Janey couldn't even imagine the scene that had gone down when Riggs and Bobbie had shown up to steal it.

"Come on, Janey," Sean said softly, and she tore her eyes from the detached garage. She let Sean guide her up the steps to the front door, where she rang the doorbell.

She wasn't sure who she expected to answer it, but it wasn't Miles, the man who the police had found unconscious on the ground. Her emotions surged as she took in the healing scrapes and cuts on his face.

"Miles," she said, throwing herself into his arms. "My goodness, how are you?" She grabbed onto his shoulders, seeing her own son and feeling all sorts of maternal over-protectiveness of him. "Are you okay? Tell me what happened."

Miles searched her face, a smile forming on his. "I'm okay, Miss Forsythe. They only kept me in the hospital for one day to make sure my vitals were strong. They are, and I'm healing up well." His accent was as elegant and strong as ever, and he stepped back to let them in.

"This is my friend, Sean Masterson," Janey said. "I said he was coming with me."

"Of course." Miles shook his hand and indicated the library where Janey had met Viola before. "She's waiting with tea. Can I get you anything from the kitchen before we begin?"

Chapter Sixty

Janey couldn't let go of Viola Martin. They wept together, and the images of Viola's black eye and bruised face would haunt Janey forever.

They finally separated, and Janey settled into the same chair she'd eaten lunch in previously.

"Start at the beginning," Janey said.

"Oh, that awful man showed up," Viola said, and none of her sass had been taken from her. She reached up to pat her hair, which looked as if she'd just gotten it set, and pursed her lips. "He wanted my boat, and I said no. This time, he had his terrible wife with him, and she told me if I didn't give her the key to her boat, she'd make sure I regretted it."

"She refused," Miles said. "Before I knew it, the blonde woman had plunged a needle into Miss Martin's neck, and she was falling to the ground. I rushed toward her, but I was too far away."

"Wow," Sean said, checking his phone, which he'd set on the table between them. He'd asked to record the conversation, and to Janey's surprise Viola had said yes.

"They made me carry her to the boat, and then they demanded the key." Miles wrung his hands. "I wasn't sure what to do, but the garage has a phone in it. I told them the key was in there, and I went to get it. Really, I was going to call the police. They attacked me from behind, and the last thing I remember hearing was Riggs saying he'd find the key and they'd be gone in minutes."

"Do you remember anything from the boat?" Sean asked, looking at Viola.

"Hardly anything," she said. "I was in an out of consciousness, and every time I woke, it seemed to be dark."

Janey wasn't going to get much information from her, but she didn't mind. "I'm so glad you're okay," she said, reaching over to pat her hand. "Did you ever meet someone named Ryan Harper?"

"Harper?" Viola's sharp eyes hooked into Janey's. "I don't think so, not with your family."

Janey had told Sean about the conversation with Dale and Joan, and he'd been helping her learn more about her father's family. "We found a record that said he lived here for a little while," she said. "Six or eight months."

"Where? In Wainscott?" she demanded, as if such a thing was absolutely preposterous. As if she knew every single person who'd ever lived in this old neighborhood for the past eighty years.

"Actually over on the west end of the island," Sean said easily.

"Oh, well, I don't know," Viola said.

Janey and Sean stayed to visit for a few more minutes, and then she and Sean left. On the way back to the cottage, Janey rolled down her window and let the summer air play with her hair. "I think Mom continued her relationship with Ryan Harper," she said. "That's why she had a house on Long Island. Did I tell you that the Harpers live only six blocks from the house she had there?"

"You didn't say that," Sean said, glancing at her. "What are you going to do? Are you going to go talk to him?"

Janey had been thinking about it for a couple of days, and she still wasn't sure. She lifted one shoulder in a shrug and extended her hand out the window to try to catch the air. She'd done this so often as a child, and she loved doing it while her daddy drove fast. Then the air would send her hand up and down, and she'd pretend she was an inchworm racing through the universe.

"Are you going to town today?" Sean asked.

"Yes," Janey said. "I need to get something for dinner tomorrow. Tessa will be back from Long Island, and we're having a big meal before I have to go back to Jersey for a little bit."

"Want to join me for dinner tonight after you get your groceries?"

"Sure," Janey said, smiling at him. Her chest squeezed slightly, as she hadn't told Sean about the money in the trunk of the car. She or Tessa had been driving to town every day to deposit more and more of the money, and the envelope in the trunk of the car was almost empty now.

The garden map still perplexed Janey, but she hadn't told Sean about it either.

Sean pulled up to the cottage and put his fancy car in park. Janey looked at him. "Sean," she said. "I have to tell you something."

He actually looked a little tired, but he said, "Okay."

"I'm not going to take the promotion at work. I actually put in my notice that I'm quitting."

Sean's eyes widened. "I don't…know what to say."

Janey smiled at him. She and Tessa had almost half a million dollars in the bank now, and Janey needed the time she'd spoken of to figure out what her next steps would be.

"I'm going to move to the island," she said. "Live in the cottage and see what life brings me next."

"You're kidding."

"I'm not." She looked out her window, and she could see the top of The Lighthouse Inn. "That inn right over there needs new caretakers, and I actually thought about applying."

"My secretary just told me he's moving with his wife to Boston."

Janey whipped her attention back to Sean. "Really?"

"You'd be an amazing addition to my office," he said.

Janey's heart pounded in excited anticipation, and while she'd never been terribly religious, this felt like God himself had opened a door and was beckoning for her to walk through it.

"Let's talk more about it tonight," she said, reaching for the door handle. "Travola's at seven?"

"I'll call and get a table right now," he said, tapping on the screen in his car.

———

JANEY SPENT AN HOUR THAT AFTERNOON LOOKING THROUGH the pictures Tessa had sorted. She got the map out and studied it, trying to see something on it that would tell her anything. There had to be something there, or why would Mom put it in an envelope in that cigar box?

She wouldn't be able to access it very quickly—certainly not as fast as simply tossing a bag in the back of the car and somehow sliding several stacks of cash into it before she boarded the ferry and left Nantucket.

The map showed the cottage, complete with the porch that went around two sides of it. The detached garage behind it. The flowerbeds along the back of the house, as well as the front. She'd bordered the sidewalk with beds too, and she'd drawn in circles for plants and bushes, almost all of which were gone now.

She'd planted three trees—two in the front yard and one in the back, besides the ones that were already there. Those were still there, with circular beds around the bases.

Janey and Tessa had cleared almost everything, because it had all become overgrown in the past few years. She looked to the left of the garage, realizing for the first time that the map continued on that side.

She peered at it, trying to figure out what the two rectangles on that side of the map could be. "I didn't even think the property went past the garage." She looked up from the map and toward the back wall of the house. A large window sat there, showing her the back yard and the garage beyond. "Bobbie and Riggs own that land."

At least, she thought they did.

Taking the map with her, Janey left the cottage and walked around it to the garage. She and Tessa had walked right past these drawn-in rectangles when they'd left the garage to come to the cottage from the beach side.

Nothing had been there.

Janey's pulse pounded into the back of her throat as she approached the corner. Not only was she a bit fearful about what she'd find there, she honestly didn't think it was their property. She didn't want to be caught on someone else's land, even if she didn't think she'd ever see Riggs or Bobbie again.

Her breath whooshed out of her body as she reached the corner, and Janey put one hand on the side of the garage before making the turn.

Nothing but grass, just like she'd remembered.

She frowned at the ground, scanning to find the property line. Out here, they were usually marked by utility lines, and Janey caught sight of it about fifteen feet from the back of the garage.

They did own this land, but she and Tessa had not taken care of the grass here. Riggs had been mowing it for who knows how long.

Janey walked toward the Friedman's house until she stood parallel with the utility box. She gazed at the side of their house, everything between her and it still and silent. No one would ever suspect that something bad had happened here, or that the cottage behind Janey had held so many secrets for so long.

Sighing, she turned around and faced the garage again. She blinked, seeing something from this position that she hadn't from the corner of the building.

The strip of grass closest to the garage was a different color than the rest of the yard. "It looks newer," Janey said, striding forward. It wasn't nearly as long as the rest of the lawn either, and the closer she got, the more it looked like someone had disturbed the land here.

"Buried treasure," Janey whispered, her muscles tensing with adrenaline. She looked down at the map, everything coming into focus now. Mom had buried something on this side of the garage and marked it on this map.

Janey went into the garage and found a shovel and a pair of gloves. Outside, she tried to judge the scale of the drawing to the real-life objects in front of her. The two rectangles definitely sat closer to the driveway end of the garage, not the beach side.

She started digging, and while she wasn't in the greatest shape and didn't regularly dig holes for fun, it didn't take her long to hit something hard with the blade of her shovel.

"My goodness," she whispered, stilling. The moment lengthened, turning more and more surreal by the moment. Her mom had literally buried money in the earth to keep it out of the hands of those she didn't want to have it.

She spun when she heard voices, and a scream gathered in the back of her throat when she recognized the first as Bobbie as she argued with Riggs, the second voice in the conversation.

Janey's brain commanded her to move, and she took the shovel with her as she darted around the side of the garage and pressed her back into it. She lifted the shovel as if she really possessed the inner strength to swing it at another human being.

Then she waited as the voices grew louder and louder...

Chapter Sixty-One

Tessa paid the driver and quickly got out of the cab. She faced the cottage, annoyance surging through her. "Why won't you answer your phone?"

She supposed Janey could be taking a nap—Tessa had been taking one every day since washing up on Cape Cod. Just because Janey hadn't spent the night kicking toward shore didn't mean the ordeal hadn't been exhausting for her. She'd been on the other end of the abduction, and she'd heard all the same conversations Tessa had.

She'd just reached the top of the steps when she heard someone yell from the direction of the back yard.

Her heart leapt into the back of her throat, and she paused for a moment. Maybe two. Her mind screamed at her to move, but in which direction Tessa wasn't as sure.

Then a woman's scream filled the peaceful summer air, and the sound of Janey's voice got her to move. She flew down the steps and around the cottage, yelling, "Janey? Where are you?"

The garage door was closed, but someone appeared at the corner of the garage.

Bobbie Friedman.

Tessa skidded to a stop, her fear paralyzing her right there in the gravel driveway. She couldn't breathe, and she couldn't think.

"I'm going to call the police." Tessa reached for her phone in her pocket.

"Janey said the same thing," Bobbie said, rolling her eyes. She turned her head. "Riggs, Tessa's out here."

Her husband took a few moments to appear at Bobbie's side, and his hair was disheveled and his chest heaved with his heavy breaths. He wore a wild look in his eyes, and she didn't like how it went with Bobbie's murderous glare.

"They've found the money," he said.

"Oh?" Bobbie took a step forward. "And where is it, Tessa?"

She lifted her chin, because she wasn't going to tell this woman anything. She pulled her phone out. "You're trespassing. Get off my property."

"It's going to be our property soon," Bobbie said. "So I don't think we'll go anywhere."

"You'll never be able to just stay here," Tessa said. "The police in two states are looking for you."

Bobbie laughed as if Tessa had just delivered a really funny joke. "Don't you know we're not to blame?" She wore a wicked smile on her face. "Those Martin sisters knocked Janey to the ground just to deliver a summons."

Bobbie shook her head in mock disappointment, and Tessa couldn't quite believe what she was hearing.

"Imagine what they'd do if they learned you girls had thousands and thousands of dollars in cash right here…" Bobbie's blue eyes glinted with malice.

Tessa scarcely recognized her. "We haven't found any cash," she said, and it sounded halfway believable.

"We'll be exonerated," Bobbie said as if Tessa hadn't spoken at all. "Dennis Martin's children knew their aunt, and they knew she had a boat." She shrugged like she'd worked out all the details of pinning the crime on Aleah, Minerva, and Lyons Martin.

Tessa didn't hold any love for the Martins, but she didn't want innocent people to go to jail. She lifted her phone. "I'm dialing now." She tapped her phone icon and the keypad, keeping her eyes on Bobbie and Riggs, still a dozen paces away.

She dialed 9-1-1, but she hadn't hit send before movement stole her attention and stalled her progress.

"She—asked—you—to—leave." Janey appeared, her hair flying in every direction and a shovel lifted over her shoulder. She swung it down and caught Bobbie in the back. The blonde woman fell, and Janey's primal yell filled the world with rage and fear.

Her chest heaved, and she dropped the shovel. "Call the cops, Tessa."

Tessa fumbled her phone, her own fear choking her.

She tapped the call button, and as Riggs stared at his wife and then Janey, she scrambled to get the shovel again.

"Don't move," Tessa said, taking a couple of quick steps forward. "Don't you dare move, Riggs."

Janey lifted the weapon above her head again, and Bobbie groaned.

"State your emergency," the woman on the phone said.

"It's Tessa Simmons," she said. "The two people that abducted me have returned to my property, and I need help."

"I have you at 17 Seagull Lane."

"Yes, please hurry. And we need an ambulance. A woman has been injured."

"I don't want to hurt you," Janey said. "But if you even take one wrong breath, I will." She didn't take her eyes from Riggs, and Tessa put her eyes back on the man.

"Who are you?" Tessa asked.

He glanced at her. "You know who I am."

"No, who you *really* are," she said. "You're not Richard Friedman. That's Bobbie's last name. Or Barbara's."

He moved his attention to Tessa fully, and she listened as the woman said she had units on the way to the cottage.

True panic sat on Riggs's face, and he took a step toward her. "I am Richard Friedman."

Tessa backed up a step, because she didn't need to pour gasoline onto a raging fire. "Whatever. I don't care," she said. "Just don't move."

Riggs kept coming toward her, and Tessa kept backing

up. She reached the house and headed for the street. He hadn't been the dangerous one before, but she hadn't challenged his identity then.

The sound of sirens filled the air, and Riggs looked down the lane. He broke into a run, and Tessa yelped as he reached her before she really knew what was happening. He simply knocked into her, and she went sprawling back toward the house.

She hit her elbow against it, but watched Riggs turn left and go in front of the cottage. "He's running!" she yelled into the phone.

She got her feet underneath her and followed him, but instead of going out into the dunes and then the beach, Tessa ran up the steps to the porch. She could see farther and better from the higher position, and she said, "He's running toward The Lighthouse Inn. I bet he has a boat at the dock there."

"I'll re-route a unit," the operator said. "Ma'am, you need to stay safe. Don't attempt to follow him."

"I won't," she said, her mind flying back to Janey. She hurried down the steps, because she couldn't see Riggs anymore anyway. Around the house, she met her sister's eyes. She'd lowered the shovel, and she stood several paces away from Bobbie, who'd sat up and crawled over to the garage door, where she leaned back into it.

She tried to get up, but couldn't. Janey didn't move either, and she said nothing.

A police car pulled up to the house, siren blaring

loudly, and two officers jumped from the vehicle. "Ma'am," one called.

"Down there," she said. "The one on the ground. That's Bobbie Friedman."

Both officers approached cautiously, and soon enough, they had Bobbie in handcuffs. More units had arrived, and Tessa had the distinct feeling she'd be answering questions for hours.

She didn't care. This was over now, and she might be able to sleep in the cottage without a dozen locks between her and the outdoors.

———

THE FIRST WEEK OF AUGUST ARRIVED, BUT RON DID NOT come to Nantucket with it. Tessa stepped out onto the porch, two cups of tea in her hands. She approached Janey, who stood in the corner of the porch, leaning against the railing, one of her elegant robes billowing in the slight breeze.

"Tea," Tessa said, handing her a cup.

"I love the Sound in the morning," Janey said. "It won't be the same on the south side of Nantucket."

"You don't have to move over there," Tessa said. "We can share the cottage. There are three bedrooms on the main floor, and two upstairs."

"Viola needs the help," Janey said. "Miles does too, and I want to learn more about the history of that house."

She gave Tessa a smile. "I like Viola. She's my kind of sassy."

Tessa returned the smile. "That she is."

They sipped their tea for a few minutes, only the sunshine and the calling of birds between them. "Are you going to go out with Sean?" she asked.

"Maybe," Janey said. "His assistant is leaving at the end of September, and I might work for him too. I haven't decided yet."

"Hm. And the kids?"

"Rachel and Travis are talking about marriage," Janey said with a smile. "They're going to stay in Jersey and rent the house from me for now. You?"

"I called my realtor yesterday. I'm going to sell the house in Pennsylvania." A keen sense of sadness moved through her, because she'd spent decades in that house. She'd raised her son there. But he'd moved on, and Ron didn't care about the house he'd barely lived in. "I'm going to live here and see if I can get on at the Whaling Museum or the Historical Society. That's almost like library work."

"You don't need to work at all," Janey said. After the police had asked all their questions and apprehended Bobbie and Riggs, Janey had shown Tessa the map and the rectangles. She'd started to dig them up when Riggs and Bobbie had arrived, and they'd made her dig a little bit more.

She'd unearthed one trunk filled to capacity with cash, and they'd then dug up a second one. With all the money in the bank, the total had added up to over two million dollars. The estate had been settled in time, and both Tessa and Janey were now each millionaires.

Barely, but they still qualified.

"Neither do you."

"I like working," Janey said.

"I do too," Tessa said. "I'm going to get the yard here in tip-top shape, and then I might move to Long Island."

"You love Esme."

Tessa grinned as two gulls soared by. "I do love her, and that's a great house there. You should come."

"I'm…I don't think I'm ready to go to Long Island," Janey said.

"So you're not going to meet your father?"

Janey shook her head, her gaze somewhere on the horizon as her mind moved through something Tessa couldn't even fathom.

"Maybe one day," Tessa said, linking her arm through her sister's. "For now, let's just enjoy our time on Nantucket."

"Yes," Janey said, squeezing Tessa's arm against her body. "That's what I'm looking forward to. Good food, and good company here on Nantucket."

After another brief bout of silence, Tessa said, "You'll always be my sister, Janey."

"I know," she said. "And you'll always be mine."

———

Read on for the first chapter of ***The Lighthouse Inn***, the next book on Nantucket Point, featuring two women who must learn to get along as they rebuild their lives… and one of them, Julia Harper, will have to deal with finding out that her father is also Janey's dad…

Sneak Peek! THE LIGHTHOUSE INN
Chapter One

Julia Harper faced the building where she'd be living soon, the pit in her stomach the kind that could swallow a person whole. She'd tried filling it with chocolate-covered raisins, but that had only left her five pounds heavier and somewhat sick to her stomach.

Outside the car she'd ferried over from the mainland, the wind tugged at the American flag flying high from the deck of the front part of the building.

The Lighthouse Inn.

Julia had spent years living in Nantucket with her family, both as a single woman, a married one, and a teenager. Sometimes she swore she had the white sand from the beaches out here on Nantucket Point in her blood, and something about this patch of land in the middle of so much water called to her soul.

She'd been planning to leave Manhattan anyway—at least she'd told everyone that so often that she'd started to believe it might have been true at some point. Whether it was or not didn't matter anymore.

She'd left.

She was here now.

"Go in now," she whispered to herself, and Julia took a deep breath, her pulse suddenly throbbing in the vein in her neck. She'd carefully applied her makeup that morning —her last in the hotel where she'd been staying in downtown Nantucket while she waited for her car and the clock to do what it was about to do.

Tick to ten o'clock on September first.

The first day of the rest of her life.

The first day of true freedom from the life she'd been encased inside for the past twenty-seven years. A life where someone else knew when to change the furnace filter. A life where someone else paid the mortgage and replaced broken doorknobs and helped the children learn how to drive.

Alan had taken very good care of Julia, and while she'd known it at the time, she'd still had quite the rude awakening when he'd walked out and she'd been faced with the enormity of taking care of their historic brownstone.

Five stories to take care of, with all of the children gone, and Julia found she didn't want to make the trips up the steps anymore. Not to empty bedrooms. Not to a master suite with a king-sized bed that only she slept in. Not back downstairs every morning for coffee in the breakfast nook that overlooked the garden—which she now had to take care of by herself.

Her mother said she'd lived a sheltered and pampered life, and Julia hadn't argued with her. Mother also had no room to talk, as she lived in a gorgeous, sprawling house in Southhampton, sipping lemonade next to the pool while Dad took care of the house, the land, the cars, and the bills.

Julia stood from her sedan, hitched her purse higher onto her shoulder, and faced the inn. The bottom portion of the building had a flat roof and could only be described as a two-story cube. The double-wide front doors sat smack-dab in the middle of the square structure, a deep, rich mahogany that actually settled her nerves slightly.

She'd been to The Lighthouse Inn first as a teenager, delivering groceries to the caretakers. Now, she was going to *be* the caretaker.

Along with someone else, she reminded herself as she took the first step toward the entrance. The Nantucket Historical Society had originally wanted a couple to live in the inn and run it, the way the previous caretakers had done. Phil and Margo Michaels had taken care of The Lighthouse Inn for over thirty years, and they'd retired at the beginning of the summer.

The Historical Society had had a terribly hard time finding a replacement couple, and the inn had been closed when suitable caretakers hadn't been found. They'd then changed the job listing, and since Julia couldn't seem to stay away from Nantucket, when she'd seen she didn't need to be one-half of a couple to apply for the job, she'd taken the bold step and done it.

Shock coursed through her even now that she'd gotten the job.

Ironically, working in and managing Alan's real estate office had been the deciding factor in her application. She was very used to a lot of moving pieces, and she'd once managed a diner as well. As The Lighthouse Inn operated as a bed and breakfast, the job required cooking skills. The inn traditionally had offered activities for its occupants as well, and Julia's old, unused marine biology degree had come in handy too.

She had not met the other person who would be living in The Lighthouse Inn with her. She didn't even know the other woman's name. She'd been told to be at the inn today, at ten o'clock to sign her contract, and then she'd be able to move into the tiny private suite where she'd be living for the foreseeable future.

A sense of giddiness and the urge to throw up hit her simultaneously, and she wobbled slightly in her heels. No one who came to Nantucket Point wore heels, but Julia had wanted to appear sophisticated and professional. At almost fifty years old, heels also firmed up her legs and gave her a sense of confidence, despite the extra pounds she enjoyed due to the chocolate-covered stress eating she did.

The breeze pulled at her dark hair, which she tucked behind her ear as the thwapping, rippling sound of the flag met her ears. She loved that sound, and she calmed further.

She reached the door and pulled it open. All the signs she'd seen when she'd come for her interviews were now gone, but the door still squealed on its hinges. That would be one of the very first things she'd fix, because why endure such a sound when a couple of spritzes of WD-40 would make this door open silently?

Pride filled her as she first tasted the air conditioning inside the building. The weather had started to cool slightly at night, and come Tuesday next week, the tourists would be mostly gone from the beaches of Nantucket.

"Julia," a woman said, and Julia turned toward the familiar tone.

"Vivian." Julia smiled and changed direction. "Good morning."

"It's good to see you again." She stood in the doorway leading into the small office where Julia would work with her partner to run the inn. The lobby of the inn sat right in the middle of the building, with staircases moving up and down behind the ten-foot counter that served as the check-in desk.

The Lighthouse Inn only had five rooms available per evening. Both she and her partner would have a private suite on the bottom floor, and while Julia hadn't lived in a basement in a very long time, she was actually ready to get her things moved in, roll up her sleeves, and get The Lighthouse Inn back open.

The Historical Society had said there would be a budget for renovations and cleaning, and that they'd like the inn open in time for the holidays. Julia couldn't imagine a scenario where she couldn't get a five-bedroom house operational in two months, because when she'd toured the inn, it wasn't in that bad of shape.

Yes, all of the carpet needed to be replaced. The walls required a fresh coat of paint. The deck off the back of the inn needed to be reinforced and re-stained. It connected via a narrow walkway to the fishing dock that extended right out into the water.

The main level housed the lobby, a public restroom, the small office, the kitchen, and the dining room. All five guest rooms were located on the second floor, and the third floor became the lighthouse tower that extended another seventy-four feet above the main building.

The lighthouse itself was no longer operational, though it had once been responsible to help guide seafarers at night. Another lighthouse down the beach and out on the isthmus of the Point did work, but no one stayed there as part of their magical visit to Nantucket Island.

Julia reached Vivian and shook her hand, her smile cemented in place now. She wasn't going to let it slip, not even for a moment, until she had all of her boxes moved in and her car parked in the single employee slot.

She'd been told that the other woman didn't have a car, and she'd readily agreed to share hers so the two of them could get to the downtown area or anywhere else on the island where they needed to go.

"Maddie isn't here yet," Vivian said, turning back to the office. "Come on in, though, and we'll get your contract signed. She signed hers last night, and she's all moved in already too." Vivian sighed with a measure of exhaustion in the sound as she sank into the chair behind the desk. "I caught sight of her leaving for a morning walk when I got here."

She flashed a professional smile and picked up a pen. "I'm sure she'll be back soon enough, and the two of you will finally get to meet."

"Mm." Julia sat in the single chair opposite the desk, perching right on the edge of it and letting her purse fall to the ground. She just needed to get her name inked on this employment contract. Then she'd be ready to take the first step into the next phase of her life.

Almost fifty. Single. Trying to figure out how to parent adult sons.

And now, instead of reading her favorite novels while Alan went to work, checking in with the progress of her children as they went to college, and going to lunch with her friends, Julia was about to become co-caretaker of The Lighthouse Inn.

"So this is a year-long contract," Vivian said, as if Julia hadn't paid attention the first time they'd gone over the requirements of the job. "If you intend to quit, you must give us three months' notice, so we can avoid shutting down the inn as we've had to do this summer." Vivian looked at Julia over the rims of her black glasses.

"I understand," Julia said.

"After the first twelve months, there is no contract in place holding you here. We simply ask for the long notice at that point." She passed Julia the pen. "You've had a chance to read over it?"

"Yes," Julia said, though she hadn't paid much attention the contract Vivian had sent earlier that week. She wasn't going to back out of this now. She didn't have anything left in Manhattan, and that chilling thought ran through her as she signed her name on the lines Vivian indicated.

The blonde woman scooped up the papers the moment Julia finished and tucked them neatly into a folder. Her smile seemed more relaxed now, and Julia looked between it and the woman's name tag, pinned neatly to her red blazer.

She worked for the Historical Society, and she was the contact should Julia and her partner need anything at The Lighthouse Inn.

"All right." Another sigh leaked from between her lips as she stood. "You're in. Done. I've put hard copies of the guest guide, policies, and anything else you need in your room. You've got the digital copies. I'll let you get moved in and settled. You and Maddie will be able to sit down and meet at your earliest convenience, and I trust that when I see you both again, you'll have a plan for the restoration and clean up that will get us open by November first."

"Yes," Julia said, standing too. "Thank you."

Vivian looked past Julia's outstretched hand, her smile widening and relaxing. She clearly saw someone she liked much more than Julia. "Oh, here's Maddie now."

With one painful thump of her heart, Julia turned toward the doorway. She took in the elegant, beautiful woman standing there, and her mind whirred as she placed once-familiar features.

Those eyes…so bright and so blue.

That heart-shaped face…could wear such a look of disgust and disdain, Julia remembered.

The blonde hair that held more gray than it once had…but still looked perfectly styled and sophisticated.

"Maddie, this is your partner," Vivian said, her voice warbling like a doorbell that needed a new battery. It had high tones and low tones in Julia's mind as a wail started somewhere inside her brain.

Vivian made it to a spot between the two women, which put the unsuspecting woman in a precarious position. She didn't even know it, if her smile was any indication.

But Julia had placed the identity of the woman in front of her, and she literally could not think of anyone worse.

Madelynne Lancaster.

She obviously recognized Julia too, because she cocked her forty-nine-year-old hip and folded her arms, as if the two of them had been transported thirty-five years into the past.

Maddie scanned Julia from the top of her head to the high heels, and just like she'd always been dismissed as insignificant, Julia could see the scoff forming in Maddie's mouth before it even came out.

Vivian didn't seem to notice, because she simply said, "This is Julia Harper." She looked at Julia, her smile almost blinding—if Julia could look at anyone but the woman who'd made her teenage life a living nightmare.

"Julia, this is Madelynne Lancaster. You two are going to be co-caretakers of The Lighthouse Inn."

Madelynne Lancaster. The woman whose boyfriend Julia had stolen and then made her husband. At the time, she'd felt nothing but vindicated. She'd gotten the last laugh. After a long string of losses, she'd finally *won*.

There was no way she could live with and work with Maddie for the next twelve months. Absolutely no way.

The silence stretching between the two women held a charge that could've called lightning from the sky, and it only increased with every passing second while each woman waited for the other to break and say hello first.

———

The Lighthouse Inn is a brand new women's fiction novel reminiscent of *Grace and Frankie,* and it's set right across the beach from Tessa and Janey!

Books in the Five Island Cove series

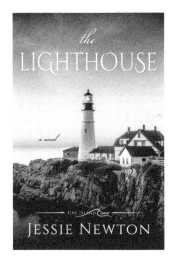

The Lighthouse, Book 1: As these 5 best friends work together to find the truth, they learn to let go of what doesn't matter and cling to what does: faith, family, and most of all, friendship.

Secrets, safety, and sisterhood…it all happens at the lighthouse on Five Island Cove.

The Summer Sand Pact,

Book 2: These five best friends made a Summer Sand Pact as teens and have only kept it once or twice—until they reunite decades later and renew their agreement to meet in Five Island Cove every summer.

Books in the Five Island Cove series

The Cliffside Inn, Book 3:
Spend another month in Five
Island Cove and experience an
amazing adventure between five
best friends, the challenges they
face, the secrets threatening to
come between them, and their
undying support of each other.

**Christmas at the Cove, Book
4:** Secrets are never discovered
during the holidays, right? That's
what these five best friends are
banking on as they gather once
again to Five Island Cove for what
they hope will be a Christmas to
remember.

Books in the Five Island Cove series

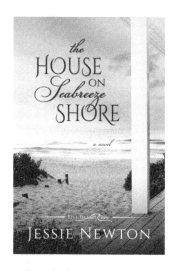

The House on Seabreeze Shore, Book 5: Your next trip to Five Island Cove...this time to face a fresh future and leave all the secrets and fears in the past. Join best friends, old and new, as they learn about themselves, strengthen their bonds of friendship, and learn what it truly means to thrive.

Four Weddings and a Baby, Book 6: When disaster strikes, whose wedding will be postponed? Whose dreams will be underwater?

And there's a baby coming too... Best friends, old and new, must learn to work together to clean up after a natural disaster that leaves bouquets and altars, bassinets and baby blankets, in a soggy heap.

Books in the Nantucket Point series

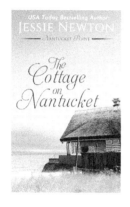

The Cottage on Nantucket: When two sisters arrive at the cottage on Nantucket after their mother's death, they begin down a road filled with the ghosts of their past. And when Tessa finds a final letter addressed only to her in a locked desk drawer, the two sisters will uncover secret after secret that exposes them to danger at their Nantucket cottage.

The Lighthouse Inn, Book 2: The Nantucket Historical Society pairs two women together to begin running a defunct inn, not knowing that they're bitter enemies. When they come face-to-face, Julia and Madelynne are horrified and dumbstruck—and bound together by their future commitment and their obstacles in their pasts…

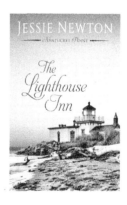

About Jessie

Jessie Newton is a saleswoman during the day and escapes into romance and women's fiction in the evening, usually with a cat and a cup of tea nearby. The Lighthouse is her first women's fiction novel, but she writes as Elana Johnson and Liz Isaacson as well, with over 175 books to all of her names. Find out more at www.authorjessienewton.com.

Made in the USA
Coppell, TX
11 September 2021

62201247R00298